MIDNIGHT HUNTERS

LIGHT AND MIDNIGHT
BOOK 1

CORT CHANNON

To Casey, my life's companion, my soulmate, always and forever.

To Deb, for giving me the push I needed to finally start writing.

To Aki, who, after hearing me talk about one book idea, said, "That dream you told me about would make a better story." Indeed it did.

To Char, for giving me the most transformative writing advice I've ever received: "Don't be a fucking role model."

To St. Jinx, for demonstrating to me that spirituality, sexuality, and creativity can come hand in hand.

A NOTE FROM CORT

Thanks to Casey for constant love and support and for help in the proofreading process, and special thanks to Melissa, Brian, Leah, and Blaze for support and advice throughout the publishing process. Thanks to St. Jinx for the wonderful cover art and for being a friend and cheerleader as I finished bringing these characters to life. I couldn't have done it without you all.

A NOTE ABOUT CONTENT

The *Light and Midnight* books are about queer identity and self-actualization. Characters suffer adversity, but the tone of the book is intended to be empowering, sex-positive, hopeful, and liberating. Additionally, the books interrogate the relationship between sex, spirituality, and religion, and there are many spiritual references throughout.

The author believes in happy endings in every sense of the term, and so these books contain a very high level of heat: there is a great deal of suggestive language, as well as very explicit descriptions of physical bodies and of consensual sex between male partners.

In *Midnight Hunters*, there are some elements of the story that readers may find distressing, such as cases where characters suffer emotional abuse at the hands of their families, instances of religious aggression and discrimination, or cases in which power imbalances are misused. Care has been taken to handle topics in as sensitive a way as possible to avoid gratuitously causing suffering to either characters or the reader.

CONTENTS

PROLOGUE

LIGHT. That was the first thing that I noticed: the light. It started as a sliver of white, a line across the blackness of my awareness. The sliver expanded as my eyelids forced their way open, then it flooded my vision, fading to a dull grey as my eyes adjusted.

The second thing I noticed was the pain. My head pounded with a dull roar, and every muscle in my body ached. My lungs felt like they were on fire; every breath was a knife in the chest.

Where was I? On the floor, for one. I felt the hard scratch of dirty concrete through the shirt on my back; felt something digging into the space under my left shoulder blade. The room was a thick, smoky fog, the kind that gets under your skin and inhabits your body, obscuring thought, breath, action. I stared up, and eventually could make out contrast—neat, ordered dark circles of recessed light fixtures marred by angry swaths of black across the high ceiling.

I moved, tried to pull myself up, and my entire body protested. Waves of pain rolled over me, followed by waves of nausea. I stopped, closed my eyes for a moment, but the darkness just made everything worse. I reopened my eyes, then tried again, pushing past my body's offended cries, and succeeded in sitting upright.

I could see next to nothing through the cloudy gray air. Everything was indistinct, and the room crowded oppressively on my senses. Cracks ran through the blasted concrete floor, over which lay a web of smeared lines in black, white, and gray. The air smelled of charcoal and sulfur.

Confusion hit. What had happened? I couldn't make out anything more than a few feet in front of me. I tried, slowly, to pull myself into a standing position. My legs wobbled as I stood; it felt like I was standing on an uneven surface. I turned my head down to look, and the whole world shifted beneath me. The room spun; my head ached; I vomited once, twice, feeling it splash on my feet. Only my right foot felt hot, and I realized it was bare. I grimaced as the acidic stench of sick wafted up to my nostrils.

Still looking down I turned away, sliding my soiled feet across the ground. I could barely see the floor through the dense air. Eventually, a lone thought penetrated inward.

Leave.

Clumsily, I put my hands in front of me and, still staring down at an angle, took a slow step. My body fought against me; the room began to spin again, but I fought back, taking another step, then another. As I made my way forward—whatever "forward" was—I began to pass dark rectangles on the floor. Their sizes varied, but their overall shapes were generally the same. Eventually I passed one that was larger, its interior white, and realized that it was an open book. I'd been passing books. I could not see them clearly from a standing position, much less make out any of the titles or text, and I wasn't about to try bending down for a closer look. I pressed onward.

I felt the wall before I saw it. Dull concrete like the floor, it pressed coolly against my hands through the mist, indistinguishable from the gray air. I greeted the invisible barrier with relief, feeling that I at least had something solid anchoring me in space. I had hit the wall at a slight angle, and so moved my way forward, easing myself along. Eventually I came to a faint polished sign on the wall, next to a darker panel.

I stared at the plaque, willing my eyes to focus. The characters were foreign to me. As I approached the panel next to it, however, I felt a glimmer of hope: there was a handle.

A door.

I stumbled anxiously toward it, letting my hand fall heavily on the handle. It turned, and the door moved slowly, as though opening against its will. The air in this new space was different: cooler, damper; it smelled of must, but not of charcoal. It was, however, as muddy with fog as the room behind me, and darker still.

I lurched forward, my feet uneasy beneath me, feeling the colder floor under my right foot. I heard a heavy thud as the door shut behind me. Another step, and I nearly tripped.

Stairs. On my left. Going up.

I groped out with my hands, and my right found a rail. I climbed, fighting the pain and the nausea that rose as I ascended each step.

A landing; more stairs doubling back on themselves. Another landing. A door.

I reached for the handle, barely able to make it out. It moved a fraction of an inch under my hand, and then stopped.

Locked.

Frustration—or was it panic?—pushed at the edges of my mind, fighting to be recognized but unable to prevail against the pain and nausea and exhaustion. I turned and found stairs again.

Another landing, another staircase. Yet another door.

I threw myself against the handle, toppling over as the door swung open easily, and I landed heavily on the floor of the room beyond. I had no idea if I had hurt myself; pain was already almost all I was feeling.

I waited on the floor as the whirling of the room slowed. The air here was crisper, but no less thick with fog. Where the fog had before been a cold, smothering gray, however, here it was tinged a shade warmer, as if yellow sunlight was trying vainly to pierce through. Dumb excitement washed over me, and I dragged myself up and began wandering forth toward the brightest patch in the fog, stumbling like a toddler, the desire to be in the light blocking out all my other senses.

Eventually, I stopped, feeling the glow directly above me, hearing a faint buzzing in my ears. I looked up, and could just make out a square shape, flickering ever so slightly as it spat out electric light.

I cursed and felt my head begin to spin again. Looking up had not been the wisest of ideas. I tried slowly to get my bearings. Some distance away, I could make out another bright spot. At least if I headed toward it, I figured, I'd be heading down the length of the building.

I wandered toward the second light, keeping my gaze fixed upon it, and suddenly tumbled forward as the ground fell away from my feet.

I put my hands in front of me as I smacked into the floor. I should have felt pain, but I was already saturated with the sensation. My face felt wet on the ground—was I bleeding?—as I peeled it off of the floor tiles, pulling my feet under me. I felt a thud as my foot jumped downward once, twice, and realized that I must have fallen down a small pair of steps. Steps in the middle of a room. Perhaps I was in a lobby? An auditorium?

Standing for a third time was agony. My entire body fought me, begging me to leave it where it was, crying out to be left alone. I forced myself forward, each step a struggle. I passed the second spot of light, and beyond it, saw nothing but a faint red rectangle slightly above head-level.

I couldn't make out the letters, but I stumbled toward it. Below, through the fog, something came vaguely into view.

A door.

A door with a push bar.

I placed my hands on the bar and pushed. The door swung open, and I was met by a welcome rush of cool night air.

I stepped outside, carefully feeling a short step down, then another. Ahead of me, all I could see was dark, spotted with a few lights surrounded by thick halos.

The fog was outside, too.

But now, so was I.

Relief and confusion washed through me, and at the momentary release of tension, pain and nausea pressed back in on my senses. I stumbled forward a ways into the night, then stopped as my stomach lurched back up into my throat and I vomited again.

I looked up to see a figure approaching briskly through the fog. A woman. Hope overcame me, and I cried out to her.

"Help me," I cried.

The woman stopped short and stared at me. I could barely make out her features, but her eyes were wide with alarm and fear.

"Help me," I said again. "What is going on? Where am I?"

The woman took a step backward, then shook her head and spoke.

I couldn't understand a word of the language she used.

"Do you speak English?" I asked. "Please, can you help me?" I stumbled toward her.

The woman backpedaled as I approached her, as if recoiling from a beast. She shook her head again, putting her hands up in front of her. She spoke three syllables I could not recognize, then turned and rushed briskly back into the fog.

"Wait!" I called. "Help me!"

As hope faded, darkness pressed in. The pain overcame me, followed quickly by a heavy numbness. As I tried to stagger forward, it felt as though the entire earth lurched beneath me, and my body toppled.

I didn't feel it hit the ground.

I

AWAKENING

THE WHOLE WORLD WAS DARK. Thick. Heavy. Closed.

Was I asleep?

Was I alive?

Everything was black silence. How long it had been that way, I didn't know. At what point I became aware of the blackness rather than simply inhabiting it, I had no idea.

What had happened?

A sensation. A memory.

I'd been tired, exhausted. I'd felt pain. That much, I remembered.

Now I felt nothing.

But why was I suddenly aware of nothing?

Something had pushed against the corner of the blackness.

Something had pushed, and was gone.

But then it pushed again. Something. Was it a sound?

A sound.

It was indistinct, as though I were deeply immersed in murky water and the sounds were coming from somewhere above the surface. What was it? Where was it coming from?

I searched outward, straining toward the sound. I felt the darkness expand ever so slightly around me, then stop.

Something was in the way; something was separating me from the sound outside.

Suddenly, I realized what it was: my body.

I pushed my awareness outward, felt it expand to fill my face, felt the cognizance of my face's presence. I had a face. If a face, then eyes. I searched and found them, felt them there, shut tight against the outside.

I needed to open my eyes.

Open.

Nothing.

Why was it so difficult? My brain was running, but I was deeply lost inside myself.

I mustered my willpower; tried again.

Open.

OPEN.

I was rewarded with a twitch; the slightest spasm in the corner of my left eyelid. Yes, that was it. Listen to me, body.

Open.

A quavering arc of light cut across the darkness, then vanished again.

The far-off voice became stronger, more intense. I wasn't certain, but I felt as though my effort had caused it.

It was enough to drive me to continue concentrating my effort on my eyes, pulling them forward.

Pull. Break. Break through.

Open.

The thin arc of light came back, and this time I caught my mind on it, willed it to stay.

More. Give me more.

It felt as though I'd succeeded in pushing a boulder over the crest of a hill. The weight gave way, my eyes opened, and suddenly my dark world was a field of light.

I felt my eyelids flutter against the sudden barrage of light. The sounds around me grew in intensity yet again.

Far away, off in a different world, another sense reached me. Touch. But what was it? Where?

My hand. I had a hand, and something was touching it. My arm began to move, be pulled; it floated in the air somewhere that felt far away from me.

My hand.

I tried to focus on my hand, but it was too far away. It was not a part of me. It was out of reach, lost behind the veil of light.

Light.

I concentrated on the light. Was it only light? Were there shadows? I struggled to bring definition, to bring the space in front of me into focus.

Focus. See.

Feel.

The white space in front of me began to gain definition. There were shadows. One was to my right, and just then it was joined by one to my left. What was it? I tried to turn to see it, but it was no good; my body wouldn't move, not yet.

The noise cut the air again:

".o…"

Had that been an "O"? Had I heard something? For the first time, something recognizable penetrated the veil.

".o…"

".o…"

".o…"

Each repetition seemed to push a little further; it was drawing closer to me.

".ol.."

".ole."

"Cole."

Cole.

What was 'Cole?'

It came again.

"Cole."

Cole. A name. It seemed familiar, this name. I knew it. I had known it forever.

My name. Had that noise had been my name?

Respond.

I concentrated, gathering all the will I could muster, then sent a message to muscles far away from me, in the throat that was a part of my body but was not me, floating off somewhere in the distance. The muscles caught the breath passing through my body, and my exhalation became a grunt. A syllable.

"Uh."

The sound around me increased.

"Cole!"

The wash of light thinned.

"Cole! .an.y...hea.....?"

The feeling in my hand tightened. I caught the sensation, and pulled upon the infant-like instinctual reaction to stimulation of the palm.

My hand closed.

"Cole! Can.yo..hea..me?"

Focus. See.

And, suddenly, the world around me slid into place.

I blinked against the sudden sharpness of my field of vision. Two faces were looking down on me, one on either side. The face on the left belonged to a handsome man with blonde hair and blue-green eyes; he was looking at me with mild concern and somewhat detached curiosity. The face on the right, however, showed outright relief. This face had a slightly more olive skin tone and black hair. The face's black eyes blinked at me, looking so relieved I thought he would well up with tears at any moment.

"Cole," the face said. "Thank God."

"Hunh?" Was all I could manage. I pulled myself up into a sitting position. It was more difficult than it should have been; my body was still unwilling to cooperate with my mind.

I was in a small apartment, on a cream-colored pleather sofa that matched absolutely nothing else in the dingy room. The walls were a dark brown, with vertical slats of fake wood paneling. The room was strewn with clothes and a few empty dishes; through a small door I could see a kitchenette's sink, which contained what may well have been the remainder of the dishes in the apartment. A small table stood in front of the sofa, empty but for an overturned glass, as though it had been hastily cleared away. One corner of the room held a stained desk with a dinged-up office chair. A desktop computer sat atop of the desk, a media player application idling on the monitor.

I looked at the two people who stood staring at me in silence. The blond one looked to be in his early- to mid-twenties; he had attractive college-athlete features that made it hard to judge his age with precision. I could see the outline of muscles under his white-and-blue hoodie; he clearly kept in shape. The darker-haired boy was definitely younger, probably barely twenty. He had attractive features, too, but his seemed to be burning up on the inside, as though he should be more handsome but was running himself ragged. He clearly exercised; he had a black T-shirt on that clung to his torso, leaving little to the imagination, but he looked as though he were surviving solely on the merits of a twenty-year-old metabolism rather than any kind of healthy eating. He seemed frayed around the edges; there was a bloodshot twitchiness about him that was disquieting.

What was even more disturbing to me, however, was that I recognized neither of them.

"What happened?" said the dark-haired boy, still eyeing me with concern.

I stared at him, straining, feeling growing alarm. Apart

from the hazy recollection of dragging myself out of the base-ment of some building, the inside of my mind was thick and black.

"I... don't know," I said truthfully. "I don't remember."

"Can you tell me your name?" the blonde man asked.

"Cole," I replied.

"Your full name," he clarified.

"Cole..." I started again, then stopped. Nothing came to me; it was as though my brain were filled with thick fog. Or empty. "I... I don't know;" I said again.

The blonde man's face now registered genuine concern. He leaned down and looked closely at my head, his green-blue eyes searching my face, then stared at my eyes. It wasn't a pene-trating stare; rather his gaze went as far as my eyes and then stopped.

"Did you hit your head? Maybe you're concussed. I don't see any trauma, though."

"Um," I said, shying away slightly. "I don't know how to say this, so don't take it the wrong way, but... I don't recognize you."

The blond man straightened and smiled pityingly, but not unkindly. "I'd be surprised if you did; this is the first time we've met. My name's Alexander."

I heard a shifting noise behind me, and turned around. The dark-haired boy was staring at me uncertainly.

"Do you remember me?" he asked.

I stared at him, looking for some kind of familiarity. Nothing came.

"I'm sorry," I said.

The boy winced, visibly hurt.

"Don't take it personally," I heard Alexander say from behind me. "The boy has amnesia, Marcus."

"Yeah, but..." Marcus started, looking from Alexander to me. "But Cole should know me; we've been... very close."

"Oh my God," Alexander said loudly, disgust and offense

clear in his voice. "You brought me here to help your *boyfriend*?"

Boyfriend?

"He's not my boyfriend!" Marcus protested hastily. "Or I dunno yet. Or maybe. But we've been seeing each other for a while; a lot of each other."

"A while?" Alexander scoffed. "You have a weird sense of time, Marcus. We broke up the beginning of September, so you can't have been seeing him for longer than a month. At least," he added menacingly, "you'd *better* not have been seeing him for longer than a month."

"Wait," I said, trying to keep up. "I was dating you?"

Marcus looked at me, his eyes searching.

"You really don't remember?"

"I... don't remember anything," I said. "What happened?"

Marcus stared at me for a moment.

"I think you were caught in that gas explosion in the square," he said.

"Gas explosion?" I asked, confused, still trying to jog my brain. "Where you there? Are you OK?"

"No, I wasn't there," Marcus said. "I was at a party. We were at a party. Then you got a text message, and you told me you had to leave and go into the city center. Something about an errand."

"Errand?"

"Yeah, it sounded like a lame excuse to me, too. Why would you have an errand at eleven o'clock at night? I figured you just wanted to leave."

Alexander looked at him. "And why would he want to leave, Marcus?" he asked pointedly.

Marcus looked back at Alexander and said nothing for a moment.

"It wasn't his kind of party," he said at last.

"Are you using again?" Alexander's words were hot, but his

expression was one of more frustration and disappointment than it was of alarm.

"Dude, you don't understand," Marcus said pleadingly. "This guy, he can get me the most amazing shit."

"What the fuck, Marcus!" Alexander barked. "When we broke up, you promised me you were done! You said you were gonna go clean so you wouldn't lose someone again."

"Maybe you should have stuck around, then," Marcus replied, almost petulantly.

"Hey... HEY," I said, surprised by my own forcefulness. "We were talking about me, remember? And Marcus. Drugs? What the hell?"

Marcus stopped and stared at me.

"That's *exactly* what you said to me at the party."

"I did?" I asked.

"Yeah; just before you got your 'text' and left," he said, punctuating the word "text" with air quotes.

"So if I left," I asked, feeling confused again, "how did I end up here? Do I live here?"

"I guarantee you don't live here," Alexander scoffed.

"So what happened?" I asked.

"The TV was on at the party," Marcus said. "I saw breaking news pop up about the explosion downtown. I kind of freaked out; I texted you to see if you were OK, and you didn't respond. Then I tried to call you, and the phone didn't even ring; it just went straight to carrier voicemail. I got worried that something happened to you, so I went out looking for you."

"You went looking for me?" I asked, actually touched.

"Yeah. I couldn't get near the square, but I went looking around the streets near where the accident hit. I found you on the ground, passed out. Your clothes were all blasted and torn, but you seemed OK otherwise, so I carried you back to my apartment."

"My clothes?" I asked, looking down at myself for the first time. My eyes widened at the sight. "Holy shit."

Shreds of what had been a light linen button-down shirt hung over my torso, the rags singed at the edges. Beneath it, a white T-shirt was similarly destroyed, and parts of my bare flesh were peeking through, including one of my nipples. My slacks were similarly torn up. One leg was nearly bare, the pant leg having torn and dropped down around my ankle over a singed sneaker, while the other leg was still covered but the shoe and sock had burned off the foot. I realized with some embarrassment that part of my trunks had been blasted away, too; my junk was probably visible from the right angle. I shifted my legs nervously to cover myself before I was hit with what should have been a more immediate question.

"Why am I not in the hospital?"

Alexander stared at Marcus.

"I've been wondering the same thing."

"Hey, I called Alexander for help," Marcus said defensively.

"Are you a doctor?" I asked Alexander.

"Hardly," Alexander said flatly.

"He's a lifeguard in the summer; he knows CPR and First Aid."

"Because *that's* the same," Alexander said.

"So why didn't you take me to the hospital?"

"I... wasn't sure how much you'd had to drink. Or if you'd done anything else. Or had something slipped to you. I didn't want to get you in trouble."

"Seriously?" I asked, suddenly feeling irritated. "So I was unconscious, and you were worried that I might have had too much to drink or been drugged, and you didn't want to take me to the hospital to *protect* me?"

Marcus was silent for a moment.

"...I'd shot up a bit, and I bought some stuff. I didn't want to get caught."

"What the FUCK, Marcus!?" both Alexander and I shouted at once.

"Dude, chill," Marcus said defensively, showing a hint of aggression that I hadn't seen until then. "You look fine. You barely even have a scratch on you."

I paused and looked down at my body again, suddenly realizing something that should have been obvious.

My clothes were blasted, burnt, and torn. I was not. I pulled at the collar of the button-down shirt, which nearly tore apart in my hands, and looked at my chest between the shreds of my tee. Not a mark.

But on the other hand, I also couldn't remember a thing.

"What the hell happened to me...?" I asked absently.

"You don't remember anything?" Marcus asked again.

"Not a thing. About anything," I said, struggling against my brain, getting nothing back.

"Do you remember your last name yet?" Alexander asked.

I shook my head.

"No," I said, feeling frustrated. I turned to Marcus. "Help me out. What's my last name?"

Marcus shrugged.

"Not a clue."

"Seriously?" Alexander asked, glaring at Marcus. "You've been going out for a fucking month, and you never bothered to learn his last name?"

"I never said we'd been going out for a month!" Marcus protested. "We've gone on five dates."

"Great," I sighed. "So, what *can* you tell me about myself?"

"You give really good head." Marcus said.

"SERIOUSLY?" Alexander exclaimed, reaching the limits of his temper as I gawked at Marcus.

"What?" Marcus said, shirking back, shrugging. "He's like, *fantastic.*"

"How about information regarding something other than his sexual prowess?" Alexander asked.

"Um..." Marcus thought for a minute. I stared at him.

"So, did we just never talk, or what?"

"Well," Alexander said dryly, glancing at me, "apparently you spent a fair amount of time with your mouth full."

"Really?" I replied, just as dryly.

"No, we talked plenty," Marcus said. "I just..."

Alexander gave an exasperated sigh. "You just never listen," he said. Then he turned to me, fixing me with his green-blue eyes. "Sorry man, but you picked the wrong guy to go out with."

"Apparently," I said, trying not to stare too hard at Alexander. Of the two of them, he was not only clearly the more put together, he was also, to me, the far more attractive. I began to wonder what he looked like without the white and blue hoodie.

"Hey, HEY," Marcus said, putting his head in between us. "Fine, so I'm not good at tons of details. So sue me."

"And yet he's your maybe-boyfriend after five dates with you knowing nothing about him?" Alexander asked.

"I read plenty about him before we started going out!" Marcus protested.

"What?" I asked.

Marcus looked at me. "Yeah, hey, yeah. I know what might jog your memory." He turned to his computer and closed the media player, then brought up a browser window and clicked on a bookmark.

"Come here," he said.

I stood up, then quickly put a hand to my crotch to keep it covered as my torn pant leg flapped open. Alexander raised an amused eyebrow at me, and I tried, embarrassed, to avoid eye contact. I went over to the computer, where Marcus was standing aside, gesturing triumphantly at the monitor. I stared at it. A picture of some guy's face was on the screen with a ton of text underneath, and the title 'NerdyHunk21'. A logo on the top corner of the screen had one Ares symbol shoving its spear into the back end of another Ares symbol.

Oh.

"A gay dating site?" I asked, almost indignant. "What am I supposed to be looking at?"

"You."

I looked back at the screen. "What?"

"It's you," Marcus said again. "This is your online dating profile."

"No way." Alexander was pushing his way next to me, his voice filled with barely contained glee. "This I gotta see."

I just stared at the screen. The face looking back at me was, if it wasn't too immodest of me to say so, pretty cute. The short-ish brown hair, swept to one side across the forehead, over inquisitive eyebrows and chocolate-brown eyes that looked straight at the camera, made for the kind of features that were almost too common to notice except that the expression clearly demanded attention. The curve of the cheeks, the not-too-square, not-too-narrow jawline. It was the kind of face that was so average in every way as to look ideal, outstanding by not standing out. But looking at that face, I suddenly felt a wave of despair.

I didn't recognize it.

"This... is me?" I asked, staring at the face on the screen.

I heard some rustling next to me, and Marcus handed me a small mirror. I picked up the glass by the handle, and stared at the face looking back at me.

It was the same face as the one on the monitor, only with a new haircut that had short hair standing up attractively from the front of the forehead. But this face looked confused, lost. I stared at the brown eyes, searching, pleading for some shred of recognition, but they gave me no answer, instead staring plead-ingly back at me.

I reached up and touched a hand to my cheek. The boy in

the mirror did the same. I reached out to the reflection, and it reached out and touched my hand as it met the glass.

"This is me," I said, my mouth tasting the words, trying to believe them.

I felt a hand on my left shoulder.

"I'm sorry," Alexander said at my ear. They were the first truly sympathetic words I'd heard since waking up.

Which meant that they were the only sympathetic words I ever remembered hearing.

I turned and looked at him. He stared back at me, an expression of honest concern and pity on his face.

A loud snapping at my ear jarred me back, and I whipped my head around to see Marcus impatiently clicking his fingers at my ear.

"Hey," he said, "are you going to read your profile or not?"

"What is wrong with you?" Alexander demanded.

The two glared at one another, and I, uncomfortable, turned my attention back to the monitor.

'NerdyHunk21' had written quite a bit about himself:

'Age: 21. Height: 5'9". Weight: 151 lbs. (Was I really that skinny?) Hair: Brown. Eyes: Brown.'

I turned the mouse wheel and scrolled the window down.

"Ah, here's the good stuff," I heard Alexander say next to me.

'I'm a simple guy,' the profile said. 'I'm not big into parties, but I'm happy to hang out with some friends or catch a movie. I'm at my best, though, curled up on the sofa at home, having a chat, reading a book, or watching Netflix. I like classical music; and I play an instrument. If you ask nicely, I might give you a private concert. And if things go really well, I might show you what else my tongue can do.'

"Oh, *God*," I said, mortified at the bad line.

"And, *there* it is," Alexander said, satisfaction in his voice.

"See, I told you," Marcus said. "*fantastic* head."

"I'm not sure how I feel about having an audience watch me read this," I said.

"Hey," Marcus retorted, "you put it up on the Internet."

"Fair point," I had to admit.

That introduction was followed by a list of favorite movies, books and music, none of which meant anything to me. The remainder of the profile was remarkably personal. Judging from the tone of the profile, I had *really* wanted some physical attention.

"And look, Marcus," Alexander said, pointing at the screen, "he clearly says that drugs are a deal breaker for him. And yet you dated him anyway."

"Yeah, well, I didn't think it'd be that big of a deal," Marcus said. "Besides, I wanted a piece of that. *Look* at him."

Marcus took the mouse and clicked on the screen, and there I was by a pool, wearing a pair of goggles and a towel.

It definitely felt like committing some kind of impropriety, being turned on by a picture of myself. But I couldn't help it. I was thin, but I was in shape. Really good shape, by the look of it. I didn't have a six pack or anything, but the shape of my muscles was clear enough under my abdomen, and my chest was firm and well-defined.

And Marcus clicked the mouse again, and suddenly I was in a pair of speedos, walking away from the camera. The focus of the picture was clearly my butt, which the swimwear only nominally covered, leaving little to the imagination.

"OK, are we done?" I asked, grabbing for the mouse.

"There's one more picture," Marcus said, clicking the mouse.

I stared at the screen.

"You have *got* to be kidding me."

There I was, sitting on a plush sofa in what must have been my apartment, reading a book, completely naked. All that was covering me was a white sheet, artfully placed like one of those sheets in a classical painting. The sheet bulged enough to send a straightforward message.

"Desperate for attention, were we?" Alexander asked.

"And, we're done," I said, grabbing the mouse and clicking the window closed.

"Did it help?" Marcus asked.

"Not at all," I said miserably, embarrassed by the desperate profile, frustrated by my inability to recognize myself, and slightly bothered by the fact that my own online dating profile had turned me on.

"I want to go home," I said.

"Do you know where that is?" Alexander asked.

"No," I admitted.

Marcus was silent for a moment.

"I do," he said at last.

"What?" I asked him.

"I know where you live," he said. "You took me back to your place on our second date."

"Really?" I asked, the feeling of encouragement at possibly being able to get home overpowering my disgust at knowing that I was someone who would bring a guy like him home after only two dates.

"But how will you get in?" Alexander asked me. "I assume you didn't just leave your place open when you went out."

I fished around in my pockets one hand at a time, the other still firmly keeping the ragged trousers over my crotch.

"I don't have a wallet," I said.

"That's probably because you're missing one of your back pockets," Alexander said from behind me, and I realized that he was probably staring at a bare ass cheek. Great.

"I don't have a phone, either," I said, still fishing around. Then I felt something in my right pocket. "Hold on," I said, pulling it out.

A set of keys. The plastic keychain was melted beyond recognition, but the keys themselves were intact.

"Will these get me into my apartment?"

"Probably," Marcus said with a shrug. "One way to find out. Come on; I'll take you home."

"Um," I said tentatively. "I can't go out like this."

Marcus rolled his eyes.

"Fine," he said, opening a door into a small bedroom. "Come with me; I'll find you something."

I walked into the bedroom as he dug through a drawer and pulled out a pair of dingy sweatpants and tossed them to me. I caught them with one hand, then turned to put them on.

"Do you mind?" I asked Marcus.

"Yes," he said.

I glared at him. "You're really going to make me strip for you?"

"I think it's sexy," he said. "I want to see you put on my clothes."

Alexander popped his head into the room. "Seriously?" he asked, glaring at Marcus. "You're not going to give him a moment of privacy?"

"He fucking sucked me off right here just before we left for the party," Marcus said defensively. "He had no problem stripping off for me every chance he got. The guy's practically an exhibitionist, and now he's changing into MY clothes in MY apartment. Why shouldn't I watch?"

"Because even if that is true, he doesn't *remember* any of it," Alexander growled. "Give him some privacy."

"Or," Marcus said, a twisted grin forming on his face, "the three of us could have some fun right here on the bed."

"You know what? Never mind," I said, dropping the sweatpants to the floor, no longer wishing to wear any clothes of Marcus's. I hadn't been entirely sure they were clean anyway. I replaced the keys into my one intact pocket. If people stared at me on the street, so be it. "Can we just go?"

"Sure thing," Marcus said, grinning. "Let's go to your place."

"Not without me, you're not," Alexander replied.

Marcus rolled his eyes. "Fine" he said. He tossed me a pair of bedroom slippers.

I stared at them, then at him.

"It's all I have," he said.

I sighed and put them on, and we left the apartment. I was glad to be out of there.

II

HOME SWEET SOMEPLACE

It was brisk outside; brisk and dark. I wondered what time it was. The streetlights were still burning brightly, and the roads were all but deserted. Marcus walked ahead of us, turning this way and that, not saying a word. I wondered if he was sulking more because I had been unwilling to strip for him, because I had wanted to go home, or because Alexander was coming along with us.

I was grateful for Alexander's presence, however. I didn't trust Marcus, and I found myself wondering how I'd managed to go on five dates with him. Perhaps he'd been different when we first met. Perhaps he *had* actually gone clean, and hadn't relapsed into drugs until that party. Or maybe I'd just been that desperate.

"You're shivering."

Alexander's voice brought me out of my reverie. He was watching me with a concerned expression; then shook his head with a small smile.

"I'm so stupid; I didn't even consider that you'd be cold."

With that, he pulled off his blue and white hoodie,

revealing a tight white and gold T-shirt underneath. He handed the hoodie to me.

"But *you'll* be cold," I said dumbly.

"I'll be fine," he said with a smile. "My shirt doesn't have holes in it."

I looked at the hoodie, then to him, then back to the hoodie.

"Thank you," I said, taking it and pulling it on. It smelled of chestnut and warmth.

Ahead of us, Marcus began to stalk down the street at a faster pace, and we hurried to keep up with him.

I looked around as we walked. Everything was completely new to me; I had no frame of reference with which to orient myself. I struggled to form any kind of mental map as we moved, but Marcus slipped down side streets and between buildings with the skill of someone familiar with back-alley dealing, confounding my attempt to learn the roads. I had to spend more effort keeping pace than I wanted to, leaving precious little time not only to learn the streets, but also to talk to Alexander.

Eventually Marcus brought us to a red brick apartment building, with a large "48" in brass numbers on a concrete awning above the entrance. The building had a bunch of buzzers and nameplates by the front door. I looked them over, but figured that they all had to be fairly out of date: they were all first initials and last names, but none of those first initials was C.

"Are you sure this is where I live?" I asked.

"You're the one with amnesia, not me," Marcus said. "You have a key; see for yourself."

I pulled the ring of keys out from my pocket by its misshapen plastic mound of a keychain, and stared at the keys as they jingled in the incandescent light.

"Well, here goes," I said.

It only took three tries before I found the key that opened

the door. I made a mental note of its bronze color and clover-leaf head and slipped it back into my pocket.

The interior of the building was dim, with sickly yellowish walls that only looked more oppressive in the harsh electric light. The center of the foyer had a stairwell leading up next to a dark, faux-wooden door that read only "MAINTENANCE." On either side of this central feature, a hallway ran parallel to the stairs, with a pair of doors on either side.

Marcus ignored this floor, walking instead up the stairs to the next landing. At the top of the stairs, he turned to the right, stopping in front of a dingy door with a "22" on the front.

"This is you," he said.

I fumbled for the keys in my pocket again, then started trying them in the door.

First one. No luck.

Second, no luck.

Third, no luck.

And so it continued along the key ring, until suddenly, much to my surprise, I heard noise at the other end of the door. The knob turned, and the door pulled open, and I was left gawking, key held out in front of me, staring at a gruff, angry-looking middle-aged man with a full, black beard and a sleeve-less undershirt.

"Who the fuck are you?" he demanded.

"Um…" was all I could muster.

"Why the fuck are you trying to break into my apartment?"

"Um…"

As the man advanced menacingly on me, Alexander spoke from behind me.

"Sorry, man," he said, a surprisingly easy tone in his voice. "My friend here had a bit too much to drink; I was trying to get him home. Guess he's trying the wrong door."

"You're damn right he's trying the wrong door," the man growled. "Get the hell out of here!"

Alexander pulled on my arm, and, obediently, I stumbled toward him, trying to play up the drunk image.

Next to me, Marcus stared dumbly, looking completely stoned.

The gruff man glowered at us, then slammed the door. As soon as the door shut, Marcus snapped back to me, and I realized the whole stoned look had been a very clever ruse.

"Well, that sucked," he said flatly.

"Nice tenants," Alexander mumbled, as I straightened up and turned to Marcus.

"I thought you said I lived here," I demanded.

"I got the wrong room; so sue me," Marcus replied, throwing his hands up. "I've only been here twice, you know." He turned to the stairwell. "I'm sure it was the second door down after the landing. It must be up another flight."

"It had better be," I said as we ascended the stairs.

"Here," Marcus said, after we reached the door directly above the one we'd just knocked on. "This is definitely you."

I stared at the door doubtfully. White plastic numbers reading "32" were nailed just below a peephole set in the otherwise featureless brown door. Marcus stared at me expectantly. I glanced at Alexander, who simply shrugged.

I pulled the keys out once more. This time, the second key, a silver color with a pentagonal top, turned in the lock with a satisfying click.

I opened the door, and there was my apartment. At least, I assumed it was mine, since I had the key that opened it. Its contents, however, were unfamiliar.

I stepped into the dark room and fumbled about on the wall for a light switch. Eventually, I found one, flipped the lights on, and looked around. It was a modest studio apartment. The walls were a dark olive green, almost brown, contrasting with the sparse brown furniture. There was a sofa, but rather than facing a TV, it faced a tall bookshelf packed with books. A tall mirror adorned the wall next to the bathroom, and a bed was tucked in the corner, but there were no pictures on the walls, no posters, no photos. I must not have been much for art.

"Anything ring a bell?" Alexander asked, stepping next to me. "Anything bring back any memories?"

"No," I said grimly. I suppose I'd hoped that coming home to my apartment would bring a rush of recognition, but in that I was disappointed. "I don't remember this place at all."

"Well, I sure do," Marcus said, walking across the room and plopping down on the full-size bed against the wall. "Especially over here." He turned to me, a lascivious grin on his face. "Now that we've got you back home, perhaps we should celebrate with a bit of fun? Perhaps I can jog your memory."

"You have some nerve, Marcus," Alexander said angrily.

"Hey, hey," Marcus said, putting his hands up in front of him. "I didn't say you're not welcome to join us, too. I'd be happy to have that big, blond body again."

I stared at Marcus as he regarded me with a tone-deaf smile, and wondered if he wasn't still under the influence of whatever he'd taken at the party.

Alexander whirled on Marcus and roughly grabbed his upper arm. For a moment, I thought he was going to slug him. But then he seemed to catch himself, and stared at Marcus's face. His eyes softened, though it looked like it took some effort. Then he opened his mouth, and his words surprised me.

"Why should I have to share you?" he asked Marcus, his mouth in a little half-grin.

I gaped.

Marcus smiled broadly. "I knew you'd come around," he said.

"So why don't we get out of here, and I'll cum all around your face," Alexander replied.

"Um...," I managed.

Marcus turned to me. "Sorry, Cole. You're cute and all, but... at least Alexander *remembers* me."

I glared.

"Do you mind if I use your bathroom?" Alexander asked, walking past me without waiting for a response. He turned over his shoulder. "Do me a favor and go down and get us a cab," he said to Marcus. "I don't wanna walk back to your place. Besides, the sooner we get there, the sooner we can get busy."

Marcus didn't miss a beat. Without further ceremony, he rushed out the door, letting it slam behind him.

As soon as Marcus was out of sight, Alexander turned back to me, his face showing concern and a little regret.

"I'm sorry, Cole," he said. "I didn't know how else to get him out of here. I didn't think he'd leave willingly otherwise."

"So you're going to sleep with him to get him to leave?"

Alexander made a face. "Oh, fuck no. I'm ditching him as soon as I get to the street. That cab's for him alone."

I stared at Alexander, who looked back at me with his bright blue-green eyes. He was standing so close to me that I could smell him—a golden kind of scent, colored with chestnut. As it filled my nostrils, I felt myself stirring, waking up in a way that I hadn't yet since regaining consciousness. I realized then why the scent was so strong—it was not only wafting over from Alexander, it was surrounding me in his hoodie, which I still wore. Before I could move to take it off, though, Alexander put a hand on my arm.

"I'll check in on you tomorrow, OK?" he asked.

"Sure," I replied, and then before I could say anything more, he was gone.

I sighed as the door shut behind him. I would have to return Alexander's hoodie tomorrow. At least, I would if he came back like he said he would. It suddenly occurred to me that I had no way of contacting him otherwise. I never got his number. And even if I had, I'd no phone to call him with.

Everything was blank. But at least now I had an apartment full of potential things to trigger my memory. It was time to start searching.

I looked around the modest apartment—home, but not home—hoping to find something that sparked a glimmer of recognition. Failing that, perhaps here I could start to piece together who I was. The studio apartment was a simple one, large enough to not feel entirely claustrophobic while mercifully small enough to mean that I wouldn't have to dig through too many nooks and crannies to find things.

But where to start? There were a few boxes under the bed, books and notebooks and boxes on the bookshelves. There was the small nightstand, the chest of drawers, the small wardrobe, the closet. There was the kitchenette, which I hadn't even ventured into yet.

While I was looking around, I heard shouting from outside the window, and I went over to look. There, in the twilight, I could see Alexander and Marcus, the latter gesticulating wildly. Alexander appeared to have been true to his word—to me, anyway, because he turned away from Marcus and walked off in the opposite direction from which we had come. Marcus shouted after him, once, twice, then turned and stalked off in the opposite direction. The cab he'd hailed idled for a moment, then sped off, its driver likely miffed at having been denied a fare.

I turned back to the room, looking at it from the new angle, hoping that something would catch my attention. My eyes went to the desk at one wall of the room. It had some things on it, a blank pad of paper, a few pens, a stack of books. But the center of the desk was empty. Just to the side of the chair below the desk was a backpack. I opened it up and... bingo.

Laptop.

Eagerly, I rummaged through the bag until I found the

power supply. I plugged in the computer, opened the screen, then found the power button and jabbed it with my finger. The computer whirred to life. I gripped the back of the chair I was standing behind as I waited for it to finish starting up. After a few seconds that felt like an eternity, I was presented with a solid-color screen, with a single line of text followed by a text box.

"ENTER PASSWORD:"

My heart sank. I was stymied by my own security. It was possible, I supposed, that I had written the password down somewhere—perhaps I would come across it while looking around the rest of the apartment. One could only hope.

I moved the pointer over "Shut Down" on the recalcitrant machine and stabbed the trackpad with my finger, watching the screen go black shortly afterward. Without my wallet, my phone, or my computer, my three shortest paths to my own identity were blocked. I would have to search harder.

I found nothing useful in the desk, and so I turned my attention to the backpack. Apparently, if I normally carried much in it, the items did not live in it while I was at home. The front pocket was mostly empty except for a few coins and a pair of ballpoint pens. The back contained a small, portable umbrella, a wireless keyboard, and—Eureka. A portable tablet. I pulled it out and opened up the case, then fiddled with the buttons on the side until I found the one that powered it on.

I was presented with the current time and an array of nine dots.

Another password.

I sighed, staring at the dots. How many patterns could there be? Perhaps I used something simple and meaningful to me. But what carried meaning, I had no idea. All I really knew about myself was my name: Cole. I took my finger and traced a "C" across the dots.

"INCORRECT PASSWORD. 2 ATTEMPTS REMAINING."

Well, that was discouraging. I decided to refrain from further attempts for the time being in the hope that something might jog my memory later. I slid the tablet back into the backpack and turned my attention to the rest of the room. Perhaps the bookshelf would have something of greater value.

I walked over to the shelf and took a closer look. The very top shelf had a handful of what looked like fiction novels. The titles meant nothing to me, but the images on the covers looked like they were mostly fantasy books. Mixed among them were a few more serious books and a very large tome entitled *The Complete Sherlock Holmes*, which looked like a collection of detective stories, printed as reproductions of old magazine pages.

The second shelf was more interesting. It held a number of religious books. At first glance, I thought I must have been a very religious person, but if that were the case, wouldn't the books all belong to a single denomination? Instead, I had a breadth of material: along with three translations of the Holy Bible, there was an Episcopal prayerbook and hymnal, a Book of Mormon, a set of magazines from the Church of Latter Day Saints, another set of magazines from Jehovah's Witnesses, a book called *The Teaching of Buddha*, the Tanakh, a number of books on Jewish mysticism, one on Islam, and one called *Witchcraft Today*. This was followed by a number of books on general religion, a book of angels and demons, and an encyclopedia. The next shelf was filled with books on mythology: general books first, then ones specializing in Greek, Roman, Celtic, Egyptian, Norse, Japanese, and Native American mythology. I pulled the first Bible out, a large one with very thin pages and a red dust cover, and flipped it open. It was covered in notes: underlinings, highlightings, scribbles in the margins. There were a number of notes also referencing other books, some of which were on the shelf, some of which were not. I was clearly fascinated by religion. Indeed, I felt a draw toward the books, and had to fight the temptation to sit down and start poring over them. Instead, I went to the next shelf.

This one was filled with books and folders. I pulled out a few and set them on the floor as I leafed through them. Every one of them held sheet music, all for a clarinet. I looked them over, pages and pages of music. Some of them had sticky notes or writing on them, and some of the books had small adhesive tabs stuck in them to mark various pages. I looked at the music itself, and something shook within me. While I did not recognize the titles of any of the pieces, the notation made perfect sense. Clearly, I could read music as well as I could read English.

I cast my gaze around the room again, looking for an instrument case. Nothing jumped out at me. Then my eyes fell on the closet door. Perhaps I would find something useful in there?

I pulled open the door, and beneath the coats and shirts, my eye fell on an instrument case and a portable music stand. Those were, in turn, resting upon a large fireproof safe. With a combination lock.

I let out a frustrated scream. My entire identity was locked behind security walls—passwords, locks, and combinations—while Marcus could easily pull up a complete description of my sexual proclivities on his gay dating website.

I opened the case and found, as expected, a clarinet and a packet of reeds. I pulled out a reed and then reached for the instrument, removing each of the parts of the clarinet from its case.

At some point in the process I realized that I had been keeping the reed in my mouth, that I had put it there unconsciously as soon as I took it out of the case. At the same time, I realized that my hands were working automatically, putting the instrument together just right without my actually thinking about it. I tried to consciously not worry about what I was doing, which in turn made me falter; I had to distract myself by looking over the music in order for my hands to take over again.

Finally, I had an assembled instrument. I picked up the sheet of music I had selected—a weathered sheet covered with pencil markings and annotations—and set it on the music stand. Then I put the clarinet to my lips and blew.

At first, the attempt was disappointing. My fingers fumbled over the instrument, stymied by my brain. I stopped, took a deep breath, then started over again. This time, it was different. My hands, mouth, and lungs took over, and a melody emerged from the bell of my instrument, filling the room, rolling along as quickly as my eyes could pass over the dense notes on the page. My brain did not remember the music, but my body did; the piece was clearly one that I had practiced again and again until I had learned it by heart. I let my mind relax, enjoying the unfamiliar melody as my body automatically breathed it into the clarinet in my hands. I reached the end of the page and, without missing a beat, reached out and flipped the paper open. It unfolded across the stand, multiple pages taped together in a musical panorama. I let my body get carried away on it as the melody built to a natural crescendo—

—And then it all came crashing down as a pounding started on my door.

"Do you know what the hell time it is!?" an angry male voice roared from the hallway. "Keep that up and I'll have you evicted; I'm warning you!"

The music died on my lips, the enchanting melody line broken. Playing the instrument had been the first thing that had felt natural to me since waking up, but there would be no more music tonight. I sighed and pulled the instrument apart, setting it back into its case. I laid the case on the empty coffee table and then walked over to the kitchenette. Nothing sparked familiarity here either, not the boxes of cereal nor the ice cream in the freezer nor the contents of the fridge. I took a glass from the shelf and filled it from the sink, drinking down the water.

I went back into the main room, and my eyes went to the boxes under the bed. I approached and pulled one out; it slid heavily on the floor. I lifted the lid and stopped.

I don't know what I had been expecting, but it wasn't this.

There were books. Not just any books, but glossy coffee-table sized photography books whose covers sported naked or near-naked men, alone, in pairs, and, in one case, in a group.

These were accompanied by a handful of smaller books on varying themes including being a better bottom, topping like a stud, and giving amazing head. I also found a hardbound copy of an erotic comic book, a deck of tarot cards all featuring male nudes, and a small collection of pencil sketches. Whoever had drawn the sketches (was it me?) had some talent, but was rough around the edges.

Next to all of these was a smaller box. I lifted it out and opened it up, and felt my jaw drop. Inside was a box of condoms with lube, a jar of coconut oil, and a very impressive model of a penis molded in hard rubber, with a suction cup on its base. I looked from one item to another, then picked up the coconut oil and looked at it with curiosity. It was the thing that did not match the others. What was it for?

Wait.

Oh.

As the realization hit me, I started to feel a bit of a draft. That was when it finally occurred to me that I was getting hard.

I looked down, and the shreds of my trousers were standing out from my torso. I wasn't just getting hard, I was there. I picked up the smaller box and walked over to the side of the room, where I had a large, floor-length mirror on the wall. I had noticed it earlier, but hadn't really thought to pay it much heed. Perhaps I had been avoiding it.

I went and stood in front of it now. The twenty-one-year-old who stared back at me was a stranger, one whom I should know intimately, but who held no familiarity for me whatsoever. I stepped close to my reflection and studied my face.

"So you're Cole," I said, as my reflection mouthed the words back to me.

I... was handsome, if it wasn't immodest of me to think so. Mine was the kind of face that was good-looking without being distinctive: short, dark brown hair, eyebrows that were thick without being bushy, rich brown eyes, defined cheekbones, and full lips.

I took a step backward and took myself all in. My clothes were the picture of shabbiness. The blue and white hoodie that was so snug on Alexander's large frame was loose and baggy on my thin torso. Below, my trousers were tatters, but between them I could see a pink erection starting to peek through.

Time to get a better look at myself.

I crossed my arms in front of me and grabbed the bottom of the hoodie, then lifted it over my head, getting one last whiff of Alexander as I did so.

The shirt underneath was so damaged as to be barely worthy of being called clothing. In its tattered state, I could see one of my nipples peeking through, and a bit of my abdomen. The strips of clothing were burned and charred in places, and the tears in the fabric were jagged and violent.

If this was what I was wearing, how was I not dead?

I pulled at the collar of my T-shirt and it split apart, its remains falling around me. I stared at my bare torso in the mirror. With my clothes on, I was unassuming; there was nothing about me that really stood out. With my shirt off, I was in shape. Good shape. The reflection in the mirror was thin, but had good definition in the chest; I had clearly spent some time on both it and my arms. My reflection's skin was a light, smooth cream, which made the dark red nipples stand out in stark contrast. The abdomen was cut and defined—while there hadn't been a visible six-pack in the images on the site Marcus showed me, in the intervening time one had started to assert itself; there was a hint of texture down the abdomen in the mirror. I raised an arm and saw a thin brushing of brown underarm hair in the mirror, but my entire torso was hairless. I ran a hand over my chest, and it felt smooth to the touch, suggesting that the smoothness was natural rather than achieved with a blade.

I stared at the mirror, awestruck as I continued running my hand over my chest. Until I had begun doing so, I hadn't really been sure that the reflection was me. It was a strange sensation, seeing my reflection without a hint of recognition. It was like having a body to explore that would obey my every thought, connected to me and yet still new in every way.

I had to see more.

I pulled on the button of my ruined trousers and they came apart in my hand, the tatters falling to the ground among the remains of my shirt. A tug on the waistband of my shredded trunks, and those too gave way, leaving the reflection naked in the mirror.

I stared at the person in the mirror, pale and exposed, firm erection pointed straight at me, straining forward about seven-and-a-half inches from its base, which was ornamented by a dusting of dark hair at the bottom of the natural V of the hips. The balls hung low and large underneath. I forced a cough and watched them rise and fall with the motion. It was enticing.

I turned and went to the dresser, where a smaller mirror was sitting, and took it in my hand as I returned to my spot near the wall. I turned around and used the combination of mirrors to examine myself from behind. My back was smooth, with only a hint of lean muscle, and my legs were similarly lean and tight, with strong thighs and calves. Most notably of all, however, was my reflection's butt: in spite of my thinness, it was quite shapely, standing round out from my waist before sloping back in where my legs began.

I placed the small mirror on the floor and turned my attention back to my reflection. Slowly, I began to run my hands over my body, watching the boy in the mirror do the same, exploring myself in time with the reflection. I watched the expression in the mirror change as I found the spots that elicited the strongest response: nipples, neck, sides, the low-hanging balls. I teased a nipple and brought the other hand to wrap around my cock, watching pleasure write across the face as my breathing deepened and my warm member sent waves through my body in response to my touch. I ran my thumb over the pink, wet head and felt the wave hit me, watched my reflection's eyebrows knit and mouth drop open, breathing deeply, wanting more.

I turned to the box, pulled out the tub of coconut oil and the large dildo, felt the weight of the large rubber shaft in my hand. I took it and slapped the suction cup base below the rubber balls onto the floor in front of the mirror; it stuck into the faux-hardwood floor perfectly. Opening the coconut oil, I rubbed some between my hands until it began to liquefy, then slathered a generous amount onto the length of the toy. I turned my attention to the mirror as I applied some of the coconut oil to my ass, watching my face twitch with pleasure and anticipation as my fingers teased around my hole.

Then I squatted down in front of the mirror, and, carefully, eased the rubber cock into me. The reflection's face winced as the dildo made its way inside. I brought the hand that wasn't busy steadying the toy to my own member, felt the slick coconut oil pass from my palm to my already dripping erection, slickening it further and eliciting an involuntary pleased groan.

Slowly, gradually, the rubber cock parted me, working its way further inside, and just as I felt my ass cheeks land on the rubber balls, the top of the dildo hit something that released a surge of pleasure through me, bringing forth a deep moan. It was all I could do to continue watching my reflection as I pleasured myself with both hands, one on my cock and one on my nipple, moving up and down on the rubber erection, feeling it push up against my prostate over and over, slowly at first, and then faster and faster as I quickened my pace.

My reflection panted, sweat forming on its forehead and shoulders, cheeks going red as blood pounded through me with more and more force, my bucking keeping pace with my quickening breath and hastening heartbeat. The toy and my hand felt good as they were, but the experience of fucking myself in front of the mirror, in front of an attractive body that I owned but did not recognize, intensified it immensely. Drop after drop of clear precum began forming on my erection and dripping to the floor, sometimes getting thrown some distance by the momentum of the stroking. Pleasure welled up inside me, pressure building, as the glans and balls in the mirror went a deep red. My reflection bucked, and then, finally, my balls rose up, tightening, as the sensation rose to a crest. It hung there for several seconds, balanced on the precipice of pleasure, until at last it burst forth, my cock shooting a blast of creamy cum into the mirror, which spattered loudly against the glass as I cried out in self-inflicted orgasm. The second spurt hit slightly below the first, and then the third and fourth splashed onto the floor, followed by stream after stream down my hand as the orgasm continued rocking through me.

Eventually the waves of feeling died down, and I pulled myself off of the dildo and plopped down on the ground in front of it, suddenly keenly aware of my aching calves and thighs. No wonder my legs were in such good shape. I stared at my exhausted reflection, which met my gaze, panting, face red, heavy brown eyes spent but satisfied. My hands and legs were a mess, to say nothing of the floor and mirror. Slowly, I forced myself up, washed myself in the shower, dried myself with one of a stack of towels in the bathroom, then hunted around the apartment until I found things to clean the floor and mirror— and dildo—with. I packaged the box back up, slid it under the bed, and then collapsed on top of the sheets and fell asleep in an instant.

III

THE EVENING PALE

I AWOKE to the sound of a loud buzzer echoing through the room. I pulled myself up, bleary-eyed, and tried to get my bearings. I was in an apartment. Right. My apartment, apparently.

The buzzing noise repeated itself. It was coming from a panel on the wall near the door. Groggy, I pulled my naked body off the bed and stumbled over to the brass panel. It had a speaker with two buttons underneath, one labeled "TALK" and one "IN." I pressed my finger to the TALK button and spoke.

"Yeah?" I asked blearily.

"Cole?" came the staticky reply. "It's me, Marcus. Can I come in?"

I hesitated, staring at the speaker in the panel as though it were going to give me advice. Marcus. He had found me out in the street, had taken me to his place and made sure I was safe. He knew where my apartment was when nobody else did. He was also the tool who had to be coerced out of the apartment by Alexander with the promise of sex before he would stop trying to get in my pants. I pressed my finger to the "TALK" button again.

"I don't think that would be a good idea," I said.

There was a pause.

"I'm sorry," Marcus said at last. His voice sounded sincere. "I was still a bit high last night; I was acting like an ass. It's... hard for me to see somebody I thought I really connected with, and to have him not remember me, you know? I... I like you, and you're pretty hot, and when I... have a bit of stuff in me, it's hard not to... Hard to control myself. That's not an excuse; it's just what happened. I.. I'm trying to go clean. I hope you'll give me a chance to start again."

I didn't know what to say to that. Maybe we *had* connected, but I didn't remember any of it. All I knew of Marcus was his being a jerk to me, and his having a drug problem. But he was also the only link to my past that I had right now, even if that past only went back a month.

"I... don't know," I said.

There was quiet on the other end of the intercom again.

"Please?" came Marcus's voice at last. It was small, pleading.

"I... I don't think I'm ready to see you again this morning, I said finally. "I still have too much I'm trying to sort out."

"...Can I come by later?"

"Maybe," I said.

And then there was silence. I turned my attention back to the room. I was buck naked, standing in the light that crept through the sheer modesty curtains that were hanging over the windows. The apartment looked different in the morning, if it even was morning. I looked around, but there was no timepiece in sight. I walked into the kitchenette and noticed a clock on the microwave.

2:30 PM.

OK, so not morning. What time had I fallen asleep last night? For that matter, what time had it been when we got back to my apartment?

Standing in the kitchen, I suddenly realized that I was ravenously hungry. I hadn't eaten a bite since—well, literally since I could remember. There wasn't much food in the kitchen. A bunch of frozen dinners, some boxes of macaroni and cheese, half a jar of peanut butter, a few stray apples. The refrigerator had a half-empty carton of skim milk (thankfully unexpired), an unopened bottle of orange juice, some butter, grape jam, and a loaf of bread.

So a chef, I was not.

I took out two slices of bread and popped them in the toaster on the counter. While waiting for them to toast, I walked out into the main room and turned my attention to the dresser and its four drawers. I didn't particularly mind being naked in my own apartment—in fact I kind of liked it—but I hadn't explored the dresser before getting distracted by the things under the bed.

I pulled open the bottom drawer of the dresser. Inside were several pairs of trousers, neatly folded. There was one pair of black jeans, two pairs of blue jeans, and four pairs of khakis. I clearly had a style.

The second-to-bottom drawer had shirts and sweatshirts. Most of the shirts were button-down. Everything was muted colors, browns and tans and grays and whites. There were a few black shirts mixed in among them, and a few dark blues and dark greens, and one dark red and violet.

The second drawer from the top had T-shirts and socks, all plain white, solid black, or brown. There were no other colors, no fancy images, no decorations. Everything was simple, functional.

I opened the top drawer, expecting the same. The left side of the drawer was populated by underwear, trunks, and briefs, mostly white or black, similarly neatly folded and organized. To my surprise, however, a few bright colors were in the mix, including blue, red, and purple. The right two-thirds of the drawer appeared to be towels; one white one was neatly spread across the top of the drawer.

But wait; hadn't there been towels on a shelf in the bathroom? I had seen them when I came out of the shower. I lifted the towel up to reveal what was underneath.

"Oh, *hello*," I said in spite of myself.

Tucked under the towel were clothes that were not remotely as conservative as the ones that filled the rest of the dresser. Here were brightly colored briefs, mesh trunks, silk boxers, thongs, and jockstraps, along with a mesh t-shirt, a leather vest, and two pairs of pants that looked to be made from some sort of stretchy material. The outerwear was clearly designed to get noticed. The undergarments also demanded attention, but of a different sort. I recognized one or two of them from the pictures on the dating site that Marcus had shown me.

I rummaged through the undergarments in the drawer, feeling myself get a little hard as I examined some of them more closely. I pulled out one unusual pair, which looked like it was made of leather and had a crotch that was basically just a flap held closed with a snap. I pulled the pair on and turned my attention to the mirror. It fit snugly—quite snugly—and I filled out the snap-closed pouch in the front very nicely. The back was basically a jockstrap, supporting my cheeks and emphasizing my already shapely butt.

As I was admiring myself, the panel near the door buzzed again, making me jump. I walked over and pressed my finger against the "TALK" button.

"Hello?" I asked.

"Cole? It's me, Alexander," came his baritone through the staticky speaker. "I said I'd come check in today; can I come up?"

"Sure," I said, then pressed on the "IN" button, realizing as I did so that I was standing in nothing but a pair of extremely erotic leather underwear. I raced to the dresser and hurriedly pulled on a pair of khakis and tugged on the first T-shirt I could get a hold of, which was a dark brown. I was just getting it over my head when I heard knocking at my door.

I went to the door, unlatched it, and pulled it open, and there was Alexander. He was in very formal clothing, his curly hair combed as neatly as he was able. He wore brown corduroys that were slightly darker than my khakis, and a light blue button-down shirt, coupled with a gold necktie accented with a slightly darker blue stripe at a diagonal angle in the middle. It really brought out his eyes.

"Hi," I said, smiling, feeling a little breathless. "Come in."

"Thanks, he said, walking by me into the apartment. "I can't stay long, but I wanted to see how you were doing."

"I'm... doing OK, actually, I think," I replied.

"I'm sorry I didn't stop by earlier," Alexander said, giving me a sheepish look that only accentuated his handsomeness. "I couldn't get in earlier. Sunday," he said, as though the day of the week were a full explanation.

"Don't worry," I replied. "I only just got up a little while ago." As I said the words, my stomach growled, and I suddenly remembered the bread that I had put in the toaster. It was probably cold by now, but it was still food and I was still hungry. "I was making something to eat," I said, turning to the kitchenette. "I don't have much, but do you want anything?"

"No, thank you," I heard Alexander say from the main room. "Like I said, I can't stay long today; I just managed to get away for a little while to stop in like I'd promised. I have... family stuff to get back to."

I pulled one slice of room-temperature toast out of the toaster and looked quickly at the peanut butter. I could make a sandwich later. If Alexander couldn't stay long, I didn't want to keep him waiting. I walked back into the main room, crunching away on the plain toast.

Alexander was looking at my bookshelf when I walked back

in. His eyes went over the three Bibles, then I noticed his eyebrows arch when he reached the books on other religions.

"You like religion, huh?" Alexander mused as I approached. "What religion are you?"

"Your guess is as good as mine," I shrugged.

He looked at me with more than a hint of sympathy.

"Still can't remember anything, huh?"

"Not a thing," I said. "I had hoped to find something helpful here, but my computer is password protected, and my strongbox has a combination lock."

Alexander turned his gaze to the room and chewed his lip thoughtfully. "There might be a technician or a locksmith that can help with one of those things. I could ask around if you'd like."

"Sure, I guess."

"Nothing else that was helpful?"

"Well, there's nothing that jogged memories, at any rate," I said. "Though apparently I can play the clarinet."

"Really?" Alexander asked, his face registering interest. "I'd love to hear you play sometime," he added.

"Sure," I replied. "I'd be happy to oblige you."

There was a pause, the kind of awkward moment in a conversation where two people wonder if they may possibly be talking about more than they are putting into words.

"You... you look much better, today," Alexander said at last. "Though that's probably because you're dressed in actual clothes, instead of rags."

"Yeah, that helps," I said, smiling at him. Then I remembered that some of what I'd been wearing yesterday was his.

"Hold on," I said, looking around the room for the blue and white hoodie, and finding it on the floor by the bed where I had thrown it off in order to stare at myself in the mirror. I put the last bit of toast in my mouth, then picked up the rumpled fabric and turned back to Alexander.

"Here," I said, swallowing the bread. "You can have this back."

"I can't take it now," Alexander said; "I have to run, and I have nowhere to put it." He put his hands on mine to push the hoodie back to me, and his touch lingered a little longer than I'd expected it to. "How about I check in and pick it up tomorrow?"

"Sure," I said. Then I remembered the other person who had wanted to call again. Perhaps Alexander could provide some perspective.

"Marcus also wants to come by later," I said. "He rang the buzzer earlier today. I didn't let him up."

Alexander took his hands off mine and turned his head, studying my bookshelf.

"...Was he sober?" he asked at last.

"As far as I could tell," I said.

Alexander sighed.

"Marcus is like a different person when he hasn't been snorting or shooting up," he said, still looking at the bookshelf. "He's... a nice guy when he's himself. I mean, I like him a lot; that's why we were together. But he's been really fucked up lately. I wish I could help him. Sometimes I think he's a lost cause, but sometimes I still feel like maybe there's something I could do."

"Are you responsible for him?" I asked. It was a genuine question, but Alexander looked at me in surprise, as though I were asking something aggressive or snarky. He looked... upset? Hurt? Angry? I couldn't tell; it was an expression I hadn't seen on his face before.

"I... guess not," he said. "But I care about him. I still wish I could help him somehow."

"Well, maybe... we can figure something out," I said, not sure if I was being subtle or obvious in the use of 'we'. I had only just met Alexander, but he was definitely attractive, and definitely considerate. I didn't know what would come of him, but if there were any coming involved at all, I figured I'd be pleased. I felt a jump in my trousers and caught myself, trying to keep my mind—and my libido—from spinning out of control.

Alexander just smiled. "Thanks," he said. "Unfortunately, I really do have to run now. I gotta get back to church."

"Church?"

"Yeah." Alexander said. "You know," he added, turning his gaze to my bookshelf again, "if you like religion so much, maybe you'd like to see my church. But not today; today... isn't good. Too busy. Maybe tomorrow?"

"Um, OK," I said, not sure what to make of that.

"Anyway, if there's nothing that's jogging your memory in your apartment, maybe you should take a walk for a bit?" Alexander suggested. "Maybe something will spark some recognition. Just don't get lost, don't stay out late, and don't get too close to the site of that gas explosion; it's not safe."

"That's a good idea," I said. I'd just have to make sure I could find my way back to the apartment. Maybe I should draw a map? "I need to eat something more substantial, but maybe I'll go out later."

"Good," Alexander said, smiling. He put a hand on my upper arm. His touch was firm, warm, reassuring. "I'll see you tomorrow."

"See you tomorrow. Thanks for coming by," I said. There was an awkward hesitation, as though he wasn't sure what to do next. But then he let go and turned to the door, pulling it open.

"Enjoy church," I said as he went out the door.

"I'll do my best," he said, turning quickly to smile back at me as the door shut. I heard his footsteps go down the hall, and then he was gone.

I went back into the kitchen and made myself a proper peanut butter sandwich, then took an apple from the counter and crunched into it, catching the juice with the back of my hand as it dribbled down my chin. I took the apple and the plate with my sandwich back into the other room and plopped down on the small sofa, looking around the room again as I ate.

I really didn't recognize it. Not at all. It felt as though I was a stranger in my own body, my own mind, my own home, inhabiting them for the first time and learning everything all over again. I had thought that my memories might have been like a jammed door that just needed the impact of familiar surroundings to force open, but that hadn't been the case. Had I needed something more personal? But then, I had found a box of erotic photos and a dildo; what could be more personal than sex?

I poked around again, turning my attention to the backpack again. When I opened up the front compartment this time, I noticed another zippered compartment inside, one that I had missed. I opened it up and found a wad of bills.

Money.

That would be very useful. I slipped the bills into my pocket, for want of a better place to put them, then I glanced around the apartment again. I wondered if there was another location where I had been keeping things; perhaps I had an office or something? Come to think of it, I didn't even know what I did for a living.

With nothing else to occupy my attention, I returned to the thing in my apartment that I'd found the most interesting—apart from the box under my bed, of course.

I went to the bookshelf and scanned over the books on religion. I pulled out the second Bible, next to the one that I had opened earlier, and plopped onto the small sofa.

At the sudden shift in momentum caused by my landing on the cushion, an envelope slipped out of the Bible and fluttered to the floor. It must have been placed in as a bookmark, though I couldn't say what page it had been saving. I picked up the envelope and looked at it. There was no return address, but there was a label on the center. It had the address where I lived on it: 48 Oak Street, Apt. 32. It was addressed to Cole Hamilton.

Cole Hamilton.

So that was my name. I traced it with my finger, then said it aloud, tasting it as it rolled off of my tongue. Did it feel familiar? Or was I just wishing it did?

I opened the envelope and looked inside. Nothing. Whatever the envelope had once contained was gone; it now served as nothing more than a simple bookmark. But it was also my identity. I clutched it to my chest for a moment as though it were made of gold; then I turned my attention back to the Bible.

Where to start? At the beginning, I supposed. I skipped through the forwards and the preambles for the time being and opened to the first page of proper text: The book of Genesis.

It had clearly been read before. In detail. The chapter was covered in boxes, highlightings of different colors, with markings like "P writer" and "JE writer" scrawled across the side, and annotations like "Creation Story 1" and "Creation Story 2". I felt a tingle of excitement, a sense of stumbling into the middle of something, with hints at a deeper meaning or a detailed deconstruction that I was looking at without the background to understand what I was seeing. Someone had done a lot of work.

A thought occurred to me, and I set the Bible down, clutching the envelope in my hand. I went to the desk and pulled a pen out of a cup that sat on its surface, then turned the envelope over to the back.

"My name is Cole Hamilton," I wrote. "I know absolutely nothing else about myself."

I took the envelope and opened the Bible back up to Genesis, holding the scribbled note up in front of the notes and annotations scrawled across the Bible pages.

The handwriting matched.

These were my notes.

Fascinated, I dove into the book, reading the text, the annotations, and my own scribblings, piecing together a picture of the work I'd been doing. There were a lot of references to other books on the shelves scribbled in the margins, notes where aspects of Genesis coincided with historical record or with the religious tales of another group.

I read about Adam and Eve, Cain and Abel, the tower of Babel, Joseph and his colorful coat. Each section was covered with notes, but none more so than the section on Babel, covering the interactions between the denizens of heaven and earth. Similarly, any time the Elohim or any angel interacted with people, I had notes covering the section in detail. Reading them, I felt a twitch somewhere inside. I had put a lot of work into this. What had I been trying to learn?

When I looked up from the book, long shadows were being cast across the apartment. I had been so engrossed in reading that I'd completely lost track of time. If I was going to go out and get some air or look around a bit, now was the time to do it.

I grabbed my keyring off the nightstand and thrust it into my pocket along with the envelope that had my address. I had no wallet, no identification, but at least with my keys, a wad of bills, and my address, I could go out without only minimal worry of getting home again. I opened up the closet and selected a nice-looking brown windbreaker before heading out.

I walked out of my apartment and locked the door behind me. The building was quiet in the evening; a little claustrophobic, perhaps, with its low ceiling and glaring yellow lights, but definitely quiet. The street outside was similar: there was activity; a person walking here and there, a car driving down the road, but the air didn't seem to want to move. I walked along amid the lengthening shadows. I had no idea where to go. I was even unsure of the location of Marcus's place, what with all the back alleys we'd ducked down on our way to my apartment last night.

I made a rough mental note of the direction from which we had approached and decided to explore at a direction about 90 degrees from it. Perhaps something there would spark my memory.

There was nothing fancy about the first two blocks: a convenience store, a Chinese restaurant, a burger joint. One block further, however, the city seemed to grow quieter. I had seen a little activity on the streets near my apartment, but here the place was... dead.

I came around one of the buildings and I soon realized why: whatever awful accident Marcus had been referring to—the one that he'd found me near—must have happened here. An intersection and the surrounding buildings were cordoned off with yellow tape that read "POLICE LINE - DO NOT CROSS"; the tape extended out into the street beyond the far side of the intersection, then crossed the street and extended into what looked like a park. At the sight of the tape, something stirred inside of me. Marcus said he had found me around here, right? Had one of those buildings been the one that I had woken up in, amidst all the fog and confusion?

None of the buildings seemed familiar, but then I also couldn't get too good a look at things without crossing the police tape. Even with no one around, I didn't want to go rummaging about in a restricted area for fear of creating more trouble for myself than I already had. After all, what was I to do if a police officer started questioning me? I had no identification to speak of beyond an envelope with an address label, and that would certainly be viewed with suspicion. And what could I say in my own defense? That I was an amnesiac looking for answers? I decided instead to follow along the edge of the police tape and see if anything sparked recognition.

The tape ran along the edges of several buildings, but whatever had happened must have shaken people, because there was no one in the surrounding area. Even the buildings just outside the perimeter of the tape looked empty. Eventually I reached the end of the street and found myself at another, larger street, which was as empty as the previous one had been. I began walking across the road, but when I turned to glance past the tape I saw something that stopped me in my tracks.

Something had happened there. Something big. The area past the tape was a city square, but the pavement had been torn up, with chunks of asphalt jutting out from the surface of the road at sharp, violent angles. Lampposts were overturned; a newspaper stand had been blasted apart, and pages of newsprint still blew over the street, carried on the odd, convoluted currents of wind created by the arrangement of the surrounding roads and buildings. The more I stared, the more it seemed that the ground had exploded from below, as though a pipe or something had ruptured in a giant fireball. Considering the black blast marks radiating outward from the square, the explosion had been fierce. Unsettled, I turned my attention from the square and pressed onward into the park.

Like everything else near the police tape, the park lacked activity and people. It was a nice park, with enough trees to feel wooded but not so crowded as to make one feel as though they were lost in the woods. The paths wound around through gardens and between trees, occasionally around small, shuttered buildings, meandering through open spaces and narrow paths by bubbling streams. The evening had settled in force, now. The sun had finished dipping below the horizon, or at least below the level of the buildings, and the stretching shadows and orange strains of sunlight had merged into a pale gray that hung over the park like a shroud.

As I approached a small crossroads near where the police tape, still within view, veered off to the right, I stopped. Something felt off. I stood and listened, thinking perhaps I'd heard something without quite noticing it, and it was a moment before I realized what it was that had caught my attention.

It wasn't a noise.

It was the lack thereof.

Until now, while my immediate surroundings had been devoid of activity, I had still been able to hear the ambient noise of a city: the sound of distant traffic, an occasional car horn, a dog barking, the wind rustling, and the constant chatter of birds preparing to set down for bed. Now, there was none of that. It was *silent*. And it had happened all at once.

Unnerved, I turned to leave, and felt my breath catch in my throat.

Behind me, not 20 feet away, was the figure of a woman. She was unearthly; the air around her billowed and quavered like a cloak, blurred and frayed at the edges and floating on some unseen and unfelt current of air. Where the air stopped and her clothing began, I did not know; she was dressed in a shredded gown which almost seemed to float around her as she moved. And move she did, coming ever closer, her face hidden behind thick, agitated strands of black hair. She seemed to glide rather than walk; if she had feet I could not see them. Only then did it dawn on me that what I was looking at might not be human.

I wracked my brain, my memory, throwing myself against the walls of my mind as I stood rooted to the ground, panic settling over me. Every instinct told me that what I was seeing was unnatural, but without my memory, how was I to know? Maybe phantoms such as these were an everyday occurrence, and people paid them no mind?

Even as I thought it, however, I knew, somehow, that it wasn't true. The phantasm floated closer as the seconds dripped past; she was now perhaps only three yards away. Do I run? Do I wait?

Indecision and horror took the choice away from me, and I stood not moving, not breathing, as she glided closer, closer. I could feel the air grow still and chilly against my skin, felt the sweat on my brow turn to frost.

And then the apparition drew up alongside me, so close that I kept waiting for her to brush against me, but I felt no contact with her hair, her dress. And she paid me no heed, but simply continued by.

At last, after a few brief seconds that felt like an hour, I felt the temperature on my skin rise as the icy coldness of her presence pulled away from me. Barely able to breathe but still mesmerized, I found myself turning around to stare at her departing figure.

The phantom floated onward ethereally, moving deliberately toward some destination known only to it. And then, with a suddenness that made me jump, the figure jerked its head sharply up and to the right, its entire posture changing to that of an animal ready to fight.

I had no idea what had captured the wraith's attention until it darted backward a second later, just as a blur pounced down from among the trees and landed right where the phantom had been floating. Only for the instant that the newcomer landed was he still enough for me to clearly make out the figure of a man wearing some kind of indigo-colored clothing; a half-second later he turned and leapt at the wraith again, moving almost too quickly to see as he struck out with his bare hands, the phantom dodging and whirling away from each strike.

I watched in awe as the man swiped and kicked again and again at the phantom, occasionally dodging himself as the wraith shrieked and slashed out with hands that looked like talons. The newcomer's movements were sharp, swift, almost animal-like.

The tussle moved across the lawn of the park, back one way, then another, with the two locked in close combat. The phantom was clearly trying to move away, but the newcomer closed the distance every time the wraith made to retreat, dogging the phantom as it moved. As it dodged, the ghost seemed to flow from one place to another, with parts of its body fading into mist, sliding away, and reforming nearby.

As I stared, I found myself wondering how the newly arrived figure was even engaging in combat: this was a ghost, after all, was it not? It seemed nonsensical that a human being could strike mist, and this was a human... wasn't it?

Eventually, the wraith seemed to collect itself enough to keep its head relatively steady, even as the figure darted around the flapping shreds of cloth and flailing talons. Out from under the mess of limp hair opened a huge, gaping maw, that seemed to widen more and more as the creature inhaled. Before it could do whatever it was preparing to do, however, the newcomer turned suddenly and made a jabbing motion at the phantom's neck. I couldn't see if he was holding something, but nonetheless his aim was true, and the phantom's neck tore open, black smoke pouring out from the wound. The phantom reeled back, its head lolling, and the newcomer, his figure still blurry in the mist and smoke, leapt back for a moment and put his hand to his waist, grabbing something out of a small pouch. Whatever it was started to gleam in the newcomer's hand, and he tossed it forward at the phantom.

The one-and-a-half-second reprieve of the of the newcomer's disengaging, however, was enough to allow the phantom to collect itself, even with its lolling head, and the creature swirled into mist and dodged away from the trajectory of the tossed item. The moment's clarity let me see that it was a small silver sphere covered with engravings, with a small round button. As I watched, the etchings became laced with light, and then the entire sphere began to glow, shining more and more brightly as it flew into what was now empty space, the phantom having already disappeared into the departing breeze. I could only see the sphere for a second, however, before it exploded in a flash of light so sudden and so bright that it completely blinded me, reducing my vision to nothing.

"GAH!" I cried involuntarily as I rubbed my blinded eyes. "Fuck. FUCK!"

I blinked, once, twice, waiting for my vision to return. And when it finally did, it took my mind a moment to recover from the sight. Standing in front of me was a guy roughly my own age, maybe a year or two older, with a lopsided grin on his face. He was pale, with a sleeveless shirt of some sort of dark violet non-stretchy material that hugged his torso snugly. His arms were pale and sculpted, and he sported a dark elastic armband around one of his upper arms. He wore what looked like indigo compression pants, which squeezed his lean, muscular legs so tightly that he might as well not have been wearing anything at all—though they obfuscated his crotch just enough that I couldn't make out more detail there beyond a general (and generous) bulge. He had on a black belted pouch at his waist that had an open silver clasp. He was lean—so much so that I couldn't imagine him having much body fat at all—though the vest was such that it made it hard to make out the general phys-ical shape of his chest. Judging from his arms, however, he was in good shape indeed.

All of this, however, I noticed *after* his face, with that lopsided grin. He was handsome, with shaggy red hair that hung over his forehead like bangs, but fell around his ears on the sides and hung partway down his neck in the back. What was most striking, however, were his eyes: they were a bright gold color, and even without my memory I could tell that the color was unusual. He was extremely attractive, with a cut and trim figure that contrasted somewhat with his uneven, ragged hair. I got the vague impression of a jungle warrior raised in the wild (whoever that is; the image just kind of came to me), but with the body of a swift predator rather than a powerful ape.

"Hi," he said, nonchalantly. He had a dimple when he smiled. It was cute.

"Um... hi?" I managed back.

"Sorry; I didn't mean to catch you in that. I almost forgot you were standing there. Did I startle you?"

"Jumping down from the trees and playing tickle touch with the ghost of Miss Havisham? Yeah, a bit," I said.

He arched a red eyebrow, seemingly impressed with my response, while I stood there wondering what had gotten into me to make me so sarcastic, as well as who Miss Havisham was and why her name suddenly popped out of my mouth.

"Well, it sucks that she got away, but..." he stepped closer, nostrils flaring ever so slightly as he did so. "Looks like the evening wasn't a total loss."

Wait, was I being hit on?

"Um, what?" I asked.

"I'm Cuan," he said, easy smile still on his face. "I've been looking for you."

IV

CUAN

I STARED at the attractive young man with the golden eyes who had just tousled with a flailing phantom before casually introducing himself to me.

"You were... looking for me?" I asked.

"That's right," Cuan said, the half-grin still on his face, dimple in his cheek. He really was cute.

But wait; I had more important things to worry about. A sudden thought shot into my head.

"Wait, do you know who I am?" I asked, almost too eagerly.

"Um... no," he said, cocking his head and knitting his eyebrows. "But I think it's you. Were you on the green near Elm two days ago?"

I honestly couldn't answer that question. Instead, I responded with one of my own.

"I... I'm sorry," I said. "Have we met? Or were we just at the green—whatever that is—and you were cruising me from afar?"

"I've never seen you before," Cuan said. "Not that I mind seeing you now," he added, his mouth taking a little bit of a cocky turn. His bright white teeth glistened as he spoke. He had prominent canines. "But you fit the description."

"Description?" Was this some clumsy way of trying to pick me up? Or... God, was he out looking for NerdyHunk21?

"I'd been asking around," Cuan said by way of awkward explanation. "A woman saw someone staggering across the green around the time of that whole explosion in the square two nights ago. She came over to help, but then ran away because she thought he was possessed. She said the guy was vomiting and speaking in tongues."

"Um, the only tongue I know is English," I said. But my head was spinning as I relived that first night. Parts of it matched.

"Well, the rest of the description matches," Cuan said. "Young male, early 20s, brown hair, fit."

"Fit?"

"Well, you know, for someone wearing shredded clothes, I guess. But yeah, you're definitely fit." Cuan stepped closer and sniffed at me.

"Most importantly," he added, "you smell right."

"What?" I asked, indignant but distracted. Cuan was so close that I could smell *him*, a dark, seductive musk that made it hard to concentrate. It threatened to make me hard in other ways, too—there was just something *about* him. "What... what do you mean, smell right?" I stammered.

"That pool of vomit," Cuan said matter-of-factly. "It was definitely yours."

So much for the hardness.

"Well, I'm glad I smell like puke to you," I said, drawing back.

"No, no, that's not what I meant!" Cuan replied, waving placatingly. He leaned back, considering me. "Are you sure you don't speak any ancient languages?"

"I don't," I said. "The lady was the one speaking in tongues, not me."

"So it *was* you!" Cuan said triumphantly.

"Yes... no... maybe." I said, shaking my head. "I don't know. My memory of that night is hazy."

"What about before then?"

I paused. "My memory of before then is gone."

Cuan paused, fixing me with an expression of genuine concern.

"That... that sucks," he said simply.

That was just about the most accurate summation of my situation I'd yet heard.

"What were you doing out here?" he asked me.

"I was looking for something that would jog my memory," I admitted.

"Well, you walked right into danger," Cuan said. "You'll have to learn to be careful really quick."

"And what were *you* doing here?" I asked.

"I was hunting," he said simply.

"Huh?"

"I should explain," Cuan offered. "You see, I'm part of a group that... well, I guess you've seen some of what we do for yourself."

"You have wrestling matches with ghosts?" I asked.

Cuan's brows knit. "To make a gross oversimplification, yeah, you could say that." He sighed. "Of course, the reality is more complicated than that."

"Sometimes you box."

Cuan gave me a flat look. "Are you done?"

"Sorry," I said. The sarcastic responses just came naturally to me. Was this a defense mechanism? If so, then I liked it. But then again, perhaps it wasn't a good idea to use it on someone who was obviously quite dangerous.

"Are... are those things common?" I asked, looking toward where it had disappeared.

"No," Cuan said. "At least, they're not supposed to be. But things like that are becoming more and more common recently. Which is why we've been more active of late." He looked back at me again, scrutinizing my face.

"...What is it?" I asked.

"I don't know," he said. "Were you standing there the whole time I was fighting that thing? Did you hide at some point?"

"No," I said. "I was standing on the path, and she walked—or floated, or whatever—right by me."

Cuan blinked at me. "Seriously?"

"Yeah, I was too scared to move. Didn't you see me?"

"I did, at least at first. I mean, I smelled that you were nearby, and I did glimpse you on the path, and I knew on some level you were there the whole time, but after she showed up, you kind of faded into the background until you reacted to the flash. I'm so sorry; it's not like me not to notice someone, especially when a predatory phantom is about." He looked generally apologetic, but that wasn't what concerned me at the moment.

"You smelled that I was nearby?" I asked. "But why did you —wait, did you say *predatory*?"

"Yeah," Cuan responded. "That thing that you say floated right by you, that thing is a killer. It seeks out and slays the living, sucking the life right out of them."

"I..." I felt my blood run cold. Had I really been that close to death? "It must have been focused on something else," I said at last.

"No, I don't think so," Cuan said. Did you see how it suddenly stopped and turned toward me before I even could attack it? It sensed me from quite a ways away. It should definitely have noticed you. The fact that it didn't is kind of remarkable."

"I'm... I'm not sure I like being this kind of remarkable," I said.

"Well, the alternative tonight would have been having the life sucked out of you," Cuan replied.

"OK, starting to have less of a problem with the remark-ableness."

Cuan smiled that lopsided smile at me. "I think Cedric would like to meet you, even if you hadn't been the person we'd been looking for. Would you mind coming home with me?"

It wasn't exactly the kind of proposition a guy would hope for, but what the hell. Besides, if there were more things like that life-sucking phantom out in the night, I'd feel a lot safer with Cuan than I would on my own.

"Sure," I said. "By the way, my name's Cole. Cole Hamilton. That's about the only thing I know about myself."

Cuan gave me a sympathetic smile, but then extended his hand, and I took it. His grip was firm, warm.

"Nice to meet you, Cole." He said. "I'm Cuan Ingolf."

"So," I asked, as we turned and began walking out of the park, "How were you fighting that ghost, anyway?"

"Training," Cuan replied.

"Helpful," I said dryly.

"Sorry," Cuan chuckled, "but it really is about all I can offer. Each of us has our own way of fighting that draws upon our own abilities."

"And you... punch ghosts?"

"No," Cuan said. "I can't really do much to incorporeal phantoms, though that ghost was more solid than I'd expected. I was a little surprised I was able to slash its neck. I was trying to throw the thing off balance enough to catch it in the burst from the flashsphere."

"Flashsphere?"

"It's a... kind of light-generating device, I guess," Cuan explained. "I don't really know the details, but when it explodes it creates a burst of light bright and pure enough to banish a ghost."

"Banish it from the park?"

"Banish it from the world," Cuan clarified. "Straight into the afterlife, or wherever ghosts go when they're done here. In any case, it wouldn't be hunting around the park anymore if I'd managed to hit the thing square on. As it stands, the thing is out there, and people are still in danger." His expression was downcast.

"Don't be hard on yourself," I said. "What I saw was pretty damn impressive."

Cuan smiled at me, a kind of sad smile. "Thanks," he said.

"And your fighting's good, too," I added.

Cuan cocked an eyebrow at me, but the sadness left his smile.

We emerged from the park into the city street. It wasn't the way I had come in; in fact, I couldn't see any sign of the police tape. Night had fallen properly now, and the streetlights dotted the dark, empty roadway with intermittent pools of light. We walked into the road, when suddenly Cuan stopped in his tracks, his expression alert.

"What?" I asked.

"Shh."

Cuan turned to look down the length of the street. I turned to follow his gaze, but saw nothing. Nonetheless, Cuan must have sensed something that I didn't, because he tugged on my arm.

"This way," he said quietly. "Quickly."

He moved briskly ahead of me, almost at a trot, and I hurried after him toward a gap between two of the buildings. I was somewhat alarmed by his sudden change in behavior, but being able to follow behind him provided a pleasant distraction. I couldn't see the detail of the muscles of his back under the material of his sleeveless top, but his compression pants hugged his ass perfectly, the tight fabric pushing the cheeks into prominence as they bounced up and down while he moved. He had a very nice butt—tight and muscular for someone so lean, but still with enough shape and volume to provide a good handful. I wanted so badly to grip it in my hands and knead, but it was neither the time nor the place for such thoughts. At the same time, something about Cuan was compelling, and so I continued to stare at his ass as we moved. The back of his compression pants also seemed to have an odd seam near the top, but he was moving too quickly for me to get a good look at it.

At the other side of the road, Cuan slipped into the alley between two buildings, and I followed. The alley was tight, only wide enough for us to go down single file. We squeezed through alley after alley in a winding path before we finally emerged back into the open.

This street had houses, some with a tiny shred of yard on them, others a bit closer together. Cuan stopped in front of one of the houses, a dark brown home with an enclosed porch and a bit of space to its yard.

"This is us," he said.

I stared at the house. It was taller than it was wide, but also at least as long as it was tall. It seemed large for a city home, as though it could have been one house plus an in-law apartment. I suspected that it was older than the rest of the buildings on the street; not only did it look a bit aged, it also was situated on a slightly larger lot.

Cuan walked up the front steps leading to the enclosed porch, reaching into the band on his arm and slipping out a single key. He opened the porch door with a click and then walked across to the proper front door of the house. Cuan turned the key in this lock, too, and with his other hand, turned the doorknob. The door swung open. He turned around and looked at me.

"Come on in," he said.

I hesitated for a moment as Cuan walked into the dark front hall ahead of me. But I had come this far, hadn't I? I stepped into the doorway.

"I'm back," Cuan announced to the dark interior of the house.

Even from the inside, the house looked perfectly normal. I hadn't been sure what to expect when Cuan was talking about living with a group of hunters, but this picture of normalcy was not it. A stairwell ran up the right side of the unlit foyer, leading away from the door, and beside the stairwell a hallway stretched forward, rooms branching off from the sides here and there. The building wasn't spotlessly kept by any means, but neither was it in disrepair. It looked, for all intents and purposes, like a well-lived-in home. I found myself thinking that, when lit, the hallways would probably be warm and comfortable. As it was, though, the darkness was a bit forbidding. Cuan kept walking to the end of the hall, where incandescent light peeked out of a small diamond-shaped window in a door set ajar. Cuan pushed the door open, and the light spilled around him, the edges of his hair glinting a bright, fiery red. I heard a gruff, slightly gravelly male voice from the room beyond.

"You are back. How was it?"

Cuan turned his head to the left to address the unseen speaker. "It didn't go as well as I would have liked," he said, his voice slightly subdued. "The phantom noticed me. I nearly had it, but it got away."

"Great," came another voice, this one sharp, young, and female. "What a waste of resources. And now you're home with your tail between your legs, and the evening is a total loss."

"Well, maybe not a *total* loss..." Cuan began.

"Cuan," the gruff male voice interrupted. "You do understand the situation that we are in. We are fortunate at the moment that we can operate without fear of witnesses or bystanders."

"That's the first time I've heard anyone refer to a massive explosion in a public square as 'fortunate'," Cuan responded. His silhouetted shoulders drooped, his posture submissive.

"You know what I mean," the gruff voice said sharply. "But it will not be long before people start frequenting the park and the campus again, no matter how hard the police try to discourage them. It is much harder to work in the shadows when there are eyes everywhere."

"I know," Cuan replied. "I'm sorry. But the phantom could see me coming a mile away. Perhaps we're going about this the wrong way."

"Or sending the wrong person," The sharp young female voice offered from the other side of the room.

Cuan ignored the interruption and continued. "We need a different approach, one that isn't so direct."

The gruff voice cut in again. "We do not have time to brainstorm new approaches, Cuan," it said. "Every night we fail to contain that creature is another night that people could get killed. And every night we waste by missing our chance is another night we are not spending going after other threats. Do you at least still have the flashsphere?"

Cuan's head fell.

"So we cannot try again tomorrow. We need another sphere, first. If you have nothing else to report, have some dinner and go rest."

"Actually," Cuan started, with the slightest hint of hesitation in his voice, "there is something else."

He turned, beckoning me forward.

"I found someone in the park," he said as I moved into the light of the doorway. I felt Cuan's hand resting against my back as he presented me. In one way, I felt like his hand was there to reassure me, but in another way, it felt as though it was there to reassure himself, like he was claiming an ally.

"Um, hi," I said awkwardly as I looked into the room for the first time. It was a simple kitchen-slash-dining-room running along the back wall of the house, done in dark greens and browns with lighter highlights. It smelled of deep, rich tones, like tomatoes and beef and root vegetables. The centerpiece of the room was a long, wooden table under an electric chandelier-style hanging lamp. Walking from the stove at the far left corner of the room to the table was man in a brown cloak, carrying two sets of silverware. His head was covered by a wide-brimmed hat over what looked like slicked-back brown hair. Upon my announcing myself, he deposited the silverware on the table, which clattered noisily.

"You brought someone back here?" the man hissed.

"I did," Cuan replied simply. "I thought he might be able to help us."

The man stared at me, looking me up and down. At least, I thought that's what he was doing: in spite of the dim light, he wore a pair of sunglasses that obscured his eyes. His hidden stare made me uncomfortable. The man's age was hard to pin down: his features were not aged, but he had a ruggedness about him, as though his edges were roughened from use. His expression—what I could see of it, anyway—was unimpressed.

"You brought me a boy," the man frowned. "What about him is so remarkable?"

"Nothing," Cuan responded simply.

"Hey, thanks," I shot sarcastically over my shoulder.

"Nothing?" The man replied, one eyebrow arching and his frown deepening. "Are you mocking me?"

"No, that's not what I meant," Cuan clarified. "I mean, there's nothing about him that you would look at and find remarkable."

"You are not helping your case," The man growled.

"No, listen," Cuan responded, clearly flustered. The hand on my back clenched slightly. "There's something about him that... defies attention. He was nearby when I was fighting with the phantom, and I might not have noticed him at all if—"

"He was there?" The man interrupted. "So, there was a bystander. Did you bring him here to preempt his spreading confused rumors?"

"No," Cuan responded. "I'm trying to tell you that he was right there, and I almost didn't notice him."

"HA!" came a voice from the other end of the room. "Some tracker you are. So are you just totally useless, or what?"

It was the female voice that I'd heard earlier. I had completely forgotten about it. Startled, I looked into the corner of the room where the voice had originated, and saw a young woman sitting comfortably in a very large easy chair. She looked barely out of high school, though there was a worldliness about her that suggested a little more age. She wore a black tank-top with frills and a plaid skirt, the latter of which may or may not have been part of a school uniform. She had rich, long black hair that cascaded over her shoulders, and sharp, piercing black eyes with long lashes. Dark eyeshadow and a beauty mark under the corner of her mouth, which was now curled into a cruel smirk, stood out in stark contrast with her milk-white skin. Around her neck she wore a black lace choker. She was leaning back in her chair, lounging like a cat, looking disdainfully at Cuan.

"I didn't know Cruella de Vil had a daughter," I blurted flatly. The girl sneered and sat back in her chair, looking actively uninterested, while I tried to figure out who Cruella de Vil was and why I knew her name.

Cuan looked askance at the girl, an uncomfortable expression on his face.

"You don't understand," he said. "The phantom didn't notice him either. At all."

"Hm?"

I turned back toward the table, immediately and uncomfortably aware that the man was now suddenly standing directly in front of me. He placed a rough hand on my chin and stared curiously into my face. His breath was hot and stale, and I could feel his eyes boring into me, even obscured behind the sunglasses.

"Um, may I help you?" I asked.

The man ignored me and turned his face to Cuan. "How close was he?"

"The phantom passed right by him," Cuan replied. "It may have even brushed him on its way past."

"Truly?" The man said, turning back toward me, his hand still on my chin. "OK, you have piqued my curiosity." He released me and stepped back, looking at me expectantly. "Well?"

"Well what?" I asked.

"Well, go on," he said. "What are you?"

I cleared my throat. "Well, I'm a simple guy; I'm not big into parties, but I'm happy to hang out with some friends or catch a movie. I'm at my best, though, curled up on the sofa at home, having a chat, reading a book, or watching Netflix. I like classical music, and I play an instrument. If you ask nicely—"

"What is this, a fucking dating profile?" the girl on the sofa interrupted. She leaned forward, the smirk back on her lips. "So, you want to play?"

"Sorry, Little de Vil;" I replied, deliberately dismissive, "but you aren't my type."

"What?" she asked, leaning forward, pushing her shoulders forward to accentuate her chest. "You don't want me to serve you up a helping of woman?"

"Believe me, there's *nothing* on that menu that I find appetizing."

I heard a snort behind me as the girl scowled and flopped back into her chair.

"Glare at me all you want," I said, "but when I wake up in the morning, I want sausage, not muffin."

"Your loss," she frowned.

"You know, I really don't think it is," I offered.

"You'd love my muffin," she said tauntingly. "Can't you just picture it?"

"Dry and flaky; lots of crumbs?"

"The hell it is," the she glared. "My muffin is warm and moist."

"And probably full of yeast."

There was silence for a moment. I marveled inwardly at myself. Her disdain toward Cuan had immediately rubbed me the wrong way, but even so, I was surprised at my sharp responses toward this person I'd never met. Was I always so edgy?

"I like you," the girl said at last.

"Congratulations," I replied offhandedly.

"If you are quite finished," the gruff man growled, "can we get back to the point at hand?"

"And what is that?" I asked, turning to him.

"Why did the phantom not notice you?"

"Perhaps she prefers muffins?" I asked.

The man slammed his hand sharply on the table, anger flashing across his features. "Take this seriously!" he barked.

"Take what seriously?" I barked back. "I haven't a fucking clue what's going on here. All I know is that the nice one here —" I gestured behind me at Cuan, whose reassuring hand hadn't left my back, "—asked me to come back with him because he thought I might be of help. Then I walk in and you all start peppering me with questions and waving girl parts at me and haven't even bothered to tell me who the hell you are."

"And why should we be telling you anything?" the man asked menacingly.

"Because he's the one you've been looking for," Cuan said from behind me.

The man looked past me, over my shoulder, at Cuan.

"What?" he asked.

"On the green, two days ago," Cuan summarized. "After the explosion, woman encounters a guy in his early 20s, can't understand a word he says, guy starts puking, woman runs away. This is the guy."

The man looked at me, then turned to what looked like a half-pantry, half-supply closet at the right end of the room. He grabbed an old, dusty hardcover off of one of the shelves and tossed it roughly into my hands.

"What does that say?" he asked.

I stared at the book; an old, hard-bound volume with a cloth cover. On the front were characters in embossed gold; I didn't recognize a one.

"It says 'How the Fuck Should I Know? Volume 1'," I replied.

The man lunged forward and snatched the book out of my hands.

"This is not the guy," he growled.

"I'm telling you, it is," Cuan said. "He doesn't have any memory of speaking any tongues; to him, the woman was speaking in tongues. But it's the guy. He smells right. It's part of why I noticed him."

The man's expression changed slightly in a way I couldn't figure out.

"You did not notice him until you recognized the smell?" he asked.

"Do I need a shower or something?" I asked, feeling vaguely insulted.

"Silence," the man said to me. He turned back to Cuan. "Well?"

"More or less," he shrugged. The hand on my back tightened a bit again.

The man turned toward the wall and pressed a button on an intercom of some sort.

"Come down here a minute," he said into the intercom, then let go of the button. He turned back to me. "Go stand in the hall," he instructed.

"What?" I asked.

"Just do it," the man demanded. "Stand against the wall and don't move."

I turned, and Cuan met my gaze and nodded. I walked into the dark hallway, pressed my back up against the wall, and waited.

A moment later, someone came briskly down the stairs on the opposite side of the hall. I couldn't see his features well, but he looked like a fairly normal middle-aged man, with thin grey hair, balding somewhat. He turned at the bottom of the stairs and walked straight past me into the lit room.

"What is it?" he asked.

"Have you noticed anything out of the ordinary here tonight?" the gruff man asked.

There was a pause, and then I heard the man reply, "Can't say that I have."

"OK, that is all. It must be my imagination. Sorry to bother you."

The balding man reappeared in the hallway, walked past me once again, and then turned up the stairs, muttering "... waste of my goddamn time..." as he did so. I heard his footsteps on the landing above me, and then he was gone.

I turned back to the room to see the gruff man in the doorway. His expression was a mixture of curiosity and something else—admiration?

"OK, I am convinced," he said. He outstretched his hand.

"You may call me Cedric. I think you could be of help to us, after all."

V

THE MIDNIGHT HUNTERS

I LOOKED Cedric up and down, from his wide hat to his outstretched hand to his booted feet. His features were still hard, but his face had lost its expression of cool disapproval. It wasn't a friendly face, but it was at least cordial, more so than it had been before. I hadn't felt particularly welcomed thus far, but Cuan had clearly gone out on a limb to bring me here, and if he had truly been looking for me, perhaps someone here would be able to tell me something about who I was.

I took the man's hand. "Cole," I said. "Now do you mind explaining what you mean by 'help you'?"

Cedric turned and led me back into the lit room. Cuan was still immediately to the left of the door, waiting quietly with his arms folded behind his back, while the young woman was still slouched in a chair in the corner of the room, off to my left. Cuan met my eye as I followed Cedric into the doorway, but he said nothing.

"I was surprised when Cuan said he had almost not noticed you," Cedric said as he headed to the stove and began spooning something out of a pot into a pair of bowls, "and Lester's missing you in the hall confirms it. There is something unusual

75

about you, if two of our most perceptive members were not aware of you right away."

"Oh, is the bitchy one back?" the girl said lazily, looking up from her chair.

"And here again, Bianca did not notice you reenter until I drew attention to you," Cedric added.

"Or maybe I just don't give a shit about him," remarked the girl, apparently named Bianca.

"And yet you have interacted with him more since he arrived than you do with nearly anyone else here," Cedric responded.

There was a pause.

"Shut up," Bianca said at last, looking away.

Cedric walked over to the table and plunked a bowl down in front of me, then one in front of Cuan. "Dinner. Would you like some stew, Cole?"

"Um, sure," I said, and took a seat at the table. Cuan sat down next to me, uttered a quick "Thanks for cooking again," and dug in, eating hungrily.

I eyed the stew in front of me. This had clearly been the source of the rich smell that had filled the kitchen. It looked to be a beef stew with a tomato base. I was a little leery of these new people, but the rumbling in my stomach was insistent. I took a big spoonful of stew and lifted it to my lips.

It was good. Very good. The ingredients—tomato, beef, a little cream, and some other things I couldn't quite place—blended perfectly.

"This is fantastic," I said, looking up. "Thank you."

"You are a guest, and guests eat," Cedric said simply, settling into a chair across from me. He watched me eat for a moment more, and then asked, "So, what has Cuan told you of us?"

I looked at Cuan. He looked up from his dish to meet my eyes, licking a bit of tomato off his lip, expression otherwise blank. He gave a half-shrug.

"You fight ghosts?" I offered to Cedric. "You use something called a flashsphere?"

"Sometimes." Cedric nodded. Anything else?

"Not really," I admitted.

"Good," he said. I felt my eyebrows raise. "Do not misunderstand; that has nothing to do with you. I am just pleased to know that Cuan has been appropriately circumspect."

"That's very nice for you," I said, "but 'circumspect' is not going to fly if you want me to help you with whatever it is that's going on. Apparently an undead death machine moseyed right past me in the park tonight, and now I'm being treated like I'm the strangest thing that you guys have run into today."

"Not just today," Bianca added.

"Stop it," Cuan snapped at her.

"Bite me," she snapped back.

"We are the Midnight Hunters," Cedric explained. "We combat the forces that are encroaching upon this world; things that should not be here. It is a quiet battle that, if all goes well, is never seen by the people it is waged to protect."

"And if it doesn't go well?" I asked.

"People die," Cedric said simply.

"And this..." I added, gesturing at nothing in particular, "this encroachment has been ongoing for a while now?"

"It is always ongoing," Cedric said. "The ordered world that humanity thinks it knows is an illusion, a necessary lie that people tell themselves to keep their sanity. Reality is frayed at the edges, and all manner of things can weave themselves into the fabric of our world. But lately, here, things have been unusually active."

"Unusually active?" I asked.

Cedric watched me behind his sunglasses. "Tell me, Cole, what have you noticed in the last several days?"

"I don't know," I said.

"Typical ignorance," Cedric sighed. "Think."

"That's not it," I replied. "I mean, I don't remember."

Cedric raised an eyebrow.

"I have no memory of anything before two nights ago," I said.

Cedric turned to Cuan, a question on his face.

"That's what he told me," Cuan said through a mouthful of stew.

"What do you know of yourself?" Cedric asked.

"Honestly, pretty much what I told you earlier. I play the clarinet. I live by myself in an apartment. I have a lot of books on religion. I—" I was going to say 'own a box of erotic comic books,' but thought better of it. "I don't know much more than that."

"What is the earliest thing you remember?" Cedric asked.

I hesitated, but then realized that, if anyone was going to hear my story and not think I was insane, it was probably the three people in this room. I described waking up in the building filled with fog—or perhaps smoke—and my struggle to find my way out, my encounter with the woman whose speech I couldn't understand, about losing consciousness, about being found by a 'friend' who knew little more about me than where I lived. I was sparse with the details after that.

"This 'friend' of yours didn't take you to the hospital?" Bianca asked sharply.

"He... apparently isn't on good terms with the authorities and didn't want to get himself in trouble," I said evasively.

"Huh," Bianca said. "I bet I'd like him."

"I'm sure you would," I said honestly.

"So," Cedric concluded, "you are the person that was seen out on the green, after all."

"So I'm told," I said.

"It is a shame you have no memory," Cedric said. "The way the woman described what you were saying, I thought you might be able to read script like the one that book is written in."

I shook my head. "I don't know what I might have known before, but now I just know English." I looked at the book on the table. "What language is that, anyway? Greek?"

Apparently I knew that 'Greek' was a language, at least.

Cedric gave a low laugh. "Hardly," he said.

"I wonder..." came Cuan's voice at my side.

"What is it?" Cedric asked.

Cuan placed a hand on my shoulder. His touch was reassuring. "It must be terrible to have lost your memory. I can't imagine how frustrated you must feel. But I wonder... I wonder if there might be something in that building where you awoke that can help. Perhaps we can find that place, and maybe a clue to what happened."

"That whole part of the city is cordoned off," Bianca said. "There are police all over the place since that explosion in the square."

The explosion.

"I've been hearing a lot about that explosion," I said. "What happened?"

"The city is claiming that it was a gas pipe that ruptured," Cedric said.

"You don't believe them?" I asked.

"Who knows?" Cedric responded. "In situations like this, the authorities cannot be trusted to act effectively, if they act at all. Most people are unwilling to accept what they cannot see or prove. And even those who do believe are often unable to accurately filter the grains of truth from hearsay and rumor."

"Why don't you talk to them, tell them what is really going on?" I asked.

Bianca scoffed. "Are you for real? They would put us away! Think about it. Why didn't you go to the police or the hospital right after you woke up, after that asshat friend of yours didn't get you treated?"

I said nothing. She was right, of course; even without my

memory, I knew that nobody would have taken me seriously. I simply nodded.

"I am sure we can find a way to get you back where you awoke," Cedric said. "And so, perhaps we can help one another out. You help us; we help you."

"And... what exactly is it that you need?" I asked.

"We need you to help us with that phantom," Cedric said.

"Um, come again?" I asked, nearly dropping my spoon.

"That phantom," Cedric repeated. "It seems that you are, for some reason, beneath its notice, at least if you do not draw attention to yourself. If it passes by you, you could toss a flashsphere to it and eliminate it without its even having a chance to react."

"Hold on a moment," Cuan interjected, looking up from his bowl. "I'm not sure I'm comfortable requesting this."

"You're the one who brought him here," Cedric said matter-of-factly.

"Yes, I did. But I thought he might be able to help track the phantom safely, not actually engage it."

"What help would tracking be?" Bianca asked. "We already have a good idea of where it shows up."

"But engaging it isn't safe," Cuan insisted. "What if he misses? Tossing a flashsphere out isn't exactly inconspicuous. The phantom would come right for him."

"Do you have a better idea?" Bianca asked.

"We can cover Cole in case things get difficult," Cedric suggested.

"I don't like it," Cuan said. "We'd be putting him in danger. There must be something else we can do."

"What, like have you go in and embarrass yourself again?" Bianca said. "I'm surprised you even bother coming back here; all I've ever seen you do is fuck up."

I felt my hackles rising again. "I don't see you volunteering," I said to Bianca.

"I have other things to worry about," she said to me, a sneer on her face.

"Oh, like waving your breasts at guys you just met?" I asked. "Seriously, who would go for that?"

"You just don't know sexy when you see it," Bianca responded. "You're lucky I even gave you a second glance; I bet that's more than you usually get. Being ignored seems like your specialty."

"And what's yours?" I asked. "Giving half-rate handjobs behind the stadium of your old high school to toothless old guys with a Lolita complex?" The words were out of my mouth without my even having any idea of who the hell Lolita was.

"Hey, any straight man would be *begging* for what I could give him."

"Begging, or paying? Not that you're talented enough for sex work, anyway."

"Oh, please. If I charged, it'd be way more than you could afford, you little shit."

"Yeah, right," I said dismissively. "I bet guys hand you a fiver and get back four-fifty and an STI—"

She moved faster than I could see. One instant, she was sitting in her chair, snarking at me. The next moment, there was clattering, and she was on the table, her hand with its sharp nails less than a foot from my face. Cuan was standing, one knee up on the table, his hand grasped tightly around her wrist, arresting her movement. He'd moved faster than I could see, too. I blinked, stunned.

"That's enough," Cuan stated, his voice a low growl. If I hadn't been so shaken I would have found it damn sexy. "Sit down, Bianca."

Bianca didn't move. She smiled at me, darkly, sweetly, menacingly.

"I like you," she said through her teeth, "but that doesn't mean I won't fuck you up."

"I'll keep that in mind," I said flatly, trying hard to keep my voice steady. I took a breath. "I'll do it," I said to Cuan. "I'll help you."

"I am glad to hear it," Cedric said from his chair. He hadn't moved.

Bianca began to withdraw from the table, and Cuan released her wrist. She slid back down into her chair, her eyes never leaving my face.

"You've got balls, I'll give you that," she said.

I was suddenly aware of a wet feeling in my lap. I pushed back from my chair to see that both my bowl and Cuan's had been overturned in the commotion, and both of their contents had been deposited in my lap.

"Aw, man," I said, pushing my chair back and looking down at the mess.

"That is going to stain," Cedric said.

"Dammit," I said.

"That's a mess," Cuan said. "Here, you and I have somewhat similar body types; I'm sure I have something that can fit you."

Yet another person lending me clothes. I didn't want this to become a trend. On the other hand, I had a lot of soup in my lap, and it was getting cold fast. And while the tomato stew smelled great in the bowl, it didn't smell nearly as nice on my khakis.

"Sure," I said, "That'd be very kind of you."

Cuan stood up and I did the same, feeling the soup soak into me, a tomato and a hunk of beef falling from my lap onto the floor.

"Do not worry about that," Cedric said when I started to bend down to pick up the chunks of food. "Go find something dry to wear. And be quick about it; we have planning to do."

I nodded, then followed Cuan out into the hall, deliberately avoiding eye contact with Bianca as I left the kitchen. Cuan turned and led me up the stairs, which turned to a dark, narrow hallway with doors lining both sides. He went two doors down and turned a knob on the left.

"This is my room. Come on in," he said, stepping inside. I followed him. The door swung shut behind me.

The bedroom was sparse, which probably made it look larger than it actually was. It featured a bed and nightstand, a small shelf, a dresser, and a door that perhaps led to a closet, but apart from a small window with drawn curtains, it had no other furnishings. The walls were completely bare. A single light fixture was set in the ceiling, which was turned off, but there was a lamp on the nightstand, which shed a low incandescent glow across the room.

Cuan went to the dresser and began rummaging through its contents.

"Are you OK?" He said as he searched, his face buried in the drawers.

"Huh?" I asked.

"Bianca. She doesn't usually lash out like that."

"Oh," was my reply. "She's a peach."

"You think so?"

"Did I say 'peach'? I meant 'bitch'."

"You really have a mouth on you," Cuan responded, pulling up a pair of what looked like dark indigo lounge pants and looking them over appraisingly.

"Oh. Sorry," I said.

Cuan turned and looked at me, his mouth curved into a half-smile, the dimple back in his cheek.

"I didn't say I didn't like it," he said, as he tossed me the pants. "Will these do? They're Wushu pants."

I caught them and looked them over. They weren't lounge pants at all; they were the kind of flowing, roomy pants that practitioners of Tai Chi might wear. The material was light and roomy, and the fabric felt like it might be a mixture of cotton and silk with a heavy emphasis on the latter. They were well-worn; there was a hole in the back just below the waistband, though nothing that would present a problem. I pulled the sides to appraise their size. Cuan was taller than me, so they would be a little long in the leg, but they would fit my waist fine.

"These'll do nicely," I said. "Thanks."

"Good," Cuan said. "And don't worry about your trousers; I'll wash them for you and you can get them back next time I see you."

For some reason, the words 'next time I see you' made me feel warm.

"Thanks, that's really kind," I said. I turned my back to him and undid my belt. I thought for a moment about asking Cuan to turn away, but then I thought, what the hell—it's just me in my trunks, what's the big deal? I'd still be more covered than when Marcus and Alexander found me. "Much kinder than the other people here," I added, as I unzipped my fly and let my trousers drop to the floor.

"They just—" Cuan began, and then immediately stopped. "Well, hell-*O!*" he said appreciatively.

"Huh?" I asked, confused, turning toward him as I did so. Or at least, turning as best I could with the fabric around my ankles.

"You dress plainly enough, but peel back a layer and *wow.*"

Cuan was staring, his dancing golden eyes focused below my waist. I looked down, confused, and then suddenly realized: I hadn't been wearing any of the trunks I had found in my drawers; I was wearing a leather jockstrap. And I had just given Cuan a very clear front-and-back view.

"Oh, SHIT," I said, flustered, turning away from him, pressing the Wushu pants against my crotch, then, realizing that I was giving him a view of my bare, jockstrap-augmented ass cheeks again, turning back to face him.

"Hey, now; hey," he said quickly, softly, placatingly, concern on his face as he crossed the space between us. "I'm sorry; don't be embarrassed."

I looked at him, his red hair and brows; his apologetic expression; his bare, muscular arms; his vest-clad torso; his tight, muscular legs in the dark blue spandex with the generous bulge. The bulge seemed to be getting bigger, taking on a more specific shape as it did.

"Cuan," I said, staring him in the eyes, "are you turned on?"

He stopped, standing maybe a foot and a half from me. "Who wouldn't be," he said, half-smile creeping across his face again, "after seeing an ass like that?"

"Cuan..." I breathed uncertainly. He stepped forward again, tentatively, his eyes searching my face, my torso. I felt my arms drop to my sides, the Wushu pants still gripped in my left hand, giving him a clear view of the front of the now-tight jockstrap. I liked his eyes on me, I realized—liked it a lot. I could smell him; a dark, sweet, musky scent that filled my nostrils and made my head spin. Lightly, Cuan placed a hand on my left side, over my brown T-Shirt, as he moved slowly closer to me. Our bodies were nearly touching. The hand slid down slowly, slowly, to the hem of my shirt. His eyes lifted from my crotch, tracing over the front of my shirt before rising to my face and locking on my own.

"Can I...?" he asked, his voice almost a whisper, sonorous and sweet.

I nodded as his face came closer to mine, his lips parting ever so slightly.

We were interrupted by a loud rapping immediately behind my head; I jumped sharply at the sound, nearly headbutting Cuan, who darted back out of the way with an expression that was a mix of surprise, irritation, and disappointment.

"Hurry it up in there!" came Bianca's pointed voice from behind the closed door. "How long does it take to choose a pair of pants? Cedric is waiting for you!"

The moment was broken.

"We're coming," Cuan called.

"I wish," I muttered under my breath as I lugged the Wushu pants onto my legs. I wasn't sure if Cuan heard me or not. I grabbed my keys, the old envelope, and the wad of cash out of my old pants, then turned and pulled open the door. Bianca was already gone from the hallway.

Cuan and I descended back to the open room where we had been eating. There was no sign of the spilled stew; the table and floor had been cleaned in our absence. Bianca was back in her chair; Cedric was standing on the opposite side of the table. He did not invite us to sit, but rather began talking as soon as Cuan entered the room, his voice brusque and businesslike.

"Right, then," he said. "The plan is simple. Cole, you will take a flashsphere into the city another night, back to where the phantom appeared. You will wait for it to pass close by, and detonate the sphere right beneath it. It will not have a chance to escape because you will be unnoticed you before you throw the sphere."

"Hold on," I said. "If I detonate the sphere right next to me, what happens to me?"

"Nothing," Cedric said. "The sphere is basically concentrated light. I suppose it could harm you if you were physically holding the sphere when you detonated it, but as long as you are not immediately on top of the blast, the most you will get is some UV exposure."

"So wear some sunscreen," Bianca said from the chair.

"OK, next question," I said. "Didn't you say to Cuan earlier that you needed another flashsphere, that that was the only one you had?"

Cedric's face darkened as he looked pointedly at Cuan. Cuan seemed to shrink slightly under his gaze. "Yes," he said. "The flashsphere is a delicate technology, one that we do not have the ability to manufacture ourselves. We are, essentially, a small team living in a small house. We can procure a sphere, but it may take a few days. We will contact you when we have one in hand."

"And how will you contact me?" I asked. "I don't have a phone right now. I don't know my own e-mail address, and I can't access my own e-mail even if I did." I felt frustration growing inside me as I thought of my computer. My entire identity, locked behind passwords and keycodes.

"Cuan will escort you home," Cedric said. "That way, he will know where to find you when we need you."

"And I'm supposed to just sit in my house all day, waiting for you?"

Cedric glowered at me. "Go about your business. We will find you."

"And what if I need to contact you?"

"You won't," Bianca said.

"Hey," Cuan cut in. "We're essentially asking Cole for a favor here, and we know what the city has been like lately. The least we can do is give him a way to reach us."

Cedric sighed. He reached into his pocket and produced a small, gold sphere, about the size of a marble, and handed it to me. "I assume you have a window, yes? Put one of these on the windowsill if you need to signal us."

"Really?" I asked dryly.

"You have no phone or e-mail, right? And those are not secure modes of communication anyway. This will suffice."

"But how—"

"Enough questions," Cedric said, turning away and waving his hand dismissively. "Cuan, take Cole home and come right back. Do not dawdle; we have tomorrow's work to discuss." He turned his head and looked Cuan sharply in the eye. "And it goes without saying, but keep a low profile; do not speak with anyone."

"Instructions you clearly followed quite well earlier this evening," Bianca said.

I turned to give her a piece of my mind, but felt Cuan's hand on my arm.

"Come on," he said softly, "let's go."

I glared at Bianca, then followed Cuan down the hallway and out of the house. The clear night air was a refreshing change from the closeness of the kitchen. I breathed deep.

"So," Cuan said to me, "where do you live?"

I thought back to the brick apartment. The address came easily, probably because there wasn't much in my memory to compete with it.

"48 Oak," I said, "Apartment 32."

Cuan smiled. "So, you do remember something!"

I shook my head. "Not really. I re-learned it when I found my apartment the last time." I looked around. Cuan had ducked down a number of alleys and side streets on the way to his home, and besides, I had been far more focused on Cuan's tight butt as he trotted ahead of me than on my surroundings. "I don't know how to get there from here, though," I admitted. "Do you know where 32 Oak is?"

Cuan frowned. "Do you know anything that it's near?"

I thought for a moment. "I know how to get to the city square from there, though I might have a hard time navigating at night."

"That wouldn't be safe anyway," Cuan said.

"Wait," I said, remembering some of the places I had passed while on my way to the city square. "It's about a block away from a Chinese restaurant called the Jade Dragon."

Cuan's face brightened. "I know that place!" he said. "I ate there once. Really good sweet and sour chicken, really bad lo mein." He turned his head, as though sniffing the air. "This way."

We began walking along the streets, Cuan now keeping

more to main roads and less to alleyways. He didn't trot ahead of me, but rather walked at my side. As he walked, he turned his face up into the breeze, as though enjoying the cool air on his face.

"It's a nice night," he said, that dimpled half-smile appearing on his face for a moment before his expression dimmed. "I'm sorry that it wasn't a more relaxing evening for you."

"So those are the people you spend time with?" I asked him.

"Yeah," he said to me. "The Midnight Hunters."

"Pleasant bunch," I said dryly.

Cuan looked at me. "Sorry," he said. "Cedric can be harsh, but that's because he has a lot to worry about. He's a good leader, and he takes care of us."

"By talking down to you?"

Cuan frowned. "He was being fair. I messed up tonight. I deserved that."

"I don't think so," I said. "From what I saw, you took on a monster and are still here. And hey, you were looking for me, and you found me, right?"

"Yeah, I guess that's true."

"It is true," I said. "And I'm sorry, I know I only just met them, but Bianca is a complete bitch."

Cuan sighed. "Bianca's been through a lot," he said. "We all have."

I looked at him quizzically. "What do you mean?" I asked.

"Just that... we all have a past."

I frowned. "I don't."

"Hey," Cuan said, stopping and putting his hands on my shoulders and fixing me with his bright, golden eyes, "listen to me. You have a past. You might not remember it, but that doesn't mean it doesn't exist. Cedric said we would help you after this, and he always keeps his word. And so do I."

"Cuan..."

For the second time that night, I felt the urge to kiss him, but Cuan released my shoulders and turned back down the street, walking us down and around a corner. "I know you have no reason to trust us yet," he continued. "I know you have no reason to trust *me* yet. But I promise I won't steer you wrong. Look," he said, big half-smile, pointing ahead of him. Down the street, the neon sign for the Jade Dragon restaurant shone in the night.

"You're really something," I said, grinning at him. I looked around to get my bearings for a moment. "There," I said, pointing at a familiar corner. "Oak."

"Nice," Cuan said as we rounded the corner onto the street. "That didn't take long at all. Cedric will be pleased."

"Do you worry that much what he thinks of you?" I asked.

Cuan looked at me. "I guess I do, yeah. The Midnight Hunters are more or less my family."

"You're related to them?"

"Nope," he said, "but Cedric raised me. My parents gave me up. I never knew them."

"Parents, huh..." I mused. Come to think of it, in my entire apartment, I hadn't seen a single picture on the wall or on my desk, nothing that would indicate a family member. I wondered if my parents were out there, waiting to hear from me. Perhaps soon they would be worried and show up at my door, and then suddenly I'd remember everything. Or maybe they wouldn't? Hell, I didn't even know if my parents were still alive.

"Hey," he said again, guessing at what I was thinking, "I told you, we'll help you find your past. We all will."

He slipped a hand down my arm toward mine. I took it, and he squeezed. His grip was warm.

"You seem like the only one who's really eager to help," I observed.

"They just aren't sure about you yet. We're... not really your everyday group of people. They're just especially wary of outsiders." He smiled his half-smile. "But I have a feeling you won't be an outsider for long."

I smiled as I looked down the street. "I hope not," I said. "I much prefer having a nice guy like you inside—oh, shit."

Marcus was sitting on the front steps of my apartment, giant paper bags resting on either side of him. At the sight of him, I instinctively let go of Cuan's hand.

"A friend of yours?" Cuan asked.

"Not exactly," I said.

"Are you in danger?" He asked, more pointedly.

"No; he's harmless, I think," I said. "Just annoying."

"OK then," Cuan said. I felt him give my shoulder a squeeze. "I should go. I'll talk to you later." When I turned my head around to reply to him, he was gone.

"What do you want?" I demanded of Marcus when I got to the steps of my apartment. While it was not necessarily Marcus's fault, I was still irritated that his presence had made Cuan vanish.

"There you are," he said, a disarming look of genuine relief on his face at the sight of me. "I was worried."

"Huh?"

Marcus stood, hefting a full paper bag in each arm. "When I was here yesterday, I noticed that you had no real food in the house. I figured you probably didn't have money, what with your wallet destroyed, and I'm guessing your credit cards went with it, and you wouldn't have remembered your PIN even if you still had your ATM card, so I went out and bought you some groceries."

"I... Huh?" I said again, completely nonplussed. "Wait, how long were you waiting out here?"

"Um... about two hours, I guess," Marcus said. "But don't worry about that. I'm just glad you came home before I gave up and left."

I honestly didn't know what to say. "Thanks," was all I could muster, but it was genuine.

Marcus smiled at me. I had to admit, he had a nice smile. In fact, looking at him cleaned up like this, he was pretty cute.

"Mind opening the door for me?" he said. "It's cool enough out here that the cold stuff should have kept fairly well, and I got an ice pack that's helping, but it'd still be better to get some of this in the fridge."

"Uh, yeah, sure," I said, unlocking the door and holding it open for Marcus.

"Thanks," he said, then followed me up the stairs.

"You really didn't have to do this," I said as I walked ahead of him. "But don't get me wrong, I really do appreciate it."

"I was worried about you, but it's... I guess it's kind of an apology?" he offered.

"Apology, huh?" I said as we reached the door to my apartment. I unlocked it, and he walked in and set the bags on the counter, and then, before asking for permission, started unpacking them.

"I know you only know me as the creep who carried you unconscious to his apartment and then was an ass to you," he said, putting groceries in the cupboards with the confidence of someone who'd had at least one meal in my apartment. "But yesterday was kind of a wake-up call for me. I realized that I wasn't able to be there for you enough when I had that crap in me. That's why I'm trying to turn over a new leaf. I flushed everything I had when I got home the other day. I'd like to make a fresh start. Hey, do you keep your bread in the fridge?"

"Uh, what?" I asked as Marcus held up a loaf of bread. "Honestly, how the hell should I know?" I said, finding a smile crossing my face. For the first time, I was able to find humor in my situation.

"Oh, good point," Marcus said, an apologetic smile on his face. "Well, I'll put it in the fridge. It keeps longer." As he said it,

I remembered that I'd found bread in the fridge the day before. I wondered if I'd learned to store it there from Marcus. He pulled out a few more things: pasta, cheese, canned goods, juice. "I got some of your favorite foods," he continued. "You might not know them, but I do. You told me what you liked to eat on our second date."

A wave of genuine gratitude washed over me. Here was someone who knew me, even if only a little. And he was making an effort.

"Thank you," I said. "I mean it." I walked over to him and took a can out of his hand, setting it on the counter. "You don't have to put everything away. I'll finish it later."

"Well, I got all the cold stuff put away, anyway," he said. "So you can take your time." Gingerly, he put his hand on mine.

I hesitated.

"Look," he said, "I know I messed up. But I mean it when I said I'm starting over. And in that spirit, I want to be completely honest with you. I talked to Alexander today, too. I told him I'm trying to clean up, asked him for help." He ran his arm up mine. "And I asked him if we could see one another again—just casually, nothing exclusive—to see where things are going."

I drew back slightly. "You're seeing Alexander?"

"Nothing exclusive," he clarified. "Just starting things out. And I want to see you, too. I messed things up with both of you. You're a really good guy, Cole, nice and sweet and hot as fuck. I feel like we connected. But Alexander is a good guy, too. I don't know where things will go with either of you. So I want to go out a bit with each of you, and see what happens."

"And Alexander is OK with this?"

"Yeah," Marcus nodded. "He's kind of wary—justifiably, I guess—and he doesn't want to dive back into something right away. And who is exclusive from the first date, anyway? That just doesn't make any sense. But if you don't believe me, ask him tomorrow. He said he's seeing you tomorrow, right? So ask him then; tell him everything. If he gets mad, says I'm lying, then never see me again."

"So you want to date us both?"

"Just while we're still testing the waters," he said. "Is that so bad? I don't expect you to be exclusive, either. Hell, go out with Alexander too if you want. Or anyone else. But Cole, I'm telling you I won't be like yesterday. I think you're great. And I'll prove it. I'm here now, and I'm not asking you to do anything to me. Let me make this all about you."

"What are you talking about?" I asked.

Marcus stepped in front of me, his fingers tracing the side of my shirt. I watched him, feeling my breath catch in my throat. Perhaps I was still turned on from the near miss with Cuan. Perhaps my body remembered what it was like to have Marcus touch me. Whatever the reason, I let him continue as he reached down with his hand, sliding it inside the waist of the Wushu pants. I breathed sharply as his fingers teased the outside of the jockstrap, pressing the leather down onto my cock, sending a wave of sensation up through me.

"I'll show you that I can make it all about you," he said, stepping closer against me, his mouth breathing over my neck. He kissed my neck once, twice, and I moaned in spite of myself.

"I remember that you like this," he said. "Even if you don't remember what you like, I do."

"Marcus, I..." I started.

"Tell me to stop, and I'll stop," he said.

My head started to fill with lusty haze. I'd been wanting something like this since Cuan's bedroom. Now a guy who knew me, a guy who was, at least, much nicer now than he had been the day before when he was drugged out of his mind, a guy who was honestly pretty cute, had his hand down the front of my pants. My body wanted the release, and Marcus clearly wanted to provide one.

"Keep going," I said.

Marcus reached his hand around, his fingers grazing my buttocks as he worked the waistband of the Wushu pants over my behind. The pants slid down around my ankles. He placed his hand on my abdomen, walking me out of the fallen pants, back until I hit the bed, which I sat down on with a thud, leaning back on my hands.

He sat sideways on the bed next to me, leaning on his left hand, moving his right down over my shirt back to the front of my leather jockstrap, cupping the front firmly in his hand and giving it a flirtatious little shake.

"I love this jockstrap," he said to me softly, a smile on his face. "You wore it on our first date."

"Oh?" I asked, interested but finding my attention hard to divert from the feeling of his hand on my crotch.

"Yeah," he said. "We started fooling around, I sat you down, I did this—" he kissed my cheek gently, then kissed my neck again, making me moan, my growing erection jumping beneath his hand, "—and then when I took your pants off, you had this thing on underneath."

"You like it, huh?" I asked.

"It's amazing. It keeps everything nice and tight, which can make this a lot of fun," he said. He moved his hand off of the front of the jock and then slid it along my inner thigh, upward, sliding his fingers under the strap until they teased the tip of my cock head. I gasped at the sensation, dropping to my elbows.

"Yeah, you like that," Marcus said, his smile widening. His hand forced its way under the strap until he had my erection wrapped in his fist. He began to move slowly up and down, sliding my foreskin onto and off of my glans, which rubbed slightly against the inside of the leather. The feeling was electric.

I began to moan and squirm slightly as Marcus's speed increased, his movement causing my balls to rock inside the cradle of the leather. My growing erection caused the material to pull tighter, cupping my balls closer against my body. I could feel pressure welling up inside them.

Marcus continued to stroke up and down until there was a POP, POP, POP as the three snaps that held the front of the jockstrap to the waistband snapped open, and my cock and balls leapt forth like an uncaged animal.

Marcus looked at my straight, hard cock and grinned ear to ear. "*there* it is," he said, glee in his voice.

He had a cute grin.

He resumed stroking up and down, faster, teasing my cock head with his thumb, as I watched breathlessly, wide-eyed, half in disbelief that another man was jacking me off. The dildo in my ass had felt good, but this was even better, being literally in the hands of another guy whose sole goal was my pleasure.

Beads of liquid formed at the tip of my cock, rising up and spilling down the sides of my shaft with each of Marcus's upward strokes, which he marked by a light squeeze of his fist at the top. The sight of the clear, slick liquid spilling over Marcus's fingers turned me on even more, and I felt pressure building inside me.

Marcus, sensing the quickening of my breath, increased his pace, stroking faster and faster until his tight fist was almost a blur as it ran up and down my length. I felt my balls rise, tightening, and the sensation hung at the peak for a moment, before—

I cried out as I shot a long, sticky stream, which spattered over my T-shirt and across my face. It was followed by another shot which splashed over Marcus, onto his cheek and into his hair. Marcus grinned even wider, stroking faster, the continuing orgasm making my head loll back as I cried out again and again, shooting several more times as the waves of sensation rocked through me.

Eventually, the waves died down, and Marcus's fist slowed. He released me, still grinning.

"You made a fantastically nice mess," he said, looking me up and down, then looking at his hand, which was covered in white froth. He brought it to his mouth and sucked on his fingers, one after another.

"Mmmm," he said, still smiling. "I love your taste."

The sight was almost enough to get me hard again. A smile crept across my lips. "Thank you, Marcus," I replied.

"It was my pleasure," he said, still smiling.

"No," I said, "I can honestly assure you that the pleasure was mine."

Marcus did not stay long after I painted his face. He washed his hand, wiped off his face with a wet paper towel, and then, to my surprise, thanked me again.

"What are you thanking me for?" I asked as I sat on the bed, flap of my jockstrap still lolling open, cum streaked across my shirt and covering my now softened cock. "I'm the one who just got serviced."

"Yeah," Marcus said, smiling again. He really did have a handsome smile. "But you gave me the chance." He bent down and gave me a peck on the cheek. "Have fun with Alexander tomorrow. You're going to his church, right? I'll be thinking of you both."

"I'm sure you could come too, you know," I offered.

Marcus's expression changed. "It's not really for me."

"You're not religious?" I asked.

"It's not that," Marcus said, frowning. "It's just that... Alexander's church is kind of intense."

"Intense?" I asked.

"Yeah," Marcus replied. "And also, I don't really think they accept Alexander." Before I could ask him what he meant, however, he sighed and shook his head, then smiled at me. "But you'll form your own opinion. I shouldn't skew your impression of them before you get a chance to meet them."

I watched Marcus as he walked to the door. He was very different from the asshole who had hit on me relentlessly just after I woke up. He still looked a little frayed around the edges, but he was much more together than he had been previously. I found myself warming to him, even as he unlocked the front door of my apartment, opening it carefully to make sure that there was nobody outside. I didn't think we was worried about being seen leaving, but rather didn't want to give anyone a full view of me sitting exposed on my bed.

"Be safe going home, Marcus," I said to him.

"Thanks," he said. "Sleep well." He gave me a wink and left, the door clicking shut behind him. I smiled in spite of myself. Perhaps I'd been quick to judge him. I had, after all, gone on more than one date with him before I lost my memory; I had to have seen something in him. But on the other hand, I remembered that Alexander had said he'd tried to clean up his act before and had failed. I supposed, though, that Marcus deserved the chance to prove that he could be true to his word.

I stood up, stepping out of my now-sticky jockstrap, lifting my wet shirt over my head and setting it on the top of what I assumed was a hamper of dirty clothes. I showered, brushed my teeth, and headed to bed.

VI

THE CHURCH OF THE HOLY GUARDIAN

I SLEPT SOUNDLY for most of the night, though I woke early as light crept into my apartment through the windows. I climbed out of bed, suddenly concerned about the time. I had told Alexander that I would go to his church that day, but we hadn't specified a time. I looked over at the clock on the microwave.

7:25.

I stood up and stretched, catching sight of myself in the full-length mirror as I did so. I had slept nude, and the sight of my naked body stretching in the morning sun made my semihard dick twitch. Automatically, I reached a hand for it, but then stopped myself. I had no idea when Alexander would be stopping by. It wouldn't do to have him ringing the buzzer wanting to go to church while I was frantically fapping away in front of my reflection.

I opened the drawers of my dresser, this time taking care to select a pair of reasonable-looking trunks instead of a jockstrap, and put on some deodorant. I selected a nice looking button-down shirt, a pair of trousers, and some white socks. I was just brushing my teeth in the bathroom when the buzzer sounded. I hurried to the intercom and pressed the button.

"Yesh?" I asked, mouth full of toothpaste.

"It's Alexander," came the crackly reply.

"C'monup," I said, pushing the buzzer, then rushed to the sink to spit and rinse.

I got back to the door just as he knocked.

I unlocked the door and pulled it open, and there was Alexander, in a button-down white shirt with blue sleeves over brown khakis, jacket slung casually over his shoulder. His blue-green eyes twinkled under his golden hair as he smiled at me in the doorway. I felt my breath catch in my throat: damn, was he handsome.

"Hey," he said. He looked me up and down. "I was worried that I might be catching you in bed, since I realized on the way over here that I never really told you a time. But it looks like I didn't have to worry."

I smiled at him, trying my best to look as though I had been ready and waiting.

"Shall we?" He asked.

"Sure," I said. I picked up my keys and the wad of bills from the bedside table and left the apartment, locking the door behind me.

"So, did you have a good day yesterday?" Alexander asked as we walked out from the entrance of the building and into the sleepy Sunday morning streets.

It was idle small talk, but it immediately sent my mind back over the previous day's events. Even if I'd had more than a day or two's worth of memories, meeting a phantom in the city streets and then finding a secret group of monster hunters seemed like the kind of thing that would stick in my head. I wondered if I should tell Alexander about it, but I feared it was the kind of thing that would get me sent to a mental hospital. Then again, what did I know? I couldn't remember anything beyond a few days ago; maybe ghosts wandering around the city at night was a commonly recognized occurrence.

Perhaps a phantom in the middle of town would be something that Alexander wouldn't find bizarre—or, at the very least, would be something that he could explain to me. I decided, however, that I might be better off waiting and seeing if he or the others at his church brought anything up. I let my mind drift back over the rest of the evening and suddenly realized that there was indeed something that I ought to immediately mention.

"It was a crazy day," I said truthfully. "But," I added, "Marcus came by last night."

Alexander's brow knit and he kept his gaze fixed in front of him. "Oh," he said quietly. He swallowed hard. "There's something you ought to know about Marcus. It's that..." He paused uneasily.

"You and he are seeing each other?" I said for him.

He swallowed hard and nodded. "Yeah," he said, still staring ahead. "I know I shouldn't have agreed to it; I know you two were kind of dating when you had your accident, and it's kind of shitty of me to jump back in. But I knew him when he wasn't messed up like he was a few days ago. He was a really nice guy. And really good at... stuff. And... I kind of have a hard time meeting guys like that."

He ran a hand through his blond hair and continued, "But it's not just that. He said he's trying to get cleaned up. I really don't think he can do that on his own. I think he'll need someone to help him. And if he came to me for help, I shouldn't really turn him away, should I? I mean, what would Jesus do?"

"Who?" I asked.

Alexander turned and gaped at me. "You don't remember Jesus?" he asked. "You know, from the Bible?"

"Oh, yeah," I nodded, remembering the books from my shelf. "I think I read a little about him. Isn't he the guy who cut the loaves and fishes into a thousand itty bitty pieces?"

Alexander gave me a flat look. "Exactly how much of the Bible did you read?"

"I just skimmed it," I admitted with a shrug. "It was interesting, but it seemed kind of cobbled together, like parts of it were kind of slapdash."

"*EXCUSE ME?*" Alexander was aghast.

OK, so clearly that was the wrong thing to say. "Well, I just mean," I began, trying to clarify, "I don't think they even finished editing the edition I had. Especially at the early part of the New Testament, they published it while still having all this markup in red."

Alexander's mouth closed as he studied me closely. "That amnesia must be really bad," he mused. "But don't worry, you'll learn all about Jesus soon enough." Then he paused. "Or... are you just baiting me because you're upset about Marcus?"

The memory of Marcus's hand in my pants and his breath on my neck came flooding back to me as the blood rushed to my groin. "Um..." I started.

"He... said he doesn't want to be exclusive," Alexander added hurriedly. "Which, really, is fine by me. I need time to get him cleaned up and he needs to prove he can stay that way before we can talk about anything serious."

"I know," I said. "Marcus told me. He said he wanted to see me, too."

"Oh," Alexander said. "And what did you say to that?"

"I... didn't really get the chance to say much. Marcus was... persuasive."

Alexander got quiet. "Did something happen?" he asked.

"He... reached in my pants. And jacked me off," I said, caught between the arousal of the memory and the awkwardness of telling it. "I let him," I admitted.

Alexander swallowed hard and stared straight ahead again as we continued walking.

"Lucky," I heard him mutter under his breath.

"I'm sorry, Alexander," I said. "I didn't mean to make you mad; I just thought I should tell you about it."

"I'm not mad," Alexander said. "I'm a little jealous, is all."

"Well... maybe you don't want Marcus to see other people after all?" I asked.

"That's not what I mean," Alexander said simply. Then he stopped and pointed ahead of him. "But here we are."

I stared at Alexander, not following his gesture. I wanted him to finish his thought. "Are you jealous of—"

"Shh," Alexander interrupted, visibly uncomfortable. "No sex talk at church," he said hastily, still looking in the direction he was pointing. "Please," he added, and then his expression suddenly changed into a big smile as I heard footsteps rapidly approach from ahead of him.

"Alexander!" came a woman's voice, big and gregarious. "You're later than usual today!"

I turned, finally, in the direction Alexander was pointing. A tall, thin Black woman with long, styled hair was heading toward us, a big smile on her face. She had just passed through a gate in a low stone wall, behind which was a modestly sized stone church. The wall enclosed the building and a garden around it, leaving the church itself set back a small distance from the street. The building featured a stone belltower and several stained-glass windows. While some of the smaller features such as modern windows and roofing were clearly recent, the church had definitely been around for a long time. It looked like it may have had an addition since its original construction, as the section of the structure set farthest back from the street featured different stonework, but even that appeared ancient compared to the neighboring buildings. It didn't fit in with the architecture of the nearby buildings, nor did it stand out like a sore thumb. I guessed that much of the city had grown up around it over the decades, if not centuries.

I was not able to look at the building in much more detail,

however, as my attention was quickly being diverted to the rapidly approaching woman, whose presence could not be ignored.

"Good morning, Julia," Alexander said to the woman, his initially forced smile easing itself into a genuine grin as she approached.

Julia smiled in return and then scooped Alexander toward her in a hug. "Good to see you," she said. The rapidity with which she swept up Alexander surprised me, and I stepped backward, letting out a "Whoa" in spite of myself. At the sound of my voice Julia released Alexander and turned her attention to me, as though noticing me for the first time. She put a hand on her hip, looking me up and down with piercing brown eyes. "And hello to you," she added, flashing me a smile of white teeth. It's not often that Alexander brings someone with him to Church, never mind a weekday service. I'm Julia Orla. What's your name, honey?"

"Cole," I said, slightly cowed by the woman's presence. She seemed to have an abundance of energy that found expression in sharp, rapid movements. "Cole Hamilton."

"Cole," Julia repeated. She looked at me quizzically, then suddenly gasped, whipping her attention to Alexander.

"Is this the Cole you were praying for yesterday? The one who lost his memory?"

Alexander visibly reddened, his expression alone providing a perfectly clear answer.

"It *is!*" Julia exclaimed, turning back to me. "I'm so sorry, that has to be so awful! But don't worry; Alexander is on it, and we can all pray over you, and—"

Pray over me? "I'm sorry, what?" I asked, suddenly feeling a little ambushed.

"Let's not get ahead of ourselves," Alexander said on my behalf.

"No, it'll be fine," Julia said. "Unless... oh God, I'm sorry; are you not Christian?"

Before I could open my mouth to reply, the church's bell rang out from the tower, capturing Julia's attention.

"Oops, we've got to get inside; service is about to start!" she said.

Alexander looked visibly relieved at the interruption. As Julia rushed off ahead of us with long, sharp strides, Alexander leaned to me and quietly offered an apologetic, "Sorry, Julia can be very intense."

I offered a weak smile and said nothing, walking alongside Alexander as we passed through the gate and up the stairs to the large double doors of the church, which stood open to the morning sun.

We stepped inside, and my eyes struggled to adjust to the different light. The interior of the sanctuary made such a powerful impression that it felt like being physically hit by the energy of the space; it almost knocked the wind out of me.

It was hard to say exactly what it was about the interior that gave it such presence. Most of the space was composed of wooden pews on either side of a wide aisle, which was carpeted in a deep red. Every few rows, the pews were marked by tall brass rods topped with glass-ringed lit candles, flames tall and still. There was a large cross of dark wood on the high far wall, gilded in gold and draped in colored fabrics.

The lower half of the back wall of the sanctuary was obscured somewhat by an altar and a tall, decorated partition behind it, also adorned with a cross, this one painted red. Like the pews, this partition was flanked by candles; tall red shafts on tall golden stands. On the right wall, in line with the altar, was an unassuming door, next to which hung a simple wooden cupboard with a cross emblazoned on the front.

The altar itself was wooden and draped in cloth. Upon it stood a golden pedestal that looked like it was meant to hold something; a smaller, similar pedestal that held a black leather-bound book; two tall, yet-unlit white candles; and another object of some kind that was concealed by a draped cloth with a gold cross embroidered on it.

This altar sat just on the far side of the center of the cross-shaped sanctuary; to its immediate left and right from my view were an enclosed pulpit and a tall lectern. The transept that crossed the sanctuary featured a row of pews on its right side facing a smaller altar and another cross and collection of candles; on the left were doors, what looked like cupboards, and another set of pews, these facing the main altar rather than an altar of their own.

The stone walls and floor were accented by dark wooden supports that crisscrossed a high ceiling, from which hung several lantern-shaped electric lights. These were lit but redundant; the illumination they provided was nothing compared to the spray of colored light that shone in from the dazzling array of stained-glass windows lining the walls. Each window showed a colorful image that contrasted with the gray stone and dark wood of the church interior. Fourteen of the windows featured a man in white robes struggling under a large wooden cross. These were complemented by larger panes higher up on the walls, which featured more complex scenes. Some of these showed men—and, very occasionally, women—draped in robes in various states of action or repose; these were captioned with names and sometimes dates. Others depicted scenes of conflict, with one or more angels wielding weapons and claiming victory—always victory—over demons or (presumably wicked) humans.

Alexander had waited patiently with me at the door to the church as I took all this in. I realized suddenly that I'd been looking around gaping, and self-consciously shut my mouth and swallowed hard, then looked at Alexander. He was smiling with no small hint of pride.

"Nice, huh?" he said.

"It's breathtaking," I replied honestly.

I followed him to the center aisle with its red carpet. As we walked up the aisle my attention began to shift from the architecture to the people. There were only a handful present, perhaps twenty-five or thirty, a number that seemed small considering the size of the sanctuary. Alexander walked past most of them to the second of a set of three empty rows of pews, then turned to me and smiled. "After you," he said, gesturing to the row. I turned and headed in, moving about halfway down the row. This row, like most of them, had a stained-glass window at its end. This particular window showed an image of an angel with a billowing robe and spread wings, a long, gleaming golden sword in its right hand. The angel's left hand was clutching the throat of a red-skinned demon who was shrinking back into a pit of flames. The angel's expression was remarkably serene, its head wreathed in a golden halo of light that stood out against a blue sky. Beams of light shone down from the sun depicted above, piercing through the clouds and penetrating the flaming pit below.

I heard a throat clear behind me and turned to see Alexander sitting, looking up at me. I shifted to look over my shoulder at him, and when I did, my hips shifted and my butt moved under my trousers, the right cheek thrusting forward a few inches from his nose. His eyes moved from my face to my ass, and then his cheeks reddened as he cleared his throat again and turned his face quickly forward.

"Hurry and sit down," he urged in a loud whisper; "the service is starting."

I did as Alexander requested, just as the door behind the transept opened and two men emerged. The man who came first carried a pole topped with both a snuffer and a candle wick, upon which a flame quietly danced. He was clad in a plain white robe and wore a solemn expression. The man behind him wore more ornate robes; these were embroidered with vines and, like most everything else in the building, prominently featured a cross on the front. He looked about two decades older than the man in front of him; his hair was gray and flecked with white, and a very short ash-colored beard garnished his cragged chin. He carried a large velvet-covered tome cradled in his arms; a red ribbon dangled from between its pages.

Upon the second man's entrance, everyone in the pews stood, and so I followed suit. Alexander stood beside me, visibly stiff, staring silently at the robed men. The first man lit the candles on the altar, bowing deeply as he passed in front. He then extinguished his torch, set it in a holder on the left wall, and sat on a wooden bench next to it, facing the altar.

The more ornately robed man had at this point walked to the center of the room. He stood behind the altar and placed the large velvet book on the large golden pedestal, and then raised both arms over his head and began to speak in a loud, deep voice that echoed across the church.

"We greet Thee, O Father, in the name of your Son our Lord Jesus Christ—"

"That's the fish guy, right?" I asked, leaning over to whisper in Alexander's ear.

"Shh!" he hissed tensely.

The man at the altar—clearly the church's priest—continued speaking his words of praise and supplication, stating that we were all gathered together in worship and thanksgiving. This was followed by an exhortation that we should all join in prayer, and Alexander responded by drawing a book from a holder in the back of the next pew and opening it to the page that the priest indicated. We read aloud then that we were all grateful servants and pledged ourselves to Christ's service.

"Just what am I agreeing to?" I asked Alexander quietly.

"It's just a prayer," Alexander replied, seeming slightly frustrated. "What matters isn't what you do with your mouth; it's what you feel in your heart."

"So, it's like the opposite of those 'straight guys going gay for pay' porn videos?" I whispered.

"What did I say about no sex talk in church?" Alexander hissed. "Besides, we actually have a ritual for pledging oneself to Christ's service," he continued. "Baptism."

"What's Baptism?" I asked.

"We immerse you in water and welcome you into Christ's fold."

"I thought you said no sex talk," I replied.

Alexander coughed loudly and shot me an irritated look, but now his eyes were dancing.

At the altar, the service had continued unabated. The man in the white robe stood and crossed behind the altar to the lectern, then proceeded to read what he announced were the words of a prophet. This was followed by a letter from someone named Paul to the Romans, in which he entreated the people to reject darkness and don the armor of light.

Following this, the priest in the elaborate robes finally moved from the altar, taking the large velvet-bound book with him. He stopped right at the row of pews where we were standing, then raised the book above him, tracing a pattern on his head and chest with his right hand as he did so.

With the book raised in his left hand, I could get a better look at the cover. The velvet was decorated with gold leaf, forming a cross that separated the cover into quadrants. Each quadrant featured a stylized image of a different creature: An angel, a winged ox, a winged lion, and an eagle. Along the spine were the words "Holy Gospels: King James Version."

The priest opened the book to the page marked by his red ribbon and announced that he was reading from the Holy Gospel of our Lord according to Matthew; Chapter six. He read in an even more booming voice, the sound of it rebounding off the stone walls and wooden ceiling as he spoke about alms and prayer, and how they should be performed behind closed doors. The passage continued with instructions of how to properly pray. Something about the prayer itself caught my attention, and I listened closely to the words, intrigued.

"Hey, you all right?"

The sound of Alexander's voice snapped me back. He was looking at me with interest, and I suddenly realized that the priest had finished reading, returned the Gospels to their place on the altar, and was now ascending the pulpit.

"Yeah," I said, shaking my head. "Something just... felt familiar."

"Good," Alexander said, a warm smile crossing his face.

"In the name of the Father, the Son, and the Holy Spirit," came the priest's voice. He was now ensconced in the pulpit, and clearly expected the people's attention. We turned toward him. "Please be seated," he said, and we obeyed.

When the priest spoke next, it was with a very different demeanor than the formal resonance with which he had spoken at the altar or read the gospels. His voice was no less loud, but now it was urgent and almost conspiratorial. He entreated us to consider the words of Paul, to reject darkness and don the armor of light. But he also harkened to the Gospel of Matthew, warning us that the armor was not a spectacle for the benefit of others. The parishioners' responsibility was to themselves, he claimed, not to those beyond the church's walls. It was the believers' privilege to be saved from the darkness, and while it was doing God's own work to spread the Word (what word, I wondered?), prayer and holy works were for members of the flock alone.

He continued thus for about half an hour, after which he finally retreated with an emphatic "Amen." This was followed by a series of simple prayers, which he concluded by entreating us to confess our sins before God and one another.

"What sins?" I whispered to Alexander as we knelt. "My memory barely goes back two days."

"Well then ask forgiveness for those you can't remember," Alexander whispered back. "Just read the prayer, and feel the Spirit in your heart."

I read the prayer, but nothing resonated. After this was an exchange of peace. Everyone stood and began shaking hands.

Alexander stood and looked at me with a smile. "You're certainly a handful," he said.

I opened my mouth to make a snide remark about how Marcus certainly thought so the previous night, but before the words came out Alexander pulled me into an embrace. My nostrils filled with the warm scent of chestnuts as his lips brushed my ear.

"Peace be with you," he said softly as I, struck dumb, managed at least to hug him back.

Presently, Alexander released me and stepped back, his expression as casual as ever.

"I'll be right back," he said, "I'm just going to exchange the peace with the others." He slipped out of the aisle and I watched him go, neat and tidy in his white, blue-sleeved button down and brown khakis, still feeling as though his arms were around me.

He turned into a pew two rows back and exchanged a hug with the elderly woman there. I realized then that while some people were shaking hands, nearly everyone was hugging. I suddenly felt a little less special. But there was something in that hug that just felt—different. Or, then again, what did I know? It was the only embrace I could ever remember having, after all.

I waited, wondering if anyone else would come to offer me the peace. Nobody approached for about a minute. The priest and the man in the white robe were making the rounds in the nave, but they both passed my pew without so much as a glance. As I turned to watch them pass, I accidentally brushed the little book Alexander had been reading from, which he'd left balanced on the back of the pew in front of us, and it fell to the ground with a thud. I quickly bent down to pick it up, and straightened to see Julia swooping across the aisle in my direction.

"There you are," she said. "I suppose you're one of those who likes to blend into the background, huh?" Without any warning, she scooped me into a hug.

"Peace be with you," I said awkwardly. Her embrace was friendly, even warm, but it lacked the intimacy of Alexander's.

"And also with you," she replied, releasing me. She smiled and then swooped away as suddenly as she had appeared, passing Alexander at the pew's end, who stepped aside with a smile to let her by. They had evidently already exchanged peace.

Alexander approached me with a shy grin, but before either of us could say anything the priest rang out with a "Please be seated," making it clear that he was once again due our undivided attention.

After everyone had found their seats, the priest asked all present for an offering. Two people in plainclothes appeared from the back of the aisle with large brass plates, and began passing them down the pews.

"What is this?" I asked.

"The Offertory," Alexander explained. "It's a collection of money."

"Oh," I said, pulling out the wad of bills I had been keeping in my pocket. Alexander's eyes widened in surprise at the sight of them. I suppose it was unusual to be carrying to much money around. But it was, nonetheless, a comfort. Without memories, without wallet or ID, without being able to access the laptop or safe in my room, I found myself taking solace in having money on me, like some sort of security blanket. I couldn't remember who I was; I didn't know how to find anyone who knew me better than Marcus, but I could buy stuff. As long as I had this wad of cash, I wasn't helpless.

I reached into the pile of money and pulled out a fifty. At the sight of it, Alexander started gesturing urgently.

"That's way too much," he hissed, pushing my hand down into my lap. As he did so, his hand brushed my crotch, and I felt my cock cushion his palm through the layers of fabric. His cheeks reddened and he immediately pulled away, eyes nervously darting from my lap to my face.

"Y-you don't have to give anything," he stammered.

"I feel like I should, though," I said simply, allowing him to ignore the fact that he had just pressed on my manhood, and ignoring the fact that the residual feeling combined with his flustered expression was making me a little hard.

"Well, then, just like a one or a five is fine."

I exchanged the fifty for a fiver and returned the wad of cash to my pocket just as the collection plate started down the row. Alexander, immediately stoic, placed a small envelope in the plate, then passed it toward me. I deposited the five dollar bill, and Alexander returned the plate to the plainclothes usher.

After the offering was collected, the brass plates were handed to the man in the white robe, who held them while the priest prayed over them, then set them aside.

At this point the priest finally removed the draped cloth from the item on the altar, revealing a large golden chalice with a plate atop it. The priest then took a large white wafer off the plate and held it up, explaining that this is what Christ did before he died, and that he commanded his followers to partake of his body.

"Wait, what?" I asked quietly, turning to Alexander.

"It's the transfiguration," he explained. "Or transubstantiation, depending on what you believe. The wafers become imbued with the body of Christ and are Holy."

"So Christ wants to be in our mouths..." I started.

"Don't you dare finish that thought," admonished Alexander.

The priest, meanwhile had continued by holding aloft the chalice and explaining that Christ had instructed his followers to drink from it, for it contained his blood.

"Seriously, what the hell?" I said to Alexander. "What kind of religion is this, where you eat people and drink their blood?"

"Not people. The Son of God."

"So that makes it OK?" I asked. "'Oh, we're vampires, but with hubris.'"

"It represents the Covenant," Alexander said patiently. "It is symbolic of our new relationship with God through the sacrifice of his Son."

I looked at him skeptically.

"Think of it this way," Alexander said. "God is in all things, yes? And God and his Son are one, so—"

"Sounds vaguely incestuous," I said.

"Shut up," Alexander snapped. "I mean God and his Son are one and the same. But God exists in the world he created; it is infused with his presence. So all things are a part of God. In the Eucharist, we are sort of 'activating' that Godly element of the food and wine we drink, and in so doing partake of unity with Christ through the Spirit."

"Is that dogma?" I asked.

"Maybe. Or maybe it's just something I came up with to shut you up," Alexander said with a smirk.

The priest now stated that we would all join in prayer as Christ had taught us. Alexander, clearly anticipating this, had the little book from the pew open to the correct page. I knelt beside him and read it aloud. It was similar to the one in the

Gospel reading, but worded ever so slightly differently. Again I felt a humming familiarity, like a tuning fork had been struck in my soul. When we finished, Alexander stood up next to me. I looked up at him, then moved to stand.

"Oh. Um..." Alexander started awkwardly. "This is the Eucharist; I'm going to take Communion. The thing is, while I know some churches believe that everyone is welcome at God's table, here the rule is that you can only take Communion if you've been baptized. And, well... do you remember ever being baptized?"

I looked at him flatly. "If it didn't happen in the last two days, then I have no idea," I replied.

"Then stay here please," Alexander said. "I'll be right back."

He looked genuinely apologetic as he slipped into the aisle and moved to kneel before the altar. The robed priest was administering wafers; the man in white held the chalice. I watched as the priest said some sort of prayer over Alexander before placing the wafer directly in his mouth. Alexander held it there until the other man stood in front of him, and again Alexander did not take the chalice but waited for the it to be held to his lips before drinking.

Alexander returned, and we had one more prayer, after which the priest lifted the velvet-bound gospels from the pedestal, walked to the main doors of the sanctuary, and gave one final blessing to indicate that the service was over as the man in the white robes snuffed the altar candles. He stepped out through the door on the right, returning a moment later without torch in hand.

People stood. Some of them left right away, exchanging a few pleasantries with the priest as they passed. Others mingled and talked to one another.

Alexander stood up and stretched absently, raising his blue-sleeved arms over his head. As he did so, his shirt lifted slightly and I could see that he wasn't wearing an undershirt. From where I was sitting, I got an eyeful of his lower abdomen, tan skin with a little bit of golden fuzz that would have been invisible were it not glinting invitingly in the light from the windows. His skin was stretched tight over his abdominal muscles, the gold-lettered blue waistband of his underwear peeking out over his brown-belted khakis. From the close distance I could make out a little of the definition of his ass from under the loose-fitted trousers. After he finished his stretch, he dropped his arms with a sigh, then turned to me and cocked an eyebrow.

"I'd ask 'So what did you think of the service?', but you've been making your thoughts pretty clear as we've gone along," he said.

"It was definitely an experience," I said. "There's a lot that doesn't make sense to me."

"So I've gathered," Alexander replied dryly.

"Still," I said, "thank you for inviting me. I'm truly glad I came."

Alexander smiled broadly and genuinely. It lit up his face so much that I wanted to ask him anything, say anything, to keep him smiling like that.

"So, who were the people at the altar today?" I asked. "Are there two priests?"

"Oh, no," Alexander explained. "He's just assisting today," he said, gesturing to the man in the white robe. "Our Priest is Father Jacob, the one in the embroidered robe, who read the Gospel and administered the Sacraments."

"'Father'?" I asked. "He's your dad?"

"Oh, that's a title," Alexander explained. "We call priests by an honorific like 'Father', 'Reverend', or 'Pastor'." He shifted uncomfortably. "But... yeah, he's also my father as in 'Dad'."

Well, holy shit. I stared at the stern man in the embroidered robes by the door, coolly exchanging pleasantries with people as they walked past him and left the church. He clutched the velvet-bound book in both hands against his chest as he stood, and I wondered if he did so as an excuse to not embrace or shake anyone's hand. "No wonder you're always at church," I mused.

"It's not just because he's my father," Alexander protested. "Church is a big part of my life."

Something about his expression, something about the tone of his voice, said to me that I might have touched a nerve. I smiled politely and said, "Well, thank you for including me in such a big part of your life."

Alexander smiled back, apparently mollified. "You're welcome," he said.

"So... what happens now?" I asked.

"Well," Alexander mused, "after services on Sundays we usually have a big gathering where everyone greets one another and spends time together. But on days like today, it's usually just... family. My father is pretty strict about inviting others."

"Yeah, I kind of got that from his little speech," I said.

Alexander's brow knit. "Perhaps I should have thought this through better. But maybe we can catch up afterward?"

"Um, sure, I guess," I said, unsure of whether I remembered the route we'd taken well enough to be able to make my way back home on my own.

"OK then," Alexander said with an apologetic smile. "But you don't have to leave right this second. Stay until I have to go join my family meal?"

"Sure," I said, though it didn't seem like that would be long. The sanctuary was mostly empty. Father Jacob and the white-robed man were having a clipped conversation with an elderly man by the door; from their body language I suspected that they just really wanted the man to leave, but he seemed in no hurry to go. Other than them and Alexander and I, the only others left in the sanctuary were a pair of people who seemed to be busying themselves with arranging items on the altar. One of them had picked up the black leatherbound book and was dusting the pedestal it sat on.

"Your religion uses a lot of books, huh?" I mused.

"No, not really," Alexander said. "We only have one Book that matters."

"But you have two on the altar," I said. "Well, I mean usually; there's only one now. Is that the book that matters?"

"Oh, that?" Alexander said, stepping out of the pew. "That's not it. That's our prayer book." Alexander walked toward the altar, gesturing to me to follow. As he approached the altar, he stopped to genuflect in front of it; I haltingly followed suit. The people working at the altar smiled politely at Alexander and then, ignoring my presence, left the sanctuary.

The person who had cleaned underneath the book had been careful to leave it open to its current page, and Alexander made no move to touch anything. I recognized on the page a script from the end of the day's service.

"This book is kind of a guide to worship," Alexander explained, "but it is not sacred in and of itself. That honor belongs to the Holy Bible."

"The book Father Jacob is carrying?" I asked, looking down the aisle to where the priest and his white-robed attendant had finally extricated themselves from the elderly man who had been speaking with them and were now walking purposefully back toward the altar.

"Those are the four Gospels. They're not the entire Holy Bible, but a part of it—the most important part, in fact. It's the start of the New Testament, the story of Jesus. It's full of parables he told himself."

"Wow," I mused. The editors of the Bible really didn't like him, huh?" I asked.

Alexander looked at me with legitimate confusion. "What could possibly make you think that?"

"I mean, that's the part of the Bible with all the red editorial markup, right? And plus, didn't they kill him off something like four times across the four chapters? That's overkill. That's like *The Cat Came Back*."

"You don't remember the Bible, but you remember *The Cat Came Back*?"

I searched my mind, trying to figure out where that reference possibly came from. I came up with nothing.

"...No?" I offered.

Alexander's expression was somewhere between amusement and exasperation. "Following your logic is impossible," he sighed.

"*My* logic?" I asked. "I'm still trying to understand why flesh-eating and blood-drinking in Church is fine, but we can't even *talk* about fuc—"

"ShhhHHHH!" Alexander hissed frantically, suddenly stiff, arms at his sides but gesturing frantically with his hand in what even I, in my amnesiac state, recognized as the universal symbol for 'Shut-the-fuck-up-before-my-father-hears-you-and-loses-his-proverbial-shit.'

I immediately clammed up and stayed behind Alexander's shoulder as he stepped back from the altar. Alexander was clearly cowed by his father. Jacob and the man in white approached, genuflected, and then, with a curt nod to Alexander, continued tidying. The man in white lifted up the chalice from the Eucharist and, in one gulp, downed the remainder of its contents. Father Jacob, meanwhile, lifted the golden tray of white, round wafers and carefully emptied it into a small silver canister with a cross on the lid. This he closed, speaking a few silent words, and then carried it to the small cupboard to the far side of the altar, by the door leading out of the sanctuary.

I watched with interest as he reached into his pocket and removed a golden key, which he turned in a lock just to the right of the cross embossed on the cover. A click resounded through the sanctuary, and then the doors opened to reveal a pair of shelves. As the priest carefully set the silver canister on the lower left shelf, I could see that the cabinet held three other items: one was a small silver chalice, the top of which was sealed; another was a glass bottle with a cross-topped stopper, filled with liquid that danced so brightly in the sun and candle-light that it seemed to possess a light all its own. These were new to me. The third item, however, I had seen before: a small silver sphere, covered with engravings, with a little round silver button on the front.

"Is that a flashsphere?" I asked absently.

As soon as the words were out of my mouth, everyone froze. I looked to Alexander—for whom my simple question had been actually intended—and he was staring at me, gaping. Some ways away, the man in white had been opening the door leading out of the sanctuary, chalice in hand, but he, too, was now staring at me with piercing eyes, his expression a mixture of shock and accusation.

Slowly, stiffly, Father Jacob turned from the cabinet, and his eyes focused on my face. It was the first time we had made eye contact—indeed, possibly the first time he had looked at me at all—and his steady, solid gaze was unnerving.

"And who might you be?" he asked slowly.

Alexander cleared his throat and turned to the priest. "F-Father, this is Cole," he said hesitantly, a tiny hint of a stammer in his voice. "I... prayed for him yesterday, you may remember. I invited him to church today and so... here he is."

"I see," Father Jacob said to his son, his expression unread-able. Then he turned his attention back to me and smiled a broad, tight-lipped smile.

"Welcome to the Church of the Holy Guardian, Cole," he said, his voice smooth and low. "Come; break bread with us."

VII

THE ORDER OF LIGHT

THE SANCTUARY of the Church of the Holy Guardian struck a careful, deliberate balance between Spartan coldness and ceremonial opulence. The dancing sunlight, burning candles, and golden accoutrements in the sanctuary lent some brightness and reverence to the otherwise forbidding gray stone walls and wooden supports. Outside of the sanctuary, however, the church offered nothing to soften the stern, hard lines and relentless grays and browns.

I had agreed to Father Jacob's request to break bread for three reasons: First, I wasn't sure I would be able to find my way home by myself. Second, I wanted to know why they had a flashsphere. And third, I didn't want to leave Alexander just yet.

Alexander was silent as we walked down the empty stone corridor on the other side of the small door in the side of the sanctuary. Jacob disappeared through another door on the immediate left, taking his assistant's woolen robe with him, but the assistant himself—who had been wearing a sweater and slacks under the robe—remained with us, ushering us down the passageway. He did not speak, and so neither did I. I was sure Alexander had a number of questions for me after I recog-

121

nized the small silver sphere, and I certainly had questions for him, but I preferred to ask them without the others around. The three of us walked on in silence, the sunlight coming in from the plain rectangular windows evenly spaced along the right wall our only company.

At the far end of the hall stood yet another door. Our guide pulled it open, gesturing for us to pass through. I did so, and found myself in a large dining room.

The decor of the room was much the same as the hallway: austere grays and browns of stonework and wood. The dark hardwood of the building's supports were mirrored in the simple long table, which was set with cold metal dishes. Bold red curtains lining the sunlit windows and brass candleholders with unlit candles offered a small bit of warmth. The wall opposite us featured a door and a long opening with a raised shutter which looked in on a simple kitchen.

The space was populated by a handful of people. Julia was in the kitchen with another woman, cooking away at the stove. The man who had assisted Father Jacob with the service stepped past me and moved to greet them both. Apart from the three of them, and Alexander who still stood by my side, two others were seated at the table, talking to one another. Or, rather, one was talking at the other. The older-looking of the two was speaking animatedly while the younger, with dusty-brown hair and attentive olive eyes, was nodding in response to each sentence, like a typewriter snapping back to punctuate the end of every line.

In the brief moment in which everyone else was occupied, Alexander gripped me tightly by the arm. I turned toward him to see an intense, anxious expression on his face.

"How do you know about flashspheres?" he whispered intently.

"I saw one yesterday," I replied, slightly alarmed. Alexander had been a little on edge at church, but I had chalked most of that up to my relentless series of amnesiac questions about his faith. His discomfort had to this point been tempered by amiability, but this was different. This was pure, urgent apprehension.

"Where in the world did you see one of those?" he asked, but no sooner was the question out of his mouth than his gaze shifted past me and his expression immediately snapped into a tight smile. I turned around to see Julia approaching.

"You took your time," she said. "Seeing your friend off?"

"Um... no?" Alexander responded, and Julia looked nonplussed for a moment.

"Hello, Julia," I said.

Only after I spoke did her Julia's eyes focus on me. "Cole!" she cried, breaking into a big smile as her voice filled the room. "Sorry; I didn't see you there. Joining us for a meal, are you?"

She wrapped me up in a tight hug, but behind her the energy of the room changed. The two men at the table and the other woman in the kitchen stopped what they were doing and stared at me, their bodies still, their eyes piercing and suspicious. It was a very disorienting sensation when combined with Julia's warm hug.

The only stranger who didn't stop moving was the man who had led us in. He nonchalantly strolled to the kitchen space, taking a plump, slightly charred sausage off of a large plate, and, leaning back against the counter, bit it in half.

"Yes; Father Jacob invited him," he said casually as he chewed, and at his words the tension in the room relaxed, as the cold stares softened into expressions of greeting and curiosity. It had all happened within the span of that single hug—though, to be fair, Julia's hugs were quite long—but it left me with some understanding of Alexander's unease.

"Cole, did you say your name was?" the dusty-haired man asked as Julia released me. He stood from the table and walked toward me, extending his hand, his expression relaxed. He was handsome, clad in a white button-down and tan slacks. I guessed that he was about Alexander's age, maybe a year older. "Welcome," he said, as I took his hand and shook it. "I'm Thomas."

"Hi," I said in reply, slightly more at ease. Up close to his face, I felt a glimmer of recognition, like I'd seen him before. Then I realized that of course I had: he had been at the church service, and we had passed his pew on the way in. In fact, everyone present had been at the service. But I supposed that would only make sense, since they were now gathering to eat after it.

Before any further pleasantries could be exchanged, a door at the far end of the room opened and Father Jacob emerged, now in a more modest flannel button-down over his black trousers. The soles of his black leather shoes clicked against the floor as he entered; at his approach everyone immediately stood and faced him.

"Greetings, everyone," Jacob said, his gravelly voice tinged with a hint of hospitality. "You may have noticed that we have a guest today." He extended both arms in a gesture of welcome. "Let us break bread together."

Jacob sat at the head of the table, and Julia immediately returned to the kitchen with the fair-skinned woman, shooing our guide aside as she picked up the plate of sausages. The man went to the table and sat in the spot Thomas had occupied, while Thomas sat on the other side of the man he had previously been speaking to.

Alexander led me to the other side of the table, and only then did I notice that the table was not flanked by chairs, but rather by two long wooden benches. The only chair, then, was the high-backed chair at the head of the table, where Father Jacob was seated.

Alexander gestured me into the bench, and so I scooched in. Julia, meanwhile, had set the plate of sausages and another plate of scrambled eggs on the table, and then scooched in from the other side, meeting me in the middle. I slid back slightly and stopped when I was in front of a plate, looking up to see Thomas across from me as Alexander settled in on my left. The fair-skinned woman had somehow managed to balance a tray with a pitcher of pineapple juice, a pitcher of orange juice, a pitcher of milk, a decanter of syrup, and a plate of toast in one hand, and after she expertly transferred those items to the table, she took a seat at the edge of the bench on the other side of Julia.

As soon as everyone was seated, Father Jacob bowed his head, and in a commanding voice, announced, "Let us pray."

The others bowed their heads as well, and so I did likewise.

"Lord, commend us this food unto our bodies," Father Jacob said, "so that we may continue to do your works in accordance with your will. We thank you also, Lord, for the gift of your Word, and the gift of those who receive it. In Jesus' name, Amen."

"Amen," said the rest of the table, and "Amen," I repeated a half-second later. The heads lifted, and the fair-haired woman immediately took Jacob's glass and filled it with orange juice, while Jacob took the plate of sausages and deposited some on his plate. I moved to reach for the eggs, but felt Alexander's hand on my thigh—not in some clandestine erotic gesture, but rather as a warning—and stayed my hand.

Starting with Jacob, each plate moved around the table, passing counter-clockwise, first down the row of men on the left before reaching me. By now the plate of eggs was looking a little empty, and while I wanted very much to take a generous helping, I took only a small portion before passing it to the two women who had yet to help themselves to any food.

"Now, that just won't do," Julia said as soon as I handed her the plate. "Here, have more eggs," she said, scooping half of the remaining eggs onto my plate. "Rebecca and I will share."

"That's right," the other woman repeated. "I'm sorry we didn't cook more, but we didn't realize we would be having a guest joining us." Both women shot a pointed look at Father Jacob.

"It was a spur of the moment invitation," Father Jacob said with a shrug before shoveling a forkful of eggs into his mouth.

"It's quite a surprise," said the other woman, who I guessed was Rebecca. "These meals rarely see an unfamiliar face."

"Well, sometimes the unexpected is a good thing," Thomas said from across the table. Rebecca frowned at him.

Jacob swallowed his mouthful of eggs, then turned to me. "We certainly have the unexpected today," he said, "and I think it right that we introduce ourselves. I am Father Jacob, pastor of The Church of The Holy Guardian. These are my sons," he said, indicating Alexander with his right hand and then sweeping it to include the three men on the opposite side of the table.

"All of you?" I asked with surprise, then turned to Alexander. "You have three brothers?"

"Actually, I have five brothers—"

"Don't disrespect Clement's memory," snapped the man on Jacob's right.

"Six brothers," Alexander corrected, swallowing. "We're a big family."

"I am Levi," the man on Jacob's right said, "oldest son of the Lucent family." I looked at him as he said the words with obvious pride. This was the man who had guided us into the dining room, the man who had also assisted Father Jacob in the service by bearing the candle and administering the wine. He had a severe face with hard lines and black hair flecked with silver; I guessed him to be in his thirties. He was a large man, not in that he was heavy, but just in that he had a very large frame.

Levi. Where had I heard that name before? Ah, right. When

I was looking in my dresser that morning I had seen a pair of jeans with that name on the label. The connection made sense —the man for some reason made me think of denim.

"As you probably noticed this morning," the denim man continued, "I usually assist Father with the services. I also help with the day-to-day running of the Church."

"I see," I said, not sure what else to follow with.

"And I am Paul," continued the man seated next to Levi. Paul had been the one talking with Thomas when I had first entered the dining room. He had a tall head and a tall body to match. Where Levi seemed wide and solid, Paul seemed lean, like a birch tree. The prematurely gray hair on his head was neatly combed back, and, perhaps as a consequence of the shape of his face, his expression seemed simultaneously serene and haughty. Gray hair notwithstanding, he looked to be in his late twenties, as though there were nearly the same age difference between him and Levi as between him and Alexander.

Paul's name I also recognized, though I at least surmised that he wasn't the same Paul as who wrote a letter about holy armor to the Romans. I waited to see if Paul offered anything further, but he said nothing more, instead reaching his long fingers for his glass of orange juice and taking a long sip.

"And I've introduced myself already," Thomas said with a polite nod, and I took advantage of the opportunity to let my eyes rest on him a little. As he looked at me with a neutral, polite expression, I noted that Thomas was actually quite handsome. He looked athletic—not in the same way as Alexander, but rather leaner—as though he balanced Paul's thinness with Levi's thickness. There was a resemblance between the three that Alexander didn't share, as though their genes had favored their Father's features and Alexander's his mother's. Or so I supposed, anyway, considering that I hadn't seen Alexander's mother. Julia and Rebecca both looked too young to be a parent to any of the brothers at the table.

"But again, I'm Thomas," Alexander's brother said, snapping my attention back to the man across from me. "I'm glad you were able to join us."

"And I'm Julia, again," said the woman next to me with a grin. "I'm not related to this crowd by blood," she added, gesturing dismissively across the table, "but I'm still part of the larger Parish family."

"And I'm Rebecca," the woman on Julia's right said with a meek voice. She also had a thin build; the wavy black hair tied in a tight ponytail behind her head contrasting starkly with her pale skin. I waited patiently for her to offer anything more, but she remained silent.

"Well, it is nice to meet you all," I said, trying to sound sincere. I turned to Alexander, looking for a comfortably familiar face, but he looked nearly as ill at ease as I was. Hoping to ease the atmosphere at the table, I asked what I hoped was an innocuous question: "So, are your other brothers younger, or...?"

"Nope," Alexander said awkwardly. "Six older brothers. I'm the youngest one."

"Nothing wrong with that," Jacob said at the head of the table, leaning back in his chair as he took a large bite of sausage. "I grew up with six older brothers, too; they made me the man I am today."

"You must be so grateful," I said dryly, but then clammed up as Alexander jammed his fist into my thigh, simultaneously hiding his face with a big swig of pineapple juice. Paul, Thomas, and Julia all glanced at me with interest, but Father Jacob emphatically nodded.

"You bet I'm grateful," he said. They taught me how to be assertive, how to stand up for myself, how to serve God and my Church. They taught me what it is to be a man."

My brain immediately fired off something about having and being a dick but my lips managed to catch it before it came tumbling out of my mouth. I shoveled in a forkful of scrambled eggs just to be safe.

There was an odd moment of silence amid chewing and swallowing around the table, and then Rebecca turned to me.

"So, what brings you to us today, Cole?"

"Alexander invited me," I said simply.

"How do you know each other?" she asked.

I felt Alexander tense to the left of me.

"A mutual friend introduced us," I said honestly. "I really can't tell you any more than that."

"Secretive type, huh?" Paul said with interest, leaning forward.

"No, not really," I replied.

"Give the poor kid a break," Julia interjected, pointing at Paul with her fork. "This is the boy Alexander was praying for yesterday; the one who's lost his memory."

Thomas's brows knit. "Really? Gone?"

"That's right," I admitted. "I have nothing beyond about two days ago."

"Any idea what happened?" Levi asked.

"Nope. The best guess is that there was apparently a gas explosion of some kind in the square, and that I got caught in it," I said.

Thomas winced. "From two days ago? Are you hurt?"

"Physically, I seem to be fine. I don't have any scratches or bruises, and my bodily functions seem to be working all right; I've checked."

Another fist to the thigh from Alexander.

"...So apart from the memory loss," I continued, "nothing else seems wrong."

Paul let out a low whistle, and Thomas sat back on the bench.

"I can't imagine what that must be like," Thomas said sympathetically. "I'm so sorry."

"Well," said Father Jacob, "that makes this whole situation even more intriguing."

The table looked at him in interest.

"So tell me, Cole," he said smoothly, gravel rolling in the back of his voice, "how does a person whose memory extends no more than two days ago correctly identify and name a flashsphere?"

Paul's, Thomas's, Rebecca's, and Julia's heads whipped around toward me in unison so quickly that I thought someone's neck was going to snap. Eyes stared, mouths hung slightly open. On my left I heard Alexander swallow hard. Levi leaned back from the table, hands folded in his lap, a somewhat smug expression on his face.

The silence stretched taut across the room like a wire ready to snap. This was clearly the entire reason Alexander's father had invited me to his family's normally private breakfast. But the people seated at the table hadn't been exactly forthcoming about themselves during their introductions, and so if they wanted me to open up to them, they would have to do likewise.

"First, I would like to know why your church sees fit to keep flashspheres in its sanctuary," I said, keeping my voice as even as I could manage.

I felt Alexander's hand on my leg, tightly gripping my knee. Levi leaned forward abruptly in his chair, indignation burning behind his cold stare. He opened his mouth, but Father Jacob stayed him with a small gesture, a look of amusement on his face.

"Bold," Jacob said. "I like it." He chuckled softly. "Very well; I will tell you exactly why we possess such a thing."

Levi turned to Jacob in surprise. "Father, you—"

"—are in charge," Jacob said with finality. "Besides, Alexander saw fit to invite this young man into our sanctuary, and I like to think that I raised all of my children to have sound judgement." The words sounded as much a warning as a statement, and Alexander's hand stiffened on my leg.

The others at the table sat still, their eyes studying me carefully as Jacob continued.

"The six of us you see here oversee operation of the Church of the Holy Guardian," Jacob said. "We are not an everyday priest and his parishioners, however. We are also members of the Order of Light, a sacred institution charged with protecting holy places of worship and those who seek refuge there."

"Order of Light...?" I tasted the words.

"Yes," Jacob continued. "You see, there is more to the world than meets the eye, and more than humans and animals roam the land under cover of night. But, of course," he added with a knowing glimmer in his eye, "I assume you already know that."

I said nothing, and Jacob's expression hardened against my silence.

"These creatures are unholy abominations," he continued. "Monsters whose existence is an affront to God and His people. It is our duty to see that they never set foot in His house."

"So you seek out these monsters and destroy them," I concluded.

"Bah," Jacob replied with scorn. "We do not hunt—we defend." Next to him, Levi nodded in quiet agreement. "We, the true defenders of Faith, are too few in number, too valuable to risk on assailing everything that walks the streets."

"But what if there is something out there that is threatening people, yet doesn't come near your Church?" I asked.

"Then it is not our concern," Jacob said simply.

"Even if people are getting hurt?" I asked.

"The faithful will find their salvation," Jacob said. "We have told our parish time and time again that this church is a sanctuary should evil walk the earth. The flock will come to the shepherd, and here it shall be saved."

"And what about those who aren't a part of this 'flock'?" I

challenged, feeling indignation rising in my voice. "What about them?"

"We've debated that point before," Thomas said hesitantly. "Frequently." His eyes looked slightly pained.

"The Order's resources are not limitless," Paul added quietly, hands folded in his lap. "We cannot save everyone."

"Salvation isn't free," Levi stated. "It must be earned through faith in God and the Church. Not everyone chooses to be saved."

"So then, what, it falls to you to mete out judgement and salvation?" I challenged.

"No," Jacob said. "It is for God to judge; we are but his instruments."

"So that's it?" I asked, looking at Alexander. His expression was raw. "That's what you do? Protect those who come here, and fuck everybody else?"

"You will not use that language under this roof," Jacob decreed. His words were sharp razors of ice, but they melted harmlessly against the heat of my indignation.

"Fine," I said, both an acknowledgement of Jacob's admonition and a sarcastic response to the situation in general. My eyes remained locked on Alexander as I continued. "So tell me: what if, *theoretically*, there were a phantom wandering the city square at twilight, killing people by sucking their souls and doing all kinds of other horrible things, and what if, *theoretically*, a person you knew had just woken up with no memory of who he was or what he had been doing or if he had ever chosen your 'salvation' or not in his life, and he had taken a walk last night to try and get his bearings, and *theoretically* had run into said phantom in the middle of the city square? What if that person *hadn't* been rescued by a chance encounter and escaped to live to today? Would that be perfectly OK with you, just chalked up to that person's guilt in not earning your salvation?"

Alexander looked at me aghast. "Holy shit," he muttered, his voice a destroyed whisper.

"*Language*," Jacob warned angrily.

"There's a phantom out there?" Julia asked, concerned. "The square is technically in our diocesan jurisdiction. If we know about it, shouldn't we do something about it?"

"We do not sortie on search and destroy missions," Levi said gruffly.

"But is that always true?" Thomas mused. "Reuben sent that Skyler kid out to investigate that castle."

"There's more to it than that," Levi countered. "Plus, Reuben's been influenced by those Europeans."

"Reuben?" I asked, feeling like the conversation had run away from me.

"Another of my brothers," Alexander said. "He left a few years ago to join a branch of the Order of Light in Europe. But more importantly, you were *attacked*?"

"More or less," I said. "That thing nearly killed me."

"That's how you know about the flashsphere," Paul concluded. "You mentioned a chance encounter. Did someone save you with one? Is the phantom eliminated?"

"The phantom got away," I said, "But yes, I was rescued by someone who had one of those."

"Thanks be to God," Alexander said. "But who saved you?"

"Someone from a group called the Midnight Hunters," I said.

For a brief second, nobody moved, the tension in the room a taut wire once more.

"Oh, *shit*," Julia said finally, leaning back on the bench.

"*LANGUAGE!*" Jacob roared.

"You know them?" I asked.

"Some of us have had run-ins with them in the past," Paul said calmly. He had leaned forward, his elbows on the table, mouth obscured by the folded hands on which his thoughtful face rested. "The Midnight Hunters are dangerous."

"That's right," Levi said. "Faithless vigilantes who prowl the streets at night under the pretense of protecting the people. They're little better than those they hunt."

"But if they're protecting people—" I began.

"A wolf that hunts a fox is still a wolf," Paul said. "Do not be fooled, even if it comes clad in sheep's clothing."

"What is this, animal day?" I asked.

"That's what they are," Levi said coldly.

"At least they're out there *doing* something," I said.

"We're doing things too," Thomas retorted. "We're not just sitting on our hands."

"That's right," Julia nodded in agreement.

"But when a phantom is right outside, you'll do nothing unless it knocks on your door?" I asked, standing up. "At least the Midnight Hunters are trying to—"

I felt Alexander's hand on my arm. I looked at him, his expression pleading. "Cole, it's like Paul said. Those people are *dangerous.*"

Dangerous. Perhaps they were. Bianca's and Cedric's reception at their home hadn't exactly been welcoming. But they weren't who was on my mind right then.

"They saved my *life*, Alexander," I explained. "They saved me, and used their last flashsphere to do it." I knew that wasn't exactly how events had transpired, but it was close enough. "They need another flashsphere to destroy that creature before it harms anyone else. I promised I would help them."

"Help them as what?" Thomas asked. "Bait?"

I winced slightly. Wasn't that exactly what Cedric was asking of me?

"Not as bait," I said, as much to myself as to the others at the table. Then, with more conviction, I added, "I won't even be anywhere the phantom would notice me."

Silence hung for a moment at the table, and then Rebecca, who had hitherto spoken barely a word, said quietly, "It *is* important to honor your promises."

"Perhaps we could—" Julia started.

"Don't be ridiculous," Jacob said. "If Cole wants to become the Midnight Hunters' chew toy, that's his prerogative. But he's the one who was foolish enough to make a promise to them, not us. He is not a member of any of the Order's churches—"

"Well he could be, for all we know," Alexander interjected.

"He is *not*," Jacob said with finality. "If he wishes to join our fold, considering all we have shared today, then we will welcome him into the Church with open arms, and we can even discuss initiating him into the Order at some point in the future. But he is not a member now. And the Order does not consort with beasts. Under no circumstances are any of you to join in this phantom hunt; is that clear? If it crosses our threshold, we will rain heaven's fury upon it, but not before. Our meal is over. Alexander, you may see your guest home."

With those words, Jacob stood. As he did, everyone else stood immediately, and I, already standing, did not move as Jacob turned and stalked out of the room. Levi and Paul left immediately after him.

"It was nice to meet you, Cole," Thomas said, offering a sympathetic shrug. "I do hope you'll be back." He turned and followed his brothers out of the room.

Rebecca and Julia picked up the serving dishes from the table and took them into the adjacent kitchen.

"Nice family," I said dryly to Alexander. "Dad's a peach."

Alexander gave me an irritated look. Then he sighed. "Cole, I—"

"Cole, honey," Julia interrupted, suddenly behind me, "do you mind helping Rebecca finish clearing the table? I have something I need to take care of real quick." She gripped Alexander's arm above the elbow as she offered a slightly too-sweet smile. "Alexander, I need you to give me a hand," she added, with an edge to her tone that demanded obedience.

"We'll talk on the way home," Alexander offered apologetically as Julia half-led, half-dragged him toward the door leading back to the hallway.

As they left, I heard footsteps behind me, and Rebecca began collecting plates into her arms.

I reached over the table and picked up both of the heavy pitchers by their handles. Juice and milk still sloshed inside as I lifted them.

"Are you part of this family, too?" I asked her as she worked.

"Not exactly," she said. Her voice was simple and musical, with a sadness that matched her expression. "I was Clement's fiancé."

"Clement?" I asked. I remembered Levi saying his name. "One of Alexander's brothers?"

"Jacob's second son," Rebecca said, nodding. "Older than Reuben but younger than Levi. He was a good man—brave, patient, and kind. The Order was larger, then. It recruited more readily, made more exceptions to its principle of only defending within the boundaries of the Church.

I opened my mouth to ask what happened to him, but Rebecca shook her head, as though anticipating the question.

"I know the rules we live by seem cruel to you," she said as we walked into the kitchen. "But we have learned that bending those rules carries a cruelty as well." She sighed as she placed the plates in the sink and began to wash them. Her ponytail fell over her shoulder, her hair obscuring her face. "It isn't possible to save everyone," she said, the sadness in her voice cascading forth like the water running down the plates. "Sometimes you have to choose who to protect. Father Jacob isn't a bad man; he's just more rigid in his criteria than most."

She set a plate on the counter near to where I had placed

the pitchers, and I picked up a towel that was hanging nearby and dried it in silence.

"Our laws exist for a reason," Rebecca said, placing another plate on the counter for me to dry. "Breaking those laws or upholding them—both carry consequences. We have to guess as best we can which we'll be able to live with."

"Wow, you're depressing," I said before I could stop myself.

There was a splash as the plate Rebecca was holding dropped back into the water with the others. She looked at me with an expression of mild shock. Then, much to my surprise, she let out a short laugh, a single note of music, her face brightening around the sound.

"You're a bold one, aren't you?" she said. "I don't think the boys knew what to make of you."

I heard a door open and close and looked through the open shutter to see Julia and Alexander returning. Alexander stood by the table as Julia walked into the kitchen. She stood for a moment watching Rebecca wash until I was handed a plate, then her eyes settled on me and she walked over and put a hand on my shoulder.

"I'll finish that up, honey," she said. "Alexander had better be getting you home." She looked up at Rebecca. "It looks like the two of you have been getting along here," she said with a smile.

"He's a handful," Rebecca said kindly.

"Oh, I'm sure he is," Julia said with a grin. "I could tell from the moment I laid eyes on him." Then she turned, shooing me out of the kitchen. "Now go on. But you'd better come back, you hear me?"

"Yes ma'am," I said.

"And if you call me ma'am again, I'll see that you regret it," Julia admonished.

Alexander offered a small smile when I walked over to him,

and together we walked through the door back to the main hall, and then back into the sanctuary.

Now, with just the two of us in the large space, I had a moment to stop and breathe in its presence. With the sun higher in the sky, the light poured in through every stained glass window, shining in a spectrum of beams across the stone floor and red carpeting.

"There's something about this place," I mused. "It's so still, and yet it just...hums." It was the best word I could think of to describe the sense of presence I felt within the space, a kind of energy that traveled on the light and breathed with the air.

"It really is something, isn't it?" Alexander said with a smile. "Sometimes I come here just to sit and pray."

He pushed open the door, letting a flood of sunlight pour into the church, and I blinked against the light. Alexander gestured for me to exit, and I did so, breathing in the city air as he shut the door behind us. Alexander released a heavy sigh as we turned and began to walk down the empty street. It was almost as though he'd been holding his breath since we first walked into the Church of the Holy Guardian, and only now was releasing it.

"Well, that was something," he said.

"You're telling me!" I said. "Seriously, if that's how your family reacted to me, what did they think of Marcus?"

"They haven't met Marcus," Alexander said. And then off of my look, he added, "And I wasn't planning on having them meet you today, either. I mean, Marcus has come to services with me, but I never introduced him to anyone."

"Well, aren't I special?" I said.

"I had no idea you were going to see a flashsphere and then brazenly announce that you knew what it was."

"How was I supposed to know that was some sort of secret society object?" I objected. "I barely recognize my own name."

"Good point," Alexander admitted. "Still, you have quite a mouth on you."

"So I hear," I said, raising my eyebrow for emphasis.

Alexander swallowed. "My family certainly didn't know what to make of you," he said evasively.

"You have six brothers, right?" I asked, curious. "Any sisters?"

"None," Alexander said.

"And you're the youngest," I mused. "But I only met three brothers today. What's the rest of your family like?"

"Well," Alexander said, "Thomas and I are close in age; we're a little more than a year apart. But we've never been that close for some reason... he always keeps his distance from me. When we were little, he used to be afraid at night, saying I was going to attack him in his sleep."

"Really?" I asked. "He seemed like the most well-adjusted of your siblings."

"He probably is," Alexander mused. "My family is very competitive, always vying for position and attention. Maybe he was just projecting that onto me."

"And then Paul is older than Thomas," I suggested.

"Right. There's another brother in between Thomas and Paul, though: Rhode. But he's no longer with us."

"Oh, Alexander, I'm so sorry," I said.

"No, no, I mean he's no longer with our branch of the Order. He left to join another. He's doing pretty well there, I guess."

"Like Reuben," I said. "So there's more than one Order of Light?"

"There's a singular Order," Alexander clarified, "But there are many divisions. Each has its own parish, and because each has its own head who interprets the Law, each is a little different. We're all over the world. Evil is not confined to a single address, and neither are we."

"Is he in Europe, too?" I asked.

"No, just Reuben," Alexander clarified. "Reuben is Paul's older brother."

"So that makes six," I said. "And then there's... Clement?"

"Clement," Alexander nodded, his face falling. "Clement is... gone."

"And I assume this time, gone means..."

"Dead," Alexander confirmed. "I was barely a teenager when it happened. The Order was out on a mission of some kind, and it went south. At the funeral people pressed my Father to explain why he'd risked Order members on such a dangerous undertaking. As if he wasn't suffering enough, having lost his son. After that, Father became much more strict about confining our activities to parish property." He sighed. "I loved Clement," he said. "He was the nicest one."

I put my arm over Alexander's shoulder, and he titled his head toward mine as we walked.

"Sometimes it happens," Alexander said. "The Order's work is dangerous. But there were two of us who died that day, plus the people we had set out to protect died anyway or were severely injured. It was apparently the biggest disaster our Order had suffered since a successful attack on the church that happened just after I was born."

"Just after you were born?" I asked, guessing where this was going. There was one family member who hadn't been mentioned at all.

"My mother was killed then, along with a few others," Alexander said quietly. "She'd just given birth to me and so she couldn't defend herself. Sometimes I think Father blames me in a way. If she hadn't been pregnant with me and just given birth, she might have been able to defend herself."

"You know a pregnancy requires two people, right?"

"True," Alexander admitted. "Well, except for Jesus," he added.

"Wait, what?"

"Seriously?" Alexander said. "That's kind of the whole point! Mary was a virgin, but God made her be with child, his only son."

"Did Mary have any say in this?" I asked. "Sounds like there are some serious consent issues involved."

"I really don't think she minded," Alexander said.

"But she was still a virgin? Or did God come down and—"

"PLEASE don't finish that sentence," Alexander pleaded. "No, he created his son in her womb."

"Well, that sure sucks," I said.

"How do you figure?" Alexander asked.

"Well, if straight women have to carry and raise a child, they should at LEAST be able to enjoy the process of making it."

"Sex isn't exactly the holiest of acts," Alexander said.

"The hell it isn't," I said as we reached my apartment building. I unlocked the door and held it open for Alexander, making it clear he was welcome to come in. He did, and I continued talking as we ascended the stairs. "I mean, I may not remember much from more than two days ago, but I gotta tell you, nothing we did in that church made my spirit soar as much as the stuff I found in the box under my bed."

"Wait, what did you find under your bed?" Alexander asked.

Ignoring the question, I continued. "And I think any faith worth its salt would feel the same. I mean, you have a whole hymn about it. What was it again?" I asked, remembering a title I saw as we had flipped through pages in the hymnal back at the church, "Don't you have a song that's like, 'O Cum, All Ye Faithful'?"

"It's not that kind of song," Alexander said, laughing.

"Well then, it should be," I said as we reached my apartment door and unlocked it, pulling it open. "Thanks for walking me home," I said with a smile. Then I remembered something. "Oh, while you're here, I can give you back your hoodie," I said, gesturing inside. Alexander followed me in, and the door latched behind us. "I haven't had a chance to wash it though," I added apologetically, turning to pull it out of the laundry hamper. "While we're here, can I get you anything?"

"No," Alexander said behind me, "but I do have something for you."

"Okay," I said with a grin, resisting the temptation to take one more whiff of chestnut and warmth from the hoodie as I turned around, "but that wasn't even subtle—"

I stopped dead.

In the fingers of his outstretched hand, Alexander was holding a small, silver sphere, adorned with engravings and featuring a small, silver button.

VIII

GETTING (A)HEAD

"A FLASHSPHERE?" I asked dumbly, staring at the silver ball that Alexander was holding out to me.

"It's what Julia took me aside for after breakfast," Alexander said, smiling. "It's for you."

"But your Father said—"

"He said that we were under no circumstances to *join* in the phantom hunt," Alexander grinned. "He never said we couldn't help in other ways."

I continued staring. The sphere glittered in the light, and Alexander's blue-green eyes were dancing to match. He had been so cowed at the church, but here he looked much more confident and self-assured. As he stood there with that smile on his face, I was overcome by how handsome he was.

"Won't he notice it's missing?" I asked.

Alexander shook his head. "Julia is the one in charge of ordinance. She manages all of our equipment and inventory. She says we have plenty of these to spare. And if it's going to be used in extinguishing a dangerous phantom, well, it'll have been put to good use."

"Alexander, thank you. Truly." I said.

As I reached out to take the sphere, he hesitated.

"Please be careful," he said as I gingerly lifted the sphere from his fingers and turned to set it on the bedside table. "I don't know what you went through yesterday, so I really don't have any room to comment, but I worry about you going after some phantom, even if you're supposedly not going to be anywhere it will notice you, as you said. But more than that, I'm worried about you getting more than you bargained for with the Midnight Hunters."

"You know them?" I asked, setting the sphere down and turning to face him. He looked worried, but this was different from the trepidation he had with his family at the Church of the Holy Guardian. There he was nervous, but it had been tempered by a feeling of knowing what to expect. Here, his expression was one of genuine concern.

"I haven't encountered them, myself," he admitted. "But several in the Order have. From what I've heard, they act in their own interest, with little regard to order or the safety of others."

"And yet, from what I can tell, their desire to eradicate the phantom is purely motivated by a wish to keep it from harming people," I pointed out.

"You make a good point," he admitted, approaching to stand close to me. I could smell the warm scent of chestnuts rising, and felt parts of my body begin rising to match. "Still," he continued, "my family says that they are dangerous, and I have no reason to doubt the truth of their words. So please," he added, putting his hand on my arm. His touch was warm, and I felt my pulse quicken. "Please be careful. When do you think you'll use the sphere?"

"I don't know," I admitted. "Maybe in a day or two?"

"Well, I'll be back to check on you. And you can always come by the church if you need to find me. We have services every morning."

"I—wait, *every* morning?" I said incredulously.

Alexander dropped his hand. "Well, yeah," he said. "Most of the weekday services are very poorly attended, but we hold them anyway. Our faith is our shield. And our sword. But come on a Sunday, and you'll see that the church community is a lot more vibrant than just the few you met today."

"OK, perhaps I will," I said.

"Good," Alexander said. He said nothing for another moment, then chewed his bottom lip like he was debating what to do next. I wanted to invite him to stay, but his body language screamed ambivalence. I opened my mouth, but before I could speak, he said quickly, "I should probably go. I'll see you later."

Well, so much for that.

He turned to walk across the room to the door, and I followed so as to open the door and show him out.

"And please, I know I keep saying it, but be careful with that group," he said. "I would absolutely hate if something happened to you." He paused, then added awkwardly, "especially before I got to experience that fantastic head Marcus keeps going on about."

Wait. Wait wait wait wait. That wasn't a mixed signal. That wasn't even casual flirting. That was like writing "Suck my cock" in the sky. And after he'd shown me such hospitality when I was in his home, who was I not to do the same when he was in mine?

I placed my hands firmly on Alexander's hips—admiring his ass in his khakis as I did so—and spun him around to face me. "That's one thing I can take care of right now," I said with a grin. He was too surprised to respond as I pushed him down into a sitting position on the sofa we had been walking past, then knelt in front of him. I could already see something twitching beneath his fly, and reached my hands to undo the buttons of his trousers.

"Hold up, hold up," Alexander said urgently, putting his

hands on mine and pulling them away. I instantly obliged, looking up at his face with a mixture of question and apology on mine.

He took a deep breath, holding both my hands in his. "Are we doing this?" he asked, his eyes shining with sincerity and anticipation.

"I definitely want to," I said honestly. "Do you?"

"Since the moment you first woke up," Alexander said. "And that dating profile of yours didn't hurt either, Nerdy-Hunk21." He smiled teasingly.

I rolled my eyes, but grinned.

"But if we're doing this," he said, "let's do it right."

I was about to say that 'right' was a subjective concept, but before I could open my mouth, Alexander's hand was on my cheek. His eyes stared into mine, full of amity and desire. He brought his face toward mine, still smiling through his full, pink lips, and then kissed me.

I tasted the tart sweetness of the fruit he had drunk at breakfast as the kiss washed over me. It was the first kiss I could remember, and my brain flooded with emotion as I pulled him to me and kissed him back, drinking him in as our lips met again and again. I felt his strong tongue push insistently into my mouth and met it with my own, exploring his mouth as he explored mine. His hands went to my arms, then my waist, caressing me over my clothes. He gripped the fabric on the base of my shirt, and I released the kiss as the shirt rose, pulling my arms with it until they lifted over my head and Alexander tossed my shirt aside.

Even without touch, kneeling shirtless in front of Alexander seemed to heighten every sensation. Just the air on my skin felt electric as he sat back and appraised me appreciatively. I felt his eyes on my pecs, then my abdomen, and I breathed with anticipation.

"Even better than the photos," he said with a smile. He

reached his arms down and traced the lines of my torso, running his fingers along the ridges of my abs. My breath caught as his fingers lightly swept across me, and when he brought his hand back up and brushed my nipple tentatively, it sent a sharp shock of pleasure through my spine that made my cock jump.

I reached for the collar of his blue-sleeved white button down, Alexander watching me intently as I worked. The first of its blue buttons was already undone, so I gingerly, slowly, undid the second, then the third, watching his shirt fall slightly more open with each unfastening. Each button revealed more of his golden chest, the muscles rising and falling with each breath. Finally I reached the last button, and then I reached my palms inside his shirt, stroking along the surface of his skin toward his shoulders, pushing the shirt from his torso as I did so. As I drew my palms over his chest, he let out a sharp intake of breath.

Alexander had a barrel chest, but there was a pleasant soft-ness to his muscles that made them yield slightly beneath my hands. I pushed the shirt off of his broad, tanned shoulders, running my hands down the muscles of his upper arms and onto his forearms, which were dusted with the same fine hairs that garnished his abdomen and chest, invisible unless the light hit them just right.

With his shirt removed, I stood, looking down at him admiringly like an artist appraising a sculpture. And Alexander was very well-sculpted. He was muscular, but not overly so, with a body befitting a college athlete and handsome boy-next-door features to match. He looked up at me, blue-green eyes full of anticipation, pink lips slightly parted with the heavy breaths that continued to cause his torso to rise and fall. I reached down and pulled him up toward me, wrapping my arms around him and kissing him again, feeling the heat of his bare chest against mine. His hands went to my back, running up and down my skin, each stroke causing my erection to grow and stiffen in my pants as though he were stroking my cock directly.

I released his lips and moved my mouth to his neck, which elicited a grateful moan from Alexander. Then I kissed down over his chest. When I lapped playfully over his left nipple his entire body shuddered.

"Cole..." he breathed.

His reaction encouraging me, I closed my lips over his nipple, swirling my tongue over it while lightly teasing his other nipple between the thumb and forefinger of my left hand. Alexander writhed and moaned his approval, hands racing frantically over my back. At last I moved on, kissing diagonally down his waist under his arm, half-turning him and half-moving my body until I was behind him. I straightened up to admire his back, solid and tan, tracing my hands up and over the lines of his muscles, then moved forward and kissed his neck from behind, grinding my crotch into his backside. Over his shoulder, I watched him watch me caress him in the full-length mirror, and the sight of my hands running over his chest and the pleasure written on his face turned me on even more.

"Cole..." he whimpered again, "please... more, please..."

I grinned as I ran my hands down over his chest to his waist, gripping his belt from behind and slowly undoing it. I unbuttoned the top of his khakis and stood back, letting them fall to the floor. The gold-lettered blue waistband of his underwear was the sole decorative feature of his functional white briefs, simple and straightforward. Beneath the fabric, I could see the round globes of his ass rise and fall as he shifted his weight with anticipation. Slowly I reached to the back of his waistband and pulled it down. The front—presumably stuck on his erection—stayed up, but I pulled the back down over his butt cheeks and let it hug them from below, pushing them up into even more prominence.

He had an absolutely gorgeous ass, round and full and

fleshy. I placed a hand on each cheek and massaged the soft muscle, drawing more approving vocalizations as I admired it. It was the same tan as the rest of his skin.

"No tan line…?" I mused absently.

"There's a place I know," Alexander said between panting breaths, "a place outside that's nice and secluded. I go there to exercise and work out sometimes, and get an all-over tan."

My cock twitched. "You exercise naked?" I asked.

"I like to, yeah."

"That is so fucking hot," I growled, spinning him around roughly and pushing him back down into a sitting position on the sofa. He kicked his shoes off after he fell and I yanked his trousers the rest of the way off of him, tossing his socks aside as I did so. I took advantage of my kneeling position to kick off my own shoes and socks for good measure.

All that remained of Alexander's clothing was his briefs, which were now a tall urgent white tent, soaking wet at the top, twitching and shaking eagerly. I leaned forward and carefully lifted the waistband, pulling it down over the tent to reveal its contents. With the strain of the fabric removed, Alexander's erection leapt forth, tall and pulsing.

It was the first cock other than mine that I had seen in the flesh since waking up to find my memories gone, and it was *gorgeous*. Unlike mine, Alexander's was cut—though it was hard to tell the difference given how erect he was—and the pink head pointed urgently upward, its opening winking as Alexander watched me admire him. It was of a good size, perhaps slightly above average in length, though it was hard to judge because of his thickness.

I pulled his underwear the rest of the way off and eased his knees apart, the hot scent of chestnut hitting me as his whole groin opened to me. His balls hung heavy and round, with the same light down as his arms and chest, though his pubes—

which, I noted, were carefully trimmed—were a heavier brown to match the slightly darker hair on his legs.

"Very nice," I said, and Alexander swallowed, still watching me.

A pulsing vein stood out on his cock's right side and I ran my finger up it, earning a gasp from Alexander as a bead of nectar formed at the winking opening of his tip. Slowly I bent forward, parting my lips to kiss it off.

Alexander's whole body shook at the contact. I continued to move my head forward, sliding my lips over him as I took his length in my mouth.

"Oh *fuck*," Alexander moaned as his cock slid down to the back of my mouth. I couldn't remember ever having given a blowjob before, but my body remembered for me. It clearly had had a lot of practice.

My head bobbed slowly and my tongue danced upward along the underside of Alexander's length, coaxing the spot beneath his cock head with the back of my tongue when it was in the back of my throat, and swirling my tip over the top and along its ridges when it was near my lips.

"Fuck.. oh fuck..." Alexander continued, as his hips began to take over, pushing toward me with each thrust. I adjusted my movements to account for his while still allowing my tongue enough freedom to keep him tantalized.

His breathing began to quicken and I increased my speed accordingly, but then suddenly I felt his hands on my face as he pushed me off of him.

"Wait," he panted.

"What is it?" I asked.

Alexander was breathing heavily, his cock shining and glistening with my saliva. "That's too fucking good," he said, "and I don't want to finish yet. Stand up."

I did as he asked, standing in front of him as he sat, naked and dripping. He leaned forward, about head level with my crotch, and undid my trousers, letting them fall to the ground. My trunks were soaked with my own precum and straining against my own erection, and with one motion Alexander pulled them down, freeing my cock, which pointed earnestly toward his face.

"Now that's what I'm talking about," he said with a grin, and then took me into his mouth.

Now it was my turn to say "*Fuck.*"

I may have earned a reputation for good head, at least according to Marcus, but Alexander was certainly no slouch either in the blowjob department. While it couldn't have been new to me, the sensations Alexander was causing on my cock were ones that I had no memory of ever experiencing, and my body was quick to react. Each movement of Alexander's tongue was like a wave of pleasure ripping through my body, if each of those waves was accompanied by a surge of electricity. His palms gripped my ass as he continued, imitating my technique by lapping me with the back of his tongue and then swirling it over my tip each time his mouth was pulled back.

"Alexander," I breathed, feeling something rise within me, but then he once again released me. I looked down at him with curiosity, almost indignant that he had removed that amazing source of pleasure from my erection.

He smiled up at me, a string of drool on his chin. "Come here," he said, pulling me down onto the sofa, but instead of pulling my face down toward his, he lay on his back, directing my face toward his crotch.

I looked down the length our bodies and saw his face looking up at my own cock with an expression of hunger and desire.

"That is so fucking hot," I said once again, and Alexander tilted his face up to meet my eyes with his, then grinned as he opened his mouth and took me in.

My head tilted back with the pleasure of the warm, wet

contact, and his own cock slid insistently across my lips. Obediently I took it in, admiring the fact that from this position I could view his balls, which were tight and reddening.

I had to adjust my technique somewhat seeing as how I was now coming at him upside-down, but again my mouth knew what to do, teasing the topside of his cock head and pushing his cock up with the back of my tongue to drag the spot just below his glans across the hot, slick roof of my mouth near the back of my throat.

The sweet flesh inside my mouth coupled with the hot wetness enveloping my length soon caused my body to tense, the feeling of a tide rising within me.

"Alexhander," I managed around his erection, "I'mh gonna..."

"Don't shtop," he moaned, his mouth full. "Don't fughking shtop." He quickened his pace, and, riding the intensity of the feeling, I did likewise.

I felt my body near the tipping point. Everything hung at a precipice, like a freshly-poured glass of soda at that point that foam and liquid are already above the rim and overflowing is a tense inevitability, and then...

"FUGHK!!"

Alexander came first, crying out as he burst into my mouth. He was hot, sticky, and creamy, with a delicious sweetness to him. He surged into my throat and I swallowed, the sensation of taking him in combined with his firing cock and writhing body causing all the foam in my own glass to spill over.

I grunted as the orgasm hit, a shot of lightning starting from my cock and spreading out in both directions, manifesting as a wave of pleasure blasting inward through my body and a wave of cum blasting outward into Alexander's mouth.

He grunted and coughed as I overflowed, but his own orgasm continued with redoubled enthusiasm, blasting me again and again with sticky sweetness.

We continued to pour forth into one another, our bodies rocked by jolts of pleasure, a closed circuit of semen and sex. Finally the orgasms subsided and I rolled onto my side, letting his cock flop out of me, looking down at him.

Alexander lay spent and smiling, streams of overflown cum spattered across his chin and cheeks. He looked up at me and his grin widened.

"That... was... amazing," he breathed.

"Yes it was," I replied, grinning back at him. As I spoke I felt a renewed surge of the sweet aftertaste of his cum in my mouth, and felt a glimmer of recognition.

Of course.

"Pineapple," I said aloud.

"The best part of today's breakfast," Alexander said with a smile. "Or, rather, now the *second* best part of breakfast."

I spun around on the sofa and lay back on top of him, this time face to face. I kissed the gobs of my cum off his face, tasting my own salty sweetness. Then I kissed him deeply on the mouth, letting my body sink into his as our softening cocks, slick with saliva and cum, slid against one another.

Eventually he pulled back, and I rolled off of him to let him stand up.

"Do you need a shower?" I asked.

"No, that's okay," Alexander said. "I probably shouldn't be gone that much longer. I can shower when I get back. I *would* appreciate a glass of water, though."

"Coming right up," I said, heading into the kitchen. When I came back with a glass of water for each of us, Alexander had his trousers on and was buttoning his shirt. While I knew that he had to go, I still felt a pang of sadness at seeing his body covered up by clothing. I handed him the glass of water.

"Thank you," he said, downing it in one gulp and handing me the empty glass. He certainly seemed in a hurry to leave.

"I'm sorry I'm rushing," he said, as if sensing my reaction.

"It's just that I was only supposed to be walking you home, and I've been away for a while."

"Does your family get suspicious if you're away from home for any length of time?" I asked, now worried for his sake more than mine.

"No, not usually," Alexander replied. "But considering that you were asking about Order of Light things and will be helping the Midnight Hunters, I don't want my brothers wondering if I'm helping you." He pointed to the flashsphere on my bedside table as explanation. "And I really I don't want to have to explain to them yet why I gave you one of those."

"...And why *did* you give me one of those?" I asked.

"Because Julia and I trust that you'll put it to good use," he said, checking his collar in the mirror. "And," he added, turning to me, "because I like you."

He gave me a quick kiss on the lips, then looked at me with concern. "Just be careful, OK? I'd like to do more of... this," he said, nodding to my crotch. "And it'd mean a lot to have you come to church with me again. Just..." he paused for a moment. "Maybe don't mention there anything about... this." Another nod to my crotch.

"Why not?" I asked.

"I told you already," he said. "No sex in church."

I nodded, but I couldn't help feeling there was more to it than that.

"Be safe," he said, offering another peck on the lips as he opened my front door. "Let me know how it goes."

Then it shut, and he was gone.

I sighed, feeling suddenly lonely in his absence. Then I turned around and noticed his hoodie on the sofa. We'd been 69ing on top of it.

He'd forgotten it.

I picked it up, and as I did a little piece of paper fluttered to the ground. I set the hoodie back on the sofa and turned my attention to the paper. A note was scrawled on it in blue ink. "I'll pick this up next time," it said, accompanied by a little doodle of a winking face. I grinned. He must have written it while I was getting him the glass of water.

I set the note down on my bedside table next to the flash-sphere, then opened the drawer below it. The little golden marble inside glittered in the light. I looked at it skeptically. This tiny ball was supposed to signal Cuan?

Well, it was worth a shot, I supposed. I lifted it up and set it on the windowsill closest to the bed, setting it on a hardcover book to add a little height and make it easier to see.

Now I had to wait.

I was still naked, so the next logical thing was to take a shower. I finished washing and brushed my teeth, then toweled myself off and went to the dresser. It was nice to be naked, but if I was going to be expecting Cuan, I should probably at least be wearing something when he arrived. I pulled on some lounge wear, then turned my attention to my bookshelf. The morning church service had piqued my curiosity, and so I pulled the annotated bible off of the shelf. It was filled with bookmarks and notes; I picked one at random and opened to it.

Luke 7. It was a story about Christ's interaction with a Roman centurion and his ill slave. In addition to the printed annotations, the margins were filled with handwritten notes. These included underlined observations that the Roman centurion had brought his slave with him to an outpost, spoke about the slave being dear to him, and that he cared enough about him to seek healing for him when he was ill, along with historical notes about the traditional relationships between Centurions and their slaves. In red pencil were written the words "They were FUCKING" in big letters, with "FUCKING" underlined three times. Beneath that was written in smaller letters, "And Jesus was amazed by his faith. Take that, haters."

I lost myself in the books, following the trail of notes and annotations between the Bible, a set of Catholic Liturgy of the Hours, the Episcopal Book of Common Prayer, a different edition of the bible, a Concordance, a book of comparative religion, a text on theology and ministry, a book on prayerful meditation, and several more books on different Christian themes and from different denominations. Clearly I had been doing research. I tried to piece together what that had entailed—what I had been looking into and getting at. The notes were sparse and scattered; anything that consolidated them had to have been elsewhere, probably on the laptop I was unable to access.

As far as I could tell, my work was split primarily between two distinct lines: one was work on queer faith, the other was on accounts of angels. This latter line brought me to another book, a heavy book with a dusty hardcover. It appeared to be an old catalogue of angels and demons that appeared in various sacred texts. Unlike the other books, this one had no handwritten notes inside. It wasn't hard to guess why: even now, with no memory of the book or how it had come into my possession, I could tell it was too rare and special to be marred by writing amidst its pages. When I opened it, a square piece of paper fluttered to the ground. I picked it up and looked at it. It felt unusual to the touch, and when I held it, it seemed as though it wasn't paper at all, but rather a kind of vellum, yellowed with age. I turned it over carefully in my hand and saw that it was decorated on one side in all manner of symbols in gold leaf. I could make neither heads nor tails of the characters, however, so I set the vellum aside and returned to the book.

As I flipped through the tome, glancing at the names and illustrations, I eventually came to a column on accounts of angels' interactions with humans in the 'modern day' (which I surmised was some time ago, though the first two pages of the book were so damaged that the year of publication was long lost). In this spread I found a piece of square notepaper stuck in between the pages. It read simply, "Show to Professor Norton."

I stared at the slip of paper, my eyes tracing the red letters over and over again. Professor Norton. This was a person whom I knew, someone who, presumably, knew me. I had called him Professor. Perhaps it was simply his title, but what if I was a university student? That would certainly explain all the research. In that case, I was most likely a student at a university close by. I turned back to the shelf and began searching with renewed purpose, this time seeking something that might give me an idea as to what university I attended.

The books offered no clues. Apparently, if I was indeed a university student, I wasn't a fan of the library, as everything on the shelf appeared to be my own property. Perhaps I had gone digital, in which case all that I needed was locked in that unforthcoming foldable plastic box of wires that sat password-protected on my desk. I returned to the bookshelf for another pass, hoping that looking a little deeper would give me the answers I sought.

I was so engrossed in my reading that the buzzer to my apartment caught me completely by surprise. The sound made me jump so sharply that my vision blurred for a moment, and I had to take some deep breaths to recover.

It had to be Cuan. I still had no idea how the little gold marble signaled him, but clearly it had worked. I went over and pressed the button on the call box, trying to figure out if my heart was beating quickly due to the surprise at the sound of the buzzer or due to anticipation of hearing his voice.

"Hey you," I said playfully into the box, eager for Cuan's reply. For a moment, there was nothing, and I began to think that something was wrong with my call box. Eventually, however, I heard a crackly voice respond. It wasn't Cuan's.

"Did you fool around with Alexander?"

"Marcus?" I asked. I almost didn't recognize his voice: it was quiet, almost pained.

"Did you?" he asked again.

"Well, yeah," I answered honestly. "But wasn't that the idea? Or... did I misunderstand you? I thought you suggested I go out with him, since you want to see both of us."

"Yeah... no, yeah. It's fine. That's what I said."

He didn't sound convincing.

"Marcus, are you OK? Do you want to come up and talk about it?"

There was a long pause. Then, finally, "No, that's OK. I gotta go see Alexander."

"You're sure?" I asked.

"Yeah. I'll drop by tomorrow, or the day after."

"Marcus...?" I asked, but there was no further response. I wondered if I should go down to the front door, but something told me he was already gone. I sighed. On the one hand, Marcus was clearly upset, and I felt a little bad about that. On the other hand, I had no reason to feel bad, as he had given me every indication that it was perfectly all right that I explore my possibilities with Alexander. After all, he was intent on dating both of us; it would be hypocritical of him to demand that we not do likewise. At any rate, that would be something we could address in a day or so.

Thinking of Marcus made me remember the food he'd brought the day before. I had been at the books for a while, so I decided I should probably eat. As I walked toward the kitchen, I heard a tapping at the window where I had set the marble. A very large crow stood on the sill, alternating between eyeing the marble closely and turning its head to tap at the glass with its beak. I strode up to the window, and it reared back in suspicion for a moment before apparently deciding that if it couldn't get to the marble then I couldn't get to the bird, and continued to rap on the glass.

"Do you like the shiny?" I asked the bird, which shot me another look as if to say, "Why are you bothering me?" before continuing to attempt to reach the marble.

"Hey," I said again, tapping back on the glass with my finger. The bird stopped abruptly and stared at me as though it were sorely affronted. "That's not for you," I continued. "That's for Cuan. He can't see it if you're standing in the way."

The crow continued to stare at me.

"Go on," I said, making a small wave of dismissal with my hand. The crow jumped back slightly, then looked from my hand to me. It gave a disgruntled croak and flew off, leaving the tiny glinting marble in view of the street once more.

That taken care of, I returned my attention to the kitchen. I prepared a small meal consisting of a sandwich, baked potato chips, and a glass of vegetable juice, then ate it as I contemplated the best way to approach the university problem. Searching through my apartment had so far proven fruitless, but I still held out hope that I had some identifying item somewhere, perhaps an article of clothing. Another option was to see if there was a university nearby in the city. Assuming that I attended a university that I could walk to and that there was exactly one university within walking distance, that could prove a fruitful course of action. But all this was also assuming that I did indeed attend a university and that Professor Norton was a faculty member there, which was certainly not a given. I decided that I would worry about it later and returned to my books. I had had enough of Christianity for one day, however, and so after I finished my sandwich, washed the dishes, and brushed my teeth, I turned my attention to the *Tao Te Ching*. Rather than opening to a random page, I started the small volume at the beginning. This book, too, was peppered with handwritten notes, primarily annotations surrounding wind and water metaphors, as well as analyses of the plentiful statements about achieving one's end through yielding, release, or non-resistance. The original translator had also offered numerous print annotations, several of which I had annotated in turn. I was most of the way through the dense combination of text, analysis, and meta-analysis when I heard a tapping at the window again.

"Are you back, little crow?" I said, putting my book down and turning toward the source of the noise. I stopped short, however, when I saw that it was not a surly black bird in the window.

It was Cuan, squatting precariously on the windowsill in the waning light of the evening, tapping on the glass with his forefinger. I raced to the window.

"Cuan, what are you doing there?" I asked, alarmed.

"You signaled me," he said, pointing through the window to the gold marble.

"But this is the third floor! How did you get up here? You could fall. What would someone think if they saw you?"

"If they saw me fall?" Cuan mused. "That I had pretty bad balance, I guess."

"No, I mean... nevermind," I said, shaking my head. "Why didn't you just use the call box?"

"I don't know your apartment number," he said matter-of-factly.

Well, he had me there.

"How long have you been there?" I asked.

"I just arrived," he said innocently. "I tapped on the window as soon as I climbed up here."

Something about his candor told me he was telling me the truth, and I relaxed very slightly, knowing that he hadn't been squatting there watching me go about my business in the apartment. I mean, I could easily have been naked! But then, the thought of Cuan watching me walk around naked was a little arousing.

I looked at Cuan through the glass, and he quietly watched me. He was wearing a sleeveless black shirt that was tight around his torso and very snug skin-tight black pants, almost like leggings. Because of the way he was squatting, I had a very good view of a significant bulge between his legs, and I swallowed hard at the sight of it.

"What do you need?" Cuan asked, snapping me back to the conversation.

"Huh?" I asked.

He pointed to the marble again. "You signaled me. What did you need? Is everything OK?"

"Oh, Right," I said. "Hold on." I went to the dresser and took the flashsphere in my fist, then went back to the window and, unlatching it, pushed it open. I felt a rush of the cool outside air on my face, colored with Cuan's warm animal musk. He made no move to come in and instead remained balanced on the windowsill watching me expectantly, and so I opened my fist and held its contents out to him.

Cuan's eyes widened, his golden irises glittering.

"A flashsphere!" he exclaimed. "Where on earth did you get this?"

I paused. Considering the way Alexander's family had reacted to hearing about me mention the Midnight Hunters, I suspected that Cuan and his companions would not be pleased to hear that I had been to the Church of the Holy Guardian. At the same time, however, Cuan's expression of surprise was so appreciative and guileless that I didn't want to hide the sphere's source from him.

"I met someone from a group called the Order of Light, who gave it to me," I said.

Cuan's expression changed like a shutter slamming closed. He almost seemed to recoil from the sphere, and for a moment I worried that he would fall off of the sill. His balance never wavered, however, and he quickly collected himself and leaned back forward. His eyes narrowed as he studied the sphere with suspicion.

"The Order of Light?" he asked.

"That's right," I said. Then I paused. "You know them?"

"Not well," Cuan admitted. "I have seen them at a distance on a few occasions. Cedric has had several run-ins with them, however, and warned me to keep away. From what I've heard, they're insular and inflexible, and don't take kindly to outsiders. Which raises the question, how do *you* know them?"

I hesitated for a moment, weighing how to respond. Straightforwardness, within reason, seemed like my best option.

"Do you remember that guy who was sitting on my front steps last night?"

Cuan nodded.

"He's the one who found me when I was unconscious, after I lost my memory. He has this friend, and they've been looking after me since I woke up."

Cuan looked past me into the apartment. He sniffed as his eyes fell on Alexander's hoodie, still rumpled on the sofa.

"I guess they've been doing a pretty thorough job of it," he responded.

Was he that perceptive? Or was he just making a general observation? Before I could ask, Cuan looked back to me and continued speaking.

"So, what, are they both Order of Light?"

"The friend is," I said. "I didn't know until today, when he brought me to his church,"—Cuan's eyes narrowed ever so slightly at the word 'church'—"and I noticed a flashsphere there and pointed it out. I had no idea it would get the reaction it did. But they gave this one to me to use on the phantom."

"They *gave* it to you?" Cuan asked, incredulous.

"Yeah."

"That... doesn't line up with what I've heard about them," he said.

"Well, not everyone was in agreement about it," I admitted.

"Hmm," Cuan mused, eyeing the sphere. "May I?" he asked.

I held the small silver sphere out to him, and he took it gingerly in his fingers, turning it and inspecting it in the light.

"It doesn't appear to have been tampered with," he mused, "but I'll have Lester check it out to make sure."

"Lester?" I asked.

"Yeah… he's kind of our technical guy. Well, him and Cedric, I guess. I'm not so good at that stuff."

He looked at me and smiled that lopsided smile of his, dimple forming back in his cheek as he did. "You know," he added, "if this thing is in good working order, you'll have saved us a lot of time, and quite possibly saved a lot of lives from that phantom, too."

"Just doin' my part, I guess," I said with a smile.

"You're just full of surprises," he replied.

As he squatted there, my eyes traced the lines of the muscles under his shirt down to the fleshy bulge at his crotch.

"You've been on that ledge for a while," I said. "You wanna come in for a bit?"

Cuan smiled a bit more widely for an instant. "Sorry, but I can't," he said, and the words disappointed me more than I'd expected them to. "I gotta hurry back. Lester's supposed to go out tonight to investigate some things, and I need to catch him and have him look at this before he leaves." He looked appreciatively at the flashsphere, and then back at me. "You still sure you're up for helping us with the phantom?" he asked.

"That's what I got that sphere for," I said.

"Well, then, I'll come back for you tomorrow around three, and we can plan from there. Sound good?"

"Count me in," I replied.

"Great. I'll see you tomorrow, then," Cuan said.

"Oh, wait," I said, turning to the laundry basket. "You can take those pants you let me borrow back with you." I picked up the pants and turned around to see an empty window. Cuan was gone, leaving me to wonder what was up with all these guys leaving their clothes in my apartment.

IX

MENACING THE PHANTOM

I HAD a hard time relaxing that evening. At first I wasn't sure what had left me so agitated, but then I realized that the thought of facing off against a paranormal creature the next night had left me with no small amount of anxiety. I decided to distract myself by going back to the books, and it must have worked eventually, because I woke up the next day in bed, fully clothed, with the *Analects of Confucius* open upside-down on my chest and *The Teaching of Buddha* on the mattress next to me.

The sun was already high by the time I got out of bed. I stood up and stretched, then sleepily walked out into the little kitchen to make myself some breakfast. I had some milk that was still well before its expiration date, so I decided that a bowl of cereal was in order. As I reached toward the cabinet to grab a box of oat flakes, I caught the clock on the microwave out of the corner of my eye, and did a double-take.

2:14.

Fuck. Clearly I'd had such a hard time falling asleep that I slept late into the afternoon. Cuan would be showing up in less than an hour. I wolfed down the cereal, then stripped off and jumped into the shower. I finished my morning routine (is it still a 'routine' if you can't remember more than a day or two ago?) and rushed to get dressed. I didn't know how much physical activity the day would involve, so I selected some trunks that looked easy to move around in and a pair of comfortable khakis with deep pockets, then found a simple brown button-down to wear over everything. I'd been standing for a while in front of my closet wondering whether it was cool enough outside to warrant a jacket when I heard a rap at the window.

I turned to see Cuan squatting on the sill again. His deep red hair shone fiery in the sunlight, his golden eyes glittering as he waved at me with his half-smile. Today he wore another pair of his baggy dark grey Wushu pants, which I admit I observed with some disappointment after the previous day's skin-tight compression pants. His torso was clad in an indigo vest that was made of some kind of slightly shiny polyester-like material; it was snug without showing off the muscles of his chest. His tightly muscled arms, however, were bare, and his shoulders were accentuated by a little bit of brown fur lining that stuck out upwards from the arm holes of the vest. The vest looked at first to be held closed with a single silver clasp, but considering how neatly it was closed all down the front, I assumed there was a hidden zipper running its length.

"What about the door buzzer?" I demanded.

"You still haven't told me your apartment number," Cuan replied.

Oh. "32," I said.

"Fine," Cuan replied. "You 'bout ready? Come on down."

"Sure," I said. I turned toward the door and then remembered that I had been looking at jackets. "Is it warm outside?" I asked, turning back to the window, but he was already gone.

He really had to stop that.

I figured that if Cuan was wearing a sleeveless vest, it couldn't be terribly cold, so I grabbed my keys and the cash I took everywhere and went outside, locking the door behind me.

"Hiya," Cuan said pleasantly as I stepped out onto the street.

"Hi," I said with a grin. There was something about his dimpled smile that immediately erased any irritation I might have felt at his surprising me at my third-story window. "So, what's the plan?" I asked as we started to walk down the street.

"Eliminating the phantom," he said matter-of-factly. "Did you forget?"

"No, I know that," I replied. "I meant, what is the plan for *how* we're going to eliminate the phantom?"

"Oh," Cuan said. "Well, that's what we're going to discuss back at The Hunters' Home. Cedric handles tactics. But you saw it yourself, right? There's not too much to it, if you ask me. You get in there, the thing doesn't see you, you blast it into oblivion with the flashsphere, we go home and go to bed."

"I like that last part," I said.

"It'll be well-deserved," he said, and I couldn't tell whether he was responding to the flirtation or completely oblivious.

We wound through the streets, and as we did so I kept close eye on the landmarks we passed, feeling that it would definitely be in my best interest to learn my own way to the Midnight Hunters' base—or "The Hunters' Home", as Cuan seemed to call it.

Eventually we reached the old brown house with its dreary porch, and Cuan led me inside. This time he didn't gesture for me to wait, instead bringing me back through the door at the end of the dark interior hall leading to the kitchen and dining room.

"We're here," Cuan announced as he walked in, gesturing to me as he did so. Cedric was at the stove, still with sunglasses, frying up something in a large black pan. He wore a cloak that resembled a poncho over what I imagined was a sleeveless shirt, considering that his bare arms protruded from the sides. His arms looked as big around as my thighs. Even in this comparatively relaxed setting, he wore leather bracers on his forearms, like he was ready for anything. Bianca was lounging in her chair, as usual. She was wearing a bizarre outfit that was a combination of leather and lace, revealing more of her skin than I particularly desired seeing.

"It's about time," she said as we entered. "Oh, and look who you dragged in. It's Preppy Spice."

"You look like something out of the Victoria's Secret S&M line," I said to her.

"Thank you," she said, flashing me a mockingly saccharine sweet smile as I wondered who this Victoria was I'd suddenly referenced and why she had a secret S&M wardrobe.

"Have a seat," Cedric said without turning around, and we did so.

A small TV was on next to the stove, broadcasting the local news. A charismatic man in a suit was standing on a platform in front of a series of microphones. A digital caption read, "Mayor Dennis Grafton personally oversees investigation into explosion in city square."

"Our investigation team currently believes that the explosion was due to a faulty gas pipe," the mayor said. "The Department of Public Works believes that the pipe corroded due to fumes trapped in the abandoned subway line, which my predecessor failed to clean up successfully."

"Always the previous administration's fault," Cedric scoffed.

"We believe the fumes were released after the tunnels were disturbed, which my experts tell me is a result of homeless using the tunnels for shelter as the weather cools. Therefore, we are increasing security around the abandoned tunnels and are widening my homeless rehabilitation and protection plan, converting the auxiliary city hall into an additional shelter and rehab facility."

"Of course the fucker says it's all the homeless's fault," Bianca spat. "Suddenly, oh, there's even more need for police out on the streets and at the same time his whole 'clean up the streets' initiative is magically justified. Look at him!" she pointed, as the mayor on screen ushered a shy little girl in a pink dress to the front of the platform, "he's going on about protecting the streets for his precious little daughter again. He's so fucking transparent!"

"He's done some good, too, though," came a deep voice from the doorway. I turned around to see a tall, muscular black man in a leather jacket walk into the room. "He's done more to give the homeless a place to sleep than the last three mayors combined."

The man walked around the table, stopping briefly behind Cuan to rumple his hair and say "Good boy," as he did so. The gesture struck me as odd, but Cuan smiled broadly and leaned into his hand, so I assumed it was some established gesture of affection.

"Yeah," Bianca said, "but the streets are so empty now. It's weird. And besides, if it were that simple to solve the city's massive homelessness problem, why didn't someone do it already?"

"Prejudice, probably," the newcomer said with a shrug. "People always talk about the homeless like it's their own fault, like they messed up somewhere and deserve what they got."

"That's a load of bullshit," Bianca said, "but I still don't buy that the answer is that easy."

"I'm sorry," I offered, "but what are we talking about?"

The tall black man leaned against the counter by the TV and looked at me in surprise.

"Oh, hey, sorry; I didn't see you there," he said. "You must be the guy Cuan brought to help us out. It's nice to meet you. My name's Bran."

"Cole," I said as the man smiled at me. Even with the

leather jacket on I could tell that he was very well-built. He looked to be in his late twenties or early thirties. His facial features were handsome, but sharp and angular, and his deep brown eyes were intelligent and piercing. His thick black hair was heavily styled into a feathered pattern, which flowed back from his forehead. He seemed to have been briefed on my amnesia, because he explained the mayor situation without losing a beat.

"Well, Cole," he explained, "Mayor Grafton here ran on this controversial platform about getting the homeless off of the streets into state-run shelters and rehab programs, and then training them for essential roles, like this guy here."

He pointed to the TV, which was now airing a story about a man who had been living in a cardboard box in the city, but after going through the Mayor's rehabilitation program had landed a job as a street sweeper for the Department of Public Works and had recently been able to afford a low-income apartment.

"What I don't get is where they found all these jobs," Cuan observed. "Isn't unemployment at a high lately?"

"Holy shit, Cuan just made a smart observation," Bianca said. "They should get him on stage as evidence for the mayor's education initiative."

Cuan scowled as the news show continued. The commentator was claiming that the Mayor's program likely saved the street sweeper's life: his cardboard box home had been right in the area of the pipe explosion.

"Now, that I don't buy," Bran said. "That was no pipe blast. Something else is going on here. It can't be a coincidence that we're so busy lately."

"Speaking of busy," Cedric said, "I assume that if you're here, it means your task was a success?"

"Naturally," Bran replied smugly.

"You gonna join us for some chicken then?" Bianca asked.

"You know I don't eat bird," Bran said. "Besides, I gotta get to hunting the next thing on my list."

"You're not coming with us, then?" I asked.

"Sorry, kid," Bran said with a grin, "wailing phantoms aren't the only things going bump in the night these days." He opened a cabinet and grabbed a bottle of water and a piece of jerky, tearing off a healthy chunk of the latter with his teeth. "Sorry to eat and run," he said. "Catch you later. And good luck with the phantom," he added with a wink. "You'll be great."

"Bran," Cedric asked before he could walk out the door, "on your way out, tell Lester to get down here."

Bran waved assent as he bit off another chunk of jerky; then he was gone.

"You want some chicken, Cuan?" Cedric asked gruffly, still facing the stove.

"Sure," Cuan replied, and Cedric flipped his spatula, neatly tossing a breast of chicken from the pan on the stove onto a plate. Then he half-turned, sliding the plate across the table to Cuan, who waited for it eagerly. The chicken had a syrupy garnish that smelled of cranberries, and Cuan grabbed a fork and knife from a holder on the table and tucked in.

"Me too," Bianca said, rising languidly from her chair in the corner and flopping into one at the table. Her lacey-leather getup held her modest bosoms up and forward and seemed to be designed to make them bounce when she moved. The overall effect did nothing for me. Cedric tossed her a plate and she began to aggressively attack the chicken, stabbing it violently with her fork and slashing through it with quick swipes of her knife before shoveling it into her mouth.

"Do I smell chicken?" came another voice from the door, and I turned to see Lester scurry into the room. His pale skin was all the more striking in contrast to the flowing black shirt and loose black jeans he wore. He looked agitated and twitchy, as though a million thoughts were running through his head at once.

"Glad you could join us, Lester," Cedric said dryly.

"Just hurry up and give me some food," Lester instructed. "I'd like to eat before the pathetic wretch that Cuan dragged up gets here."

Bianca cleared her throat loudly.

"What?" Lester asked. "If the kid's idiot enough to get all wrapped up with the Order of Light, then I say he deserves whatever happens to him."

"You're a jerk, Lester," Cuan growled.

"What?" Lester asked again, grabbing a plate of chicken and letting it thud onto the table. "You insist I investigate a flash-sphere that some everyday outsider mysteriously acquired from the Order of Light and make sure that it's not some trap that will kill us all—it's not, by the way; the kid somehow got the real deal—when I have about a thousand other more important things to take care of at any given minute. My work can't be put on hold just because you found some moron whose one accomplishment is NOT getting killed by the phantom."

By now, Cedric, Bianca, and Cuan were all staring daggers at him.

"What?" Lester repeated.

"Hi, I'm Cole," I said, standing up from the table. "I wish I could say it's a pleasure, but instead I think I'll open with 'fuck you, you desiccated Uncle Fester reject.'"

Lester's eyes focused on me suddenly and the color—if you could call it that—drained from his face. Before he could recover, Bianca burst into hysterical laughter.

"Uncle Fester! I love it!" she shrieked. "I knew he reminded me of someone! I can't believe I didn't think of it!"

"Don't call me 'Fester'," Lester warned.

"Well now I'm *only* calling you that," Bianca grinned.

I made a mental note to ask Bianca who this Uncle Fester

was that I'd suddenly remembered and why we both seemed to know him as Lester turned back to me accusingly.

"How the hell long have you been here?" he demanded.

"Since well before you showed up," I replied.

"Well fine," Lester said, then suddenly tossed something in my direction. Cedric and Bianca shouted in protest and I reached my hands up in front of my face, but Cuan's arm was instantly in front of me as he caught the little silver ball neatly in his fingertips, holding it fast by the sides.

"What the fuck?" Bianca demanded as Cuan rotated the flashsphere in his palm and held it for me. I stared at it, still recovering.

"I was just returning his flashsphere," Lester said nonchalantly. "He's the one who's supposed to use it, right?"

"And he won't GET to use it if the button gets depressed and it detonates early," Cedric warned. "You're done; get out of here and get back to those other hundred things that are clearly more worthy of your time."

"Gladly," Lester replied, taking his plate and a fork and knife and heading out of the room.

"Later, Fester," Bianca called in a sing-song voice.

"Rot in hell, Bianca," was Lester's sing-song reply before he vanished from the room.

"He seems friendly," I said sarcastically after he left.

"He's a douche," Bianca said flatly. "But he's brilliant, so we deal."

"Well, I'm glad to see you haven't compromised your standards," I responded.

"What the fuck do you know about it?" Bianca demanded, and I could see that our short-lived ideological alliance was now over.

"Well now, shall we get down to business?" Cedric asked. He had transferred the remaining chicken to a plate and was now scrubbing the pan clean in the sink. "Are you clear on what we're asking of you tonight?"

"You want me to go out into the city, get up close to the dangerous soul-destroying monster, and then detonate this little ball near it before it notices me."

"And in return for your aid, we'll help you find the place where you lost your memory, or at least where you woke up," Cedric said. "Any questions?"

I looked at the ball uncertainly. "What if... what if something goes wrong?"

"Then you die," Bianca said simply.

"Shut up," Cuan said. He looked at me with protective concern. "I wish we could say that you'll be perfectly safe, Cole, but we can't. I wish we could be right there next to you, but we can't do that, either—the phantom would notice us. But the three of us WILL be close at hand in case something happens. We'll be watching and listening and we'll be right there for you if things go wrong. I promise."

Just looking at his sincere expression made me feel more confident. "Okay," I nodded.

"Good," Cedric said, taking a seat at the table, and transferring one of the two chicken breasts on the serving plate to another smaller plate, then cut into it. "One left," he said, pushing the plate toward me. The chicken looked appetizing and smelled even more so. "It's a big night; you shouldn't go into it hungry."

"Are you sure?" I asked.

"Of course I am," Cedric said. "You're a guest. Guests eat."

So I did. It was delicious.

Shortly thereafter we had finished our preparations and were back out on the street as the sunlight was beginning to wane. The Hunters hadn't changed before heading outside, and a few of them earned strange glances from the passers-by once we got along the main street, especially Bianca.

"Your mother would be ashamed," one cranky-looking middle-aged man called to her as we walked by.

"My mother would fuck you sideways and throw you away," Bianca retorted.

"Your mother sounds like a handful," I chuckled as the man recoiled and hurried away.

Bianca fixed me with a look of undisguised disgust. "Fuck off," she said.

Before I could reply, Cuan put a hand on my shoulder, drawing me away from her and Cedric.

"It's not a good idea to ask about her mother," he said.

"Why not?"

"We... don't really have families. Any of us," Cuan explained. "That's kind of why we're all together. The Midnight Hunters are basically my family, now. Same goes for all of us."

"Oh," I said, watching Bianca and Cedric walk ahead of us. "...Do you know what happened to her family?"

"That's for her to tell, if and when she wants to," Cuan said.

"What... what about yours?"

"Mine?" Cuan sighed heavily. "I never knew. Cedric found me when I was an infant. He said my parents abandoned me to die."

"Why would they do that?" I asked.

Cuan just shut his eyes and shook his head, and I knew not to press. "We're... basically cast offs. All of us. We don't really fit in with the rest of the world."

"I... I think I know what you mean," I said at last. "Lately, I've been feeling like I don't fit in, too."

Cuan smiled that half-smile of his, dimple forming back in his cheek. "Well, don't worry," he said. "Today, you're right where you belong."

I beamed at him.

"Here we are," Cedric said. We were back in the center of the city, which was cordoned off by yellow tape. "Thankfully, this area was evacuated, which does some of our job for us." He turned and pointed over the police tape, down the road toward the ruined square. "Head that way," he continued gruffly. "That's where the phantom will come from, if past experience is any indication. We need to go get in position."

With that, he whirled around and dashed off down a side street.

"This is it," Bianca said. "Don't fuck it up."

"Thanks for the advice," I said as she raced away.

I turned to Cuan, anxiety starting to get the better of me. He must have read it on my face, because he placed a calming hand on my shoulder.

"You'll be fine," he said. "We'll be here to make sure nothing happens." He looked over the tape and sighed. "The waiting is the hardest part."

I followed his gaze, then looked down at the sphere I still gripped in my palm.

"I've just gotta throw this at the phantom, huh?" I asked.

"That's right," Cuan said simply.

"What... what if I miss?"

"You won't miss," he said, dimple forming as he smiled his half-smile. Somehow, I found that more reassuring than anything.

I climbed over the tape and started to head down the abandoned street. After I'd gone a few steps, I looked back over my shoulder to Cuan, but he was gone. I was alone.

I continued down the street to the abandoned square. The oppressive silence had settled over the street again, and I strained to hear even a bird or a car anywhere.

After what may have been a very long time or a very short while, the lengthening shadows began to take on an orange-greyish tint. The air grew heavy. As I waited, I absently ran my thumb over the ridge of the button that triggered the flashsphere. Feeling it in my hand made me feel slightly more at ease. Only slightly.

Eventually and all at once, the air shifted. I felt a breeze, but not like the air was blowing; rather that it was being *pulled* toward something. Scattered leaves and debris began dragging along the ground toward a point some distance away. The ripples of air pulled inward and wrapped around one another, slowly gaining substance. Then the whole winding mass unfolded from itself, tattered grey shreds of cloak billowed out and down, and there she was: the phantom.

The hollow mask of the creature's face creaked around as the creature directed its gaze almost—but not quite—directly at me. Long, billowing hair floated ethereally around her as she began to move, floating menacingly over the ground.

The blood began to pound in my ears. I almost pressed the trigger of the flashsphere out of fear, but caught myself before I ruined everything. Calm down, I told myself. Focus. Wait. The moment will come.

The creature drew closer, floating toward me, as whisperings and fog began to intrude upon my thoughts. I fought to retain control of myself, concentrating on the task at hand. Even though the creature ignored me completely, the screams in my head as it passed by me were deafening, and the relief I felt even as it moved even a foot away was profound.

Slowly I turned as the creature moved onward, and as I did so I pressed the button on the sphere. Then I lobbed it at the creature's feet—or, rather, where its feet should have been, if it had any.

As soon as the ball left my hand it began to emit a high-pitched charging sound, and the phantom whirled around immediately like a ferocious animal. It was too late, though; the ball clinked to the ground directly beneath the beast and I only just thought to shield my eyes with my forearm before a bright blast covered everything in searing light. The light was punctuated by a wild, piercing shriek that left my ears ringing; it reverberated through the empty square, echoing off of buildings and seeming to cause the very ground to shake. Shreds of cloth burst upward from the site of the blast, dissolving into dingy gray wisps of mist that smelled of sulfur, and then nothing. Where the creature had been, there was now nothing but a thin billow of white smoke and its echoing final scream.

But the echoing continued, and the rumbling it had started only increased. By the time the shriek fully dissipated, the shaking was overwhelming. For a few seconds, I was able to keep my footing, but then another rumble caused me to lose my balance and fall. A moment later I heard a crack and a crash as the entire section of pavement I stood on seemed to sink below ground level, dropping over a foot from the curb. I tried to clamber to my feet but another tremor sent me back onto my ass as a few yards in front of me the street caved in.

Then, to my horror, a hand emerged from the opening. Not a human hand, but a large, yellowed fist, which grabbed onto an exposed piece of metal and pulled, bringing behind it a massive yellow-skinned creature that clambered onto the surface.

The beast was vaguely humanoid, with a distended stomach and stretched skin, and features that somewhat resembled a person's. Its eyes were sunken and red, and it was roughly twice the size of even Cedric, who was the tallest person I'd seen. The creature was clad in stitched burlap fabric, some of which had torn enough for me to see that the creature had male genitals. Its shriveled junk and the uneven swollenness of the rest of its considerable muscles gave the impression of a bodybuilder who had massively abused steroids and other growth hormones, but who also had plenty of fat that it needed to burn off. The creature never looked at me, but it immediately rushed in my direction, and I felt certain I was about to be trampled. I feebly put an arm in front of my face as I tried to get out of the way.

Before it got anywhere near me, however, a blur passed by the edge of my vision, and I heard a furious roar. I lowered my arm to see black blood splashing from a slash across the creature's face. Between it and me stood Cuan, hunched and ready for another strike. He flicked the fingers of his right hand and blood spattered off of his nails onto the pavement. An angry growl resonated from his throat.

I had never been so happy to see anyone in my life. As far as I could remember, that is.

The creature continued to stagger backward, and as soon as Cuan saw that he had the opportunity, he whirled around and crouched next to me concernedly.

"You okay?" He asked.

"I am now that you're here," I said, and I could see a flash of relief in his eyes. "What the fuck are those things?"

"I have no idea. Let's get out of here."

Before I could stand, however, the ground rumbled again, and the pavement we were on sank even lower, now at least four feet from the curb. I turned back toward the ogre-type creature and saw that it had now been joined by two others, one with greenish skin, and another pinkish-red.

"Uhh, Cuan?" I said.

Cuan turned in the direction of my gaze.

"Aw, fuck me," he spat.

"If we get out of this, gladly," I responded, but I had no idea if he heard me—he was already darting toward the creatures.

The green ogre reared up to swipe at Cuan as he approached. It moved shockingly fast, but Cuan was faster, ducking under its arm and swiping at its belly with his hand. Cuan's nails hadn't seemed sharp to me, but they must have been, because Cuan's slash opened an angry, if shallow, gash on the ogre's abdomen. He then leapt up and back in a graceful backflip as the pink ogre landed a heavy punch where Cuan had been standing. The creature howled in pain as its fist smashed into—and through—the pavement, sending a ripple through the ground that knocked me back onto my ass just as I was trying to get up.

The yellow ogre had recovered at this point, and spun around toward Cuan. Just as it moved, I heard a "THWACK" and suddenly a small fletched stud was jutting out of the creature's shoulder. It roared and whirled around, its eyes focusing on the balcony of a nearby building. I followed its gaze to see Cedric, face partially obscured by a wide-brimmed hat, loading a bolt into an impressive-looking crossbow. Before I could wonder how the ogre had possibly pinpointed Cedric's location, it dashed toward the building he was in, neatly leaping over the curb and smashing through a large display window. Cedric disappeared from the balcony, likely to address the threat that had just passed inside.

The reddish pink ogre had by this point managed to extricate its hand from the pavement and turned its attention to Cuan, who was dodging a punch from the green ogre. I could tell he was slightly distracted; he kept glancing in my direction as if to ascertain that I was still okay. I needed to get out of there, for Cuan's sake just as much as for my own, but the ground was still unstable and I couldn't get my footing.

The green ogre ripped a piece of metal debris out of the ground and swung at Cuan, who leapt backward out of the way. The pink ogre made to rush him when suddenly it was beset by a fast-moving swarm of tiny creatures rushing out of the darkness. The ogre howled and swatted at them, batting a few aside, which spiraled away and then popped into little bursts of mist. One or two of them fluttered in my general direction before evaporating and I could see that they were in the general shape of bats.

The pink ogre and I both looked in the direction that the assault had come from, and there in an alley stood Bianca, who looked far more imposing than she should have considering her ridiculous leather-and-lace getup. Somehow, however, that same outfit now made her look terrifying. The pink ogre roared and charged at her, leaping over the ever-rising curb, and she vanished back into the darkness of the alley, the ogre following.

The odds looked a little more even, now. I struggled to my feet and turned to make a run for safety, hoping to be able to clamber up the now four-and-a-half-foot ridge to the edge of the street. I only made it two steps, however, before another massive tremor made me trip. I tumbled forward, tucking my head down and rolling over my shoulder, but was unable to regain my footing and rolled sideways, winding up on my ass again. There was a cracking noise from the pavement and a fissure appeared the length of the crater that was forming. A moment later a giant spiked metal ball burst through the edge of the hole in the pavement and flew between where I lay and where Cuan was still managing to keep the green ogre at bay. The ball crashed through a lamppost and into the remains of a kiosk, both of which collapsed sideways, toppling behind me in a mass of metal and broken glass. I rolled out of the way as a spike of metal landed near my head, clattering across the pavement and coming to a stop next to me.

The ball was attached to a chain which suddenly went taught, winding back and dragging the ball over the pavement toward the giant hole in the street. As it wound back, another creature emerged.

This one was blue, and much larger than the other ogres—probably three times the size of Cedric and packed with even more muscle and sinew and fat. Its right arm ended above the elbow, and instead sported a bizarre mechanical contraption that was now spinning, retracting the spiked ball and chain.

Cuan knocked the green ogre off its feet and looked over his shoulder for an instant at the massive beast, and as he did so the fallen ogre grabbed a fallen street sign and swung it at the back of Cuan's head.

I opened my mouth to scream "Look Out!!" but before the words even passed my lips, Cuan's reflexes seemed to take over: he leapt nimbly and planted his feet on the swinging pole, then launched himself from it, using the added momentum to leap over the winding chain and across the gaps in the pavement, spinning in the air and landing neatly on his feet in front of me, facing the ogres.

"Hi there. How are you managing?" he asked over his shoulder.

"Peachy," I replied. "Can we go home now?"

"Love to. Can you stand?"

"I keep trying to," I said. "I didn't know I needed sea legs to walk through the town square."

Cuan darted his gaze around behind me, as though he were plotting an exit path through the rubble and over the ridge.

"Even if we could run, I don't think we could outrun them, not together," he said.

"None of that 'I'll sacrifice myself so you can get away' bull-shit, please," I said. "You're too cute."

I wasn't sure if Cuan registered my words. He looked from one ogre to another, then up at the half-moon that was hanging low overhead.

"Dammit," he said as he took in each thing in turn, "Dammit, dammit. Let's hope you still think so in a moment, then."

I was too anxious to ponder what he was talking about. The blue ogre had nearly finished retracting its spiky ball of death, which had left a gash in the pavement it had been dragged across. The green ogre was waiting agitatedly to rush us as soon as the ball and chain was removed from its path.

Cuan took a deep breath, then addressed me over his shoulder.

"I think I can get us out of this, but I have to do something," he said. "Please, please, PLEASE don't freak out."

"I think that ship has already sailed, hit an iceberg, and been lost at sea," I said, surprised at how sardonic I sounded, given the circumstances.

"Well, I hope this doesn't dredge it back up," he said, steeling himself. "But if so, then, well... it was worth it to protect you." Before I could make any sarcastic comment about how that line was both super cool and ridiculously melodramatic, he took a deep breath, tilted his head skyward, and howled.

And I mean *howled*.

The sound was unearthly, reverberating through the square and echoing off of the buildings. The very air seemed to resonate with its sound. And then, as the howl continued, Cuan's body began to glow, shining like moonlight. His skin and hair became brighter and brighter until I could only make out his general shape; the light even began to shine through the fabric of his clothing. Cuan's head began to elongate, and his torso and limbs thickened. His baggy Wushu pants stretched and drew taut against his massive thighs, and a tearing fissure appeared on his torso as his vest ripped open to accommodate his expanding chest. His shoes split apart as his feet lengthened and his weight rose onto the balls of his feet. Finally, light began to stream out through that odd fold in the back of his Wushu pants, taking the shape of a bushy tail.

The entire transformation took less than two seconds, and when the light subsided, I found myself staring at an animal. An animal that was upright.

A werewolf. Cuan had become a werewolf—or was 'become' even the right word? He was now covered in blue-grey fur of varying length from head to toe, except for a mane of bold red hair extending back from his head, exactly the color of

Cuan's normal mop of hair. Under the fur of his bare arms I could see his taught muscles, which twitched with energy as he flexed his dagger-like claws. For an instant, he glanced over his shoulder at me, his long muzzled face taking me in for a moment. I looked in his golden eyes and felt a pang of reassurance: those irises, those pupils—that was unmistakably Cuan. Then he turned back to the ogres, let out a low growl, and dashed forward.

The blue ogre swung upward, wielding its retracted spiked ball like a mace. Cuan dodged sideways out of the way, then pivoted and leapt suddenly at the green ogre, slashing its shoulder with his claws. The creature roared as black blood spilled out from the deep wound. It swatted at Cuan with its other arm, and Cuan planted a foot on the creature's shoulder and leapt backward, somersaulting through the air before landing back between the ogres and me.

The blue ogre rushed him, raising its arm as it did so. Knowing what was coming, I rolled sideways out of the way as the ball fired. Cuan dodged aside and the ball crashed into the pavement near where I had been lying, bouncing across the ground and tearing up the road as it did so before smashing into the pile of debris behind me.

The ogre stopped moving not far from me and spun around to face Cuan, and that's when I saw an opportunity. I picked up the large metal spike that was on the ground next to me and lunged forward, driving it deep into the back of the creature's left knee.

The monster howled as I released the spike and backpedaled out of the way an instant before black blood started spurting out from around where the spike was stuck. The back of my heel caught the massive chain that the ball was attached to and I fell backward, on my ass once again.

The ogre looked down at its leg in confusion and anger, and

the momentary opening gave Cuan the opportunity to lunge and dig his claws into the creature's working raised forearm, pivoting over it to land a roundhouse kick to the creature's jaw. He landed neatly in front of it, again positioning his body between the creature and me. The ogre staggered backwards, and as it did the pavement began to give way as the opening in the middle of the street continued to widen. It teetered on the edge for a moment, and Cuan did a neat standing backflip, kicking the blue ogre in the chest with both feet as he did so. The ogre's leg buckled where I'd stabbed it, and it toppled into the abyss, its chain, still extended, dragging down after it.

Almost at the same time as the creature fell, the green ogre swung a large metal girder it had lifted from the wreckage like a massive bat. Cuan, having just landed from his flip, was only just able to jump and plant his feet on the girder, absorbing the shock of the impact with his knees before it sent him flying off to the edge of the growing crater. I ducked as the girder swung over my head before the green ogre dropped it and raced after Cuan.

I tried to stand as soon as I was able, but before I could even move, something yanked my foot and dragged me back onto the ground.

The chain.

The blue ogre's chain, which I had tripped over, had wrapped around my feet. The moment I had needed to duck the swinging girder had kept me occupied long enough for the sliding chain to close its noose around my ankle, and now I found myself being dragged very quickly toward the abyss.

I shouted, kicking against the chain, knowing that it was futile. I heard Cuan bark in alarm, but I had no idea how close or far away he was or whether he would even have the chance to get to me with the green ogre in his way. All I could see was the chasm drawing closer and closer, and I knew that even if I somehow survived the fall, the giant spiked ball dragging behind me would certainly kill me when it landed on me. I flailed and fought as my body dragged across the ground, time seeming to slow the closer I drew to the hole. If only I could free my leg, if only I could leave the chain behind, if only I could stop being dragged...

My whole body seemed to scream at once as my every faculty melted into a concentrated desire to free myself. And then, suddenly, it felt as though the world gave way. Everything seemed to take on a weird quavering quality, leaving a little afterimage as it moved.

I, however, had stopped moving. I experienced the very uncomfortable sensation of the chain loop tightening, not around my leg, but *through* it. At the same time, I felt a wave pass downward through me, as though something were falling through my body to the ground. Even though I had stopped moving, there remained the sensation of motion, and I realized it was the chain sliding toward the chasm—but rather than taking me with it, it was passing through me. I saw my trousers, still caught in the loop of the chain, dragged away toward the hole, my trunks still inside them. Beneath the chain, my shirt was being dragged along the ground, catching my socks and shoes and sending them tumbling likewise toward the abyss.

So that was what had fallen through me: my clothes. Before I could fully comprehend what that meant, I felt an even more uncomfortable feeling, that of the large spiked ball dragging itself through my body. The feeling was not painful, but it was deeply bizarre and unpleasant. An instant later, the ball had vanished into the pit, and I realized from its speed that the entire process of the chain first looping around my leg to now had only taken a few seconds.

Dazed, I turned my head and saw Cuan loosing himself from the grip of an unmoving green ogre. I couldn't see his canid countenance clearly at the distance, particularly because of the afterimage left by every little motion, but his fear and alarm were palatable.

What had happened? I felt strangely detached from the world. My whole body was... what? Gone? No, it was still there, and yet it was as incorporeal as mist. And yet, in spite of its insubstantiality, I could see it clearly. All of it.

I was naked.

Of course I was naked. My clothes had all been pulled away. And now I was lying on the ground—or floating on the ground?—with my cock and balls out for the world to see. And Cuan was coming running. While I had no objection in principle to Cuan seeing my nude body, this was not how I pictured his first introduction to my junk.

I looked for something to cover myself with and saw a piece of discarded calendar that had fallen from the kiosk. On the cover, two men were having sex. How appropriate. As I extended my arm to reach for it, my body pivoted in place on the ground, and my hand passed through the calendar as though it wasn't even there, then continued through the pavement.

I reached again. Same thing.

Suddenly and all at once, panic set in with renewed intensity. I began flailing, desperately trying to hold onto something. I needed to touch something. I needed somehow to anchor myself to the physical world or I thought I would simply blow away.

Hold. I needed something to hold onto.

I turned my head and saw Cuan sprinting in my direction, his entire shape a quavering blur as afterimage upon afterimage traced through the air behind him. I reached out to him, and suddenly the entire world snapped back into place with extreme violence. The sensation of the cold air on my bare skin hit my body like a hammer, met with equal force by the cold, jagged pavement beneath me. Smells flooded my nose as the sounds of the collapsing battlefield went from a muted tangle to an overwhelming roar. All the afterimages I was seeing solidified and overlapped one another until my entire field of vision seemed clouded in fog.

An instant later, I felt warmth next to me, and the pavement leave me. Or, rather, I left the pavement, lifted by two strong, furred arms. The air buffeted my skin as Cuan conveyed me from the collapsing ring of pavement, clearing the now five-foot wall of the curb in a single leap. I felt the arms release me onto a strip of grass and my vision was suddenly blinded by a bright glow of moonlight close to my side. A moment later I felt a large piece of fabric cover my waist and my lolling genitals, then a bare arm moved under my shoulders and lifted me up.

I saw Cuan's face—his human face—staring at me with concern, holding me against his bare torso. He looked into my eyes, his own wide and panicked, and said something that I couldn't understand.

While I could make out his eyes, I could barely make out the rest of him through the fog that clouded my vision. I couldn't tell if he was hurt. He'd fought those things for me—whatever they were—and they had definitely smacked him around a little.

"Are you OK, Cuan?" I asked sleepily.

At the sound of my voice his head backed up slightly. I couldn't make out his expression was through the fog, but I could tell he was concerned. He said something at me again, louder this time, but I still couldn't understand him. I wanted to reassure him, to let him know that I was OK, that, thanks to him, I was still alive—or was I alive? Living bodies were solid. Shit doesn't pass through them. Well, OK, *shit* passes through them, but only in the way it's supposed to. Big metal spiky balls of death passing through them is another matter entirely.

I couldn't think. My senses railed against me as my brain

vacillated between accepting and rejecting everything that had happened since I pushed the button on that little silver globe.

A wave of nausea slammed into my stomach and I turned away from Cuan to vomit vigorously. My stomach emptied onto the ground, and my mind quickly followed, my consciousness pouring out of me until all that remained was blackness.

X

(RE)AWAKENING

THE WHOLE WORLD WAS DARK. Thick. Heavy. Closed.

Here again. The familiar questions floated up from within me.

Was I asleep?

Was I alive?

In response, just black silence. I must have only slipped into this place a moment ago, but it felt like I'd been here an eternity—an eternity before becoming aware of the blackness, rather than simply inhabiting it.

What had happened?

A sensation. A memory.

The world had passed through me. Now, it felt as though I had passed out of the world. I felt nothing.

So why, then, was I again aware of the nothingness?

Something had pushed against the corner of the blackness.

Something had pushed, and was gone.

But then it pushed again.

A sound.

A sound I knew.

I reached for it from the depths, reached to the sound at the surface. It was earnest, insistent.

It was important to me; that I knew. And so I reached.

The darkness around me expanded slightly, but then snapped back into place. Something was in the way.

Right, I remembered: my body.

I pushed my awareness outward, felt it expand to fill my face, my limbs, my core. In some places, my body was cold. In others, it was warm. I searched my body and found my eyes. I willed them to open.

Open.

They resisted. And so I listened for the sound.

The voice.

Cuan. It was Cuan's voice. And with recognition of the voice came recognition of the warmth against my body.

Cuan.

I switched from focusing on my body to focusing on Cuan. His warmth against mine. His voice in my ears.

He was calling to me, calling me back.

I recognized something. A vowel.

".o..."

".o..."

I clung to the sound, used it as a stepping-stone from which to climb my way back to consciousness.

".ol.."

".ole."

"Cole."

"Cole!"

My body stirred first, moving toward the source, toward the heat of his flesh. I clung to that one motion and used the momentum to draw my eyelids open. My eyes focused as the darkness gave way slightly to the nighttime city streets.

Cuan was kneeling on the ground, clutching me tightly against his bare chest. The first things my eyes took in were his muscular pecs, and I followed the lines of his muscles up toward his face, passing over the silver chain around his neck, to his bright golden eyes, wide and staring with worry.

"Hi," I murmured.

Relief flooded Cuan's face as he squeezed me close. I felt something wet on my torso and looked down to see a trickle of blood from Cuan's forearm.

"You're hurt," I said absently.

"It's nothing," Cuan said. "I'm just glad you're OK."

I continued staring down at my own body, trying to reassure myself it was still there. Something was different. I looked at my waist in confusion for a moment before recognizing that I wasn't naked; my waist was wrapped in a kind of makeshift loincloth formed from a torn indigo vest, which was tied in a knot around my hips, brown fur sticking out a bit from the top.

"Cole...," Cuan's voice was shaky. "What was that?"

"I don't know," I said. "I was being dragged away, and I panicked. And everything just suddenly seemed to be... less solid, and the ball and chain went on without me."

"I've never seen anything like that," Cuan said. "It was bizarre. It was... I don't know what it was."

"I was trapped on a sinking piece of street while four giant monsters climbed out of a hole in the ground and tore up the town, and then you transformed into a werewolf in front of my face," I retorted. "You don't get to be the one who's freaked out."

"I'm sorry," Cuan said, his voice laced with insecurities that I could tell went farther back than just tonight. "Can you stand?"

I did so, looking down at Cuan as he stood as well. The tight, lean muscles of his body moved provocatively under his skin as he rose. I could see the outline of every ab, every lat. He had to have almost no body fat. While normally such impressive musculature would have my full attention, I was slightly more concerned by the plentiful cuts and bruises, which were greater in number than I had initially realized.

"You... are you all right?" I asked.

"I'm fine," Cuan said as the half-smile slowly crept back across his face. "It's only a few scratches." He looked me up and down. "You look exhausted."

"I look like an anemic George of the Jungle after a gay rave," I responded, and Cuan's eyes twinkled as he chuckled slightly at what I figured must have been another amnesic pop-culture reference. I looked down at my makeshift loincloth and suddenly felt a wave of self-consciousness. I had always considered myself in good physical shape, but I was nothing compared to the golden-eyed boy who stood in front of me. No wonder he had been able to move so quickly against the ogres.

The ogres. I felt a sudden wave of indignation.

"What was that?" I demanded, gesturing at the ruins of the city square. The green ogre was gone now; it looked as though the pavement it had been on had collapsed into the giant hole in the street while I was unconscious. "You guys only mentioned the phantom. Why didn't you tell me about the Shrek Pride Parade?"

"I didn't know," Cuan said, and I could tell that he was being entirely truthful. "I was horrified when those things crawled out. I had no idea they existed. Here we were, asking you to do something entirely new and dangerous, and suddenly you're being attacked by four huge monsters just seconds after you got rid of that phantom—which, by the way," the half-smile returned, "you did an admirable job of."

I paid no heed to his compliment: my mind was already on something else. There had been four monsters.

"Where are the other two ogres?" I asked. "Where are Cedric and Bianca?"

"I'm here," came a gruff voice. I turned toward the building and saw Cedric walking out from the picture window. "I apologize for my delay in returning; disposing of a giant yellow beast in the middle of a department store is a tall order."

I wondered whether he meant dispatching the ogre or hiding its body, but I decided not to ask.

Cedric took two steps toward us and then stopped, looking me up and down. "Here I was worried I was leaving you two to fend for yourselves for too long, but it looks like you've had plenty of free time."

"That's not—" Cuan started, but then he was interrupted by Bianca's appearance, as she marched toward the city square.

"What the fuck was up with those things?" She cried as she approached. Then she took one look at me and her expression shifted from indignation to disgust. "And what the *FUCK* do you think you're doing?" she demanded. "What, is giant half-naked monsters rampaging through the city a turn-on for you?"

"Shut up," I replied. "I don't have the energy to deal with your shit."

"No, clearly you've used up plenty of energy already," she retorted.

"Listen here, you cheap Elvira rip-off—" I started.

"The fuck did you just call me?"

"Never mind," I said. "She looks half your age anyway."

"That's *it*," She said, striding menacingly toward me. "I hope you had fun with Mowgli here, Cuan, because I'm about to rip him to shreds."

"Stop it, NOW." Cuan growled menacingly, positioning himself in front of me. Bianca stopped in her tracks, clearly unaccustomed to this kind of reaction from Cuan, but she continued to stare daggers at him. "Cole has been through enough," he said. "His system just had a massive shock."

"Clearly," she said. "I'd feel sorry for anyone who has to be on the receiving end of your oversized doggie d—"

"I said *SHUT UP*," Cuan ordered. "Cole almost got dragged into that pit. He only survived by... I don't even know how to describe it. It was like his body just went transparent, and everything passed into the abyss without him."

"Cole went incorporeal?" Cedric asked, eyeing me with suspicion and surprise—at least as far as I could tell, that is, considering that he still wore his sunglasses in the middle of the night.

"Yeah, something like that," Cuan said. "Everything, even his clothes, just kind of got away, but he was left behind."

"A likely story," Bianca said.

"Look around," Cuan said. "Do you see his clothes anywhere?"

"Incredible," Cedric muttered, surveying the destruction inside the collapsed ring of pavement. "And all of your stuff is just..."

"Gone," I said. "My shirt, my pants, my... oh fuck, my keys!" I said, suddenly realizing what I'd had in my pockets. I turned to Cuan. "I can't get into my apartment without my keys!"

"We'll figure it out," Cuan said.

"You will stay with us tonight," Cedric said. "We can at least spare a sleeping bag for you."

"Oh, hooray," Bianca said dryly, "houseguests."

As I started moving, I was suddenly acutely aware of how much my body hurt. I was covered in abrasions from being dragged across the pavement. I was left to walk barefoot and cold through the city to the house. Cuan said apologetically that he wished he could have offered me his shoes, except his own were destroyed in his transformation.

As we started to walk, Cedric pulled a phone from his jacket and pressed a button. "Call Lester," he said gruffly, and then proceeded to instruct Lester to find some bedding and set it up in Cuan's room.

"And draw a bath," Cuan added, and Cedric nodded and relayed the instructions. Then he paused. "Yes, everything else as usual," he added before hanging up.

During the walk back to the house, Cedric grilled Cuan and me on the details of everything that happened from the moment the yellow ogre demanded his attention to his reappearance. He responded with alarm to our account of the giant blue ogre, then listened intently as I told him about the chain passing through my leg and dragging everything but me into the pit.

When we arrived at the house, Cedric was eager to grill me more in the kitchen. "I want you to tell me every detail about how it felt, about what you saw when it happened," he said.

"Can that wait until tomorrow?" Cuan asked. "I think Cole has been through the ringer enough tonight."

Cedric looked at me, as if demanding a response.

"I'm beyond exhausted," I confirmed. "I won't be able to make sense of what happened, even if you ask me to."

"Very well," Cedric replied gruffly. "Go get some rest."

Cuan led me up the stairs and back to his room. A mat was on the floor with a sleeping bag and pillow. Even that modest bedding looked inviting. Before I could collapse onto it, however, Cuan pushed open another door in the room, which opened onto a decent-sized bathroom, complete with a claw-footed tub that was filled to the brim with inviting bubbles. It smelled pinkish, if such a thing was possible.

"Have yourself a soak," he said. "It'll help ease those cuts and bruises, not to mention help you relax. Oh, and the blue toothbrush by the sink is for you, too. Make yourself at home." Then he left, shutting the door behind me.

I sighed, then untied the little knot that held the makeshift loincloth in place. It fell to the ground, and I looked at myself in the large bathroom mirror above the sink.

I was a mess.

I somehow managed to use the toilet in spite of my ass being one giant scrape, then brushed my teeth. Finally I moved to the bath and lowered myself slowly in.

The very touch of the water was amazing: as soon as I stepped into the tub, I felt a pleasant tingling of relief on my legs, which then met my ass cheeks as they hit the water, following up my back and shoulders until all but my head was underwater. My ankle, which had been wrenched by the chain, eased almost instantly, and the redness that had risen up around it seemed to subside. I ducked my head under the water for a moment, letting the medicinal water work its magic on my face, but the feeling of being submerged was too similar to what I felt when I was unconscious and I quickly resurfaced.

I soaked for a while in silence. Eventually there was a knock on the door.

"I realized you didn't have a towel," Cuan said from behind the door. "I brought you one."

"Thanks," I said, and then the door opened and Cuan walked in.

"Cuan...!" I exclaimed, flustered by his sudden entrance. I reached for the shower curtain which hung around the tub on a rail, then realized that it was clear plastic and would be less than useful in covering me. But then I also realized that Cuan had already seen me naked up close and personal, and figured that the pinkish bubbles were doing more to obscure me now than earlier. As soon as Cuan walked into my field of vision, however, I forgot about everything else and stared.

Cuan looked fresh and clean. The scratches had closed, the bruises subsided. Now he was carrying a light brown towel, which he walked over and deposited on the closed toilet seat.

That wasn't what I was staring at, however. Cuan was clad in nothing but the silver chain around his neck and loose white lounge pants, which were almost, but frustratingly not quite, see-through. Still, they didn't need to be see-through for me to see the sizeable mass that hung freely between his legs, swinging against the front of his pants as he walked. When he bent down to put the towel on the toilet seat, the pants slid tightly against the globes of his butt. I felt blood moving to my cock as I watched him and sunk lower in the bath, now less concerned with hiding my nudity than my arousal.

Cuan straightened up and looked at me, his red hair still wet, then averted his eyes, his cheeks gaining just the tiniest bit of color as he did so.

"You look like you've gotten cleaned up," I said.

"Yeah," he replied, his voice a little uncertain. "I used Bran's shower. That bubble bath also makes a good shower scrub."

"It's amazing," I agreed. "I feel like I was never even dragged halfway across the square."

Cuan's face fell. He walked toward the bathroom door. I didn't want him to go.

"So... you're a werewolf?" The words were out of my mouth before I could stop them.

Cuan was silent for a moment. Then he turned and leaned against the door frame, his back to me. I watched the muscles of the right half of his back—all that was visible to me—move up and down as he sighed.

"Yeah."

I considered this for a moment.

"But it was only a half-moon today," I said, knowing that that was relevant but not sure why.

Cuan paused again.

"It doesn't work like that," he said at last. "Not for me, anyway. I don't have lycanthropy, not like you see in the movies."

"I don't remem—" I started.

"Well then, not like you may or may not have seen in the movies, if you were able to remember them," Cuan corrected. "Or in books or fairy tales. I don't change into a ravenous beast every full moon and lose all sense of myself. I don't have some wild pack that I run with. It's not some disease that I can transfer through biting, and I didn't make any kind of Faustian bargain for animal strength. It's just... who I am. I've been this way since I was born. But it takes practice to control it well. Not to control myself once I've shifted," he clarified, "but to be able to transform at will. When I was little, it would just happen sometimes. And after I turned back, I'd be wiped out. Cedric has helped me to learn to control things better, and while I still can't change back and forth multiple times without exhausting myself, I can shift at will, on my own terms. Though it is easier when the moon is full."

There was silence.

"Sorry to scare you," he said, his voice small.

I didn't reply. I was scared, true, but not because of Cuan. My mind was still swimming with the events of the evening. I couldn't think straight. I decided to try to focus on something mundane.

"What... happened to the fur?" I asked.

"Huh?"

"You... were covered in fur, weren't you?"

Silence again.

"The bluish gray fur comes and goes with the transformation," Cuan explained at last. When I'm transformed, the red hair I do have becomes more pronounced, and the rest of me gets covered in that fur. When I revert, it all goes away. It's strange, I know. Normally, like this, I couldn't even grow a beard if I wanted to—which I don't, so that's fine. I'm completely hairless... except for two places."

One was the top of his head, that was clear enough. I found myself wondering where the other one was. It clearly wasn't anywhere I had seen, which left very few options. I looked at his back again. While it looked mostly healed, there were still the shadows of the bruises and cuts that had covered his body a little earlier.

I stood from the tub. Cuan turned away, facing out the door as I walked dripping and naked to the towel, then rubbed my body off with it. My own body was perfectly healed now, but it still held the memory of the abrasions.

"I'm sorry, Cuan," I said, looking at his back in the mirror as I tied the towel around my waist.

He didn't move. "What for?"

"I saw how those things hit you. Even if that scrub makes it feel better now, that... really had to hurt."

"It was nothing," He said, walking back into the bedroom.

"But I couldn't do anything to help," I said, following him.

"Are you kidding me?" Cuan scoffed, turning around and looking at me for the first time since I stood from the tub. "The way you jabbed that spike into the blue one's leg; that was pretty damn brave."

"For all the good it did," I said.

"Hey," he said, "it was because of that that I was able to kick the ogre into the pit—" He stopped, expression changing to horror and regret. "I shouldn't have done that," he said. "Because of me, your leg got caught, and—"

"That wasn't your fault, and you know it," I said.

"I should have noticed the chain. I should've protected you."

"You're not responsible for my leg getting caught," I reiterated forcefully. "It's not your fault my leg was wrapped up; it's not your fault that I... that I..."

I couldn't finish the sentence, remembering what had happened after that. I sat miserably on the edge of the bed, Cuan still looking at me with concern. I wanted to enjoy the sight of him, standing there shirtless in front of me, all tight muscle and no body fat. He looked like a professional diver, only in better shape. But I was too preoccupied to let myself indulge. My brain was swimming.

Incorporeality. That wasn't something people could do. I didn't have my memory, but I still knew that. People could not walk through solid objects. At least, not people who were alive.

"Am I... dead?" I asked, choking on the words. I directed the question at Cuan, but I was asking myself as much as anyone.

"You're not dead," Cuan said.

"But... how can you be sure?" I asked.

"Because..." Cuan began. He looked at me, hesitation in his eyes. Then he leaned down. "Because of this," he said.

Then he kissed me. Warmly, deeply. I was taken by surprise, but I kissed him back hungrily. But as soon as I pushed my tongue forward, he pulled away.

"I'm so sorry," he said immediately, his expression one of fear and regret. He looked so scared, so vulnerable.

"For kissing me?" I asked.

"You must hate me," he said, pulling away. I put my hand on his arm to stay him, to keep him close to me.

God, he had a fantastic arm.

"What do you mean?" I asked. "Because you're gay?"

He looked at me in confusion. "Of course not," he said. "I mean, of course I'm gay, but that's not what I mean. Because I'm a monster."

"A monster?" I asked, confused. I looked into Cuan's eyes. He averted his.

"A beast," he said. "An animal pretending to be a human."

"Do people call you that?" I asked, horrified for him.

He said nothing.

"I don't think you're a monster," I said. I shook his arm, and after I didn't get a reaction, I reached up with my other arm and turned his face to mine. "Look at me," I said.

Eventually, reluctantly, he met my eyes.

"You're not a monster," I said. "So what if you don't always look like a normal human? You're a better person than any human I know."

His eyes widened. A tear started to form in the corner of one eye. He started to turn away again, and I stopped him.

"I don't think less of you because of who you are, Cuan," I

said, my voice breaking, my heart breaking for him, for myself. "I think MORE of you. You're a hero. You risked your life for me —or at least what exists of me—me, who doesn't even warrant a phantom's notice, who might even be dead."

"You're not dead!" Cuan almost shouted.

"Make me believe that," I pleaded, pulling his body toward mine. "Please, Cuan; I need this. I need to feel this. From you. Especially from you. I need to believe I'm still alive. I need you to make me cum. Make me cum my brains out."

Cuan's mouth met mine immediately. I could feel the warm wetness of his lips, the coolness of the tear on his cheek. He turned me, pushed me back onto the bed, and he lay atop me, grinding into me. His bare chest was smooth, hairless like he said; it rubbed against mine like silk. He ground his waist into mine, the feeling of his cock, a sizeable mass even soft as it currently was, kneading into my own groin through the layers of towel and fabric. He kissed me deeper, and I kissed him back, over and over. His tongue pushed into my mouth, and I pushed mine back into his, running it over his canines, wrapping it around his own tongue. I ran my hands across his back, up his sides, over his arms, through the thick hair on his head.

Cuan eventually released my lips, and, raising his body slightly, moved his mouth to my neck. I leaned my head back as he closed his lips over my neck, his tongue teasing my skin and making me gasp. He took both my wrists in his left hand, looking at me as he did so, silently asking my consent. I nodded breathlessly and he stretched up, pinning my wrists over my head. The movement opened his perfectly hairless underarm to me, and my nostrils filled immediately with his musk. The scent was overpowering, like a heady cologne, raw and animal and sexual. I wanted to bury my face in his skin, to envelop myself in him, but couldn't lift my head, instead feeling the intensity of the proximity and anticipation.

He ran his right hand down the side of my torso, making me

squirm with pleasure when his hand reached the sensitive spot on my side just above my hip. Then his fingers moved up and found my left nipple, and began to lightly tease it, sending waves through my body that made me groan loudly. The light teasing turned to a slightly harder pinch and my hips bucked, my manhood hardening to a rock under the towel. Slowly, Cuan moved his head downward, and his lips grazed my right nipple, while his fingers continued toying with my left. I whimpered at the feeling, and then gasped as his mouth closed over my chest, his tongue teasing my nipple as he sucked at it, drawing the arousal forth from within me. My waist began to buck unconsciously up and down as he drove me to a frenzy.

"Please, Cuan... Please, more," I begged.

Cuan released my left nipple and slid his hands down my side to my waist, where the towel was tied. He deftly loosed the knot of the fabric and, in one motion, pulled the towel from my raised hips, freeing my urgent erection. He released his mouth from my nipple to look down at it, smiling approvingly as he slid his fingers to the base of my shaft. I gasped at the touch, my length pulsing in his hand.

"Beautiful," he said.

"That's my line," I responded, my eyes tracing his muscular arm and bare torso. Then my head tilted back involuntarily as he leaned forward, closing his lips around my chest again as he explored me with the tips of his fingers, teasing my balls, sliding up and down my dripping shaft, grazing my sensitive head. Each touch made me gasp and moan my approval, my body writhing and hardening further. He closed his hand lightly around me and I gasped harder as he gently stroked up and down. He straightened slightly, and as soon as he did so I thrust my hands forward, sliding them down his sides to his waistband, yanking it urgently downward.

He stepped out of the pants, his large, low balls swinging as he moved. He was now completely naked but for his silver chain, giving me an answer to the question of his second spot of hair: his cock was neatly highlighted by a handsome patch of deep red hair just above its base. He was hard, his cock head a deep red against his pale skin, precum pouring forth from it onto the sheets. He was big. I only had a moment's look at it before he lifted my legs up from under my knees, pushing my body up and back onto the bed.

"Are you sure you—" Cuan started.

"I want you inside me," I interrupted, answering the question for him. "I need you. Now. Please."

Cuan a grabbed a fistful of something that looked like coconut oil from a jar next to the bed and slathered it along his length, then obliged, pivoting his hips forward, his large cock pressing at the entrance to my hole. Between the warm, soapy bath and my arousal, I was slick and eager, and my tight ass readily began swallowing his precum-and-lube-soaked cock in spite of its size.

Even so, it was snug. He watched me carefully, his eyes locked on mine for every millimeter of insertion, reading from my expression when to push forward and when to relent. His gaze was so attentive, so caring, that I felt myself melting into him.

It felt so good to have him inside me that I wanted to throw my body toward him and engulf his length, but at the same time the experience of having a warm cock in my ass was new to me, even if my body clearly knew how to receive it. Instead, I carefully relaxed onto him, remembering how it felt to let the dildo that I found under my bed into me, and even more than that enjoying the intimacy of the extended penetration.

Eventually, he pressed into something inside me and I felt a gush of pleasure release into my body. I moaned aloud as my muscles shuddered along his length, allowing him to slide forward further until I felt his balls against my ass.

"That feels amazing," I said.

"Yes, it does," Cuan agreed, eyes still on me. "I'm going to move," he said.

I nodded, and he began to slide slowly out, then pressed back into me, releasing another wave of pleasure throughout my body. He pumped again and again, slowly at first, then faster, and muscle memory took over as my sphincter worked in tandem with his thrusts to intensify our shared pleasure.

"More, Cuan; more," I gasped as his rocking turned to thrusting, and he obliged, moving faster and faster, his breath growing raspy and sweat beginning to form on his skin. His heat, his scent, his expression all combined with the waves of sex crashing through my body with each pound against my prostate and I began to grunt eagerly with each buck of our bodies, our vocalizations matching in a chorus of sex.

"Cole..." Cuan said, his face beginning to contort with pleasure. "Fuck, Cole..."

At the sound of my name on his lips, my balls tightened up, sensation building up inside me, sending me to the brink, like a storm about to burst.

"I'm gonna..." I gasped.

"Cole..." he gasped again, and that was it. The orgasm hit like a lightning bolt, tearing through my body as I blasted cum all over my torso, the pillows, my face, Cuan's face. Almost simultaneously, Cuan exploded into me, his muscles shuddering and convulsing as he sprayed my prostate like a hydrant. The sensation only intensified my own orgasm, and I continued to fire over and over, the pounding causing my fully erect cock to shoot wildly and freely onto myself and my partner. I had filled to the brim and now overflowed, and I could feel Cuan's own semen leaking out of me around the edges of his still-thrusting cock as our shared orgasm carried us like a hurricane.

Eventually the storm subsided, and the pumping slowed. My body bucked a few more times as the last throes of lightning-like intensity coursed through me, and Cuan shuddered once or twice more as the final vestiges of the orgasm forced its way through his cock in a few more shots of cum.

Finally he slid out of me, then leaned forward and kissed me. I could taste my cum in his saliva where a shot of mine had hit his mouth, and I drank the combination deeply, feeling our sticky bodies press against one another. He pulled back and gave me a spent half-smile, that irresistible dimple forming in his cheek, and I couldn't help but give him an exhausted grin in return.

"How do you feel?" he asked, still panting.

"Perfect," I replied, pulling him back against me, and we slept there, curled up together, until dawn.

XI

THE MORNING AFTER

A THIN RAY of light filtered between the blinds and fell on my eyes, drawing me gently out of a deep, comfortable sleep. I stirred, feeling Cuan's strong arms around me as my head rested on his shoulder. I leaned happily into him, watching the little beam of light slowly move from the glinting silver necklace on his neck and crawl gently up his face.

This was contentment, something I hadn't felt since waking up alone and confused in the basement of that fog-covered building.

Or, I thought, reflecting on it now, maybe it hadn't been fog-covered at all. The disoriented sensation, the inability to make out anything more than detail, the nausea—everything I'd experienced then was uncannily similar to what I'd just felt after becoming incorporeal.

The only difference was, this time I'd had Cuan there to keep me safe. He'd looked after me, brought me home, and then when I had been on the verge of spiraling, had brought me back with a kiss.

Among other things.

I smiled, leaning into him, feeling my dried seed on our

bodies, his ample semen on my thighs, the residual sensations of him inside me from our night of sex.

Passionate sex.

Passionate, unprotected sex.

Fuck.

Fuck, fuck, fuck. What had I done?

"Hey... hey, are you OK?" Cuan's voice was gentle but concerned. He was awake, looking down at me. I must have been visually panicking.

"We had sex last night," I said to him.

Insecurity and anxiety immediately wrote itself in broad strokes across his face.

"I'm so sorry," he said, dread in his voice. "I thought.... Was... was it not OK?"

"No, it was spectacular," I said, shaking my head, and he relaxed slightly. "Perfect, actually. Except..."

"Except?" he asked.

There was no gentle way to broach the subject.

"We didn't use a condom," I said.

At my words, Cuan breathed a very palpable sigh of relief. He smiled at me.

"You don't need to worry about that," he said. "I don't have any STIs."

"That's good to know," I said, "but that's only half of the equation, isn't it? I mean, I have no memories of more than a few days ago, and apparently I was pretty sexually active before that. I could have given you who knows what, and—"

"Hey... hey," Cuan said, placing his hands on my shoulders, grounding me with a calming gaze. "That's a good point, and we should get you tested to be sure you're safe. But you don't need to worry about me."

"Why not?" I asked.

"It's... it's because of the way I shift," he said. "When I

change to my other form or back again, my whole body sort of... teems with energy."

"I've seen it," I said. "It's like moonlight."

Cuan nodded. "That energy is so intense that it is basically a full-body purge. It burns away any disease or infections or toxins and such that could possibly be in my system."

"Really?" I asked.

"We've verified it. Lester has this thing where he runs our bloodwork once every two weeks to keep an eye on our health. Cold, flu, tetanus, you name it: any sickness I've ever gotten vanished as soon as I shifted."

"You've had tetanus?" I asked, alarmed.

"And Lyme Disease," he responded. "And four kinds of spider venoms, and three kinds of snake venom, and the list goes on. The things we hunt aren't exactly hospital beds, you know."

My breathing calmed. So Cuan was safe, and I, at any rate, wasn't any worse off health-wise than I was the previous evening. In fact, considering the workout we'd given one another, we were both probably considerably *better* off than we had been the previous night.

"Here... if it'd make you feel better," he said, climbing out of bed, "We can make sure right now that I haven't contracted anything. Besides, you're probably curious to see this again anyway."

"I'm enjoying what I'm seeing right now; I can tell you that much," I said, watching his round bare ass as he took a few steps away from the bed.

"I don't need to summon a ton of strength right now, so I can probably do this quietly," he said, turning to face me, lolling cock and balls swinging gently. I looked him up and down approvingly. Then he tensed, pushing his chest forward and his head back, and let out the tiniest, tightest howl.

His body began to glow, his entire physical form melting

into moonlight. I could see the outline of his body lengthen and thicken, his height increasing not only due to the transformation but also due to the shift of his weight to the balls of his elongated feet. When the light faded, I was staring at Cuan the werewolf, in all his glory.

The silver chain remained around his neck, but otherwise he was completely naked. His muscular torso was covered in fine grey fur, which also covered his limbs and his canine face. The red hair on his head had formed a long mane, and similarly the handsome garnish of red above his cock had thickened and lengthened so that it completely covered his genitals like a built-in loincloth.

I stood from the bed and walked toward him. He watched me uncertainly, ears and eyes tracking me as I moved. I looked behind him, where a bushy tail stood out over his muscled furry backside, then looked back at the muscles of his pecs. Lightly, I laid a hand on his chest, and he breathed uncertainly against my touch, body tense. Amidst the grey fur I could make out a round pink nipple, and I lightly, playfully, moved my thumb down to brush it.

Immediately he jumped sharply back with a short bark, growling at me warningly. Startled by the sudden movement, I pulled my hands away.

"I'm sorry, I'm sorry I'm sorry I'm sorry," I stammered.

Cuan composed himself, and then seemed to heave a long sigh. As he did so, his whole body became subsumed in moonlight again, his form returning to its familiar proportions. The light faded, and there was Cuan the human, continuing his long, slow exhale as his body relaxed.

"I'm so sorry," I said again. "Do you not like your nipples touched?"

"It's not that," Cuan replied. "In fact, normally I like that a whole lot. But when I'm shifted to wolf form, my whole physiology changes as well. My sympathetic nervous system takes over."

"Sympathetic nervous system?" I asked. "You mean fight or flight?"

"Exactly," he said. "Everything's on high alert. All my senses are ready for battle. It was a struggle to even stand still while you looked at me."

"I... that was careless of me," I said. "I shouldn't have come so close to you."

"You needn't worry," Cuan said. "I can't speak in that form so I couldn't say anything, but I know you're you. I was never about to lash out or anything like that. Not at you."

"Still..." I said. "I must have made you really uncomfortable."

"It... wasn't pleasant, I'll admit," he said. "But I never warned you. You didn't do anything wrong."

"And now... are you still in a residual fight or flight mode?" I asked.

"It's... kind of the opposite," he said. There was a duskiness to his voice that stirred something inside me. "Being in that form puts my fight or flight response into overdrive, so afterward my sympathetic nervous system is exhausted. It's why I can't easily shift multiple times in a row: my body needs to recharge. When I shift back to my normal form, there's a kind of rebound effect. So for a little while, my parasympathetic nervous system kind of runs unchecked."

"You mean...?"

"Feed and breed," he said huskily, his chest rising and falling in front of me.

I looked him up and down. The transformation and subsequent reversion had also had the effect of burning away anything on his body that wasn't a part of him, and so his pale skin looked like that of a newly-sculpted statue, without a hint of the dried fluids that had been caked on him when he awoke and that I could still feel stuck to my chest, stomach, and face. Slowly, I knelt in front of him.

I'd had plenty of time to admire Cuan's body, but this was my first opportunity to really gaze at his equipment up close. He was—in a word—beautiful. His cock hung, thick and sheathed, over his ample balls, which cushioned it and buoyed it forward slightly. Apart from the thick tuft of deep red pubic hair, he was indeed completely hairless, and the contours of his shaft and his sack were clearly visible in his pale skin. His manhood twitched provocatively under my gaze. Even soft, his cock was sizeable, but more than that it was just... gorgeous. The graceful lines, the way his fully-sheathed head moved slightly under his foreskin, the shape of his balls as they cradled his length—I could have stared at him for hours. He smelled like freshly washed skin, colored by wafts of the rich musk that was particularly strong near his crotch. I wanted to do more than look. I glanced up at his face, and the way he was watching me, lips slightly apart, told me he wanted the same. He tilted his hips ever so slightly, pushing his crotch just a tiny bit forward.

Slowly I parted my lips, wrapping my tongue around his softness and sucking it into my mouth, tasting its clean, fleshy flavor. Cuan gasped at the sensation and I reached my hands around his hips to the mounds of his ass, squeezing it as I pressed my face into his groin.

Cuan's butt wasn't as big as Alexander's, but was still round, and it was firmer: like the rest of his body, Cuan's ass was pure muscle, whereas Alexander's had a kneadable softness to it. I squeezed the muscular cheeks and felt Cuan's hooded cock roll around in my mouth as I teased it into growth. As it stiffened, his cock head begin to peek out from its hood and I lapped it with my tongue, eliciting shudders and approving moans with each flick.

My hands left Cuan's ass and slid around to the front of his torso, sliding up the ridges of his heaving abdomen to his sharply cut pectoral muscles, until I found his red nipples, which were hard and erect. I gripped one in the forefinger and thumb of each hand and began to lightly rub, at which point I felt Cuan's hips thrust forward as his head flew back, then dropped forward again to watch me work his body. He reached out to his side to steady himself against the furniture, which also had the effect of opening his torso to me further. I took the invitation to increase the intensity of my ministrations on his cock, which was now rock-hard and pushing against the back of my mouth.

The night before was amazing, but there had also been a kind of urgency. This morning was different: this was just about enjoying his body. I drew my head back and let him slide out of me, a string of saliva still connecting my lips to his cock.

Fully hard, he was just as gorgeous as he was soft. His length was maybe an inch or two longer than me, his proportions both handsome and impressive. The pale shaft contrasted with his dark, fully-exposed cock head, which glistened with saliva. As I looked at it, it pulsed, and the lips of his head parted in a kissing motion as a bead of clear liquid formed between them. The bead grew, then, as he twitched again, turned into a dripping stream of precum.

I gently kissed the base of his firm, pulsing shaft from all sides, letting his cock roll across my cheeks and my chin, the scent of my own saliva and his sweet precum filling my nostrils. Precum splashed across my face, its sticky wetness warm against my skin, and Cuan moaned at the combination of the sensation and sight. I tilted my head upward slightly to gaze past his rippling abs, over his heaving chest to the dark nipples I continued to tease in my fingers, meeting his lidded eyes with my own. As he watched me, I took advantage of the upward-tilted angle to drop my head slightly and run my tongue over his scrotum, perfectly smooth and tasting of clean skin colored with the earthy, animal musk that was quickly filling my nostrils as his arousal intensified.

"That feels really good," he breathed as I lapped at his balls, feeling them dance away under his skin at my touch before dropping back down to meet my tongue, each lick eliciting a shudder and a moan. I took one testicle into my mouth, rolling it around and releasing it, then continued with the other, repeating the action as his breathing became more ragged and his cock jumped and danced before my face.

Presently I felt another long, thick strand of clear precum drip onto my cheek and draw lines across my face as his cock continued to bounce and move, and I knew it was time. I released his balls and moved my lips back toward his cock, giving his nipples a tweak as I took his entire length into my throat.

"Ah! Cole!" he cried as I moved on him, stimulating his shaft with the base of my tongue and gripping and releasing his cock head as I thrust my nose into the soft fiery cushion of hair at his base and pulled back again, over and over, faster and faster.

His body stiffened, and he let out a cry as he fired directly into my stomach, then filled my mouth as I continued to pull him out and push him in again, his whole length throbbing and pulsing as his body heaved and bucked. I eased the teasing on his nipples and intensified the movement of my tongue and earned myself an approving whimper amidst the orgasm. His rich, sweet, salty taste coated the back of my throat and I grunted my satisfied approval as he continued to cum, emptying himself into me. I drank him down again and again until at length the firing subsided and Cuan's breathing became less haggard, at which point I finally let his cock slide out of my mouth and slide down my chin to hang semi-hard, a string of white stickiness still tying it to my lips.

I looked up. Cuan was watching me in spent amazement.

"Wow, that was something else," he said, panting. "What was that for?"

"To thank you," I said, sliding my arms back down, wrapping them around his waist and kneeling slightly taller as I hugged him to me, pressing my sticky cheek against his hard, ridged abs. "And because I wanted to. Because you're hot. And I like you."

I turned my eyes back up to his, and he looked back at me with that adorable dimpled half-smile, his expression one of pure affection.

"I like you too, Cole," he responded.

After I took care of a few morning bathroom necessities, Cuan joined me in the shower and gently, tenderly helped me wash my body. Once we toweled off, there was one more issue to address before we could go downstairs.

"I still don't have any clothes," I remarked.

"You don't hear me complaining," Cuan said.

I grinned at him. He, too, was still naked, standing completely at ease with himself in the bedroom, and I had to admit that I resented the thought of having to put clothes on.

"Still," I said, "I don't think Bianca would necessarily agree."

"Fair point," Cuan nodded. "As much as I enjoy you like this, you should probably be somewhat covered before going down to breakfast."

He turned and rummaged through a drawer. I had to admit I enjoyed the view as he did so. After a few seconds, he pulled out something small and tossed it to me. "That looks like it'd fit," he said.

I held it up and looked at it. It was a black jockstrap with an accommodating pocket in the front.

"Seriously?" I asked.

"You don't like it?" he asked. "It's more modest than what you were wearing the day I met you."

"OK, you got me there," I said. "But is there anything else you have?"

"Sorry," Cuan said. "For me, if I'm gonna wear underwear, it's gotta be jocks or else something super low-cut." He pointed to the spot where his back met his ass. "Gotta have room for the tail."

Ah. Of course.

I pulled on the jockstrap, feeling it holding everything in place and lifting my butt slightly. I did a quick pivot to give Cuan a full view and he licked his lips approvingly. Then he pulled on a similar jockstrap and returned the favor, which I very definitely appreciated. He pulled on a pair of his compression pants, which only seemed to accentuate every line of his legs and ass.

"I usually wear these for training, and baggier pants when I expect trouble," he explained. "I need material that either has a lot of stretch or has some room for growth."

"Makes sense," I nodded.

"I generally only wear underwear with the baggier pants, though."

I felt a jump in my crotch at the thought.

"Most of what I have are compression pants or Wushu pants, but..." he opened another drawer and dug around. "How about these?" he asked, tossing me a pair of khakis and a button-down shirt.

I looked at them, then looked at Cuan.

"No offense, but... these don't exactly look like you," I said.

"They're not my favorites," he admitted, "but sometimes I've gotta blend in with the crowd a little more. Besides," he added with a wink, "lately I've come to appreciate just how hot a pair of khakis can look on a guy."

I smiled and pulled the clothes on, then a pair of socks and an old pair of sneakers that Cuan produced from his closet. The clothes and shoes were a tiny bit big on me, but after I tied a sash through the belt loops they were at least a look I could get away with.

When we went down to the kitchen, Bianca and Cedric were already there. Cedric was at his usual place at the stove, while Bianca was lounging in her easy chair, this time wearing a sheer white flowing nightgown over black lace lingerie. As before, the overall effect did nothing for me.

"Mornin'," I said as we entered.

"Have a good night, I trust?" Cedric asked as he slid a plate of bacon and eggs my way.

"Perfect," I said with a grin, and Bianca arched an eyebrow.

Before sitting down, Cuan went to the fridge and pulled out a large package of probiotic yogurt.

"Gotta replenish the gut flora," he said, pointing at the cup with a spoon when he sat down.

"Ah," I nodded as he tucked in.

Over breakfast, Cedric grilled us about every detail of what had happened the night before. I was in a much better state to discuss it after the pleasant night I'd had with Cuan, but recalling the events in the square still made me uneasy. I still had no idea what had happened to me, or why. Cuan and I took turns filling in the details, as Cedric and Bianca watched with interest.

"...and then when I got to him, I asked him if he was all right, and he said something I couldn't understand before passing out," Cuan concluded.

"Wait," I said, "I said something you couldn't understand? But *I* couldn't understand *you*. I told you I was all right."

"That's not what came out of your mouth," Cuan said. "Or at least, if it was, it wasn't in English."

The same as that first night, I realized.

"But that effect is clearly temporary," Cedric mused. "Perhaps if we can help you become incorporeal again, we can learn more."

"I don't want to be some guinea pig," I said.

"Cole," Cedric said simply, "This is to help you. You have a unique ability, and it would behoove you to master it. Though I will not lie," he added, "I am keen to learn more about it."

"Yeah, yeah, fascinating," Bianca said. "I'm more keen to know what's up with the Shrek Pride Parade."

"That's what I called them!" I exclaimed, and Bianca shot me a fleeting glance of approval before turning her attention back to Cedric.

"What the fuck were those?" she asked.

"I have no idea," Cedric said. "One thing is for sure, though... that was no ordinary pipe explosion that happened the other day."

"The mayor said he has the DPW investigating it," Cuan added, alarmed. "We need to warn them; they could be in danger."

"Right," Bianca scoffed, "because 'Hey, you've got trolls under your bridge' is never met with derision. Why don't we tell them the sky is falling while we're at it?"

"Well, we have to do *something*," Cuan protested.

"Perhaps Lester will have an idea," Cedric said. "And speaking of Lester," he added, turning to Bianca, "he needs you for your tests today."

"Hoo-fucking-ray," she said dryly.

"Tests?" I asked absently.

"Yeah, we have a weekly exam on minding your own fucking business," she said, getting up. "Maybe you'll pass next time around."

"Hey," I said firmly, "I get that you all have secrets. But if you're asking me to trust you, you gotta trust me, too."

Bianca paused in the doorway, fighting with herself.

"I was bitten," she said at last, then left.

"Bitten?" I repeated. "What does that mean?"

"Bianca was bitten by a vampire," Cedric said.

"Wait, a what?"

"A vampire," Cedric repeated. "After all you have seen in the last few days, surely that cannot be too impossible to believe."

My mind whirled. "So, is Bianca... also a vampire?"

"No," Cedric explained. "She is something in between. You see, vampires draw their energy from the life force in blood. But if they bite their victims directly, it creates a kind of negative energy flow, bonding them together. The victim provides a very small source of energy to the vampire, and the vampire remains drawn to the victim. The victim's life force holds the process in check, but if the victim dies while the bond is strong enough, usually ensured by continued feedings, then the energy sink causes the victim to become a vampire herself. If the feeding vampire dies before the victim, however, then the process is prevented."

"So... Bianca is in that in-between state?" I asked. "And... the bats?"

"The bitten gain some vampire-like powers from their hosts, courtesy of their bond," Cedric explained. "In Bianca's case, those powers are particularly strong, though only along certain lines."

"Bianca came to us for help after she was bitten," Cuan said. "If we can find the vampire who fed on her, we can stop her from turning."

"And at the same time, Lester is monitoring her blood and working on a cure, just in case," Cedric said. "Ideally, she would like us to cure the vampire who fed on her, if such a thing is possible."

"But not even Bianca knows where he is," Cuan explained.

Before I could ask anything further, Bran strode into the room.

"Hey doggo, you're with me today," he said to Cuan as he walked in.

Doggo?

"Oh, right," Cuan said. "Crap, OK. Shall we go, Cole?"

"Cole?" Bran asked in confusion.

"Yes, that is my name," I said.

Bran looked at me. "Oh no," he said. "This is no place for your pally. We're hunting a wight, remember?"

"A wight?" I asked.

"Veeery nasty," Bran said. "I don't care if you are Mr. Transparent, you're not ready for that one. So say goodbye to your buddy for a while, Cuan, and meet me outside in five minutes. If you do a good job, I might even reward you."

"Reward?" I asked.

"Bran and I would sometimes hook up after missions," Cuan explained, a hint of meekness on his face.

I looked at Bran as he shoved a strip of bacon into his face. He seemed cocky, but his tight red tank top and tighter leather pants made it clear that he was all muscles and cheeks and swagger and bulge.

"Can't say I blame you," I replied quietly to Cuan.

"Man," Bran said, "you should see this one rut after he howls at the moon. Veeeery impressive." He gave Cuan's hair a tousle, which Cuan seemed less enthused about than he had the day before.

"You gonna be all right?" Cuan asked me.

"He will be fine," said Cedric, who had been pointedly ignoring the previous exchange, "but he will not be fine here. You need to find somewhere else to idle today; I have things I need to check up on."

"But..." Cuan stammered.

"No buts," Cedric said. "He can come back this evening for training, but not before."

Cuan protested again, but Cedric stood his ground, and so we got up and left. In the dark hallway between the kitchen and the front door, Cuan stopped and held me close.

"Do you have somewhere to go?" he asked as we embraced.

"I do," I said.

"Good," he said, and then kissed me deeply. "Come back around 4?"

"I promise."

The streets were lonely, but at least I was finally learning—or re-learning—my way around. A twenty-minute walk later, and I was at the doors of the Church of the Holy Guardian. It seemed as though their morning service was getting ready to start, as a few people were heading inside. I entered the familiar sanctuary, looking around as I did so.

Standing in the center aisle, talking to a woman in a pew with his broad back to me, was Alexander, in khakis and yet another white and blue shirt. I walked up to him and lightly tapped him on the shoulder.

He turned around and, when he saw me, his expression burst into one of surprise and relief.

"Cole!" he cried. "You're OK! Thanks be to God."

"Sorry if I worried, you," I said.

"I've been by your apartment twice, but you didn't answer the buzzer," he said.

"I wasn't there," I said. "I was kind of... locked out."

"I want to hear all about it," he said, "but it'll need to wait until after the service. Come sit down," he said, and he led me to the pew we'd sat in the time before.

I didn't enjoy the service. The previous one had, at least, been interesting; this one was just annoying. The first reading was about some cities called Sodom and Gomorrah, whose entire populace God had apparently deemed irredeemable and wiped off of the face of the earth, while the Gospel reading was a passage from Matthew 24 about sacrilege and false prophecy and wicked people leading the world astray. Jacob synthesized these into a tirade about the denigration of the world in its current state, highlighting the mayor's need to create special programs for addicts and the homeless (speaking as though they were one and the same, and both worthy of derision) as evidence of the world's tumble toward oblivion, then moved on to expounding upon Sodom and Gomorrah and how it was a clear denunciation of sexual perversions.

"That wasn't what I got from that first reading at all," I whispered to Alexander, who was sitting miserably next to me.

"What do you mean?" he asked.

"It seemed to me like the problem in Sodom and Gomorrah was the failure to recognize basic cultural tenets of hospitality," I observed.

"Okay," Alexander said, "but what about the stuff in Leviticus?"

"Oh," I said, recognizing what he was getting at from my reading a few days ago, "do you mean that misogynist edict against treating a man like he was a woman, since women had few rights and were basically property?

"Huh," Alexander said, and sat back thoughtfully.

The rest of the service was fairly uneventful. I refused the collection this time, partly on principle but mostly because I didn't have a cent on me, though nobody seemed to care when I let the plate completely pass me by.

After the service, Alexander was insistent that I join his family for brunch, claiming that the Order had been worried about how I had fared. Even though I had already swallowed my fill of bacon and eggs—among other protein—I accepted. After all, where else was I going to go?

XII

BLOOD IS THINNER THAN WATER

"It's so good to see you again!" Julia said after I had walked into the dining room and offered a shy hello. "We've been worried about you. Here, sit down and have a glass of juice."

I sat on the bench in the same spot I had been in before, and Julia presented me with a tall glass of yellowish liquid.

"Is it ok—" I began, remembering that last time nobody ate before Jacob.

"He's not here now," Julia said matter-of-factly.

I took a swig, the sticky-sweet juice running down my throat.

"I do love pineapple juice," I said with a sidelong grin at Alexander, who cleared his throat awkwardly.

A moment later Jacob, Levi, Paul, and Thomas arrived, and Rebecca emerged from the kitchen with a tray laden with bowls of soup. They stopped and stared at me for a moment when I said hello. Thomas and Rebecca smiled and said hello back, and Paul gave me a curt nod, but the other two didn't seem particularly pleased about my presence.

"Sorry about the soup meal," Rebecca said as she set a bowl in front of me. "Since the mayor started the network of city-run

223

shelters, our soup kitchen doesn't get as many guests, so we have a lot of extra soup stock lately."

"The mayor is doing some good work," Paul added, "but I still feel bad for that daughter of his."

"The illegitimate kid from that affair he had?" Levi spat. "Why would you feel bad for a mistake like that?"

"It's not her fault her parents had poor judgement," Rebecca said.

"Right," Paul concurred. "But what I feel bad about is that she's clearly just some political tool. All through the election cycle we never even heard about her, even after he admitted the affair. And now suddenly he starts parading her around out of nowhere in front of the TV cameras."

"He's using her like a hammer to drive through all his new reforms," Thomas observed. "It's all, 'Oh, we need to get the homeless off the streets to protect the children; let's round them up and put them in shelters."

"Really he should be sending them to church," Jacob said. "Then at least they can learn to repent the sins that got them in their situation in the first place."

I opened my mouth to say "What the fuck?" but Alexander cut me off.

"Should we eat?" he asked.

One prayer later, and we were having our fill of bread and pumpkin soup. It didn't take long for Jacob to ask me if I was still planning to throw myself at the phantom.

"Oh, the phantom is taken care of," I said, noting Julia's smirk out of the corner of my eye.

"How?"

"The Midnight Hunters obtained another flashsphere," I said, carefully omitting where it came from. I then told them about banishing the phantom. Jacob, Levi, and Paul leaned forward with interest when I explained that the creature had passed next to me, completely oblivious as to my existence, and then leaned back in shock as I explained how its departing wail had brought forth a quartet of monsters from the depths of the square.

"I *knew* that wasn't just a pipe explosion," Thomas said triumphantly.

"There were reports of a whole second set of explosions this morning," Paul explained. "That's also why we have fewer people at church lately. The city is evacuating a wider area."

"And see," Jacob said, "Just as I predicted, the Hunters left you in grave danger."

"No," I said; "they saved me."

I continued recounting the events of the night, avoiding carefully any mention of the Hunters' names or their powers, just that they split up the creatures and, as far as I knew, eliminated them. I did, however, decide to tell them about my experience with the blue ogre and the chain, and the manner in which I escaped almost certain death.

"...And then, it was like my whole body kind of melted away," I said.

"Incorporeality?" Paul exclaimed.

"Apparently," I said.

"Tell me in detail," Jacob asked, leaning forward. "How did it feel?"

"Nauseating."

"Anything else?"

"You seem awfully keen to learn more about the experience," I said.

"If we know more, perhaps we can help you understand it better," Jacob replied.

"The Midnight Hunters have offered to train me," I explained.

Levi scoffed. "That's a mistake," he said.

"Listen," Jacob urged. "Their leader... Cedric, right?"

"You know him?" I asked, surprised at the mention of his name.

"He's merciless. He'll use you, and he won't care if you get hurt." Jacob continued. "He thought nothing of putting you in harm's way to get that phantom destroyed. Imagine what he'll use you for now that you have shown these abilities."

I thought back to the battle with the phantom. I was well aware that, on some level, Cedric had seen me as a convenient means to an end. But he had also treated me well. Seeing my hesitation, Levi leaned forward over the table, speaking in a low, foreboding voice.

"The Midnight Hunters will hurt you," he said, slowly and deliberately. "Maybe not today, maybe not tomorrow, but the day will come when they break you, and then discard you just like any other tool."

I swallowed. Hard.

"I'm worried about you," Alexander said. "First your memories, and now this? I want to be sure you're OK."

"I'm more concerned about those things in the square," Paul said, sipping a spoonful of soup. "If those creatures are under the city, who's to say there aren't more of them?"

"As long as they don't come near our church, they are none of our concern," Jacob said flatly.

"But the city is investigating the square," Rebecca said.

"Then the city will have to deal with what it finds," Jacob replied with finality. "The city square is not a place of worship. If anything, it's a seat of decadence. It's no wonder that the forces of evil have taken a foothold there."

"I really don't think—" Julia began.

"You don't need to think," Jacob interrupted. "You need respect the instructions as passed down by your leader. We are an Order, and that is how order is maintained."

"Now you listen to me," Julia said, her voice like cold steel. "You may be the priest of this Church. You may be the head of this branch of the Order of Light. You can give instructions, and I will follow them out of respect for your position and this institution. But you will not—I repeat, *will not*—tell me not to think."

Silence fell as Jacob and Julia locked eyes with one another in a standoff.

"So... brunch is *over*," Paul said quietly, flashing me a wide salesman smile. "Thank you very much for coming, and if you need a place to stay you are always welcome. However, I think this would be a good time for you and Alexander to have a day on the town. Alexander, pick up a phone for him from the office on your way out."

"A phone?" I asked as Paul ushered us out into the hallway, shutting the door behind us. As soon as the door closed, muffled voices erupted in the dining room.

"What the fuck was that?" I asked.

"You may have noticed," Alexander said sheepishly, "but Julia and my father don't always agree on how things are run around here."

"No shit," I said. "Now... what did Paul mean about a phone?"

"This," Alexander said as he led me through a few doors to a small office. He pulled open a drawer and pulled out a box with a flip-phone inside. "It's nothing fancy, but the Order uses a few of these phones when we want to be sure people can reach us." He flipped the phone open and quickly started tapping away on the buttons. "I hate these stupid keypads, though," he added, then handed the phone to me.

I looked down at the screen. It was displaying a list of contacts, though considering that there was only one entry, I think it was playing fast and loose with the term 'list'. It said "ALEXANDER" in big letters, followed by a phone number.

"This is..." I started.

"So that you can always reach me," he said with a smile.

"But if you call during a service or something, know that I might not pick up. So just leave me a text or a message in that case and I'll come running as soon as I'm able."

"Alexander..." I said, "Thank you."

"So," Alexander said as we walked through the some of the hallways leading outside, "it looks like I have the whole day free. What would you like to do? Maybe..." he said with a knowing wink, "we could hang out at your place?"

"Wow, you cut to the chase, huh?" I said, as he grinned. "You must have really enjoyed that hea—"

"SHH!" Alexander cut me off, looking around nervously as though he expected to see a family member appear at any moment. "None of that talk in church, remember?"

"Right, sorry," I said. "Only thinly veiled allusions."

"Shut up," he said, now laughing.

"But Alexander, we can't go to my apartment... I had my keys in my pocket last night."

"So?" Alexander asked, and then his eyes widened as comprehension dawned. "Oh," he said. "Oh, shit."

I nodded.

"So, what are you going to do?"

"I think I'm going to stay with the Midnight Hunters for now while they train me."

"Cole," Alexander looked at me with serious concern, "I really don't think that's a good idea. Father may be ham-fisted about it, but his concerns are legitimate. You should stay with us."

"Something tells me I'm not as meek and obedient as your father would like," I replied.

"Father has... different expectations for members of the Order," Alexander explained. "It's like in your interpretation of today's reading. Hospitality is paramount."

"I gave my word that I'd go back," I said.

"Very well," Alexander sighed. "But until then, we have

some time. Have you remembered anything? Has anything been on your mind?"

"Well, those are two different questions," I pointed out. "Though I think I have a response for each of them. First... I found something in my apartment. Something about a Professor Norton."

Alexander stopped in his tracks and looked at me. "Are you a student at the university here?"

"So there *is* a university here," I said.

"Yeah, though it's kind of shutting down at the moment. The city square is right by campus."

"Damn, that's not good."

"Don't say 'damn' here," Alexander admonished.

"Fuck, that's not good," I corrected, and Alexander's brow darkened.

"*Anyway*, do you have any idea what department you might be looking in?"

"It was in a book on angels and demons," I said. "Perhaps theology or something? You've seen all the religious books on my shelf."

"To be fair, when I'm in your apartment, it's not your books that have my attention," he replied.

"So *that* is OK, but I can't say I gave you head?" I asked, prompting more frantic shushing from Alexander.

"For a Church that you claim to love so much, it certainly puts you on edge," I observed.

"Faith is never simple," Alexander stated, slightly grumpily.

Maybe not, but something told me it didn't have to be that complicated, either.

"Anyway," Alexander said, "now that you mention it... I seem to recall hearing about a speech by a Professor Norton in comparative religion."

"How do you know the names of the professors at the university?" I asked.

"I graduated with a degree in business last year," Alexander explained.

"Business?" I asked, with no small amount of incredulity. "I would have thought you'd have studied religion for sure."

"Absolutely not," Alexander said. "Father pointed out that there was no reason for me to need to study religion at some secular university when the One True Word was being spoken right under my own roof."

"And that didn't strike you as myopic?" I asked.

"When one has a clear signal, one doesn't try to introduce noise," Alexander replied, clearly parroting something he had heard somewhere—doubtless part of this 'One True Word' of his. During this conversation we had made our way through the church from the office to the front of the empty sanctuary, and Alexander now pushed open the doors and we walked out into the sun.

"Anyway," Alexander continued, "Father felt that the Church could use someone more skilled at looking after its books after my brother Rhode left, and thus I got a degree in business."

"He must be very proud," I said dryly.

"I hope so," Alexander agreed, oblivious to my sarcasm. "Anyway, I can check the university directory and see if there is indeed a Professor Norton, and try to reach him."

"Thank you, Alexander," I said. "I really appreciate that."

"Don't mention it," he replied with a smile. "Now, you said there was a second thing?"

"Yeah..." I added as we stood in the front courtyard of the church. "Is there a place you know where someone can get tested?"

"Tested?" he asked, not following.

"You know," I said. "A clinic."

"A... OH," he remarked, realization dawning. "Yeah, but I don't think you have anything to worry about," he said. "I'm on

PrEP, and Marcus... well, Marcus may be irresponsible in a lot of ways, but he *always* wraps it up."

"Good to know," I said patiently, "but that's not the issue."

"Cole," Alexander asked warily, "Are you hooking up with someone *else*, too?"

"Yeah," I admitted, "but I know for a fact he doesn't have any STIs."

"You don't waste any time, do you?" Alexander remarked with an impressed expression on his face. "You've been conscious for... what, three, four days?" He shook his head. "Still, you can't *know* this guy is free of STIs, just because he said he is."

"But I should be satisfied when you told me you're on PrEP?" I asked.

"That's different," Alexander said; "you can trust *me*."

"Well then trust *me* when I say this guy has no STIs," I replied. "But that's not what I'm worried about. I'm worried about myself. Who knows what I was up to before I lost my memory?"

"I'm sure you had it covered," Alexander said. "You seem like you were a responsible guy."

"I was dating Marcus," I pointed out.

"We'll get you tested," Alexander nodded.

Alexander pulled out his phone and brought up a map. "There's a clinic nearby that does rapid STI testing, and they run on donations, so people in need—like you—can be tested for free."

"Really?" I asked.

"Yeah. I get tested myself about once a month. We can head over there now and—"

"Of *COURSE* you're fucking here!!" came a furious shout from beyond the church's stone wall. It was a voice I recognized.

"Marcus?" Alexander responded in surprise. "What are you doing here?"

"You mean why am I still in the picture?" Marcus demanded, lurching forward. He seemed... off. "Why haven't I just disappeared and left you two with one another?"

"That's not what I—" Alexander began.

"Sure it is," Marcus spat. "You say we can try again; you say we can see how things go, but you're really just trying to keep me away from Cole."

"Are you high?" Alexander asked, concerned. "And drunk, on top of that? Marcus, what happened to—"

"And YOU," Marcus whirled on me unsteadily, eyes wild and dilated. "Suddenly you stop answering your buzzer? You get Alexander's cock in your mouth and now I can go fuck off?"

"Quiet down," Alexander said urgently, looking over his shoulder.

"I haven't been home," I said.

"Of course not;" Marcus said. "You've been here."

"No, he hasn't," Alexander stated.

Like a switch, Marcus's expression turned from accusatory to petulant. "I'm so crazy about both of you," he whined. "Where's *my* head?"

"Hey," Alexander said, his voice a hushed combination of placating, fearful, and impatient. "Just last afternoon, you and I—"

"Until you had to run back home," Marcus interrupted with a broad, dismissive wave. "Back home to a service, you said. Sure. To service this one," He levelled an unsteady finger at me.

"I was not here yesterday," I said firmly.

"Don't lie to me!" Marcus cried. "Don't ignore me. Why don't you guys want me? I want you. I mean it. I'll prove how much I want you." He whirled around to turn his back to us. "Would I have done *this* if I didn't mean it?"

He yanked down his waistband to reveal his round fleshy ass cheeks. One of them sported, in fancy, flowering script, "Alexander" in fresh black ink. The other featured an equally ostentatious "Cole". The tattoos were new, glaring, and angry, the flesh around them red and weeping. Whatever he was supposed to be doing to care for them, he clearly had been neglecting.

Alexander frantically threw his body in front of Marcus's ass. "Pull your pants up," he hissed angrily.

"Those look awful," I said, wincing.

"You hate them!" Marcus cried.

"No, I mean they look super painful; maybe even infected."

"What the fuck do you care?" he demanded, continuing to moon us and the church windows.

"We care because we care about *you*," Alexander said anxiously. "So pull your pants up and let's get you some help."

"Fucking bullshit," Marcus responded, rounding on Alexander, pants still hanging off his ass, which now faced the street. "You don't give a fuck about that. You're just terrified of *them*," he pointed angrily at the church, "and that they'll find out that you like having guys CUM IN YOUR ASS!" He shouted the last words over Alexander's shoulder at the top of his lungs.

"*SHHHH!*" Alexander hissed, waving his arms in front of Marcus's face. Then he turned to me.

"I gotta take care of this," Alexander said apologetically. "I'm gonna take him to a clinic to get detoxed. I'm sorry, but I think if we're both there it'll just make him more agitated. Think you can find the clinic without me? I'll text you the address."

I nodded.

"Ok then. I'll call you later," he said, placing his arm over Marcus's shoulder and spinning him around, yanking his pants back up over the festering tattoos on his ass with his other hand as he did so.

"Hey, hey, it's OK; let's go for a walk," he said placatingly at Marcus's ear, steering him out from the church courtyard. As they left, he gave me one more apologetic glance over his shoulder, and I waved.

Then I got the hell out of there.

I was disappointed that Alexander had taken off, but when he texted me, he thankfully sent not only an address, but also street-by-street instructions, complete with landmarks. He must have been texting furiously with one hand while carefully steering Marcus with the other, and I appreciated the effort. I texted him a thank you but did not receive a reply, so I figured that Marcus had by that point demanded his undivided attention.

I found the clinic without difficulty, even though it was set inside an office building with minimal signage. Considering the message puked out by places like the Church of the Holy Guardian, the clinic probably felt that it was in its best interest to keep a low profile.

The interior of the clinic was sparse and clean, all simple white lines and light gray furniture. True to Alexander's description, the clinic was both anonymous and offered free rapid testing.

A friendly and patient doctor greeted me. He looked to be around forty, his black skin contrasting starkly with his white doctor's coat. He introduced himself as Doctor Peterson and invited me into a small clinic room.

After what I assumed was a standard consent form and basic information about the testing and what it entailed, I had a quick physical check that revealed nothing amiss, after which the doctor took a sample of my blood with a finger prick and collected some of my other fluids.

"If you don't mind returning to the waiting room," the doctor said, his voice calm and friendly, "I'll run these to our lab and get right back to you with the results. Sorry that you'll be on your own; we're a little short-handed today."

I returned to the simple waiting room and put it to the use

for which it was named. After a short while, Doctor Peterson reappeared.

"Um... do you mind coming here a moment?" he said.

I swallowed. that reaction from a doctor never signaled good news.

"What's wrong?" I asked, reentering the examination room. "Did my results show something the matter?"

"No," the doctor replied, much to my relief, "but I think something was wrong with your sample. Would you mind horribly if we took another sample of blood?"

I obliged, and this time the doctor collected a vial from my arm. A longer wait in the waiting room followed, and when Doctor Peterson returned, he had gauze taped in his own elbow.

"What's going on?" I asked.

"That's what I'm trying to figure out," the doctor replied. "Every test came back negative, which is what we would expect from a healthy male, but everything also had atypical markers. All the samples seem... too neat, if that's a thing."

"Huh?" I asked.

"Like your blood," he said. "I tested your blood twice, once for antigens and once for target nucleic acids. The latter test is expensive so we don't usually do it, but your blood was reacting abnormally so I did the additional check. The readings are... unusual, so much so that I ran my own blood to be sure the machines are working. Your blood is blood, that much I can tell from looking at it, but the tests came back as though it were water."

"Which means...?"

"Which means that if our tests are to be believed, your blood is so pure that it makes O-Negative blood look like mud by comparison."

I blinked at him. "Not all of my fluids can be like that," I said. "I mean, my cum definitely is thick and rich."

"Oh, well, good to know," Doctor Peterson said awkwardly. "But that's not something we're going to be checking here. If it's OK though, I'll send your fluids that we *did* collect away for a more comprehensive test."

I assented, and the doctor asked for my contact information. Since I currently did not have access to my apartment and had no idea what my e-mail address could be, I flipped open my phone and copied down my phone number. Then I left, feeling renewed unease.

According to my flip phone it was well into the afternoon, and so I decided that at this point I would probably be safe returning to the Midnight Hunters' base of operations.

I arrived at the building just as Lester and Bianca were heading out. Bianca gave me one of those not-quite-friendly-but-still-affable acknowledging jerks of the head as she descended the stairs from the front porch, but Lester took one look at the flip phone that was open in my hand and immediately started my way.

"What is that?" he demanded.

"It's something called a phone," I said. "Apparently it's like the telegraphs you grew up with, but this one doesn't need wires and can transmit entire *voices*. Will wonders never cease?"

Bianca burst into laughter, but Lester was not amused. "I mean, where did you get it?"

"One of the Order of Light gave it to me in case—"

"Nope. Uh-uh." Lester barked, snatching the phone from my hand. "These things can do tracking, GPS, all sorts of stuff. I'm sure The Order of Light would just LOVE to pinpoint the location of The Hunters' Home."

"One, they seem kind of agoraphobic, so I really don't think that should be a worry of yours," I said. "Second, *what the fuck,* give me back my phone." I reached for it but Lester dropped it into a large black bag he was carrying, then fished around and pulled out another phone, this one a smartphone still in its packaging. He ripped the phone out of its packaging and thrust it into my hands.

"Here," he said, "you can have one of our burners. It's a huge upgrade anyway, so Merry fucking Christmas. I need to keep that pocket tracking device they gave you away from this house." Then he stalked off at a brisk pace, Bianca practically having to run to keep up with him.

"Hey Fester, how come I never get a new phone?" she whined mockingly as they hurried down the street.

"Shut up," I heard him say before they left earshot.

I turned and looked at the simple, unassuming house that was the Hunters' headquarters. It had profoundly affected not only my life, but also my worldview. Werewolves. Vampires. Phantoms. All these beings that the rest of the world thought consigned to fantasy were real.

I pushed open the door to the house and walked down the now-familiar dark hall to the kitchen. As I walked, I called out a polite "Hello; I'm back," so as to not completely take everyone by surprise.

There wasn't an 'everyone' to surprise, however, just Cedric.

"Welcome back," he said as he sat at the kitchen table, looking over a newspaper, still with his sunglasses on his face. He had to have very sensitive eyes.

"I assume by the 'welcome' that it's OK for me to have come back here?" I asked.

"Correct," Cedric nodded, setting the newspaper aside. "I had finished up what I needed to do, and was just catching up on the day's events." He gestured to the newspaper. "It is critical that we stay informed, after all," he said, "otherwise we would have to rely on chance encounters like the one you had with the phantom in order to make any headway against the creatures that threaten those that live here."

"You get a lot from the newspaper?" I asked.

Cedric chuckled. "Some," he said. "And from the broadcast

news. I am more old fashioned, I suppose; I leave the social media research to those more suited to the activity, like Bianca. And of course Lester has many means of acquiring new information."

"He took my phone," I complained.

"Why would he do that?"

"The Order of Light gave it to me," I began to explain, "and—"

"Then he was right to take it," Cedric growled. "Lester is extremely cautious, it is true, but I consider that one of his finer qualities."

I harumphed, but Cedric paid my reaction no mind. Instead, he stood.

"We have some time before dinner," he said, "and Bran and Cuan have yet to return. "Perhaps we should see what we can do about your training before then."

I nodded my assent, and Cedric opened a door for me at the back of the kitchen, between Bianca's chair and the rack of drying dishes. Beyond it was a stairwell leading down and to the right, and Cedric flipped a light switch to reveal a large open room below. The room was surprisingly well-lit and bright for a basement room, with concrete walls paneled with a light-brown finish and wood-and-metal supports holding up the floor above. The floor here was inset with what looked like padded gym mats imprinted with a woven pattern that emulated bamboo. They had a little bit of give to them but were, for the most part, firm enough to support running and jumping and all manner of other exercise. The room had a pair of doors, one in the corner of the room and one that looked to be made of reinforced metal under the center of what I figured was the rear wall of the house.

Cedric noticed me looking at the doors and cleared his throat loudly. "This is one of our training rooms," he said. "We have another through that door in the corner; that one is outfitted for some more intensive training, so I advise you not to go in there just yet. And this one," he said, gesturing to the heavier door, "is a private room of mine, where I keep some of my personal equipment. I am afraid I must sound a lot like creatures of folklore such as Bluebeard when I ask that you not go in that room. However, unlike those fairy tales, this is not some test of will or exercise in temptation where you are destined to open the unattended door and be horrified by what lies within; I keep this door firmly locked. And even if you did go in one day, I fear you would be very disappointed to find that it is more or less a simple storeroom full of nothing more than items integral to our day-to-day operation."

"That was a lengthy answer to a question I never asked," I said, raising an eyebrow.

"Forgive me," Cedric said simply. "Since Bianca, I have learned to expect that others will not always be respectful of boundaries."

I nearly laughed at the thought, but managed a knowing smirk instead.

"Now then," Cedric said, "this should be a safe space to start testing the workings of your abilities. Let us see if you can go incorporeal again."

"You know that if I 'go incorporeal', as you say, it means dropping my clothes in front of you," I warned.

"What do I care?" Cedric shrugged.

I considered pointing out that 'I don't care about your body' didn't immediately make it OK to ask someone to get naked, but I also didn't give a flying fuck if Cedric saw me with my cock out, so I said nothing.

"If you are quite ready, let us continue," Cedric said. "Now, help me understand the conditions under which your body went incorporeal."

"I already told you that," I said.

"You told me the sequence of events," Cedric clarified.

"What I want to know is what was going on internally. How did the experience make you *feel*?"

"Shouldn't I be lying on a leather couch for this?" I asked.

"Stop wasting time," Cedric growled.

"I... I don't know how to describe what you're asking me to describe," I explained, fumbling for words. "I was panicked. I wanted to get away. It was like some primitive emotion in the back of my head realized that, if I wasn't physically there, the chain couldn't affect me, and then the whole world just... shifted out of place."

"Fascinating," Cedric said thoughtfully. "Do you think you can harness that feeling again?"

"I don't know, I..."

"Close your eyes," Cedric instructed patiently. "Concentrate. Feel your body. Search yourself."

I did as he instructed. I remembered what it had taken to regain my consciousness earlier, after I had gone incorporeal in the square and after fainting when I was first awake. I tried working in the opposite direction, pushing backward against my consciousness instead of clawing my way toward it. The process was entirely counterintuitive.

"I... don't feel anything," I said.

"Keep trying," Cedric said.

I closed my eyes again, but we were suddenly interrupted by the loud sound of the doorbell ringing. The noise jolted me back, and Cedric groaned with irritation.

"Who in the hell?" he grumbled, turning to the stairs.

I followed him up into the kitchen and down the hall. He opened the front door, and there on the other side of the porch door stood a man patiently waiting.

The sight of him made me do a double take. He was tall and blond, dressed immaculately in a dark suit, and... *extremely* handsome, almost to an unworldly degree. His unblemished skin was like porcelain, his blonde hair neatly parted to one side, his eyes a shockingly clear icy platinum. From the way the suit fit his body, I could tell he was in fantastic shape. I swallowed hard.

Cedric, however, seemed completely unaffected by any of this. Instead he said gruffly, "What do you want?"

When the stranger replied, his voice was a smooth baritone.

"I wish to join the Midnight Hunters."

The sentence did not get the response I expected. Cedric looked as though he were about to tear the door off its hinges.

"How do you know that name? How did you find this place?" He demanded, his voice low, intense, and threatening.

The man gave a smug, unruffled smile. He wasn't exactly cocky, just confident. It suited him. I continued to stare at the gorgeous man. He looked older than me, but I wasn't sure if I would place him at 30.

"I knew where to look," the man said simply, and for a moment the two stared at one another through the porch screen.

"This is not some scavenger hunt," Cedric scowled.

"No, but you hunt the creatures that shouldn't be here. There are more of them of late. Like in the city square."

"You saw what happened in the square?" I asked, and Cedric turned his head slightly toward me as though he were giving me a dirty look behind his sunglasses.

"No," the man said, "but I am aware of it."

"How?" Cedric asked.

"It is a difficult thing to explain," the man said. "When something isn't right, I can... feel it. It's what brought me to this city."

"I already have enough people providing me with intelligence," Cedric replied gruffly. "We are hunters. Intelligence is fine, but it will not keep you alive when those things come."

"Don't underestimate the value of knowledge," the man

said, smiling again. "But if your concern is about my martial prowess, rest assured that you needn't fear on that account."

With that, the man outstretched his arm to his side and opened his palm as if reaching for something. And instant later, the air began to quaver, and then a short beam extended from his palm. It was like a beam of light, except that it was pitch black, even though it shone and radiated. A moment later, the black glow coalesced into cold, shining steel, and the man was holding a sword with a slender blade about three feet in length. The blade had a dark glint, as though it had been polished with black oil.

Cedric stared at the blade for a moment, and then asked gruffly, "Who are you?"

"Call me Az," the man said.

"As?" I scoffed. "Are you a simile? Do you have a brother named 'Like'?"

"No," the man said, "A-Z."

"Oh, much better," I said. "What, were your parents just like, 'Who knows what to call him, let's take the first and last letters of the alphabet and be done with it'? Were they just bored of calling you 'Mistake'?"

"Shut the fuck up," Cedric barked over my shoulder.

"And who are you?" Az asked, looking at me.

"Cole," I replied.

"So you're named after a type of fuel, and you're complaining about *my* name?" he said.

"No, C-O-L-E," I said.

"So a slaw, then," Az replied.

"Ok, now I am starting to like you," Cedric grunted begrudgingly. He looked the man up and down, then at his sword. "But we are not going to take you just because you show up at our door peddling fancy knives. If you are looking for a place to stay, you are out of—"

"I have my own accommodation, thank you," Az interrupted.

"Well, good then," Cedric said. "Meet us here tomorrow at 2, and we shall take you on a trial run to see if that blade of yours is more than just a magic trick."

"Very well," Az agreed. "Until tomorrow." The sword dissolved back into black light, which then dissipated. He gave a short, small bow and turned, disappearing down the street.

"Do you get a lot of visitors like that?" I asked.

"Never," Cedric scowled. "If someone knows who we are and where we live, then it means that one of us made a mistake." He turned and stalked into the house. I followed, frowning at what was clearly a jab at Cuan.

"Do you think this Az person might be dangerous?" I asked.

"If he is not, then he is not of much use to us," Cedric replied. "I admit that I am impressed with his sword-summoning act, but I am losing patience with the number of new faces showing up of late."

"Who else has shown up?" I asked.

Cedric turned and stared at me.

"Oh," I said. "Right."

"Your apparent ability to escape everyone's notice is convenient," he said, "but that alone is not enough to make you a Hunter." He ducked into a side room. "Go downstairs and let us see if we cannot figure out how to replicate this disappearing act that you and Cuan reported."

"Disappearing...," I thought aloud as I proceeded to the stairs to the basement. I heard Cedric enter the kitchen behind me and follow me down the stairs. "I guess that's kind of what it felt like. Except that I wasn't gone. I wasn't *there*, but I wasn't gone, either. I don't know how else to talk about it." I reached the bottom of the stairs, walking into the center of the mat-lined room. I took a deep breath. "I can work on trying to feel that way again, but I think it might be slow going."

"This day has tried my patience enough already," Cedric said from behind me, his voice low and menacing. "It is time to speed things along."

I turned to face him, and found myself staring down the length of his crossbow.

"What? What, wait, what?" I stammered, backpedaling until my back was flat against the wall.

"I have always found that the best way to teach someone to swim is to toss them into the water," Cedric said flatly.

"And how many people drowned?" I challenged.

"None," Cedric said simply. "They all swim eventually."

"What makes you so sure?" I asked.

Cedric's face twisted into a smirk. "Your so-called 'friends' at the Order of Light would call it 'faith'. I call it confidence. Confidence that I do not surround myself with weak people." He raised the crossbow higher, finger poised on the trigger. "Show me I have not made a mistake, Cole."

"What the *FUCK*, Cedric!?" I shouted at the top of my lungs. Cedric squeezed the trigger. The bolt flew faster than I could see, but it left a trail that hung in the air. I heard the thwip as it found its mark, and Cedric lowered the crossbow and stared at me, slack-jawed. I looked down in wide-eyed horror to see the back of the shaft sticking out of my chest.

My bare chest.

I turned my body, feeling my torso pass over the shaft, and looked behind me. My shirt was pinned to the wall, the crossbow bolt stuck firmly through the material. The remainder of my clothes were in a heap at my feet.

The very next moment, I heard the door to the basement burst open, and Cuan appeared in a blur at the top of the stairs.

"I heard you shout from outside; is everything all—what the *hell* is going on?"

In one leap, Cuan was at the bottom of the stairs, and in

another, he was at my side. He rounded on Cedric, who was still staring at me, crossbow lowered.

"What did you do?" Cuan demanded. "You *shot at* him?"

"He was having trouble going incorporeal," Cedric explained, as if it was the most natural thing in the world.

"So you *shot at* him?" Cuan demanded again, clear rage in his voice. "What the *hell*, Cedric?"

"I would have missed his heart," Cedric said simply.

"I..." I started.

Another face appeared at the head of the stairs.

"We just got back, and were still outside when Cuan suddenly perks up and sprints into the house like a maniac—hellooooo, sexy naked white boy!" Bran exclaimed, eyeing me appreciatively after following my voice to its source.

"You might not've hit his heart, but you'd probably still have punctured a lung," Cuan barked, ignoring Bran's appearance.

"So what if I puncture a lung?" Cedric shrugged offhandedly. "He has two, you know."

"*Cedric!*" Cuan shouted.

"Wait, punctured a what now?" Bran asked.

Everything was running together; even the words seemed to leave trails behind as they traveled to my ears. I staggered forward.

"Cuan..." I managed.

Cuan whirled around. "I'm here," he said, reaching for me.

His arms passed through me.

And with that, the afterimages all coalesced, and fog took me.

I collapsed against Cuan's chest, managing, just barely, to keep my consciousness. This time Cuan's arms found purchase on my body, and he held me. He continued shouting at Cedric, and all three of them began talking over one another, but now I couldn't understand a word. My senses started to overwhelm me, and I slumped in Cuan's grip. Immediately, Cuan stopped shouting and looked down at me anxiously, uttering something I didn't understand.

"Cuan... I feel nauseous," I moaned.

All three of the men stopped talking and stared at me, though Cuan's expression of concern was the only one I could make out. Then Cedric and Bran resumed talking at once, still in the language I couldn't understand. Cuan turned and barked something at them, and they both disappeared to the floor above.

Cuan turned to me, saying something intently that I couldn't make out. A wave of vertigo hit me and I crumpled in his arms, and he leaned over me, repeating the same thing urgently over and over.

Cedric reappeared at the top of the stairs, his body a foggy blur. He held a large book in his hands, the cover of which was printed in large gold letters. These were so large and so bright that I could read the part not covered by his arm easily: "*Treatise on Angelic...*" but the rest was obscured.

Cedric said something in that language I couldn't understand, but Cuan immediately turned and roared at him, and he disappeared again.

Cuan then turned his attention back to me, and resumed repeating that same word. I stared at his face, watching his eyes on me, watching his mouth form that word over and over. I didn't recognize it.

Or did I?

Something about it sounded familiar.

I listened harder. Eventually, I caught something.

A vowel.

"O."

".o..."

".o..."

".ol.."

".ol.."

".ole."

".ole."

"Cole."

"Cole."

The fog subsided as I opened my mouth again.

"That's... my name," I said.

"That's right," Cuan replied with a smile. "Welcome back, Cole."

I smiled at him, comfortable in his arms. An instant later, indignation hit, along with a shot of adrenaline. I sprang to my feet.

"Cedric *shot* me," I shouted angrily.

"I know," Cuan said, standing alongside me. "Are you OK? Are you hurt?"

"Fuck this shit," I said, grabbing the khakis and jockstrap from the floor and tugging them on. "He fucking *shot* me, Cuan."

"He had some sick idea that it would help you go incorporeal," Cuan explained lamely.

"Well congratu-fucking-lations, it worked," I spat, ripping the bolt out of the wall and freeing my shirt. I didn't even bother unbuttoning it, instead just lugging it over my head. There was a sizeable hole near the breast pocket.

"It always does," Cuan sighed. "Cedric's training methods are ruthless, but they're effective."

It was exactly the wrong thing to say. Cuan knew it, too, and shook his head rapidly.

"I'm not saying that makes it OK," he continued. "It's fucking twisted, and he could have really hurt you, if not killed you."

"I can't stay in a house where I'm getting shot at," I said, moving to the stairs.

"I understand," Cuan said, following me up the stairs. "What if Cedric agrees not to do that again?"

"Negotiating on my behalf, are you, Cuan?" came a gruff voice.

Cedric sat by the table in the kitchen, waiting impatiently as I ascended the stairs. Bran was leaning against the kitchen counter, face expressionless.

"You shouldn't have shot at him," Cuan growled over my shoulder.

"It worked, did it not?" he said.

"Fuck you, you fucking sanctimonious asshat, and fuck the giant oversized needlegun you use to compensate for your fucking invisible cock," I spat.

Bran whistled appreciatively. "Bianca should be here to hear this," he said. "She could take notes."

"Are you quite finished with your tantrum?" Cedric said calmly.

"No, I'm not, you miserable sack of—"

Cedric slammed his fist down on the table with enough violence that Bran, Cuan, and I all jumped. "That is *ENOUGH*," he said. The impact of his fist caused the large old book on the table to jump, raising a cloud of dust around it. The book had the same gold lettering as the one Cedric had with him when he began descending the stairs, but unlike that one, this one's title was unreadable to me.

Cedric rose, staring at me from behind his sunglasses.

"Let me make a few things perfectly clear. First, my penis is around eleven inches erect, so I have no need to compensate for anything. Second, if you are going to stay here, I am going to continue to train you as I see fit, just like I trained everyone else here, until you have a satisfactory understanding of your own abilities. That is for your own good. End of discussion."

"I guess it is," I responded icily, and stalked by him down the hall and out of the house, Cuan hurrying behind me.

"Cole. COLE!" Cuan called to me on the lawn. I turned and faced him. He looked about to fall apart.

"I can't stay here, Cuan," I said. "I can't stay somewhere I'm not safe."

Cuan nodded. "I know," he said. "The most important thing is that you're safe. Do you have somewhere to go?"

"I'll stay with the Order of Light; I know someone there."

"With the one who was helping you when you woke up?" he asked. "And who gave you the flashsphere?"

I nodded.

"The same guy whose cum you were drinking in your apartment the other day?"

I gaped, taken aback. "How did you know—"

Cuan gave me that adorable half-smile of his and tapped his nose. "Don't forget I've got keen senses," he said. "There were some interesting smells when I arrived at your apartment that night. And now that I know what *you* smell like, I know that one of those scents on your breath was someone else's spunk."

I continued gaping.

"He's a lucky guy," Cuan smiled sadly. "But... just please don't count me out yet. Last night... with you... I felt something."

"That was my prostate," I replied.

Cuan laughed. It felt good to see him laugh. "That's not what I meant. I mean that you... there's something about you." He put his hand on my cheek. "You're the only person I've ever met who's seen me transform and doesn't treat me like some kind of monster, or an animal."

I looked into his eyes. His comment bothered me. Something else stirred in the back of my mind, something Cedric had said: 'Just like I trained everyone else here.' I put a hand on Cuan's shoulder.

"Cuan," I asked, "are you safe here?"

Cuan said nothing.

"Did Cedric hurt you?"

Cuan winced, but he bowed his head and shook it. It felt more like he was trying to shake away the question than he was giving me a reply.

"You don't have to stay here," I said.

He scoffed. "Where would I go?" he asked. "I don't have a sanctuary waiting like you do. Everywhere I go, people are terrified of me; they call me a monster; they try to hunt me. At least here people treat me like I'm worth *something*."

"You're worth a lot more than that," I said. "Come with me."

"I can't," he said. "The Order would kill me immediately."

"How do you know that?" I asked. "Is that what Cedric told you?"

Cuan shook his head. "I've seen some of their stuff," he said, "about how anything that's not human is unwelcome in their halls."

"You're human," I said.

"Not always," he insisted. "Here... here it's not perfect, but it's my family. And they accept *all* of me."

"It's not acceptance if they treat you like a dog," I said.

"Better than a monster," Cuan replied.

I looked at him in silence for a moment, my heart breaking for him. He truly seemed to believe that he could do no better than his current situation. And, while it killed me to realize it, I wasn't in a position to show him otherwise.

"Can I see your phone?" Cuan asked.

I handed it to him, and he tapped at the screen for a moment. Then he handed it back to me.

"That's my number," he said. "Please... *Please* use it."

"I will," I said. "I promise."

Then I leaned in and kissed him deeply, a kiss full of longing and, perhaps, a tiny bit of hope.

"I'll let you know as soon as I'm OK," I said.

He nodded, and I noticed a tear in his eye.

I turned to go, and felt his hand on my arm. I turned back toward him and kissed him again.

"You're worth more than you give yourself credit for," I whispered. "You're worth *more*—to me."

Something in Cuan's expression cracked, pain and longing in his eyes.

"I don't want you to go," he said, voice breaking.

"I can't stay where I'm not safe."

"I know."

"See you later, Cuan," I said.

"Later," he whimpered.

Then I turned and walked away from the house, Cuan standing on the lawn and watching me until I was out of sight.

I sighed, pulling the phone out again. Lester had taken the one that Alexander had given me, but I had seen the contact page that Alexander had filled, and thankfully, because the only two phone numbers I had seen since losing my memory were Cuan's and Alexander's, the number easy enough to recall.

I tapped the numbers into the screen and pressed the green call button. He answered on the second ring.

"Hello?"

"Alexander? It's Cole."

"Cole?" Alexander asked. "Thank God! I called the phone I gave you earlier and some old guy answered and told me to fuck off. Are you OK?"

"It's a long story," I sighed, "but if the offer to stay at the Church still stands, I'll tell you all about it in a few minutes."

XIII

TEMPERS AND TEMPERANCE

To my surprise, it was not Alexander who greeted me when I knocked at the door to the sanctuary, but Thomas.

"Welcome," he said, gesturing me inside. "Alexander is still putting your room together."

"My room?" I asked.

It's a room that we normally reserve for visiting priests," Thomas explained, "but we haven't had visitors in a while. Don't worry, though; Alexander is next door."

"I see," I said.

"Alexander volunteered to share, but Father insisted that guests should have their own space, and put Alexander to work setting it up."

I raised an eyebrow, but Thomas waved me off.

"It's what Father said, anyway." As we walked through the hall, he kept glancing at my shirt. "Are... you OK?" he asked.

"Yeah," I said grumpily. "But... maybe you all were right. About one of the Hunters, at least."

Thomas frowned.

"You don't look particularly pleased about being right," I observed.

"I'm never happy to be right if it means that someone else has come to harm," he sighed. Then he looked at me. "I figured something must have happened. I didn't expect you to come stay with us."

"Well, here I am," I shrugged.

"I'm glad you came," Thomas said after a pause. "Alexander needs someone like you."

"Oh?" I asked.

"He's... kind of lonely, I think," Thomas explained, looking down at his feet. "Some of it is because of the... you know, the sex thing."

"You know?" I asked.

"It's this thing the family doesn't talk about," Thomas added. "But I mean, really, we're all sure the kid's ass sees so much traffic that it should get a cut of the Highway Trust Fund."

OK—Thomas, I liked. I laughed slightly, but Thomas's face quickly fell again.

"And you don't approve?" I asked.

"I didn't say that," Thomas said. "In fact, I kind of envy how openly he lives."

"You call that living openly?" I asked.

"More openly than I do, that's for sure."

I looked at him questioningly. "Thomas, are you saying...?"

"Jacob Lucent has no gay sons," he responded.

"I *know* that's not true," I said.

"And now you know why I envy how openly Alexander lives," he said with a wink. Then he sighed. "But it's not really up to me. The Order of Light doesn't have any particular rules against homosexual behavior, but our Church's stance is pretty clear."

"But isn't your Dad the head of your church?"

Thomas nodded gravely. "So you see why Alexander feels a

little isolated. But that's not the only reason," he added. "He doesn't really have any close friends around."

"You and he aren't close?" I asked.

Thomas shuddered. "I...have this recurring nightmare." His expression shadowed with old, long-standing pain. "I know it's just a dream, but it happens so often that I can't help but think it means something. For as long as I can remember, I've had it." He gazed in front of him, seeing a memory only he could see.

"When we were little," he continued, "Alexander and I used to share a room. His crib was next to mine, and later his bed next to mine. In the nightmare, I would hear this growling, and when I would look over, there'd be a monster."

Thomas's eyes were distant. He was reliving the dream—it must have haunted him even while awake. I said nothing, letting him continue the reverie.

"Sometimes the monster would be attacking Alexander. Sometimes it was there in place of Alexander. Sometimes the monster *was* Alexander. Always shadowed, always hair and teeth and claws, always growling and frothing. And I would scream for help, or hide, and then when I woke up, it was always just Alexander, sleeping peacefully—unless my screaming woke him up, that is. Even now that I have my own room, I still see that crib in the night, with the monster and Alexander."

Thomas shuddered, and I waited for him to continue, unsure of what to say. When he spoke next, his voice was bitter.

"Father tells me I have those nightmares because I'm weak. Because my faith is weak, and he says I know it. If I prayed hard enough, believed well enough, worked diligently enough, the nightmares would go away. But they don't. He says I'm not trying enough."

"That's a load of bullshit," I said.

Thomas's eyes snapped to me, surprise written on his face. I wondered if he'd forgotten I was even there.

"You're not weak," I continued. "You're just different. Different is good." I stopped short of railing against Jacob for being a fucking horrible parent, because I didn't think Thomas was in a place to hear it. But what kind of father does that to their kids?

Thomas smiled slightly. We had reached a door that looked a lot like all the other doors in the complex, and Thomas opened it to reveal a long gray stone hall. The left was lined with wooden doors, the right with windows that looked onto a small garden.

"Well, one thing's for sure," Thomas said as we walked into the hallway, "Alexander has good taste."

I smiled.

At the sound of Thomas's voice, a head peeked out of the farthest door on the left.

"Is that you, Thomas?" he asked.

"Hi, Alexander," I waved.

Alexander beamed at the sight of me.

"There you are!" he said. "I've just finished putting your room together."

"I'll leave you two to it," Thomas said. "If you need anything, just let me know."

"Here," Alexander said, taking my hand and giving it a little squeeze, "Let me show you around."

He pulled me into the small room at the end of the hallway. Like most every part of the church that wasn't the sanctuary, it was spartan: It featured a simple bed with plain white sheets, a small nightstand with a lamp, an overhead light, a small desk with a wooden chair, and a dresser with three drawers and a mirror. The walls were simple grey stonework, and the rear wall between the head of the bed and the desk sported a single simple window.

"It's not much, but I hope it'll do," Alexander said. "As a room for visitors, it is a tiny bit smaller than the others, but since it's at the end of the hall, it's generally quiet. My room is next door. I shared it with Thomas for the longest time, but after Rhode left to join another order a few years ago, Thomas moved into his old room, which is on the other side of mine. Rhode once shared with Paul, but after Reuben left Paul moved into Reuben's old room, which Reuben had had to himself since Clement..." he swallowed. "Then Levi has always had his own room, and Father's room is next to Levi's at the top of the hall."

It was a lot of information to take in. Alexander was clearly excited to have me staying with him; he pattering on like a schoolboy. I felt like I was in one of those logic puzzles where I was going to have to later identify who was staying in what room, but Alexander's excitement was such that he summarized exactly that.

"So basically you're here at the end of the hall, then me, then Thomas, then a bathroom, then Paul, then Levi, then another bathroom, and then Father. That second bathroom was originally supposed to be just for Father, but now Levi uses it too."

"Sounds like cramped quarters," I said.

"This is nothing," Alexander smiled. "Once when I was a little kid and the eight of us were all in the hall, two monks came to stay with us. Father insisted on keeping his bathroom to himself so there were nine of us sharing one other bathroom. THAT was cramped."

I couldn't help but chuckle. Not at the story per se, but at Alexander's exuberance. "So now it'll be four of us to one bathroom?" I asked.

"Yeah, pretty much," Alexander nodded. If you really have to go, there are a few bathrooms in other parts of the church as well, so that's not a really big deal. It's more of a problem in the mornings, since we need to basically figure out so many different shower times.

"I know one way to reduce the number of showers," I said.

"I told you already," Alexander said, with a slightly annoyed, slightly amused look, "there will be none of that in church."

I pouted playfully, but then realized that I also had some pressing questions.

"What happened with Marcus?" I asked.

Alexander swallowed hard, then stepped behind me and shut the door to my room, affording us a modicum of privacy.

"I took him to one of the city's new rehab clinics," he said. "I hated doing it, but he needs it." Alexander frowned and dropped onto the side of the bed. "I've never seen him that bad," he continued, staring at the floor. "Everything was catching up with him. He was getting evicted. He hasn't spoken to his family since they kicked him out. I couldn't let him stay here if he wasn't sober. When I dropped him off, he was making a scene, claiming that I was some random person he'd never met who'd brought him against his will. But the clinic staff seemed to feel that he was a danger to himself or others, because they took him in anyway." He buried his head in his hands. "He must hate me."

I put my hand on Alexander's shoulder. "Or he'll thank you," I said. "You made a tough decision, but you've probably saved his life."

"Maybe," Alexander sighed, looking up at me. "I hope so." He offered me an uncertain smile, then suddenly switched to an expression of interest. "But how did things go at the clinic?"

"They're having specialists weigh in," I said.

"Oh SHIT," Alexander said, drawing back slightly.

"No, not like that," I clarified. "My blood is uninfected. But it's... almost *too* perfect, if that's a thing."

Alexander looked at me quizzically.

"The doctor said it was clearly blood, but he suggested it

might as well have been water," I said. "It seemed like the rest of my fluids are similar."

"Not all your fluids," Alexander said with a wry grin. When I raised an eyebrow, he continued. "I've had a mouthful of you, don't forget." Then he leaned in conspiratorially and added in a low voice, "Now, I've swallowed my fair share of guy juice, and I gotta say, yours is particularly... invigorating."

"Is that a thing?" I asked incredulously.

"All I know is," Alexander said, "most swallowing I do because it's just convenient, but you... I'd drink you up any day of the week."

"Well," I said with a broad grin, bringing my hands to the button of my trousers, "in that case..."

"Stop it," Alexander said flatly. "Not in church."

I frowned at him. "Mix your signals much?"

Alexander sighed heavily. "It really does suck that you're locked out of your apartment," he said wistfully. "Which reminds me... why did you wind up not staying at the Midnight Hunters?"

"I... didn't really feel safe," I said. "Their leader, Cedric, was trying to get me to go incorporeal again. Apparently he felt that the best way to do that was to shoot at me."

"Wait, he fucking WHAT?" Alexander asked, indignant. "Cole, is that what the tear in your shirt is from?"

I nodded.

"Though... not everyone shared his sentiment that it was a good idea," I said.

"I should hope the fuck not," Alexander nodded. "I'm glad you got out of there. We told you: they're dangerous."

"I think that might be a bit of a generalization," I said.

"Cole. Listen to me." He stood, expression dead serious. "They're monsters. My father knows what he's talking about."

"You really believe that, don't you?" I asked.

"I don't have any reason to believe otherwise," he said.

"That's because you don't know them like I do," I said. "I mean, yeah, the leader seemed nice but now I'm wondering if he's not a sociopath. Plus they have a technician who's like Doc Brown if he had Marty McFly chopped up in his freezer. And then there's the girl who's like Wednesday if they'd loaded her with Adderall and put her on Jersey Shore. Though to be honest, I kinda like her. But—"

"You're not painting a sympathetic picture here, Cole," Alexander said.

"But they're not all like that," I continued. "While the Order of Light is hiding in its sanctuary, they're the ones out there fighting these phantoms and ogres that could be killing people. They're the ones who saved my life."

"After putting you in that situation in the first place," Alexander said.

"And who knows how many other people would have been put in 'that situation' had the ogres run free last night?" I challenged.

Alexander looked at me coolly. "What's his name?" he asked.

"What?" I responded, confused by the sudden change of subject.

"I assume that the guy whom you know for certain couldn't possibly have had an STI but because of whom you nonetheless wanted to get tested today is this 'not like the other Hunters' that you're speaking of?"

I glared at him.

Alexander sighed. "Ok, look," he said more calmly as he stood up from the bed, "You have every right to sleep with whomever you want to. I'm just worried about you and your safety. Don't let a nice piece of ass impair your better judgement."

I directed my gaze, pointedly, at Alexander's backside.

"No, see, that's *good* judgement," Alexander said with a

smile and a wink. Then his expression changed, and he stepped toward me.

"Really though, Cole, I'm glad you're here," he said. "I—"

"Curfew time," came Jacob's brusque, impatient voice as he suddenly and swiftly threw open the door to my room. Alexander leapt back from me and stood guiltily by the desk, trying and failing to act as though he'd stood there the entire time.

"Bathroom and Bed," Jacob instructed, looking at Alexander suspiciously.

"Yes, Father," Alexander said simply.

"Isn't it, like, eight o'clock?" I asked.

"Special rules when a guest is present," Jacob replied blithely. "It's for your own safety. We don't want you wandering around, getting into things," he explained, staring at Alexander pointedly as he spoke.

I was overcome with the desire to reply, 'If you're referring to your son's mouth, I've already gone there, cum there, and he's digesting my babies,' but Alexander gave me a look so plaintive that I restrained myself. Instead I responded, "Do I get some bread and water, at least?"

"You will be a courteous guest while in this house," Jacob growled.

"Yes Monsieur Thenardier," I responded, bowing my head. "I will do my best to obey the master of the house."

Father Jacob stared at me quizzically, then turned and stormed away.

As soon as he was gone, Alexander glared at me. "You just can't help yourself, can you?" he said.

"You should have heard what I *wanted* to say," I responded.

Alexander gave me a flat look, then headed to the door. "I've filled your dresser with some of my spare clothes," he said, "and there's a toothbrush in a new package and some tooth-paste in the bathroom. I'll have Rebecca bring you up something to eat, since I take it you didn't have dinner. Sorry that it'll probably be soup, though."

"Speaking of Rebecca," I asked, "don't she and Julia have rooms, too?"

"Their room is by the kitchen," Alexander replied, as if it were the most natural thing in the world. Just as he was walking out the door, he stopped and turned back in.

"Also, one more thing," he added. "I checked in with the university and there is indeed a Professor Norton on staff in Comparative Religions. I sent him an e-mail explaining that a Cole Hamilton mentioned him and I wondered if the name rang a bell. We'll see if he responds." I felt a thrill at the possibility that someone might actually know me from before I lost my memory, at least better than that I give good head. Though, to be fair, that information *had* come in handy.

"Oh, and one last thing." Alexander glanced down the hall, then ducked forward and gave me a quick peck on the lips. "Welcome," he said with a smile.

Then he was gone, hurrying away to the kitchen.

I sat, alone with my thoughts. The day had been a whirlwind. It was nothing compared to the ogre-filled chaos of the previous night, and yet, for some reason, this day had left me feeling more exhausted.

I pulled out the smartphone Lester had given me and brought up Cuan's contact. I typed out a quick text message: "I have a room at the Church of the Holy Guardian."

The response was immediate. "ok. stay safe. if u need anything call".

A moment later another text came through: "i miss u".

I smiled.

"I miss you too."

There came a quiet knock on my door, and after I said "come in" Rebecca entered with a bowl of soup and some bread.

"Sorry that this is still all we have to offer," she said, "but I hope you'll like it."

"If it's like this morning's, it'll be amazing," I said.

She smiled, then looked at me for another moment and sighed. "You look like you've had a long day," she said. "You can bring the tray downstairs in the morning. Just drop it in the kitchen before the service."

"Service?" I asked.

"The church service," Rebecca explained. "Surely you didn't expect to stay here without attending services? There's no way Father Jacob would permit that."

"I see," I said. "And... what time do I need to be there?"

"Don't worry about that," Rebecca said as she left. "Someone will be sure to wake you."

The soup was, as usual, delicious. I finished the modest meal and then washed up. Surprisingly, I didn't encounter anyone in the bathroom. I returned to the bedroom and undressed before slipping into the simple white sheets. It had been a chaotic two days, and I had a lot to process. Between my suddenly becoming able to go incorporeal and my mysteriously analysis-resistant blood, my already tenuous grasp on my sense of self was beginning to weaken. Marcus was in rehab, Alexander was living in a closet with a glass door, and Cuan was trapped with people who treated him like an animal. And meanwhile, in the bigger picture, the city seemed on the verge of...something.

Whatever was happening, though, I wasn't going to find the answers in bed that night. What I would find, I hoped, was sleep.

Morning arrived without warning. My wake-up notice came in the form of Jacob throwing the door open (scaring me half to death from a deep sleep) and announcing to the room, "Church in 20."

"Whatever happened to knocking?" I asked.

"I don't knock in my own house," Jacob scowled, fixing his eyes on me.

"I thought the church was God's house," I said.

"And He has entrusted its care to me," Jacob replied. "If you wish to be the beneficiary of such care, you will behave accordingly in this house."

I was sorely tempted to reply with 'well your so-called care is absolute oppressive shit, fuck you very much', but unfortunately I needed the place to stay, so I held my tongue.

I washed up and pulled open the drawers to find some clothes. The only underwear was plain white cotton boxers with button flies, so I pulled on a pair. At least they were of the tighter variety, and they hugged my ass while still allowing a little space in the front. The next drawer had a set of brown long-sleeved T-shirts and white socks, and the bottom had a pair of plain khakis. I guessed the whole set (except for maybe the khakis) had been an acquisition by someone who had gone shopping in bulk on Alexander's behalf and had selected things not to his taste. They were, however, serviceable, so I pulled them on along with the shoes I'd borrowed from Cuan. There wasn't time to shower before the service, so I was thankful for having had a shower the previous morning as I completed what part of my routine I could and then headed through the maze of halls.

I managed to find the kitchen without too much trouble, and took two minutes to take some soap and wash and dry the bowl and utensils, which I left on the counter alongside a drying rack full of other bowls.

From the kitchen, it was an easy walk to the sanctuary.

People were still filtering in when I walked past the altar. Jacob and Levi had yet to process in, and so people were talking to one another and generally milling about. I saw Alexander standing by our usual pew, clad in a royal blue long-sleeved polo shirt and brown slacks. He was facing away from me, looking anxiously toward the double doors at the end of the sanctuary. I tapped him on the shoulder.

"There you are," he said, turning. "I was looking for you." His blue-green eyes glittered in the morning light.

"Am I late?" I asked.

"No, but just barely." he said. "Father would *not* have been happy if you'd missed service."

"'Father' seems to be very particular about the way things are done," I said. "You know, he walked right into my room this morning without so much as a knock."

"Ah, yeah, he does that," Alexander sighed. "His stance is that there's nothing any of us should do behind closed doors that we wouldn't be happy for everyone else to know about."

"So much for Matthew 6," I muttered, remembering something from my reading the other day.

Alexander looked at me questioningly for a moment, and then recall seemed to dawn. "Oh, you mean Jesus's instruction to pray behind closed doors?" he said. "Yeah, that's not really father's thing. But I think his no-knocking policy has more to do with... something else."

"Catching you in bed with Marcus?"

"Stop that!" Alexander hissed again.

Presently the door at the top of the transept opened and Levi entered, Father Jacob processing behind him.

The morning's service was oddly tense, and Jacob's sermon was particularly preoccupied with themes of authority and obedience.

"He's really trying to drive his point home to me, huh?" I whispered to Alexander.

"I don't think this is directed at you," he replied, then gestured behind us with his head. I turned and saw Julia sitting with her arms crossed, staring coldly at Jacob.

"What's going on?" I whispered.

"Whatever went down after we left brunch yesterday," Alexander said. "It apparently wasn't pretty."

I sat quietly through the end of the service. Rather than waiting to greet people after the service ended, Jacob and Levi simply left through the transept door, eliciting a murmur of dissatisfaction from some of the elderly parishioners. After a moment of confusion, people began to get up and leave.

Eventually, Julia slipped into the pew behind us and leaned over to Alexander.

"No brunch today, honey," she said.

"Is everything OK?" I asked.

Julia turned, her eyes focusing on me. "That man has some very questionable ideas about authority," she said. "Apparently he feels that if he withholds our daily late morning meal until I see things his way, I'll feel guilty on everyone's behalf and capitulate." She put a hand on her hip and cocked her head, a twinkle in her eye. "You'd think he'd know me better than that."

Alexander turned to me with a small smile. "Well, it looks like we have some extra time today."

"I guess so," I said.

"If you don't mind, I'd like to show you someplace," he said. "Maybe get out of downtown for a bit."

"That sounds nice," I admitted.

"Anything you want to do here before we head out?"

"I could probably do with a shower," I admitted. "I didn't really have time for one this morning. And what about food?"

"I'll take care of that," Alexander said with a smile. "How about you go have yourself a shower, and I'll meet you at your room in a few?"

That sounded good to me, so off I went. The small bathroom's shower was uninviting; it consisted of a simple stand-up chamber with a dingy curtain. All that was inside was a grungy bar of soap, which I rinsed very thoroughly before building up some lather in my hands and using that, not the soap bar, on my body. I spent as little time in the shower as possible and then retreated to my room. I was getting dressed when my phone dinged with a text from Cuan.

"how r u 2day", it read.

Apparently there was some letter shortage I didn't know about. I typed a simple reply:

"I'm OK. I think I'm going to get out of the city for the day."

"sounds good"

"You?"

"some guy named az came while u were here yesterday? apparently hes coming on a mission w us 2 test him out"

Right. Az. I thought of the ridiculously attractive man in the dark suit.

"I saw him," I texted. "He has a sword. I don't know anything else." Then I added, "Be careful."

"i will b. u 2"

There was a knock on the door, immediately telling me that the person on the other side wasn't Jacob.

"Yes?" I asked.

"You about ready?" came Alexander's voice.

"Yup," I replied, opening the door.

Alexander stood in the hall, carrying a backpack on one shoulder with what looked like a wrapped umbrella stuffed in the side. He had changed clothes since the service, and now wore a tight gold-collared blue ringer tee that hugged his torso tightly, outlining his muscles. Over that he had an open chestnut-colored jacket that complemented his straw-colored hair. He was wearing a pair of well-worn jeans, loose enough for movement but snug enough that they still brought out the lines of his body. I openly gave him an up-and-down look of approval, and he smiled.

"Shall we?" he asked.

"Absolutely," I replied, and we were off.

We walked two blocks from the church, and I was surprised slightly when Alexander stopped in front of a bus stop.

"OK, the bus should be here in a few minutes," Alexander said, checking his phone.

"Honestly, I kind of expected that we'd drive somewhere," I said. "You don't have a car?"

"I'm the youngest in a big family that lives in the center of the city," Alexander explained. "I'm kind of at the bottom of the vehicle priority list. Don't worry, though, it's not a long bus ride."

Alexander unzipped the front of his bag and pulled out nine quarters, a dime, and a nickel and handed them to me.

"Bus fare," he explained.

I nodded, and soon the bus pulled up.

"Where are we going, anyway?" I asked Alexander as we climbed aboard.

"We're going five stops," he explained as we slid into a little row of two seats and sat down.

I watched with interest as the bus traveled through the city. The first three stops were at various places downtown that were fairly close together, including one labeled 'University'. There was quite a gap between the third and fourth stop, however, and I watched out the window as the bus left the city proper and passed down a long road lined with suburban houses and a field or two. Finally the fourth stop came and went, and after that Alexander tapped a little button on the back of the seat in front of us. There was a loud electronic 'ding!' and little red indicators lit up throughout the bus before it pulled to a halt in front of a little bus stop on a suburban corner.

As we disembarked, I took a deep breath of the crisp autumn air. I smelled turning leaves—albeit cut somewhat by bus exhaust—and smiled at the sun on my face. Even this little distance outside the city, everything felt different. I still didn't know where Alexander was taking me, but I was certainly eager to find out.

XIV

THE ESTATE

"Enjoying the fresh air?" Alexander asked with a grin.

"Absolutely," I said. "So... now will you tell me where we're going?"

"It's right down this street," Alexander said, pointing down the side street next to the bus stop.

The cool breeze rustled the air as we walked. The street was lined with green pines and tall oaks, although the maples were already turning a glorious red and orange.

"It was a wet summer," Alexander mused. "The trees are turning late this year. But oh, are they beautiful."

I agreed. Here, away from the main road, the air was filled with nothing but the smells of autumn.

We walked alongside one another, and eventually the little street ended at a tall wall. The white plaster was a little in disrepair, and it had fallen off in places revealing the gray stonework underneath. Chains ran the extent of the wall, and at various points hung big metal signs reading 'no trespassing'. They were just chains and a wall, but they somehow meant business.

We walked alongside the wall before coming to a corner of the property. Here stood a large iron gate, the center of which was held fast by a large, ornate lock, into which the chains connected. The gate itself was very rusted, but the chains retained their shine.

"I wanted to show you my special place," Alexander said with satisfaction.

"You already showed me that the other day in my apartment," I said.

"Har har," Alexander replied with a dry smile.

"So, what, you sneak in here from time to time?" I asked.

"You'd never be able to sneak in here," Alexander stated. "These are spirit chains. They were originally forged for shackling souls, or for capturing things like that phantom you encountered. When used to secure a location, they work as a kind of spiritual boundary. They'll keep just about anything out."

I looked back along the wall. That explained the relative lack of weeds and vines on the old structure. Here and there a particularly stubborn plant had pushed through, but for the most part even the moss stopped about a foot from the line of the chains.

"So can you... force your way through?" I asked.

"No need," Alexander smiled. He reached into his backpack and drew out a very large iron key. "The couple that lived here were members of the Order of Light. Apparently, they represented two families that had been a part of the Order for generations. They specialized in protection and warding enchantments. That's where these chains came from. I could have sworn there were more of them, though," Alexander mused as he put the key in the lock and turned. There was a large click, and at the same time a sigil of light flashed faintly on the gate and I could feel a sort of energy surge. The chains wound back, seemingly of their own accord, and the gate creaked open. We stepped through and the gate closed quietly behind us. Beyond the gate a second pillar stood to the side, and Alexander inserted the key and turned it to the left. The chains didn't move, but a different sigil briefly glowed to life on the inside of the gate.

"They also set up this, making more of a one-way barrier," Alexander explained. "I don't want you to feel like you couldn't leave if you wished. No one should ever feel trapped."

"Thanks," I said appreciatively.

The inside of the compound was lush and overgrown. There was a gravel driveway that led along the edge of the property, with only grass and a row or two of trees between it and the left wall. To our right, however, was thick bushes and foliage.

"This couple was apparently pretty amazing at protective magicks," Alexander said again. "They kept their whole property extremely safe. But I guess they were also kind of paranoid, because their wards keep out the mundane as well as the magical."

"They must have been pretty amazing, though," I mused.

"They must have been," Alexander agreed. "Unfortunately, I never knew them. But it seems that when they died, Father asserted the Church's right to their estate, which is typical for Order members who've passed, and would generally have been stipulated in their wills. But then some lawyer showed up and claimed that they had a next of kin, which halted the whole process. Nobody's been able to find this mysterious next of kin, but the lawyer has nonetheless managed to keep the whole estate wrapped up in legal limbo for more than twenty years."

"So how is it that you have a key to the place, then?" I asked.

"When the couple died, they were defending the Church of the Holy Guardian from an attack. When an Order member dies, the rest of the Order normally assumes responsibility for any of their magical possessions in order to safeguard them and keep them from getting out in the world among people who might not understand them, or to keep them from falling into the wrong hands, that sort of thing."

"And conveniently for your father, that key falls under that heading."

Alexander gave me a flat look, but then sighed. "You're not wrong," he said as the path turned slightly to the right. "When the lawyers appeared and demanded that he turn over any property they'd had when they passed, Father didn't tell them about the keys on the grounds that the Order has to keep magical items a secret."

"'Keys', plural?" I asked.

"That's right," Alexander nodded. "There are three in total. Two work the gate, but they also had another one to their house." He pointed ahead of him. A large, white home was visible at the end of the long gravel driveway. It looked a little weathered, but it had held up very well for a structure that was apparently abandoned for the past twenty years.

"Whoa," I said appreciatively. "Is that where we're headed?"

"Nope," Alexander said, turning off the driveway to step between an opening in the bushes that lined the right side of the road. This was clearly not an intentional path, or at least not one that was meant to be readily apparent. It was heavily overgrown and I had to duck through the underbrush to follow Alexander, who slipped between the branches with the expertise of one who had trod the path plenty of times.

"The wards on the compound are nothing compared to the ones on the house," Alexander explained as we walked. "There's simply no way to get in while they're up, at least not one that I know of. Father says he'd be surprised if even the Holy Spirit could get into that house. Without the key, at least," Alexander added. "Father kept that key for himself, along with one of the keys to the compound, and I'd be surprised if he ever let them out of his sight."

"Why is he so interested in the house?" I asked. "Apart from greed, I mean?"

"Greed has nothing to do with it," Alexander affirmed, though I wasn't sure I believed him. "You remember how father said that the Order's holy magic has been less effective lately? How our wards have been weakening?"

"Yeah," I nodded, continuing to follow him through the brush.

"Well, the wards on the compound and the house haven't wavered in the slightest in twenty years," Alexander said. "Father goes to that house once in a while to search it, though he never lets anyone come with him, probably to keep a low profile. He's convinced that inside he might find some book or object explaining how the wards are cast and maintained so that he can use it to establish similar protections at the Church. Failing that, he also hopes he can find the couple's will, which he thinks will stipulate that they intended for the Order to assume ownership of the estate, and finally put to rest all of this 'next of kin' nonsense."

"Why would the lawyer be fighting so hard about that if there is no next of kin to be found?" I asked.

"Who knows?" Alexander replied. "Bureaucracy? Greed? Misinformation? I can't begin to guess at the reason."

"So, can I assume that what you have is the second key to the compound?"

"That's right," Alexander said. "Like most Order equipment, it was left in Julia's care. One day a few years ago I was having a hard time, and Julia came and handed the key to me. 'You look like you need some space to yourself,' she said. She never asked for it back, so I've held onto it. Since then, on days when I have the chance and I know my father is definitely going to be occupied elsewhere, I come down here."

"It is nice and quiet," I said.

"You haven't seen anything yet," Alexander said with a grin, directing me through an opening in the underbrush toward a golden spot of light.

We emerged into a wide clearing flooded with plenty of sunlight. It was filled with soft grass and clover and was surrounded on three sides by trees, but the fourth was a tall rock formation. This too was topped with brush, but from near the top of the formation a steady stream of water poured forth from within the rock, cascading down the natural outcropping before forming a wide little waterfall over a moss-ringed pool below. I didn't see any river leading out of the pool, and so I figured the outlet had to be under the ground.

My intake of breath was audible. "This is stunning," I said. "Is that a natural spring?"

Alexander nodded, setting his knapsack down in the shade before walking into the sun. "Warm water, too. I thought you'd like it." He grinned, his smile as sunny as the clearing. "This is my space, where I come to enjoy being alone with nature and my thoughts. Usually I work out here by myself, but today I thought you might want to come along."

"Wait, this is your workout spot?" I asked. "But, don't you usually do that naked?"

Alexander nodded. "Yeah, but since you're here with me, I guess I'll—"

"Oh, don't hold off on my account," I interrupted.

Alexander responded with a wide, mischievous grin. "I was hoping you'd say that," he said, letting his jacket slip off of his shoulders and onto the ground. Then he reached to his waist and with one movement lifted his shirt up over his head and tossed it aside, the muscles of his chest and abs stretching as he did so.

The sight of him shirtless in the sun was in and of itself enough to start a little extra blood moving to my crotch. Alexander looked at me with a boyish smile, eyes glinting.

"But you know, fair is fair," he said. "I shouldn't be the only one in the buff out here."

"Fair enough," I nodded, and began removing my shirt.

Alexander watched me as he lifted up his left foot, then his right, pulling off his shoes and stuffing his socks inside them. We both undid the buttons at our waists, and as my khakis dropped, Alexander pulled his jeans down over his tanned legs. The sun felt very warm on my pale skin as I stood in just the white cotton boxers Alexander had provided me. He, meanwhile, was in royal blue briefs with a gold pouch in the front. The pouch looked fairly well packed, but I didn't have long to admire how fully it was stuffed before he drew them down over his thighs, releasing his endowment from its containment.

I looked at him in admiration as I removed my cotton boxers. Alexander's body was built for the sun. The soft lines of the muscles on his torso, arms, and legs were accentuated by the sun's rays, and his soft, thick cock nuzzled between his hanging balls as they bathed in the sunlight. The fine, almost-invisible hairs that dusted his torso and limbs glinted as he moved, so that his whole body looked to be molded from burnished gold.

As I stepped out of the boxers, Alexander looked me up and down approvingly.

"Now, that's what I like to see," he said, walking through the grass toward me.

His kiss was deep and sincere, and I kissed him back enthusiastically. It was a far cry from the furtive peck he had offered the previous night at the Church of the Holy Guardian. Here, Alexander was almost a different person—forward, confident, playful, comfortable with his body and his own sexuality. When he finished the kiss and stepped back, his whole posture was relaxed, his weight shifted slightly to one foot.

"What do you think?" he asked.

"Like Michelangelo's David," I remarked, "only with a nicer

cock and carved from bronze instead of marble." I blinked at the association as it rose in the back of my mind, wondering who Michelangelo was and why he owned a David, but Alexander's laughter brought me out of the reverie.

"I mean about this place, but I'll gladly take the compliment," he said. "though I must say I enjoy the scenery here much more now that you're around—and have your kit off," he added.

"This place is incredible," I admitted. "Although, I'm worried I'll burn."

"Yeah, you do look a little pale for a lot of sun," Alexander mused. "How about some sunscreen?"

"You brought sunscreen?" I asked as Alexander walked to his knapsack and pulled a tube out.

"SPF 60," Alexander said. "For sensitive skin, since I didn't know how your skin would react." He squeezed a dollop out onto his hand. "May I?" he asked.

I nodded, and Alexander approached and began to gently apply the sunblock to my face, then began to slowly, sensuously knead it into my shoulders. The touch of the sunblock was cool, and it tingled a little in the sun, but Alexander's warm hands expertly massaged it into my muscles, removing every streak of white from my skin. I returned the favor, letting my hands slide over the contours of Alexander's chest, the ripples of his abs, and down his legs. I squeezed it into the round cheeks of his ass and drew it over his thighs and calves. By the time we had covered most of our bodies, we were both rock hard.

"That makes the last bit a little easier," Alexander said, squeezing one more dollop of sunscreen into each of our hands. "Just be careful of the tip," he added, reaching down and carefully coating my balls and shaft. I moaned appreciatively and reciprocated, stroking and massaging him as we enjoyed our mutual, dermatologist-approved masturbation. Once every trace of white cream was gone and before we began producing any of our own, Alexander released my shaft and stepped back.

"There," he said. "How are you now?"

"Horny," I replied.

Alexander grinned. "Well, let's harness that energy for a little exercise, why don't we?"

I nodded enthusiastically until I realized that Alexander probably meant 'exercise' of the type more traditionally used for physical fitness.

"Mind if I do some pushups?" he asked. "Though," he added, looking down at his full erection, "it might be a little harder with this in the way. Perhaps some stretching first."

I tried to follow Alexander's lead as well as possible as he stretched, but it was something of a struggle. Not only was he surprisingly limber for his muscular frame, but he also was so gorgeous that he was distracting. His body had glinted in the sun before, but now that he was oiled up with lotion, he positively shone. Apart from that, watching him do lunges and other stretches while he had a raging erection was almost too much to bear, though it did eventually begin to subside, returning to hang pendulously beneath his gold pubes.

I must have been in fairly good shape because I managed around thirty pushups before having to stop, but Alexander kept going. Not that I complained; I sat, panting and sweating, watching as he continued to lift his glistening body, muscles in his arms flexing and swelling as he moved. The lines of his body were those of a practiced fitness enthusiast, though the perfect straightness of his body was interrupted by his round ass, which, even clenched as it was, stood out invitingly as though he were housing a basketball.

After I don't know how many pushups, he moved to sit-ups.

"Why don't we help one another with these?" Alexander asked. "I'll brace your feet."

He did so as I did thirty sit-ups, then we switched and held his for fifty, then he held mine for another thirty. After I did four sets of thirty I was spent, but Alexander kept going, doing about a hundred in a row. It was almost hypnotic to watch him bob up and down in front of me: his face, screwed in concentration, his arms behind his head, the sweat trickling down his full pecs, the low, rhythmic grunting as his body rose and fell. I never knew exercise could be so... erotic.

When he stopped, panting heavily, the air was thick with the smell of sunscreen and sweat. He grinned at me, then looked down and chuckled.

"Looks like someone's reared his head again," he said.

I followed his gaze, but I didn't need my eyes to tell me what my body already knew: I once again had a raging erection, my exposed cock head straining pink and urgent toward the object of my arousal.

"How are you feeling," he asked, "other than horny, I mean?"

"A little spent," I admitted, "but my sweat is starting to make the sunscreen sting."

"Yeah," Alexander nodded. "Perhaps we should wash off," he said, nodding to the waterfall.

"That sounds great," I said, "but is it really OK to wash this off there?"

"Oh, don't worry," he said, standing up, "I only buy ecologically safe sunscreens."

He stood up and went to his bag, pulling out a leather pouch, then walked to the water. I watched him for a moment, enjoying the sight of his ass cheeks rising and falling as he moved, then stood and followed him. He set the leather pouch on a rock at the edge of the pond, then got into the water.

He turned under the fall, stretching up and running his hands through his hair as he leaned his face up into the water. He must have been as excited as I was at the prospect of being naked in the spring together, because he now sported an erection to rival my own, and the water cascaded over his cock and down his shaft, dripping off of his balls and down his legs.

My first sensation upon stepping into the water was one of pleasant warmth: Alexander was not kidding when he had said that the spring featured naturally heated water. It was not the intense heat of a hot spring, but rather warm enough to be inviting without causing me to sweat more, and cool enough to be refreshing without causing my balls to tighten up.

My second sensation was equally warm and welcome—that of Alexander's lips on my own. Our bodies slid against one another as the water washed away the sweat and lotion, and his mouth moved to my neck as our cocks pressed against each other in the cascade. Pleasure washed through me as the water washed over me, and we ground our bodies together; I squeezed his ample ass as he massaged my own while we continued frotting in the sun. He pulled his head back and met my eyes, water pouring down his face and dripping from his nose and chin as our cocks continued to slide over each other.

"There's something I've always wanted to try here," he said, panting heavily.

"I'm all ears," I replied.

"Oh, you're much more than that," he grinned. "Mind looking in that pouch?" He gestured with his eyes to the leather pouch by the rock.

I was loathe to release his body and leave the cascade of water and sex, but I did as he asked and walked over to the pouch and opened it.

It contained only two things: a condom in an easy-open packet, and a bottle of eco-friendly, condom-safe lube.

I picked them up and turned around. Alexander was now standing with his back to me, legs spread, hands against the slick rock face. The cascading water was splashing onto his shoulders and running down his back, the stream parting neatly at his ass, running down either side and also in between his robust, spread cheeks. He was looking at me over his shoulder through the curtain of falling water.

"I really, *really* want to feel you inside me," Alexander said. "And I really, REALLY want to be fucked under this waterfall."

I couldn't say no to that. The sun gleamed off of the cascading water pouring down his body, making it shine like a golden trophy. His whole being was waiting for me, pleading for insertion.

I walked over to him. He continued to crane his neck to watch me as best as he could over his broad shoulders, but between his own body and the curtain of water, he couldn't have seen much. I set the condom and the lube down on a nearby dry outcropping and placed a hand on each cheek of his ass. He moaned approvingly at my touch as I squeezed. But then, rather than reaching back for the lube to slather over him, I knelt behind him and leaned forward.

His waiting hole, bathed in the falling water, was the same golden tan as the rest of his body. I opened my mouth and lapped at it.

Alexander cried out and his body shuddered, and so I continued my ministrations, the taste of fresh skin and mineral water filling my mouth as I buried my face between his cheeks.

Alexander positively writhed.

"Fuck... fuck, Cole, fuck!" he cried as I worked on him. Once I was sure I could let go without losing my ability to rim him, I released his cheek from my left hand and reached around to find his erection. His shaft was firm and hot, with a slickness that I recognized was not caused by water or lotion, but rather copious amounts of precum. The feeling of his body at my hands and tongue turned me on further, as did Alexander's increasingly frantic cries of appreciation and encouragement. I reached up with my hand and ran my fingers over the ridges of his swollen glans and his whole body jumped.

"Cole, please..." Alexander begged. "Please fuck me."

Obligingly, I released his hole from my mouth and stood. I pulled the rubber over my attentively waiting cock and then slathered it and Alexander's ass with the lube. I placed a hand on either side of his waist and tilted my own hips forward.

At the feeling of my cock teasing his entrance, Alexander shuddered with anticipation.

"Are you ready?" I asked.

"Yes, please," Alexander nodded, frantic with anticipation.

I pushed forward, guiding myself inside Alexander. I slid in smoothly if not quickly, though Alexander's insides were pleasantly tight.

"FuuuuuuuuuuuuUUUCK!" Alexander let out a long, protracted moan of pleasure as I pushed my way inside, his flesh yielding before me only to envelop me once I was in. I half-groaned, half-sighed with appreciation as his body squeezed the entire length of my shaft, and finally my hips met his full ass cheeks, the water cascading down his body now moving to my own and running over my balls.

"I'm going to move," I said.

Alexander grunted, nodding furiously enough that I could see it through the curtain of water. And so I did, moving my hips slowly at first, then faster, feeling Alexander's body react and caress me, the rhythmic pulses of pleasure his sphincter delivered to my length matching my own movement. Each time I completed a thrust Alexander cried out, and I knew I was hitting his prostate, and his body was reacting the only way it knew how.

I increased my pace, enthralled by the feel of him, the heat of him. The sight of the water cascading down his muscular back, his full cheeks behind my gripping hands, the sound of his voice, the sun on my back and my legs and my ass, all conspired to drive me further and further into the passion of the sex.

I began to thrust harder and harder, faster and faster,

pounding like a piston into his eager body, feeding his hungry ass my cock again and again.

Alexander's cries were growing louder and more pitched, and I felt him tighten inside. I knew what was coming, and my body responded in kind.

"Fuck, Cole," he wailed, "I'm gonna—"

"Do it," I cried back, and Alexander yelled as his entire body shuddered. Even through the curtain of water I could see the spray of cum splattering on the rock face outside the outline of Alexander's body, and the sight combined with the increased pressure inside and outside my cock pushed me over the edge.

I grunted and gasped as the orgasm exploded, cum bursting forth into the rubber. My body nearly buckled as the sensation rippled through me, but I kept my footing, squeezing Alexander's waist as I pumped into him again and again. The condom was unable to contain my essence, and soon semen began spurting out from the base, running down my leg and into the pool where it mixed with Alexander's own ample offering.

Again I fired, again and again, as the shudders continued to rock me and Alexander's own orgasm continued causing his body to work on mine just as I was working on his. Finally, however, the intensity died down, and my pumping slowed before I finally slid out of him, the overextended condom falling limply into the spring. I fished it out, and when I straightened up Alexander was facing me, panting, with a huge grin on his face.

"Was it everything you'd hoped?" I asked.

"And more," Alexander replied. He gently placed a hand aside my head and pulled me into a kiss.

We washed off for the second time under the water, then walked back to where Alexander had set his bag in the shade of a tree. Alexander opened it and pulled out a little plastic baggie, which he held out to me to insert the spent rubber into.

"We thank you for your sacrifice, little rubber," he pronounced playfully as he zipped the bag shut. "You served honorably, even though I'm not sure it was entirely necessary given what the doctors said about Cole's blood."

"I'd prefer to hear what the specialists have to say about that," I said. "Until then, I don't know *what* is going on."

Alexander gave me a shrug that said 'fair enough', then returned his attention to his bag. This time, he pulled out a soft, plaid blanket and an insulated lunch bag.

"What... what is this?" I asked.

"Since we didn't have our usual brunch today," Alexander explained, spreading the blanket in the shadiest part of the clearing, "I thought perhaps we could have ourselves a picnic."

"That is... ridiculously sweet of you," I said.

"I have... ham and swiss, or peanut butter and jelly," Alexander said, looking into the bag.

"Oooo, peanut butter!" I exclaimed, and Alexander grinned and handed me the sandwich.

We ate and laughed, and shared a thermos of pineapple juice. I asked Alexander more about his college life and we chatted a bit more about religion. He seemed intrigued, if unsure, when I told him about the Tao Te Ching, but he perked up with interest at my interpretation of Luke's and Matthew's recounting of the Centurion and the Slave.

After we finished eating—including a delicious brownie Alexander had provided for dessert—we lay on the blanket together, me perpendicular to Alexander, my head resting on his chest as he ran his hand through my hair.

"You're so different here," I mused as I looked up at the orange maple leaves overhead and the green oak canopy beyond.

"What do you mean?" Alexander asked.

"I mean, you're so high strung most of the time," I said. "Even out and about in the city, but most of all at the church.

There, you're so tightly wound you make Donald Duck look like a Xanax commercial."

Alexander sighed. "This is... the only place I can really be myself," he said.

I turned my head to look at him. "Is that really true?" I asked. It was only partially a challenge.

"I dunno," he replied, still looking skyward. "That's how it feels, though. With my family, it's hard. I mean, I try to be a good Christian."

"What does that entail?" I asked.

"Well, not doing what we just did, for one."

"I only have about a week's worth of memories," I said, "and even I know that's not universal doctrine. I think that prohibition is just a way to exert control over people."

"It doesn't matter if it's universal," Alexander said. "It's my family."

"But do *you* believe it?" I asked.

He paused. "I guess if I really believed it, I wouldn't do it." he admitted. "I mean, sometimes it's just physical, but there's something about sex with a guy that can just be..."

"Sacred," I nodded.

"They don't see that," Alexander lamented. "And I'm not about to be the one to try to show it to them. Even if some of them come around, Father won't. Or Levi."

"You're really cowed by them, huh?"

"They're my father and my big brother. You gotta respect Family. It's all over the Bible."

I wasn't sure of the universality of that interpretation either, but I didn't think it was the right time to go off on a tangent by challenging him now.

"You're just so closed off at church," I mused. "Not just to your family, but to everyone."

"Marcus said the same thing," Alexander admitted. "So did

every other guy I dated. They always feel like I'm hiding something, like I'm ashamed by them."

"Are you?"

Alexander paused. "Hiding something, or ashamed?" he asked.

"You tell me," I said.

"I don't want trouble with my family," Alexander said at last. "Marcus is a good guy—sometimes—but he's also trouble. I need a guy to respect my boundaries, even if they aren't ones he understands."

"And if your expectations transgress the other guy's boundaries?" I asked.

Alexander shrugged. "I... I didn't think of that," he admitted. "But it's not just that part. I can't really be myself with the other guys, either."

"What do you mean?" I asked.

By way of response, Alexander leaned up on his elbow, turning to his bag. I sat up from his chest and watched as he removed the wrapped long packet from the side of his backpack. He laid it on the blanket and then gently, slowly, unwrapped it.

"This is...?" I gasped, looking at the beautiful blade that lay inside the cloth. It was a short sword, with a modest blade of about a foot and a half in length and an ornate golden hilt. The blade was so polished that it was almost blinding, even in the shade.

"Meet Candela," Alexander said.

"It has a name?" I asked.

"Every member of the Order of Light has a personal weapon with a unique name," Alexander explained.

"Are they all swords?" I asked.

"Far from it," Alexander replied. "We each have one that is suited to our specific abilities."

"Well, I see why you have this one, then," I said.

"Why's that?" he asked.

"It's like your cock," I explained. "It's a little thicker than one would expect for its length."

"Fuck you," Alexander laughed, punching me playfully in the arm.

"Why did you bring it here?" I asked.

"Partly to show it to you," Alexander said. "But mostly because I usually practice with it here."

"It's beautiful," I said appreciatively. "Again, like your cock."

Alexander levelled a dry look at me, but then couldn't help but laugh.

"Anyway, the point is... I can't show this to most guys I date."

"To be fair, I don't think that's the sword they're interested in anyway."

"What I *mean* is," Alexander clarified with mock impatience, "the Order of Light is a pretty big part of my life, and not one I can just ignore. But it's also a secret order. Cole, you're the first person I've been able to share *both* parts of myself with— the gay part *and* the Order of Light part."

I was silent for a moment as that sunk in. That had to be hard. But it also didn't feel right to me. Yeah, it made sense for Alexander to need to keep the Order secret, but living in the closet to do it? Hiding the Order was protecting the institution and the people he dated. Hiding his sexuality was denying *himself*.

"I know it doesn't seem right," Alexander said in response to my silence. "And it's not. But until I figure things out, that's just the way it's going to be," he said.

"Well," I said, scooching toward him on the blanket, "here's to sharing everything."

I kissed him, and he responded in kind.

As I was reaching forward to take his cheek in my hand, however, a tinny chime rang out, repetitive and insistent.

Alexander pulled back apologetically and walked to his discarded jeans, pulling his phone out of the pocket.

"Hello?" He asked, holding the phone up to his ear as I watched him. I couldn't help but admire him, standing with head cocked and one hand on hip, muscular torso and thick thighs glinting in the sun.

He nodded into the phone, then looked at me as he replied to the person on the other line.

"Yeah, that's right," he said, and something told me I was the subject of the conversation. "Sure, OK... how about... 45 minutes? OK, Bye," Alexander beeped the phone off, then lowered it and looked at me in a combination of anticipation and surprise.

"What's up?" I asked.

"Professor Norton responded to my message," Alexander said. "It turns out you're his student. And he happens to be on campus today even though the university is closed. He asked if we could come by."

"Seriously?" I asked, trying to process the possibilities.

Alexander nodded. "Cole," he said. "This could be your chance to remember your past."

XV

ENCOUNTERS

THE 'UNIVERSITY' bus stop was unassuming enough. I had expected to find something along the lines of a large welcome gate or big official signage, but instead we just seemed to be back in the middle of the city. Alexander explained that one of the conditions set by the city on the university was that its buildings blend into the cityscape as much as possible.

"So... how do you even know where to go?" I asked. "Did the professor tell you where to find his office?"

"We're not meeting him at his office," Alexander explained. "Professor Norton is meeting us at the coffee shop on the corner. Most of the university buildings are closed, and technically the staff isn't supposed to be in. And honestly, he's probably also worried that we'll have trouble if security sees us on campus."

"There's a lot of security?" I asked.

"Maybe?" Alexander mused. "I mean, I've only seen a few security guards around in my time there, but I also haven't been on campus since all this happened. Anyway, here we are," he said, pointing to a small shop on the corner.

The interior of the coffee shop was a simple white with pink and red trimmings. It clearly had once been, or now was, a pastry shop. The interior seemed large, though that was perhaps due to how empty it was. Even though I had no memory of him, I had little trouble identifying Professor Norton: he was the only customer in the place.

The professor sat at a round table in the middle of the coffee shop, occasionally lifting the cup of coffee that sat on the saucer in front of him to his lips and taking a sip. Mostly, however, he was absorbed in a book in front of him, but I couldn't discern the title as he had it wrapped in a plain paper book cover.

The professor looked in his mid-fifties, with salt-and-pepper brown hair and a face cragged from years in academia. He sported a serious but serene expression, one that was marred somewhat by sunken, haunted eyes. When we approached his table, the man stood up in his tweed suit and politely turned his attention to Alexander.

"You are the young lad who wrote me, I presume?" he asked, his voice soft and just the slightest bit raspy. "Alexander?"

"You must be Professor Norton," Alexander said, smiling politely. "Thank you for meeting us."

"Us?" Professor Norton gave Alexander a confused look.

"Hello," I said.

The professor turned his head sharply, eyes focusing on my face. His mouth opened slightly as he stared at me uncertainly.

"Sorry if I startled you," I said. Professor Norton said nothing, but continued to stare at me as though he'd seen a ghost.

"I... I don't know how well you know me," I said hesitantly, "but I was hoping that you at least recognize me."

"Cole...?" Professor Norton said, still staring.

"That's right," I said, "or at least, so I've come to believe. I'm sorry if I'm not treating you with more familiarity, but... well, I don't know how much Alexander told you, but I have no memory of anything beyond a few days ago."

Professor Norton blinked at me. Then suddenly the tension seemed to fall out of his body, as though he had been waiting for some explanation of why I had been acting so stiff and unfamiliar.

"I'm so glad you're all right," he said, suddenly taking me by the shoulders and looking me up and down. My body tensed at the unexpected contact. "I haven't been able to reach you since the day of the pipe explosion," Professor Norton continued. "I was afraid you'd died."

"I lost my phone," I said.

"I figured," the professor nodded. "I've been calling since I first heard the explosion, hoping you'd pick up."

"You heard the explosion?" Alexander asked.

"I was on campus that night," Professor Norton explained.

"That must be the errand Marcus mentioned," Alexander realized. "The one you ran out on the party for."

"You never showed up," Professor Norton said sadly. "I assumed the worst." He looked me up and down again. "You look like you managed pretty well, though."

"What was the errand?" Alexander asked.

"Oh, it was just a research thing," Professor Norton said. "I needed him to help me look through some texts I'd found. Another pair of eyes, and all that."

"In the middle of the night?" Alexander asked, raising an eyebrow.

Professor Norton sighed. "It's a habit academics get into when we become really engaged in a project and have students as diligent as Cole," he said. "It's easy to forget that they might have lives outside of the university."

"Is... is that usual?" I asked. "For us, I mean."

"You were—sorry, are—a very eager student," Professor

Norton said. "You've always been very interested in my research."

"What is your research area, anyway?" Alexander asked. "You're in religious studies, right? What is it that you're working so hard on?"

"You know the way to an academic's heart," Professor Norton replied with a smile. He gestured to the round table. "Have a seat and I'll tell you all about it."

We sat at the table, and Professor Norton waved over a twenty-or-so-old staff member with red hair, big ears, and freckles, who approached from behind the counter to take an order from us. I got an iced tea. Alexander ordered a glass of strawberry milk, which I thought was adorable. The professor tapped the side of his partially-empty cup of coffee agitatedly with his finger and scowled, and the freckled boy frowned and removed the cup from the table. I figured it was a kind of short-hand the professor had developed; clearly he was a regular at this establishment.

"My interest is in human understanding of the afterlife," Professor Norton explained, "particularly in the entities we believe populate these existences."

"You mean like ghosts and spirits?" Alexander asked.

"Angels and demons," I realized, remembering the book I had found on my shelf.

"Very good," Professor Norton remarked with approval. "Even sans memory, you're quick to follow my line of thinking."

Alexander looked surprised. "This is something Cole was interested in?"

"But it is fascinating, isn't it?" I said, a surge of enthusiasm rushing through me. "So much academic scholarship considers traditional conceptualization of beings like angels to be metaphor and allegory," I explained, remembering what I had read in my notes back in my apartment. "But what if it's not?"

I figured this line of thought would click with Alexander, and indeed it did, for he leaned forward with interest.

"Exactly," Professor Norton said. "What if these beings are real? Just because humanity hasn't had modern encounters with angels doesn't mean that they don't exist. What if the ancient texts aren't just allegory, but contain the secrets of having these spiritual encounters on earth?"

"But they do," Alexander said. "The Bible is all about connecting with God."

"But not in any observable way," Professor Norton countered.

"I respectfully disagree," Alexander insisted, and the Professor rolled his eyes.

"Ok, but not to any degree that skeptics can't just deny it," he said. "It's like the religious 'queer coding' that is Cole's primary area of study." I felt a twinge of irritation at the professor's use of finger quotes when saying 'queer coding', but said nothing as the professor continued. "David and Jonathan, the Centurion and the Slave, all of these are examples of same-sex romantic or sexual relationships, and yet people who don't wish to acknowledge them or who believe them to run counter to their own spirituality continue to challenge the validity of such interpretations."

"Wait, that's what you're studying?" Alexander asked me.

"Apparently," I said. "Makes sense to me, anyway; my apartment is full of notes like that."

"He's looking across multiple religions, not just Christianity," Professor Norton explained. "It's amazing work for an undergraduate, really. It could easily transition into a Masters' Thesis or a Doctoral Dissertation." I felt my cheeks redden slightly at the praise, particularly because I had no idea what work I had done. "Personally, I have little interest in the topic," the professor continued. "Not because I have anything against it, mind you. It just isn't important to me." Another twinge of irritation. "But his work is sound, and I can relate to the reasoning, since it bears similarity to my own. Also, he also has been very engaged in furthering my own research, which makes him an excellent research assistant."

"I... see," Alexander said.

"Anyway, the point is, what if someone were able to prove the existence of these spiritual beings beyond a shadow of a doubt? So that even the atheists would have to acknowledge them? Imagine: proving the existence of angels and demons would not only definitively demonstrate the validity of millennia of theology, but would also firmly establish that an Abrahamic—and particularly Christian—worldview is correct, and other religions' views of the world are not."

"That would be... amazing," Alexander said.

"Except if it didn't establish that at all," I interjected. Alexander and Professor Norton both looked at me, the former with interest and the latter with irritation. "Even if you were to, for example, prove the existence of angels, unless that angel came down and said to you specifically that Christianity was the only valid religion and that the others were flawed, you wouldn't have any evidence to say that the theologies couldn't coexist in some form."

"Except that God says that you shall worship no other gods but Him," Alexander said.

"Even if that is a direct decree from God-as-man-upstairs-in-bathrobe, that doesn't preclude the existence of other spiritualities," I countered. "It's no different from a country decreeing that its citizens swear allegiance to that country alone. It doesn't mean that no other countries exist. In fact, establishing that angels exist may actually give *more* credence to other religions, as different religious expressions could coexist."

"What religions coexist with others?" Alexander scoffed.

"Buddhism, for one," I said, thinking back to my bookshelf.

"I mean, nothing's universal, but Buddhism has historically been very compatible with other religions."

"Yes, yes, very good," Professor Norton said with a wave of his hand. "But regardless, that is a debate for after I prove the existence of otherworldly beings."

"So, when you say 'otherworldly beings', you are specifically concerned with heavenly beings?" Alexander asked.

"And infernal ones, as, from the existence of one, we could logically infer the other," Professor Norton said.

"Not necessarily—" I started.

"One could logically infer the other," Professor Norton repeated with impatience.

"What about other creatures?" Alexander asked. "Things like ghosts and ogres?"

"Superstitious nonsense," Professor Norton said with a dismissive wave, and Alexander and I exchanged a glance. "I have no time for fairy stories."

"And yet you are confident in the existence of angels?"

"Yes," Professor Norton said. "Without a doubt."

"That's strong faith," Alexander mused.

"It's only faith when you're not sure," Professor Norton replied. "I have proof enough for myself; I just need to prove it to others."

"Proof?" I asked.

Professor Norton waved his hand again. "Not demonstrable proof. But enough of that. I'm glad to see you safe, Cole. University is technically not in session with the current volatility of the pipes, but I am trying to continue my research as best I can. Do you have a new phone or some other means of contacting you?"

"Before that," Alexander asked, "What about Cole? He has no memories of anything more than a few days ago. Can you tell him anything about his life? His past?"

"He's a very good student," Professor Norton said. "Diligent and hardworking; insightful, sometimes irritatingly so. We don't always see eye to eye, but it's good to be challenged once in a while."

"That's great and all," I said, "but what about life *outside* of University? It does exist, you know."

"Oh, and he has a mouth of him," Professor Norton added.

"Yeah, tell me about it," Alexander said, and I winked at him.

The professor sighed. "I don't concern myself with students' personal lives, so there's not much I can tell. I believe you used to live with an aunt, or uncle, or both, and they largely left you to your own devices."

That made sense. At least, if I was not close to my family, it would explain why they hadn't been banging down the door looking for me.

"Anything else?" I asked.

"I suppose you pretty much kept to yourself," Professor Norton said. "I never saw you with any friends on campus, and you always responded to e-mails or texts promptly. Honestly, I was surprised when—Alexander, is it?—reached out on your behalf, because I didn't think you had any social circle to speak of."

"I probably didn't," I admitted. "But I have met people since the accident."

"Good people, I see," Professor Norton said with a small smile of approval. "That's always encouraging. I do hope, however, that you will continue to approach your studies with due dedication. Once you have recovered fully, that is—though you do look fine." He eyed me with interest. "You really weren't hurt?"

"Well, I guess that depends on how you see complete and total memory loss," I replied flatly.

"At least your sarcasm seems to have survived intact," the professor frowned. "Nonetheless, I would appreciate being able to reach you going forward. A professor worries, you know."

I exchanged phone numbers with the professor, who was then kind enough to treat us for our drinks. We parted ways with a smile and a handshake outside the coffee shop, and the professor disappeared among the university buildings.

Alexander sighed after he left.

"Well, how do you feel, Cole?" he asked.

"I don't know," I said honestly. "I don't know what I was expecting. I guess... I guess I hoped he'd have known more about me."

Alexander put a hand on my shoulder as we walked down the sidewalk. "Well, it sounds like there might have not been much to know," he said.

"Hey!" I protested.

"I didn't mean it like that," Alexander replied with a chuckle. "I just meant that it sounds like you led a pretty simple life here. Going to University, coming home, reading and studying, trying to get laid as NerdyHunk21..."

"Hey!" I said again, this time laughing. But yeah, Alexander was probably right. "Judging from that dating profile, I must have been pretty desperate for some sex," I mused.

"Well, at least *that* need's been met," Alexander said, giving me a playful squeeze.

"Indeed," I agreed.

"So... we're in the city now," Alexander said. "Good to walk?"

"Yeah, sure," I said with a nod. "Let's just... steer clear of the square."

We passed the bus stop and continued onward. It was evening now, and the shadows lengthened along the street.

"Still, though," Alexander added thoughtfully, "something about that professor kind of bothers me."

"What do you mean?" I asked.

"Well, he had asked you to come to University late one night, and then became really worried when you never arrived," he said.

"Sounds right," I nodded.

"And furthermore," Alexander continued, "he says he was within earshot of the explosion, and so feared that you were hurt, or worse, and so started trying to reach you, but couldn't because your phone was damaged or destroyed or lost."

"Wow, what a criminal mastermind," I said, throwing up my hands in sarcastic outrage. "What a devilish, horrible man, worrying about his missing student. Mr. Holmes, you've done it again."

"Are you quite finished, Watson?" Alexander responded flatly.

"Who's Watson?" I asked.

"Oh, for fuck's sake," Alexander shook his head in irritation. "Look, the point is, say you're a college professor. You have every reason to believe that one of your students has just been injured or possibly killed in an accident on their way to university. You can't reach them. Who're you going to call?"

"The Ghostbusters?" I asked. Then, off of Alexander's exasperated look, I added, "What? You tell me; you're the one with the functioning memory."

"You seem to have very good recall for an amnesiac," Alexander responded.

"Oh, I'm sorry," I said, "My brain clearly isn't paying attention to all the rules for how an amnesiac's brain is and isn't supposed to work. Must have forgotten them. Maybe it happened when I *lost my fucking memory*."

Alexander crossed his arms and watched me. "Are you done?" He asked.

I thought for a moment. "Yeah," I said.

He smirked at me and suppressed a chuckle.

"What?" I asked.

"Have you noticed how you become a cheeky, sarcastic little shithead whenever you're uncomfortable?" He said, smiling. "I'm guessing you've always had that personality. You may have lost your memories, but you're still you, Cole."

"That's... one of the most encouraging things I can remember hearing," I said, honestly moved. "Also, fuck you," I added, and Alexander laughed.

"Anyway, my point is this," he said: "If Professor Norton couldn't reach you and thought you had been injured, the logical course of action would be to call the authorities or to at *least* reach out to campus administration. In any case, *someone* should have come by your apartment, and continued to do so until they found you."

"But I haven't been at my apartment in a few days," I noted.

"But you *were* there for a number of days following the accident," Alexander pointed out. "It would have been plenty of time for someone to find you. And the university has been working closely with the city to account for missing people. Anyone they couldn't pin down after a day or two, they added to a list that they e-mailed to the student body asking for information about. It could be construed as a huge privacy violation, mind you, but emergencies are emergencies. The point is, I don't recall seeing you on it."

"So... why didn't Professor Norton report that I was missing?"

"Exactly," Alexander said.

"Perhaps he was just preoccupied," I said. "It might not have occurred to him."

"Perhaps," Alexander said. "I mean, it's not proof that anything underhanded is going on, but still, I'd be careful."

I nodded.

Just then, I heard a ding, and felt a vibration in my pocket. I pulled out my smartphone and saw a text notification.

"Someone is texting you?" Alexander asked.

"No, it's a remote vibrator," I said dryly. "I just forgot how to insert it properly."

Alexander fixed me with a stony look of impatience as I unlocked the phone.

It was Cuan.

"u at church?" it read. It was followed immediately by another: "if so stay there"

"And what if I'm not?" I responded.

A pause.

"dont go near the umivrsity"

I assumed that the last word was supposed to be 'university'. Was he texting in a rush?

"What if I'm there now?" I texted back.

Another pause. I stared at my phone. Then a simple reply: "run"

Who's that? Alexander asked.

"We have to get out of here. Now," I said.

"What's going on?" Alexander asked as I grabbed his arm and ran. "Who's texting you?"

"One of the Midnight Hunters," I said.

"Oh, well we should *definitely* listen to them," Alexander responded sarcastically.

"Shut up," I said. "We need to get away from the University. It's not safe here."

"Why?" Alexander asked.

"I don't know why."

"Well, *that* sounds trustworthy."

"Now who's a cheeky sarcastic little shithead?" I asked impatiently.

Alexander stopped. "Seriously," he asked, "why are you trusting them? They put you in danger and used you like a tool to kill some ghost. Then, sure, they came to your rescue when all hell broke loose, but that didn't stop you from losing all of your clothes AND the key to your apartment, not to mention experiencing whatever horrible trauma was involved with going incorporeal. Then when they brought you home, they shot at you with a crossbow. Why do you keep listening to them? What, is one of them just stupid hot or something, and so you lose all sense of rationality around them?"

"That's not fair," I responded, temper rising.

"Well tell me then, Cole," Alexander demanded. "Apart from those texts, what evidence do you have that we're in danger?"

As if in answer, an explosion rang out from around two streets away. The ground shook, and we struggled to keep our footing as an unearthly screech echoed from building to building.

"There," I said. "Satisfied?"

Shaken, Alexander nodded, and we started to run. We had only gone half a block before I heard my name.

"Cole!"

I turned in the direction of the voice and saw Cuan bounding toward me. He was wearing his usual baggy wushu pants and sleeveless shirt, only this time the strap around his upper arm contained what appeared to be a smartphone.

"Cuan!" I exclaimed as he ran up and took both my hands in his.

"Are you all right?" he asked.

I nodded. "How'd you find me?"

He tapped his nose. "I'll always find you," he said, and I couldn't help but beam at him.

"So... stupid hot it is, then," Alexander muttered.

"Hi, I'm Cuan," Cuan said, turning to Alexander with a friendly expression and extending his hand.

"Stay away from me," Alexander said, recoiling.

"Friendly," Cuan chirped sarcastically. "I can see why you're so taken with him."

"What's going on?" I asked him.

"We were taking Az on a kind of trial run," Cuan explained quickly. "We brought him on a hunt to clear out a minor haunting. Everything was going smoothly, but then those things showed up again."

"Things?" Alexander asked.

"You mean the ogres?" I said, alarmed.

"That's right. We don't know where they came from this time, but there are six of them, and we're having a hard time containing them."

"What about the people?" Alexander asked.

"The university is closed," Cuan said, "and that section is cordoned off. Thankfully I don't think anyone is in danger."

"But only if those creatures *stay* in that area," I pointed out. "We just met my professor from before I lost my memory. He went off that way," I said, pointing. "And there's a coffee shop open in that direction, so at least a few people must still be active up there."

"Wait, you met your professor?" Cuan asked excitedly. "You're a student here? Did you remember something?" Then, suddenly, he shook his head. "No, later. The important thing right now is stopping those ogres."

"Well then, *you* should go do that," Alexander said. Then he turned to me. "We need to get out of here."

I looked from Alexander to Cuan. I hesitated.

"Cole," Alexander urged. "We need to get back to the church."

"Not two minutes ago, you doubted that we were actually in any danger," I pointed out.

"Well I don't doubt it now," Alexander replied, looking pointedly at Cuan.

Cuan, however, was looking at me.

"Go while you can," he said, with a slight hitch in his voice. "The most important thing is that you're safe."

I hesitated for another moment. But, when push came to

shove, what could I do? If Cuan was worried about me, then he'd be distracted. The best thing I could do *was* to leave. What else would I be capable of?

"Let's go," I said to Alexander.

Alexander shot Cuan a glance that was both scornful and triumphant, then turned and ran.

"Be safe," I said to Cuan before I turned to follow Alexander. Behind me, I heard Cuan run back in the direction from which he came.

Alexander and I hadn't even made it a block, however, before there was a giant crash, and a massive creature came tearing through the glass doors of a building next to us.

The creature was giant and yellow, with tattered rags hanging from its body.

"W-wha-what the *fuck is that*!?" Alexander cried.

"That's an ogre," I said, my body tensing.

"Holy fucking shit," Alexander gasped as the creature fixed its gaze on him. "Run!"

We turned, but there was a crash from the corner ahead of us as a streetlight sparked and smashed to the ground. Behind it was another ogre, this one green.

"Shit," Alexander swore again, looking behind us. The yellow ogre let out a low roar, and then charged.

The building on the right side of the street offered no cover; there wasn't even an alley to duck down—and if we did, we'd most likely be trapped there. The left side of the street was slightly more open, but a parked car was overturned across the front of a gap between buildings next to a broken dumpster. Clearly the battle had been waged here already. Our current location offered the most room to maneuver.

I braced myself and prepared to dodge the ogre's rush— assuming it had even noticed me next to Alexander in the first place, that is. Alexander, however, was wide-eyed and terrified.

I took his arm, steeling myself to yank him out of the road

with me. However, the ogre hadn't crossed half of the distance to us before there was a flash of movement, and suddenly Cuan's powerful thighs were wrapped around the creature's neck, his body twisting in the air, using the creature's own momentum to send it crashing to the ground. Just before it hit, Cuan pivoted his body, releasing his legs from the ogre and doing a one-handed handspring off of the pavement, pivoting in the air to land before us.

"Are you all right?" he asked for the second time.

"I am now," I said gratefully.

"What... what the fuck is going on?" Alexander asked, looking on the verge of panic.

"You're under attack, is what," Cuan said hurriedly. Then he pointed behind us. We turned around and looked down the street, where the green ogre was ripping the sparking stoplight out of the ground like some kind of unwieldly club.

"I can handle one of these, piece of cake," Cuan said, panting slightly. "But two, flanking us? That's a problem even if I transformed."

"Transf—what?" Alexander asked.

Cuan fixed him with a look. "You're Order of Light, aren't you? Aren't you trained for combat? Defending your home, and such?"

"Yeah, but—" Alexander started.

"I'm not interested in your 'but'," Cuan said. "Well, then again, maybe," he added, tilting his head, "though I'd have to see it first."

"It's nice," I said, and Alexander shot me an angry look.

"—but not in the middle of combat," Cuan said. The yellow ogre began to stir behind him. "The point is, you need to fight."

"Fight..." Alexander repeated quietly, half to himself.

Cuan turned toward the yellow ogre and prepared to strike it while it was down. However, just as he was about to land his blow, the creature suddenly moved like lightning, swatting

Cuan aside with his hand. Cuan flew sideways toward the brick face of a building, but spun in the air and landed on the wall with both feet and one arm, absorbing the shock with his limbs. Even so, the impact had to hurt.

"Cuan!" I shouted.

"Fight!" Cuan ordered Alexander before springing off the wall, becoming a blur again as he darted back toward the ogre.

Alexander shook his head violently. "Fight..." he muttered again, turning back down the street. The green ogre had loosed its prize, and was now advancing toward us holding the tall street light in both hands, red, yellow, and green lights dangling impotently from the bar.

"Alexander?" I asked.

"Fuck it," Alexander spat. "Father is going to kill me for engaging in combat outside of defending church grounds. But fuck it." He reached his right arm up over his right shoulder and pulled the wrapped sword out of the pouch in his backpack. Then he stood up straight.

"Atta boy," I heard Cuan say quietly. I glanced over my shoulder to see him shooting Alexander a satisfied glance as he belted the yellow ogre across the jaw.

"Hey, Jolly Green," Alexander shouted. "Time for me to chop off your beanstalk."

I winced. "Jeez," I said, "I have no memories of what you're referencing and even *I* know that taunt is bad."

"Hey, we can't all be amnesiac pop-culture-encyclopedic banter machines like you, OK?" Alexander replied in an exasperated tone as the green ogre roared and rushed down the street toward us. It raised the stoplight over its head and started to swing it in an arc. However, it clearly hadn't judged the width of the street well, as the light smashed through a building window and lodged there, wrenching the ogre's arm backward. It staggered, then recovered, pulling the stoplight free and rushing us again, now holding the beam like a clumsy spearman or an extremely awkward pole vaulter.

I stepped to the side of the road as it approached. The ogre paid me no mind, instead staying focused on Alexander. It lunged inexpertly, thrusting with the stoplight. Alexander dodged nimbly as the light embedded itself in the pavement, then reached to the wrapped blade and tossed his hand forward. The wrapping fluttered off in the air before the stunned ogre, which blinked at it distractedly. Immediately afterward, Alexander pierced the fabric with a thrust of his sword, Candela's blade erupting with light as it flew through the air. It was a blind thrust, but it would have been true, had the ogre not drawn its head back at the sight of the fluttering material. Candela instead found the creature's shoulder, the ogre's own movement turning the lunge into a slash that tore into the skin.

The creature roared and staggered backward. Alexander slashed with Candela again, and though he missed the creature the blade flashed brightly. Even from where I was standing I had to blink against the light; the ogre, meanwhile, seemed blinded entirely. It recoiled backward, pulling the stoplight from the pavement as it did so. It attempted to swing the light around but instead sent it crashing into a parked car. One of the suspended stoplight tops snapped off and clattered to the ground several feet from me. Alexander rushed the ogre but the creature, recovering from Candela's flash, pushed forward with the beam of the stoplight, causing it to pivot sideways like a park gate with the parked car as a fulcrum. The beam slapped into Alexander's chest, knocking him onto his back. Alexander struggled to his feet with the wind knocked out of him, but the green ogre, encouraged by the sudden shift in momentum, lumbered forward.

I glanced in the opposite direction. Cuan was, true to his word, managing the yellow ogre with minimal difficulty. The creature was still standing, but it was clearly tiring, while Cuan continued to zip around the street, harrying the frustrated creature. No, Cuan was fine.

Alexander needed my help.

I ran to the broken-off stoplight. It was a full red, yellow, and green array, of the type that normally suspended from a cross-beam, but this one had been severed when the beam hit the car. It would do. Bracing myself, I hefted the large rectangular light box. Man, these things were so much bigger up close.

Alexander managed to dodge a swipe from the green ogre and swung his sword at its face. The ogre dodged back, this time shutting its eyes in anticipation of Candela's bright flash. The creature succeeded in not blinding itself, but caught its foot on some debris and lost its balance. It started to fall backward, but then reached out and caught the beam of the streetlight post, which was still embedded in the parked car. The beam pivoted at its free end, and the creature instead started to fall sideways, catching itself with its other leg and managing to stumble onto its knees. Alexander tried to follow it but the ogre pushed the beam forward, which swung out at him, forcing him to dodge backwards.

The ogre was struggling to get up. It placed its arm on a nearby broken car hood and bent forward, trying to get off of its knees.

This was my chance. I ran forward—as quickly as I could while holding a massive stoplight, anyway. I ran up the car hood, then used the creature's own back as leverage and leapt off of it, bringing the heavy stoplight crashing down on its head. Metal splintered and cracked and glass shattered at the impact, and I heard the crunch of bone. I thought for a moment that I had felled the beast, but suddenly I felt a large hand close around my ankle, and with a roar the creature spun me around. My leg yanked painfully in my hip socket as my body twisted. I yelled as the creature whipped me through the air before loosing me to send me flying toward the intersection it had come from, where a truck was overturned.

I knew I was going to hit it. I heard both Cuan and Alexander scream my name as I careened toward the tractor trailer head-first. I lacked the superhuman athleticism that allowed Cuan to pivot his body mid-air to land feet-first, and even if I did, I suspected that rather than absorbing the shock with my limbs I'd wind up swallowing my own kneecaps as they burst through my skin. I braced myself for impact as my mind whirled. My life probably would have flashed before my eyes if I could've remembered any of it.

I heard the dull thud as my body reached the truck. The noise, however, wasn't of flesh and bone cracking against metal, but rather that of clothes and shoes thumping against material. There was dark, and I had a quick glimpse of what looked like crates of Oreos and Cheez-Its before I was flying through the open air again. The truck had been like flying through thick fog —if thick fog was made of gelatin—and it had slowed my momentum somewhat. The trajectory of my flight slowly curved downward until I was gliding along the surface of the pavement. I reached my hands down through the ground, and slowed to a stop.

Here, too, there was fighting. A large red ogre was whipping a slab of concrete around and roaring angrily. Everything had an odd afterimage to it.

Everything, that is, except for whatever the ogre was fighting.

I did not see a person, or a creature, or anything. Instead, I just saw a vaguely human-shaped mass of glowing black light. It was whipping around, nimble like Cuan, only one of its arms seemed much longer than the other.

"Cole!"

I turned back around to see Cuan leaping over the overturned truck, leaving an afterimage trail behind him.

"Cuan...?" I managed. My voice was a hiss. Talking was difficult. It felt like my lungs had to work overtime to make any noise. But then, of course they would... my body wasn't exactly airtight.

"I'm here," he said, kneeling next to me. He glanced up, quickly surveying the situation.

"What... is that...?" I asked, pointing in the direction of the red ogre.

"Can you not see it?" he asked with concern. "It's another ogre."

"With...?" I managed.

"Oh, that's Az," Cuan said, an impressed smile crossing his face. "Isn't he something?"

I turned back and stared at the mass of black light. It slashed with the extended limb, and the red ogre staggered backward, falling to the ground.

"Black...?" I managed.

"Huh?" Cuan said. "No, Az is pale-skinned. It's Bran who's Black."

I shook my head.

"Do you mean his suit? His sword?" Cuan asked, clearly confused.

I turned back to the figure-shaped black light. Why didn't Cuan seem to be seeing what I saw? I tried to see Az as he did.

Then, suddenly, the world seemed to solidify. My body felt weighty, the pavement solid under what I suddenly realized was my bare ass. The afterimages seemed to fold over one another, but remain, like a fog. And as all that happened, the mass of black light seemed to coalesce and take form. There was Az, with blond hair and blue eyes, clad in his impeccably neat suit. What I had perceived as an extended limb was his long black sword, which he held neatly in his left hand. He was heading toward us through the fog.

And as he approached, I suddenly realized that, while my whole world was enshrouded in fog, Az was crystal clear.

Az didn't spare me a look, but said something to Cuan in a language I couldn't understand. Cuan replied in kind, then looked down at me with concern. Only then did Az's eyes fix on me, his eyebrows shooting up as he beheld my naked body.

Suddenly a loud crash came from behind me, and I turned to see the tractor trailer being bashed apart from the truck cab, the yellow ogre tearing metal aside as it rushed forward. Cuan said something sharply that I couldn't understand and, standing up, leapt at it as it rushed forward. Az, sword in hand, strode behind him.

"Cuan!" I called, still too disoriented to get to my feet. "Be careful!"

At the sound of my voice, Az stopped in his tracks. He turned back toward me, body still oddly sharp in contrast to the fog that clouded the rest of my perception. He leaned down close to me and opened his mouth, and his words, insistent and demanding, were clear as day:

"Where did you learn that tongue?"

"What are you talking about?" I asked, confused.

"That language," Az said. "Where did you learn it?"

"I'm speaking English," I insisted, panic creeping into the edge of my voice.

"No, you're not," Az stated.

I heard a dull thud and turned to see the yellow ogre fall sideways to the ground. It didn't move. It had a bloodied arm, but otherwise showed no overt signs of trauma. Cuan continued to watch it for a moment, then, satisfied that it wasn't about to move again, rushed back to my side, shouting something I couldn't understand.

I reached up with both hands, and Cuan embraced me,

holding my bare chest tightly to his. He turned over his shoulder and said something urgently in that mysterious tongue to Az, who replied coolly in the same incomprehensible language, never turning his hard stare from my face.

Cuan held me tightly again, whispering in my ear, that same word over and over.

I knew by now what it was.

My name. I focused on my name.

".o..."

".ol.."

".ole."

"Cole."

The world firmed up, the fog coalescing and solidifying until everything was as clearly defined as Az.

"I'm here," I said faintly, holding Cuan to me. "I'm here, Cuan."

Cuan squeezed me close.

"The slaw returns," Az said.

Cuan looked up at him. "Slaw?" he asked, then recognition took. "Oh, of course. Cole slaw. Veeery cute, Az."

"So, this is your power, Slaw?" Az asked. "Showing up naked out of nowhere?"

"My clothes... I lose them when I go incorporeal."

"Normally I wouldn't complain about having him naked," Cuan said, still holding me, "but in the heat of battle, it's a little dangerous."

Az looked me up and down, eyes plainly lingering on my crotch.

"Yes, I imagine you'd have little cause for complaint," he concluded, a hint of approval in his voice. "But... incorporeality?" He nodded. "That would explain why I didn't notice you. And this is... something you can do at will?"

I shook my head. "It just... happens."

Az flexed his left hand and his sword melted into a beam of

black light, which then dissipated. "It shouldn't just 'happen'. And it shouldn't come with exhibitionism. Unless you wanted it to, that is."

"What are you talking about?" I asked.

He took out a slip of paper and a pen from his pocket and scribbled something on it, then handed it to me. It was an address.

"Meet me there tomorrow," Az said. "I can train you to understand your abilities better."

"Um..." Cuan looked at Az suspiciously. "What are you trying to do here, Az?"

"Yeah, I'm not sure that's a good idea," I said. "I'd rather not get shot at, thank you very much."

"Shot at?" Az asked, leaning back in surprise. He looked almost affronted. "Why would someone shoot at you?"

"That was Cedric's training regimen," Cuan said.

"To force me to go incorporeal," I continued.

"Are you kidding me?" Az exclaimed, momentarily dropping his veneer of imperturbability. "That's possibly the least helpful thing he could do!"

"Right?" I said, as Cuan sighed unhappily.

"Look," Az said. "I promise that your training will not involve you being attacked in any way. Besides," he said, crouching close to me, "I think we have a great deal to *talk* about."

"What the hell does that mean?" Cuan demanded, but Az straightened, offering no response.

"What the *FUCK* was that!?"

The three of us turned to see Alexander walking toward us from the truck wreckage, carrying my clothes in a bundle in his arms along with Candela.

"And *what* are you doing with Cole?" he continued.

"He was helping me come back," I explained.

"Come back?" Alexander asked.

"I have trouble after I'm incorporeal. I get... disoriented. Confused."

"Are you OK now?" Alexander asked, genuine concern evident in his voice.

"Yeah, I think I'm all right."

"Good. I brought your clothes," he said. I stood and walked to collect them, knowing full well that I was giving Alexander a great view of my cock and the other two an eyeful of my ass as I walked. Honestly, I didn't mind.

"But *you*," Alexander glared at Cuan as I began to dress myself. "You just *left* me with that fucking monster and ran to the other side of the truck?"

"Oh, please," Cuan said. "After the blow Cole gave that thing? That was really nice, by the way," he added with a smile at me, and I grinned at him. "That creature could barely stand. It fell over as soon as it let go of Cole."

"Yeah, fell *on* me."

"It wasn't moving. You were fine."

"And then there was that yellow one that you left behind! What about it?"

"That thing seemed pretty fixated on me," Cuan said. "I figured it wouldn't even notice you were there. You were mostly covered by the green one, anyway."

Alexander was fuming. "And what if it *had* seen me?" he asked. "What then? I was still struggling to get out from under the green thing; I would have been helpless."

"You'd have been fine," Cuan said.

"The fuck I would have!" Alexander said. "I can't fight like you, even when I'm *not* trapped."

"Oh," Cuan said. Then he shrugged. "Sorry."

Alexander glared at him.

"Had you called for help, I would have come for you, though," he added.

"The fuck you would have," Alexander said.

"You seem to really like that word," Az observed.

"And who the hell are you?" Alexander demanded.

"You don't bother to introduce yourself first?" Az asked. "Isn't that simple courtesy?"

"Yeah, come to think of it," Cuan said. "You still haven't told me your name."

"So what?" Alexander replied coldly.

"Generally I've observed that those who do not identify themselves are ashamed of who they are," Az stated calmly.

"What do you know?" Alexander spat.

"A good deal, actually," Az replied.

"Well, I'm Alexander, and I'm not ashamed of anything."

"Sexinchurch," I sneezed.

Alexander glared at me.

"Well, Alexander, I would say it is a pleasure to meet you, but you are quickly proving that to be a falsehood," Az said. "Even Slaw here made a better first impression. My name is Az."

"And what, are you a Midnight Hunter too?" Alexander asked.

"He aspires to be."

We turned in the direction of this new voice and saw Lester walking toward us from the shattered door of a building.

"Though I must say, he has acquitted himself admirably tonight," he continued.

"Lester?" Cuan asked. "What are you doing in the field?"

"Combat's over," Lester said matter-of-factly. "Who do you think does the cleanup? But more importantly, what are you doing talking to the Order of Light, Cuan?"

"He's with me," I said, and Lester's gaze focused on me.

"Ah. Cole." Lester frowned. "I have a message for you. Your doctor called the phone the Order planted on you."

"We didn't plant anything," Alexander said.

"Nonetheless, he left a message," Lester said. "He wants you to go into the clinic when you have a chance; your STI results came back from the lab and he wants to discuss them."

"Oh, shit," Cuan muttered.

"It can't be like that," Alexander said defensively. "They had to send it out to a specialist because his blood was like water, or something. So don't worry, you can't have caught anything."

"I wouldn't have caught anything anyway," Cuan replied, and Alexander looked at him, nonplussed. Only then did I realize that Alexander had likely been fishing to see if Cuan had slept with me, and Cuan's response was not what he had expected.

"Well, if we're quite finished here," Lester said, "I think you had all better clear out."

"And what will you do?" Alexander asked.

"Wait for you to leave," Lester said flatly. He turned and waved over his shoulder as he walked back into the building. "Cole," he called at the doorway, "if you have any sense, you'll come back with Cuan."

"I shall depart," Az said. "Until next time," He nodded at the slip of paper which was still in my hand, and I tucked it into my pocket. Then he turned and disappeared down the street.

"Cole," Cuan said, taking a step toward me.

In a flash, Alexander whipped Candela forward, pointing it toward Cuan. "Don't come near him," he demanded, and Cuan stopped in his tracks, eyes on the glowing blade.

"Alexander, what are you doing?" I asked.

"Don't come another step," Alexander ordered. "Don't come anywhere near him."

"Don't you think I should be the judge of who can and can't come near me?" I demanded. I walked defiantly to Cuan and embraced him, as Alexander glared angrily.

"I wish you'd come back with me," Cuan said.

"Will Cedric still try to impale me with arrows?" I asked.

"Probably," Cuan admitted, releasing me from the hug.

"I can't go where I'm not safe," I said.

Cuan nodded, and I walked back to Alexander.

"Is he keeping you safe?" Cuan asked.

"Better than you could," Alexander spat, still pointing his sword at him. I gestured with my hand for Alexander to stand down, but he ignored me, continuing to stare at Cuan.

"Well, I haven't been shot at since staying at the church," I admitted.

Cuan's shoulders dropped slightly. "If that's where you feel safe, then that's where you should be," he said.

"Damn right," Alexander said.

"Ok, that's enough," I said firmly. "Let's clear out before Fester does whatever mad science he has planned."

Cuan nodded sadly. "I'll text you," he said.

"Don't bother," Alexander replied.

"Oh, I'll bother," Cuan bristled. "I'll bother *hard*."

"Good," I said, and we exchanged a smile. Then we parted, Cuan disappearing in one direction and Alexander and I heading off in another.

We walked for a block or so, Alexander angrily wrapping Candela back in a cloth from his bag and stuffing it into his backpack's side pouch.

"You were kind of a dick, you know," I said.

Alexander grunted angrily as he finished securing Candela.

"What's the matter with you?" I asked.

"I don't trust them," he replied in a surly voice.

"Why?" I said.

"Father has told me all about Cedric. He's in opposition to all that we stand for. He's waging a war on Christianity. I don't trust anybody who follows him."

"I trust Cuan," I said.

"Why?" Alexander asked. "Every time he's around, you're put in danger. Look at tonight."

"He didn't make those ogres appear," I said.

"No, but he led them to us," Alexander countered.

"He was trying to protect us," I insisted.

"That again," Alexander sighed. "You're so convinced that Cuan is trying to keep you safe." He sighed, his voice heavy.

"What?" I asked.

"I'm trying to protect you too, you know," he said quietly. His fingers brushed mine as we continued down the street. "I care about you, Cole."

"I know," I said, taking his hand, and we walked the rest of the way to the church in silence.

XVI

AZ

IT WAS AN UNCOMFORTABLE NIGHT. Jacob had been waiting for us when we walked into the sanctuary, and demanded to know where we had been all day and why we looked a mess. Alexander explained that we had gone to see my old professor and on the way back had been caught up in the attack in downtown. He did not, however, mention anything about going to the old estate, which I suspect was a very wise decision, considering Jacob's reaction to what we *did* explain.

He was furious that Alexander had taken Candela out of the sanctuary without permission. When I asked "Isn't it his sword and he can do with it whatever he damn well pleases?" I earned Jacob's ire for having the gall to talk back, Alexander's for making things worse, and both of theirs for saying 'damn' in church.

Alexander pointed out that it was good that he'd had Candela with him because of the ogres, but Jacob seemed even angrier that we had engaged them, even when Alexander insisted we hadn't had a choice in the matter. "There's always a choice," Jacob said, whereupon I made the choice of rolling my eyes.

More than anything else, however, Jacob was furious that we had spoken to and fought alongside the Midnight Hunters.

"How *dare* you consort with such godless sinners?" Jacob roared.

"They were already there," Alexander said.

"They were helping us," I said.

"You." Jacob leveled his gaze at me. "It's bad enough that you associate with those monsters, even after they assaulted you. Yes, I know about that." I gave Alexander an irritated sidelong look. "But it's worse still that you have now dragged Alexander among them. I allow you to stay here because you need a place that is safe. You are not a poison, but those whom you associate with are. Do not allow them to taint this house."

He turned to Alexander.

"Alexander, you are confined to the church tomorrow."

"You're *grounding* him?" I said in disbelief. "He's not a child."

"He behaves like one," Jacob said. "My house, my rules."

"God's house, you mean." I said.

"Don't make this worse," Alexander said. His voice was calm, but his eyes were pleading.

"We're done here," Jacob said. "It is past curfew. Get to your beds."

The next morning I didn't have the stomach for another session in the sanctuary, but I bore it for Alexander's sake. He sat next to me in the pew in stony silence as Jacob railed in the pulpit about sin and corruption, continuing to go on about Sodom and Gomorrah.

"He seems to really like Sodom," I mused.

"I prefer sodom*y*, myself," Alexander whispered.

"You're getting better," I said with a suppressed grin. "*That* was funny."

Still no brunch to follow service. Rebecca offered me a granola bar and an apologetic look, and I accepted the first and dismissed the latter.

"Honestly," I said, "I'm happy to not have a prolonged meal today."

"Things *are* pretty tense around here." I turned to see Thomas behind me. "I heard you guys had quite the adventure yesterday," he added, walking to the pantry and picking up an apple, then polishing it off before taking a bite. He seemed more casual today, and looking at his face, I felt another odd twang of recognition.

"What?" he asked, and I realized I was staring at him.

"Thomas, we never... met before now, did we?"

"Um... you do know you *have* been here for several days, right?" he said.

"No, I mean, before I lost my memory. It just... feels like I've seen you before."

"Nope," he said. "Believe me, I'd remember you. Maybe it's just something with your amnesia? Like... things you see feel familiar, because your brain is trying to make up for its confused memories?"

"I don't know," I mused. "Maybe."

"Have you had any luck remembering anything?" he asked, taking a bite out of his apple.

"Nope," I said. "I mean, the Midnight Hunters were *supposed* to help me, but..."

"But then they shot you," Thomas nodded. "Yeah. Look, I know you're hearing this a lot, but I really do think you should be careful around them. Even if one or two of them are nice, if the leader is toxic, then the whole organization suffers."

"Yeah, I'm beginning to see that," I said, though I didn't think we were talking about the same group. But then, from the way the corner of Thomas's lip twitched, maybe we were.

I passed through the sanctuary on my way out, and said a cordial goodbye to Alexander, who was busy dusting off the pews and reorganizing the hymnals.

"You going to be all right?" I asked.

"Yeah," Alexander said. "I'll do my penance and then things will be back as they should be." I looked at him doubtfully, but he ignored my concern. "You're not staying around today?"

"I have to get to the clinic, remember?" I said.

"Right," Alexander nodded. "Let me know how it goes, OK?"

"Sure," I said. I wanted to give him a hug, or a peck on the cheek, or something, but Levi was straightening up the altar, watching us disapprovingly. So instead I just waved and left.

The testing clinic wasn't difficult to find the second time around. I checked in, then sat in the waiting room until Dr. Peterson called my name. I called an affirmation as I stood up.

"You have me completely confounded," Dr. Peterson said after we entered his office. I could tell he had given my case a lot of thought, as he hadn't even needed to consult my chart when I entered. "And not just me," he continued; "our entire lab has never seen blood like yours."

"How so?" I asked.

"I... don't know how to begin to describe it," he said. "First off, your blood, strictly speaking, would probably be considered O-Negative, but only in the sense that it doesn't *have* anything."

"What do you mean?"

"Well, at first I thought it was unreactive, as all of our tests came back as though we were testing water. But the lab results were even stranger. Your white blood cell count is zero."

"Zero?" I asked.

"That's right. Normally that would indicate a really serious medical condition. But it's not just your white blood cells that are missing. Your blood consists of red blood cells and plasma; nothing more. And not only that, but the lab wasn't able to introduce anything into it, either."

"I don't understand." I said, trying to wrap my mind around what I was hearing.

"White blood cells. Pathogens. Proteins. Vitamins. Lipids. Anything they put into your blood just... evaporated. Within seconds, it was completely undetectable."

"Lipids are fat, right?" I said. "But... that can't be right. I mean, I have at least *some* fat." I lifted up my shirt and pinched my abdomen. I was skinny, yes, but I wasn't 0% body fat by any means—that was Cuan, if anyone.

"No, and that's what confuses me," Dr. Peterson said. "Under any normal circumstances, if someone had a blood profile like yours... they'd be dead."

Dead. I swallowed.

"If I didn't take your blood myself, I would be sure it was faked," Dr. Peterson continued. "As it stands, you're some sort of medical marvel. Honestly, if you'd consent to more testing, I think the medical community could learn volumes from—"

"I don't think I'd like to undergo that kind of testing right now," I said.

"Right. Of course," Dr. Peterson said, shaking his head. "I'm sorry; I didn't mean to put pressure on you. You remain complete control of any and all things that happen to your body, and to your results."

"Thank you, Dr. Peterson," I said. I stood, and he stood with me. I shook his hand. "I appreciate your respecting my wishes."

"That's what the clinic is all about," Dr. Peterson said with a smile. "It's important that people feel safe coming here when they want to know about their risk regarding STIs." Then his face turned thoughtful. "Speaking of which: I hesitate to say this, as it is really irresponsible of me to even suggest, but... given your blood profile, I don't think you even *could* catch an STI. Not one that infects the blood, at any rate."

When I left the clinic, those words were still circling in my mind. What really concerned me, however, wasn't the notion that I didn't seem able to catch an STI: it was the assertion that if someone had blood like mine, they'd be dead.

What was I?

Shortly after I was out on the street, my phone rang. It was Alexander.

"Hey," he said when I answered. "I'm just checking on you."

"Hi back," I replied. "I'm doing fine. How's being grounded like a high schooler?"

"It's not like that," came the somewhat sulking reply.

"You're right, sorry," I said. "How's being grounded like a middle schooler?"

I heard Alexander's frustrated groan from the other end of the phone. "I'm fine," he said. "Anyway, did you go to the clinic yet?"

"Yeah, good timing," I said; "I just finished up there."

"And?" he asked, then added in a hushed tone, "what did the doctors say about your tests?"

"It's the weirdest thing," I replied. "The short of it is, I apparently *can't* catch an STI. Or any infection, at least not one that travels in the blood."

There was a pause. A long pause. Then, finally, "Wow."

"That was my reaction," I said.

"How... how do you feel about that?" Alexander asked.

"I don't know, really," I replied honestly.

"Well, we can talk about it when you get back," Alexander replied. "Lunch should be ready soon."

"Yeah, about that," I began, as I pulled the crumpled piece of paper I had received the night before out from my trouser pocket.

"What?" came the wary reply.

"I won't be back until the evening," I said, "I'm meeting Az."

"Az?" Alexander asked. "Who the fuck is Az?"

"You met him last night," I said.

There was another pause. "Not the guy in the suit."

"Yes, the guy in the suit."

"Holy shit, that must be what happened," Alexander replied

dryly. "The Men in Black came for you, and they already erased your memory once with a neuralyzer, and now they want to do it again."

"I have no idea what the hell you're talking about."

"Oh, come on!" Alexander cried. "I finally make a *good* pop culture reference, and you and your amnesia don't even get it."

"You thought that was *good*?" I responded.

There was a long pause.

"I'll see you at dinner," Alexander grumbled. But before he hung up, he added, "be safe, OK?"

"I will," I promised.

The address on the paper was to a hotel. It was unfamiliar, but thankfully I at least had a smartphone. Lester had locked down most of the functionality—including the Internet—but at least the map worked with data.

The hotel itself was very large, and—if the lobby was any indication—a little on the fancy side, even if its external facade was relatively unassuming. Inside, it featured a hanging chandelier with what I assumed was cut glass decorations and gold-colored brass-gilded elevator doors. The overall aesthetic was just on the tasteful side of gaudy.

What surprised me more than the decor, however, was the person seated in a velvet chair between the doors and the elevator, who looked up and waved as I walked into the lobby.

"Cuan?" I asked.

"Hey there," he said, standing up and stretching before smiling at me with that lopsided grin of his. He shook out the stiffness in his shoulders and kicked his legs once or twice each, leaving me with the distinct impression that he'd been there a while.

"What are you doing here?" I asked.

"Waiting for you," he said.

"But... why? How?"

"When Az handed you that address last night, I made sure

to get a look at it," he said. "All I really needed was to catch the name of the hotel. I thought you'd be here sooner."

"The Order starts the day with church," I said, and Cuan grimaced. "After that, I was at the clinic."

"Oh, for your test results? I hope that went OK," he said, and I noticed with appreciation that he hadn't actually asked me directly to tell him what the results were.

"It was... odd," I explained. "Apparently, I'm like you."

"Huh?" Cuan cocked his head blankly.

"I... don't seem able to catch anything."

Cuan beamed. "Well, that's a fun discovery," he said.

"But back to my original question," I said, "What are you doing here?"

"Az said he was going to train you," Cuan explained. "Last time someone tried that, it didn't go that well. And... and I wasn't there when I should have been. I wanted to make sure I was there for you this time, in case something happened. But," he added, "only if you want me to be. Say the word, and I'll leave." The earnestness of his expression was irresistibly endearing.

"No," I said, punching the button on the elevator. "I'm glad you're here."

The elevator ride up to Az's room on the 13th floor was a long one. As the doors closed, I couldn't help but look at Cuan, who was in his usual outfit of Wushu pants and tight sleeveless top. We'd only just passed the second floor when I wrapped my arms around him, burying my face in his neck. He seemed a little taken by surprise, but he hugged me back, holding my body to his.

"I really am glad you're here," I whispered, and he held me even tighter. I felt safe and secure in his arms.

On the 13th floor, I walked down the hall and rapped on the door to Az's room.

"Yes?" came Az's serene baritone.

"It's me, Cole," I said.

The door opened. It was Az, dressed in his usual impeccable black suit.

"Ah," he said, "Welcome, Slaw; I have been awaiting you." Then his eyes fell on Cuan. "And... what are you doing here?" he asked.

"Well, let's see," I said. "The last time someone offered to train me alone, I was nearly shot. Forgive him for worrying. Is his presence a problem? Because if it is, then perhaps *my* presence is a problem, too."

"No, no," Az said, shaking his head. "It was just unexpected. Though I must admit that I fear Cuan will have little to do while here."

"That's fine," Cuan replied. "I like to watch."

I coughed slightly at the—probably?—unintentional double-entendre as we entered the hotel suite. I say 'suite' because, while it featured a single king-sized bed against one wall, it looked more like a studio then a simple hotel room. It had a fair amount of floor space, a sink and kitchenette, and a small side room with a toilet. The shower, however, was prominently featured, a wide stand-up chamber in the near corner of the main room with glass walls extending not quite to the ceiling.

The room had a small table and a pair of upholstered chairs, but Az gestured toward the bed when he addressed Cuan: "Have a seat there, if you don't mind; it's out of the way."

Cuan did as Az requested, and perched on the bed in a tight squat, elbows resting on his knees and hands hanging close together. Az then directed me to stand by the far wall, with the window behind me and bed on my left, and stood for a moment, as though sizing me up.

"So," he said. "Tell me what the process of becoming incorporeal feels like for you."

"So... we're just getting right into it, huh?" I asked.

"Why waste time?" Az said. "We're well into the day as it is."

"Everyone's acting like I was expected to be here at a specific time," I responded. Az shook his head.

"No, you're fine," he said. "Now just... what has it been like?"

So I told him. I started with the first time I went incorporeal, with the ogres. Thankfully, Az had experienced enough yesterday as to not require a lot of background for that. I followed with the other similar experiences, adding how difficult it was to come back, how it was like being lost in a fog similar to what I felt after I woke up with no memories. Az listened to everything thoughtfully, but when he spoke, his response was not at all what I was expecting.

"You may not have realized, but you don't need to drop your clothing every time you 'go incorporeal', as you put it," he said.

"What?" I asked, nonplussed.

"Your disrobing is probably a result of the involuntary manner in which your transitions have triggered," Az surmised. "I shall use the term 'go incorporeal', I suppose, as that seems to be the framework that works for you. If you are able to initiate a transition yourself, then all that you identify as 'you' should be a part of that transition."

"How do you know all this?" Cuan asked from his perch on the bed, a slightly suspicious expression on his face.

"You are here as an observer," Az said to him. "He is the one who may ask questions," he said, pointing to me.

"No, what he said," I insisted. "How *do* you know all this?"

"It's currently a working assumption derived from other similar cases," he replied, somewhat evasively. "It's all theoretical, at the moment, until I can observe you make a transition up close."

"If you want to see me naked, just ask," I said.

"That is not the goal here," Az replied flatly. He sighed. "Let's try this: what goes through your consciousness just before you 'go incorporeal'?"

"Alarm, usually," I said, thinking. "It sort of... happens when I'm in danger."

"Immediately?"

"Not always," I realized.

"And those times when it's not immediate... what is that like?"

"It's like..." I tried to remember not just the events, but also how they felt and what I was thinking. "It's always in a situation that I want to get out of. Desperately, for my own safety. I just don't want to be there. I just want to... disappear."

"Ah," Az replied. "I see. So it's like eliminating your sense of presence."

"That... makes a lot of sense," I realized.

"It would also explain why, when you transition, only the bare minimum of what you identify as 'you' makes the transition with you."

"But... that *is* all that's me," I said. "My body is me."

"And yet, the food in your stomach comes with you," Az said.

"Yeah, but... that's part of me," I said, confused. "Isn't it?"

"That is a good question," Az replied. "It is simply a matter of perception. Of identity."

"I don't get it," I said.

"Here," Az mused. He turned to the nightstand next to the bed and pulled out what looked like a permanent marker. Then he walked over to me. "Hold still," he instructed. Then he pulled the cap off and started drawing all sorts of little symbols on the sleeve of my button-down.

"Um, why are you drawing on me?" I asked.

"I'm not," Az replied, continuing to make strange marks. "I'm drawing on your shirt."

"It's not my shirt," I realized. "It's Alexander's." Shit.

"Oh," Az mused as he replaced the cap on the pen. "Hm. Should've drawn a penis, then."

Over on the bed, Cuan burst into hysterical laughter.

"But that's not the point," Az said. "The point is, you experienced it as me drawing on *you*. Humans are socialized into perceiving the clothes they wear as a part of their identities. Recognize that. Think of yourself, right now. Allow that sense of self to include the clothes you're wearing; the shirt, the socks, the shoes, everything. Picture yourself, right here in this room, right as you are right now."

I labored to get a sense of myself in my mind's eye. It might have been easier had I closed my eyes, but I wasn't comfortable enough in the situation for that. So instead I concentrated.

Az slowly stepped toward me. "That's it," he said calmly. "Picture yourself." He reached out and placed his palm on my chest. "Now," he breathed. "*Fade.*"

He breathed the word, drawing it out in a long breath. It was a command, one that echoed in my ears, and I felt the air move through me, as though my body were melting away. I felt a sense of detachment, as though the world simply weren't as concrete as I'd always believed it to be. At the same time, Az's body seemed to dissolve into the same black light I had seen the previous night. Everything else gained that weird afterimage, and I heard the quiet sound of fabric hitting the ground. I looked down, where a pair of white boxers lay on the ground. All the rest of my clothes, however, remained on my body.

Cuan had straightened up, cautiously alert. "You OK?" he asked.

I nodded. "Yeah," I managed to breathe, and he relaxed, but only slightly.

Slowly, the light in front of me solidified into Az's familiar form. Unlike everything else, however, he left no afterimage. He looked down at my boxers. "Not bad," he said approvingly. "Odd that you should lose those, though."

"Not used to 'em," I breathed, each word a struggle in my incorporeal form. "Not mine."

"Wait, what?" Cuan asked.

"Borrowed from Order," I said.

"Ah." Cuan settled back down.

"Try not to talk so much in this state," Az said. "You'll exhaust yourself."

"How did you...?" I asked, but Az shook his head.

"Let's bring you back first," he replied softly. "Focus on the room. Focus on yourself in this room. Feel the floor. Remember its solidity." He reached out with his foot and lightly kicked the white boxers aside, and I realized that I hadn't been standing on them, but rather had been standing *in* them, and so it was probably good that they not be there when I returned. "Feel the air," Az continued. "Focus on your sense of place. Remember how it all feels. Focus on the room, the furniture, the people."

The people. I looked to Cuan, who was watching me silently. I remembered what it was like to touch him, to have his body close to mine, the sense of his warmth, the solidness of his muscles...

And the world slid back into place. And with it, came the fog, layer after layer of afterimages all overlapping one another until they completely obscured my perception. My ears felt buffeted by wind, my throat thick and heavy. Even Cuan, who continued to watch me with concern, seemed to be behind a veil of mist. Everything was a fog. Except Az.

Az was clear as day.

"Why aren't you like everything else?" I asked him. In my periphery I could see Cuan's silhouette lean forward, and then he spoke in that language I couldn't understand. So, we were back to that. Az simply looked at me, studying me as though he were a doctor trying to come to a diagnosis.

"Who are you?" I asked him again.

Silently, he pointed to my sleeve, where he had drawn all the strange marks. I looked down. Only now, they weren't strange marks at all: they were letters, and I comprehended them perfectly.

I AM DEATH.

"Well, that's *super* fucking creepy," I said, staring at the words.

"So you *can* read them," Az replied. As soon as he spoke, Cuan did a double take. I looked at him as he looked from me to Az, asking some question that I couldn't understand.

"What happened to Cuan?" I asked.

"Nothing," Az replied. "Rather, he's concerned with what happened to *you*."

"Why, what's he saying?" I asked.

"You don't understand?" Az said. "Interesting." He looked at Cuan and said something in that mysterious language. Cuan paused. As best as I could tell, he was eyeing Az cautiously, but it was hard to be sure with the fog pressing against my senses. Then Az turned back to me. "Cuan is speaking English, you know," he said, still serene as ever.

"What?" I replied. "No he's not; I'm speaking English now."

Az chuckled. "That again. Is that how it appears to you?" He asked. "Ah, human perception is such a tricky thing. I take it you don't speak any additional languages?"

"Not fluently," I said.

"Ah, privilege," Az mused. "How your mind must be scrambling to make sense of what it is perceiving. You only know one language, and so therefore you are experiencing this tongue as that language. Fascinating."

"Ok, Wile E.," I said, beginning to get annoyed. "I get that you're a *suuuuuper* genius, but could you please stop talking down to me and explain what's going on?"

Az gave me a wry smile. "You are speaking in the Tongue of Souls," he said simply.

"The what of what now?"

"The universal divine language," Az said. "The tongue of

those who are attuned to the divine. Humans spoke it once, at least in legend. Many human religions mention it... you may know it as the language spoken by those who erected the tower that would later be known as Babel."

I blinked at him, but then I realized that this tower and its history was not my most pertinent question. "Why do I understand it now?" I asked.

"All souls understand it," Az replied, "only they generally must be free to comprehend it. When a soul is incarnate, perception becomes what the incarnation can perceive, and so understanding of the Tongue is lost. But the divine know it, as do the dead."

"The dead," I said, blanching. "Is that what I am?"

Az didn't reply, instead looking at me thoughtfully.

"And what about you?" I asked. "How do you know it?"

He gestured at my sleeve.

"Yeah," I said, shaking the creepy transforming letters at him. "I'm gonna need more than that."

Az straightened, leveling me with an imperious stare. His eyes seemed to penetrate through me, and when he spoke, his voice echoed inside me.

"I," he announced, "am Azrael."

I blinked at him again.

"Who?" I asked.

Immediately the serene veneer cracked, and Az massaged his temples in frustration with his left hand.

"Stupid amnesia," he groaned. "Azrael," he repeated with impatience. "The Angel of Death."

I looked at him incredulously.

"Wait, seriously?" I asked.

He nodded. Over on the bed, Cuan watched us in confusion.

"Wait, does he know?" I asked, pointing to Cuan. At the gesture, he looked at me and made a one-syllable remark that, even with my understanding of language shifted, I still recognized as "Huh?"

"No," Az replied, "And you can't tell him."

"What do you mean, 'can't'?" I demanded incredulously.

"I am revealing myself to you because I need you," Az said, "but I can't complete my objectives if everyone knows my identity. So you must keep it a secret."

"What is this, *Death Takes a Holiday*?" I demanded. "Do I look like Duke Lambert?"

Az groaned in frustration. "You don't recognize the name Azrael, but you know *that*?" he moaned. "Also, I *hate* that movie."

"And what do you mean you 'need me'?" I demanded, ignoring his exasperation. "And you have some 'objective'? What are you talking about? Are you here because of the ogres?"

"No, that's unrelated, as far as I know." Az said, "Though it serves me to try to understand that situation as well."

"So you just casually come down and announce that you're an angel, and I'm just supposed to tell no one and do whatever you say?" I said.

"See, I knew it would go like this," Az said to no one in particular. "They never had this kind of trouble with Mary."

"Oh, right, because that has integrity written all over it," I moaned. "'Hey, just so you know, God's impregnated you even though you're already about to get married, so go wander off into some manger and give birth with the goats and the sheep, but don't worry because we're going to have some pretty star send you creepy men bringing gold and drugs and shit, and who cares about consent, because this is 1BC, and women are basically property.'"

"You—" Az bristled, but then he stopped and blinked at me. "You make a good point, actually," he said offhandedly. "But still, it worked out pretty good for Mary, don't you think? People *worship* her."

"Well, is that what Mary wanted?" I asked.

"Well, I can bring you to ask her yourself," Az retorted, "But then you'll be *dead*, so think *very* carefully before you respond."

"Oh, well then won't that just suck for you, since apparently you need me alive," I mocked. Then I stopped. "Wait, *am* I alive?"

Az sighed. "Will you just help me?"

"And what if I don't want to?" I asked. "What if I don't want to keep some big secret you've just foisted upon me against my will? What if I want to tell Cuan who you are?"

"Then I'll... harvest your soul?"

He didn't sound convincing.

"I don't believe you," I responded. "Let's look at this another way. You're clearly here because you need me—so, thanks for the training, by the way, *very* philanthropic of you."

"There's nothing philanthropic about me," Az interjected. "I hate humanity. It's a blight."

"I don't disagree with you on principle," I said, "but we'll circle back to that. The point is, you said you need me. And you clearly *really* need my cooperation, or you wouldn't have revealed yourself to be the Angel of Death—which I'm still not entirely convinced of—when you yourself claim that you don't want anyone to know your true identity. But now you want me to keep a pretty big secret from one of the only people I've found really trustworthy since losing my memory. Don't you think it would be a much better idea to try to cooperate with me and, oh, *not* casually threaten to harvest my soul, and just maybe I'll help you out of some genuine sense of camaraderie instead of under duress?"

Now it was Az's turn to blink at me. "You'd really just... help me because you like me?"

"Well," I said, "I don't particularly like you right *now*, but...

yeah," I said. "I'm not stupid enough to make any blanket promises, but why don't we start by telling Cuan who you are, and see how things go from there?"

Az paused. For a long time. Then, at last, he said, "Fine."

"Good," I nodded. "Now, can we get me out of weird Babel-babble fog land? I'm kinda gonna puke."

Az shrugged. "You're already solid. Try finding something to ground you."

I breathed in, and breathed out. Something to ground me. I knew instinctively what that was.

I walked over to Cuan, who still sat on the bed with a concerned expression, and took both his hands in mine.

"Find me," I asked.

He looked searchingly into my eyes. I knew he couldn't understand my words, but he nonetheless seemed to know what I needed.

".o..," he said.

It was my name, and I knew it. He repeated it, just as he had so many times before.

".ol.."

".ole."

"Cole."

The fog snapped away like a projector coming into focus.

"Hi there," I said, looking into his bright, sincere eyes.

"Hi," he said back. "Now, will someone please tell me what in God's name is going on here? Is everything OK?"

"Maybe?" I said, looking over my shoulder. Az was watching me with a somewhat petulant expression on his face. It was kind of adorable. "I think Joe Black here has something to tell you."

"I hate *that* movie, too," Az groused.

"Yeah, but Brad Pitt at the height of his sexy?" I pointed out. "You can't be *too* mad at that. Though, I do have one question."

"And what's that?" Az asked.

"Who's Brad Pitt?" I responded.

Az glared at me.

"Will someone please clue me in here?" Cuan insisted.

Az sighed. He slipped off his suit coat, setting it on the back of the chair by the desk. Then he reached up to the collar of his white button-down shirt and slowly started unfastening buttons one by one.

Um... what's happening?" Cuan asked.

"Your guess is as good as mine," I said. "Not that I'll ever complain about a good striptease."

Az continued silently undoing his shirt until it hung open over his torso. Both Cuan and I swallowed at the sight of his chest. It was beautiful, lean and lightly muscled, white and smooth as though it had been carved from living marble. Then Az let the shirt fall off of his shoulders to the small of his back, and for an instant—just an instant—I forgot all about the gorgeous muscles of his torso.

Because the very instant that the shirt left his back, two snow-white feathery wings sprang from behind his shoulder blades.

Cuan's eyes shot open like two golden saucers, and he gaped. I totally understood why: we were standing in the presence of a hot, shirtless angel. Even folded, his wings were sizeable; the tops of them were about level with his ears, while his wingtips went down almost to his knees. Had he spread them fully, he'd likely have hit the walls, or at least knocked over the bedside lamp, which I'm sure housekeeping would not be particularly pleased about.

"So..." I said slowly, "I guess you were telling the truth."

"You..." Cuan stammered at Az. "You're..."

"My name is Azrael," Az said.

"The archangel of death...?" Cuan gasped.

"Now, see, this is the reaction I was hoping for," Az said.

"And yet you didn't want to tell him," I said.

"Is that what you were arguing about?" Cuan asked. "He told you who he was, and then didn't want you to tell me?"

"Yup," I said. "He said he'd harvest my soul if I did."

"He *what*!?" Cuan growled, rounding on Az.

"Well, obviously I'm not going to do that," Az asserted, lifting his shirt back over his shoulders. As he did, his wings seemed to fold in on themselves and vanish. "It was an empty threat, anyhow. But I was running out of patience with Slaw here," he explained as he did up his buttons. "He was running off his mouth like some sort of snark cannon."

"Yeah, that sounds like him," Cuan nodded with a hint of admiration.

"He's not the most cooperative human," Az concluded.

"And you're not the most angelic angel," I said.

"Well, what are you here for, then?" Cuan asked.

"There's a soul that's stuck here," Az explained.

"Oh shit," I said. "So I *am* dead?"

"It's not you," Az replied.

"Oh," I relaxed. "Then, who is it?"

"That, I'm not sure."

"Wait, you're *not sure*?" Cuan asked incredulously. "Then, how are you supposed to find them?"

"I know where they are, just not who they are," Az explained. "And I can't get to them. But Slaw can, perhaps, if he can master his abilities."

"And that's why you're training me," I realized.

"One of the reasons," Az said. "But also because I'm not sure what your situation is, and I'd like to figure it out. Plus you're struggling, and I thought I could help you."

"I'm still not sure I trust you," I said.

"Fine," Az replied. "How about this? I hereby pledge before

the Divine to not harm you in any way through my action or inaction, and to look after your well-being to the best of my ability for as long as I am here, whenever I am here." The air around him seemed to shimmer as he spoke.

"And Cuan," I said.

Az looked at me flatly, then sighed.

"And Cuan," he nodded. The shimmering around him faded. "So there. And note that I did not make this promise under duress or by force, but rather of my own free will."

"Do angels *have* free will?" I asked.

"Everything has free will," Az insisted, "at least as long as it isn't snatched away by some tyrant. The Divine is not a tyrant. Angels are different in that we are divine, but not *the* Divine; we exist as servants of the Divine and Its will."

"So... wait," I said, suddenly remembering my conversation the previous day. "My professor has been trying to prove the existence of angels. He said that would prove that Christianity has the right of it."

"Ha!" Azrael scoffed. "Which of the countless branches does he mean? Not that it matters, anyway," he added; "Christianity has been a mess ever since humans started mucking about with it, staring with Paul. And besides, what about the other religions that recognize angels, that predate Christianity? And what about my existence means that *other* religions are suddenly invalid?"

"That's what I said," I remarked proudly.

"So, then, what, all religions are wrong?" Cuan asked.

"No," Az replied. "The Divine infuses everything, but thousands of years ago humans developed a society so obsessed with power and artifice that human perception of the Divine became tenuous at best. But all are still connected to the Divine, and as that connection became strained, humans sought more and more to understand the Divine in the context of their new society. For those who sought this understanding, to reaffirm this connection, the Divine manifested in ways that were comprehensible to those societies."

"So... what," I asked, "Angels exist because people wanted them to?"

"Yes and no," Az replied. "We have always existed in some form, just as the Divine has always been there. But the Divine is both proactive and reactive. It responds to the wills of all souls. Otherwise, what would be the point of prayer, of intercessionary entreaties, of magic? All of those are interactions with the Divine, in the hopes that the Divine will move. And so when different individuals seek the Divine, the Divine meets them in ways that they can understand. All are the Divine, but all are compartmentalized in comprehensible ways. And then, of course, there is human perception and interpretation and desire and greed, making a mess of it all and complicating those understandings and misusing them." He scrunched his face in disgust. "The Divine is Universal, Unconditional Love. Do you think the Divine would judge someone for loving another of a different race or of the same gender? Do you think the Divine would tell humans to rampage across the landscape on a murderous crusade to get a holy cup or expand an empire? Or to waltz into a foreign land and convert people by sowing discord and division? All that was done by humans, sick to the core and desperate for power."

"Wow you really don't like humanity, do you?" I asked.

"Not as a general rule, no," Az replied. "So many humans cling to hate and power, and claim it in the name of the Divine even as they destroy countless lives, human and otherwise."

"So why doesn't God just strike them down or something?" I asked.

"That's the tricky thing about unconditional love," Az said. "It means loving no matter what happens, no matter how bad things get or what choices someone makes. The divine isn't just going to wipe people off the face of the Earth because they've fucked things up. That's part of the whole message Christ was trying to convey, that you humans seem to have missed completely. There is no 'I love you, but..." with the Divine."

"And yet you're here, professing a hatred of humanity," I said.

"I'm not the Divine. Unconditional love is not really my thing."

"Clearly," I said.

"Are there more like you?" Cuan asked. "Here on Earth, I mean?"

"Do you mean Angels, or aspects of Divinity?" Az asked.

"Aspects of Divinity?" Cuan gave Az a confused look.

"Incarnations. Avatars," Az said. "Call them 'Gods', perhaps, but understand that they are all reflections of a greater interconnected whole. And yes. Angels like me are servants of the Divine, but the Divine itself is manifest here in various forms, often with so much of an identity as to be a distinct soul. The Gods of the Land are always present in their native soils in one form or another, and some of them incarnate regularly. The Green Man, for example, is spreading his virility around Ireland at the moment, I believe."

"He's just wandering about, covered in leaves?" Cuan asked.

"Heavens, no," Az said. "He's a redhead, looks around your age, I think. He also has a name like yours or Slaw's; something beginning with the same letter, anyway." He shook his head. "It's not my duty to keep track of every Divine incarnation that walks the earth. I have my hands full enough with the humans and their souls and keeping the Wheel of Life in motion."

"The Wheel of Life?" I asked. "What is that, some kind of game show where you drive a little car around a board and get colored pegs while some lady in a dress turns letters on a board? 'Hey, Spin the Wheel of Life, hope you don't go Bankrupt.'"

Az glared at me. "It is not a physical wheel." He said.

"No," Cuan observed, "But you can't truly be responsible for ferrying every soul out of this life."

"Absolutely not," Az said, "No; I'm only responsible for those difficult cases, when something isn't working as it should."

"And... one of those is now?" I asked.

"Indeed," Az said, "Which is why I'll need your help."

"Why me?" I asked.

"Your 'incorporeality', as you put it, puts you in a unique position to assist me."

"How? And why can I do this anyway? What is up with me?"

The answer to the former will come later," Az stated. "As for the latter two questions, the short answer is that I don't know. My first instinct was to believe that you were a spirit, because you can pass from the physical realm and manifest your spiritual identity ethereally, much like a ghost. But spirits speak the Tongue of Souls, and yet when in that state you retain an understanding of English, and only speak the Tongue of Souls when you return to your physical manifestation."

"Wait," Cuan asked. "Tongue of Souls? Is that what you were speaking? What *is* that?"

Az glanced quickly at him. "Babel," he said.

"Ah. Gotcha."

"Now you see how easy that was?" Az replied, looking at me with impatience. "Things are much easier with people who haven't lost their memories."

"Well, I'm sorry," I exclaimed, picking up the white boxers off of the floor and waving them at him. "I must have left them in my other shorts."

"Well, speaking of shorts, put those back on, and let's try this transition again."

"Wait," I said, "you're not going to explain anything else?"

"Not now, no," Az said. "I'd like to try this again. I'd like to see if you can take all of your clothing with you this time."

"Fine," I said, unzipping my trousers and dropping them. Both Az and Cuan blinked in surprise, but what did I care? It wasn't anything they hadn't seen already. And Cuan, at least, had had some close-up experience. "Stupid big white boxer shorts," I groused as I lugged them on. "I'd never wear something like this myself."

"No," Cuan agreed. "You look much better in tighter trunks. Or a jockstrap."

Az cleared his throat impatiently—though his eyes hadn't left my crotch—and so I pulled the trousers back on, buttoning them as I stepped back into my shoes.

Once I was put back together, Az took a deep breath, and I followed suit.

"Now, try to gather an image of yourself once again," he said.

I did so, closing my eyes this time.

"Remember the feeling you had the last time. I am not going to nudge you toward incorporeality this time; do it yourself. Remember the feeling of fading from your physical form. Remember your identity. Take you, your whole self, and step into the ethereal."

"It is a step," I said, my eyes still closed. "But it's not one of losing my physical form." I searched my imagination. "It's one of stepping with my physical form out from the physicality of everything else. It's not *me* that fades; it's the *world*."

I felt a shift. I opened my eyes. Az was staring back at me, gaze clear and steady. But everything else had an afterimage to it.

"I... I did it," I realized.

Az smiled, and I could make out Cuan beam from where he sat on the bed.

"Well done, Slaw," Az said. "Now, step back."

"This... is the hard part..." I breathed. I willed the world back into solidity. Suddenly I had a feeling of familiarity. This step, the return, was the same process as when I clawed my way back to consciousness. I strained, struggled, trying to feel the ground solid beneath my shoes, the air on my face. For the world to be solid, *I* had to be solid, but this was the hardest step.

"Focus on something you want to return to," Az urged.

I turned my gaze, looking at Cuan.

"Come back to me," Cuan requested.

And I did. The afterimages converged, overlapping, and then the fog returned.

I looked from Cuan to Az and back again. Az alone remained clear.

"Am I back?" I asked.

Cuan frowned, then said something I didn't understand.

I looked down at my sleeve, where the letters were eminently readable.

I AM DEATH.

"This again," I sighed.

"Yes," Az said. "The Tongue of Souls."

"It's like... It's like I'm in some third state," I said.

"Indeed," Az mused. "This is what I can't comprehend. It feels like I should understand it, but I don't."

"Don't you have some heavenly wisdom or some such?" I asked incredulously.

"The Divine is omniscient. I am not the Divine." He sighed. "I don't understand this state you're currently in, so I don't know how to guide you out of it. But it seems that there is someone who does." He looked to the bed.

I followed his gaze, turning to Cuan. I walked over to him, I took his hands in mine. Az said something I couldn't understand, and Cuan looked at him and nodded. Then, to me, he said one syllable.

".o..."

That familiar syllable.

".ole."

"Cole."

"Cole," I said back, as the world came into focus. "I'm Cole."

"Yes," Cuan said with that adorable half-smile. "Yes, you are."

"Well done," Az said approvingly. "The return needs work, but you seem to have managed the transition into an ethereal state seamlessly, undergarments and all."

I smiled. I don't know why. It just felt right. I may not have been any closer to understanding what had happened to me, but at least I felt, for the first time, some modicum of agency over my own situation.

"And you, Cuan," Az added, turning to him. "You've been a great help after all." He sighed, then offered a small smile. "I'm glad you're here."

Cuan smirked. "Me too. You're kinda our guardian angel now, huh?"

Az grinned. It was a handsome grin. "You assume I wasn't already."

"That's an unsettling thought," I mused; "Death hovering behind me, sword at the ready."

"I thought Death used a scythe," Cuan observed.

"Oh, no, usually it's Quietus here," Az said, forming the sword out of black light and looking at it fondly. Then, with a mischievous twinkle in his eye, he added, "the scythe is only for *very* special occasions."

Just then, there was a ringing in Cuan's pocket. He reached down and pulled out his phone. Just as he was answering, my phone started to buzz.

"What?" Cuan said in alarm into his phone as I pressed the talk button on mine.

"Cole, you need to get back here, fast," Alexander's voice came on the other end of the line.

"Why?" I asked.

Cuan looked up from his phone, his face ashen. Both he and Alexander spoke at the same time:

"Ogres are attacking the Church."

XVII

WAR ON THE CHURCH

WE COULD HEAR the conflict before we could see it. The crash sounded like stone being smashed. It echoed across the buildings and through the empty streets. While I was relieved to see that there weren't bystanders, it struck me as odd: Were people in hiding? Had they evacuated?

We rounded the corner. The church was straight ahead; we were coming up toward the left side of the churchyard on a street perpendicular to the property. Between it and us were three of the now-familiar (to me, anyway) massive ogres: one a pinkish red, one orange, and one yellow. They all wore tattered rags in various arrangements, and they all were angry. It appeared that they had dismantled a truck and were now wielding its various components, for the red creature was holding what looked like a truck cab's exhaust pipe and the orange one had an axle with a single tire still attached. The yellow one was holding what could have been part of an engine; but honestly I had no idea what it was other than that it looked big and metal. The street was littered with debris, including shattered windows and a busted storefront.

The three ogres weren't facing us: instead, they were advancing menacingly toward the church.

"Cuan!" came a call to our right, and above us. We looked to see Bianca calling from a low balcony. She was in a skin-tight suit that seemed like some cross between nylon and leather, and yet fit more like a bustier on her torso, and somehow sported frilly cleavage. "Cuan, we need you this way! The front is having a much harder time of it."

"What's going on?" Cuan called back.

"Massive numbers of these things showed up tonight. We've been cutting off their access routes to the rest of the city, but for some reason now they started heading here."

"Why?" Cuan asked.

"How the hell should I know?" Bianca said. "Maybe they have a pen full of goats or something? Now get the hell up here."

Cuan looked at me. "Not... all of us can leap like that," he said to Bianca.

"It's OK," I said, "I'll meet you at the front of the churchyard."

Bianca suddenly turned her attention to me. "Well, if it isn't Casper the Friendly Ghost," she said. "Welcome back." Then she looked me up and down. "But really, that's what you're wearing? Can you even move well in it? What kind of battle outfit is that?"

"You're one to talk," I called back to her. "That getup doesn't even reach your shoulders. What, did you run out of puppies when you were making the coat?"

She grinned at me. "Yeah, the pet shop wouldn't sell me any more. Also, fuck you." She titled her head at me. "But hey, can't you just walk through the wall or something?"

"Now that you mention it..." I started.

"No," came Az's voice from behind me. "You've already

made that transition twice in very close succession. It's a process that expends a lot of energy; you'll exhaust yourself."

"Well, you heard the man," I said. Then I turned to Cuan. "Don't worry. I'll be fine; I'll see you in a few minutes."

Cuan nodded. "Be careful," he said, and then like a flash he bounded onto a car hood, then up onto a street lamp and from there to the balcony. He and Bianca disappeared inside.

I turned my attention back to the street. The ogres now appeared to be engaged in combat, but I still couldn't see whom with.

"I can get to the front of the church building if we go past there and then along the church wall," I said to Az.

"Well then, that's what we'll do." Az extended his left hand and Quietus formed in his palm. The blade glistened, covered in black liquid.

"By the way," I mused, "What is on your sword?"

"Black gall," Az replied. "Don't touch it. DEFINITELY don't get it in your mouth. Or eyes. Or anywhere."

"Got it," I said.

Just then, some kind of impact sent the orange ogre staggering backward. The creature spun around, the weight of the axle it carried wrenching its arm as it fell to the ground. The creature hefted it back up, looking up as it did so. It focused on Az, and with a roar, leapt forward. I stepped lightly onto the sidewalk and out of the fray as Az strode forward to meet it. The creature roared and swung the axel in a wide arc, but Az neatly dodged it, then swiped forward with Quietus and slashed the creature's arm. The monster roared as black blood splashed from the wound and retreated back toward the church. We gave chase, and finally I could see that this particular end of the church was being defended by Julia and Thomas.

Julia was clad in tight black leather pants with high boots and a thick brown leather jacket, her hair tied up away from her face. She looked *fierce*. In her hands she held a glistening spear. Thomas, meanwhile, had white pants with gold accents, and a slim shirt to match. It wasn't clearly made for combat like Julia's, but it looked easy to move in. Plus, the way it hugged his chest, I didn't see much need to complain. Where Julia wielded a spear, Thomas held what looked like a formidable chain whip with a wicked spiked ball for a tip.

"Reinforcements?" Julia called as we approached. "Reinforcements are always welcome. You *are* reinforcements, right?" She added warily, readying her spear.

"Don't worry; he's with me," I said.

"Cole!" Julia exclaimed, looking at me with a big smile. "I'd give you a huge hug, but, you know, monsters."

"You two all right?" I asked. "Where is everyone?"

"Alexander and Levi are guarding the front of the church," Julia explained, "While Paul and Rebecca are in the rear. There's a lot of these things, though, so we're stretched a little thin."

"Where's Father Jacob?" I asked.

"Hiding," Thomas said offhandedly.

"No," Julia corrected; "He's inside praying."

"So... hiding," I said.

"Yes, he's hiding," Julia sighed. "But we can't worry about that right now. What we need to worry about is the three giant monsters charging us down."

She was right: the three ogres had regrouped and were now rushing toward the church wall. Julia tensed and then darted forward, leaping over the orange ogre's truck axle and bringing her spear down toward the creature's head. It dodged awkwardly, but the spear pierced its shoulder, and suddenly it was a vertical beam of light, stretching straight to the heavens. The creature roared and Julia pulled the spear out of the wound, then backflipped neatly off of its shoulder back in front of the church.

Thomas, meanwhile, swung the chain over his head and then lashed out at the red ogre. As he struck with the whip, it burst into bright orange flame, the arc of fire blasting toward the creature. The ogre blocked with the exhaust pipe, and the whip coiled around it, but when the ogre tried to wrench the pipe backward and pull the whip out of Thomas's hands, the center of the pipe melted away. The ogre staggered backward from the sudden loss of resistance, splashing molten metal onto its forehead in the process. It roared and covered its face as it retreated to regroup.

Az, meanwhile, was slashing at the yellow ogre, which managed to parry the first strike with the engine block. The second, however, cut into its arm, and the black gall left a hissing, seething wound. Az moved to strike again but the ogre tore off the door of a nearby car and brandished it like a shield, both deflecting the strike and pushing Az backward.

"Not bad," Julia said appreciatively in the brief moment of calm.

"That's quite a spear you have," Az remarked.

"This is one of the weapons of the Order," Julia explained. "The spear of light, Gratia."

"And this guy is Prominence," Thomas said, stroking the whip affectionately.

"Oh, I get it!" I said. "Like a solar flare."

"Wow," Thomas said, the corner of his mouth twitching upward slightly. "Yeah. Nobody *ever* gets that." I blinked at him. Again, I was *sure* I had seen him somewhere before, but with the dust in the air and the smudges on his face, I was having trouble placing him.

"Those are cool and all," I said, "but why not just use guns?"

"And bless all those bullets?" Julia asked. "How much anointing oil do you think we have?"

"Can't you just bless the gun?" I asked.

"Sure, if you're gonna pistol whip the things," she said. "Me, I prefer Gratia, thank you."

"Huh," I replied, facing the creatures and steeling myself for their next onslaught.

"We can handle things here," Az said to me. "Go to the front of the church."

"Yeah," Julia nodded. "With your friend here, I'm liking these odds." She smiled darkly. "These guys are cake. Alexander needs you."

I nodded and turned, running down the length of the property wall. As I ran, I could hear more sounds of fighting. I rounded the corner and stopped short.

There were four of the creatures here: another each of orange and yellow, plus a green one and a purple one. The green and the purple were facing away from the entrance; the yellow and orange ones facing front.

"What is this, ogre rave night?" I asked once I had run toward the entrance.

Alexander was standing there, clad in another blue and white hoodie, brandishing Candela in his right hand. At the sound of my voice, he turned toward me.

"Cole!" he exclaimed. "I have no idea what's going on, or why these things are descending on the church." As he spoke, the yellow creature rushed forward, raising its fists, but suddenly a large hammer slammed into its side and knocked it back.

"They are descending on the church because they are monsters, and we are righteous," the owner of the hammer said. As the creature staggered out of the way I could see Levi, clad in black denim jeans and what looked like a bomber jacket. He pulled the heavy hammer back. It had a long, thin handle like a sledge, only it was about a yard and a half long and looked crafted out of obsidian with an ornamented butt. The hammerhead itself was uneven, flat, polished black on one end and the hint of a claw on the other. "That is why I visit Perdition upon them," he declared, twisting his large square body and swinging the hammer into the ogre's side again. There was a crack and the ogre staggered back a few feet and then fell.

"Ok, thank you, Ronan the Accuser," I said.

"Who?" Levi asked.

"Behind you!" Alexander shouted, and Levi leapt to the side as the purple ogre brought a cement block crashing down where he had been standing. Levi hefted the hammer again, then ran forward. The purple ogre dodged aside, and the green ogre moved in next to him, separating us from Levi once again.

"I just came from Julia and Thomas," I said. "They're fine. She said your Father was inside and Rebecca and Paul were in the rear. Where's everyone else?"

"What, the citizens?" Alexander asked. "They were evacuated earlier today. But we stayed. The Order's entire purpose is to protect the Church."

"Isn't the church wherever the people are?" I asked.

"Hey, we're people too," Alexander insisted. The orange monster, meanwhile, rushed toward him, and Alexander dodged sideways and slashed at its arm with Candela. The sword shone with light, causing the creature to stagger backward, both from being blinded and from the cut Alexander had made in his arm, which the sword had also instantly cauterized.

"But I mean, where are the others?" I asked. "Cuan and them?"

"Why would Cuan be here?" Alexander asked warily.

"He got a call the same time you called me," I explained.

"You were with Cuan?" Alexander responded, slightly more accusatorially than I liked.

"And so what if I was?" I said. "I was training. And that's not the point. The Midnight Hunters were trying to contain the creatures when they suddenly headed this way."

Levi appeared again after whacking the green ogre aside.

"So," he said, "the Midnight Hunters are behind this? Leading the ogres here?"

"You know that's not true," I scowled.

"I assume nothing where the Hunters are concerned," he replied before the purple ogre mercifully drew his attention back away from us.

"They're supposed to be here," I said.

"I haven't seen them, Thanks Be to God," Alexander replied, and I frowned at him.

"Then... where are they?" I wondered.

As if in answer to my question, the plate glass window of an apartment building half a block down burst outwards, and Cuan came flying out of it as though he'd been shot out of a cannon.

"Cuan!" I screamed, but Cuan spun in the air, catching a lamppost in his hands and swinging around it, letting go to send himself careening in our direction. Expertly, he turned in the air and landed in a run, heading toward me. I was relieved to see that he was ok, but from his gait I could tell that he had been smacked around a bit.

"Cole!" Cuan shouted, running toward me. "Everyone, Look out!"

"What—" Alexander started to ask, but a moment later the shattered window was blasted out of the wall, bricks flying across the street, and from the gaping opening emerged a giant hulking ogre of a size slightly larger than the massive ball-and-chain wielding one that had been responsible for my first bout of incorporeality. This one was red, and where it should have had hands it instead sported two large metal blocks like hammerheads. I recognized the metal mechanical pieces that replaced the creature's wrists, however. The creature levelled its left arm at us.

"Get down!" I shouted, leaping at Alexander and throwing

him to the ground as the monster's hammer-like fist flew over our heads and smashed into the low wall marking the church grounds a few yards behind us. Stonework flew everywhere and I scrambled out of the way, making sure this time to not get caught in the chain that fell where my legs had been.

"Oh, *fuck*," Alexander croaked, scrambling to his feet.

"Language!" Levi admonished as the green, purple, and orange ogres stepped back to make way as the red hulk raised its right arm. "But, yeah."

We scattered as another giant hammer-like fist crashed into the wall behind us. Then came the telltale sound of clanking chains as the metal hands rewound.

"Don't let him pull those back in!" Cuan shouted. He, Levi, and Alexander rushed forward. Levi was quickly intercepted by the green and purple ogres, and Alexander was stopped by the orange one. I had a sudden idea and scanned the ground, looking for something I could put to use. I spied a metal pole that looked like a length of pipe long enough and thin enough to work, but the arms dragged through the ground past me as I was scrambling over to pick it up. Cuan, meanwhile, ran forward, darting around debris, but just as he was about to reach the ogre, two more figures sprinted out from the hole in the apartment wall, and Cuan had to dodge back to keep from getting slammed in the head by a piece of thrown concrete.

The newcomers were two more ogres, one a sickly gray and the other blue, both of roughly the same size as the multicolored menagerie that was blocking Levi and Alexander. Cuan braced himself, watching them.

"Where's Bianca?" I asked when I'd caught up with him, metal rod finally in hand.

"With Bran," Cuan said. "They're covering the other side of that building," he said, pointing forward. "That's toward the square, where the creatures have been spilling in from. Cedric and Lester are out here, too."

"Wait," I asked, "Lester's in the field?"

"It's all hands on deck," Cuan explained.

The red ogre's metal fists retracted past where the gray and blue ogres were standing, and as soon as they were clear, the two creatures rushed forward.

"Is it me," I said, running out of the way, "or are these things becoming more coordinated?"

"It's definitely not you," Cuan agreed. He backflipped out of the way as the gray ogre swung at him. He leapt gracefully up to the roof of a truck but then had to leap back down over it as the red ogre fired a fist at him, which smashed into the wall beyond. We retreated back toward the church, where Levi and Alexander were continuing to struggle with the ogres there. I noticed that the yellow ogre had rallied, though its side already sported a nasty black bruise where Levi had hit it, and I suspected several of its ribs were broken.

"Why isn't Perdition working?" Alexander cried to his brother as they continued to fight off the monsters. "Shouldn't your hammer banish these things as soon as it touches them?"

"Evil is strengthening," Levi growled. "It's because humanity continues to stray from the path of righteousness. Even something as powerful as Perdition doesn't seem to faze them."

"I don't understand," Alexander said. "Candela is still effective." He brandished the sword in front of him and it flashed brightly, confusing the orange ogre which stumbled into its green companion, giving Alexander an opening for a slash.

"Your little prick of a sword?" Levi responded scornfully. "Sure, it's blinding, but it barely scratches them."

"What are you guys talking about?" I asked.

"Perdition," Alexander said. "It crushes wickedness; sends it spiraling into the abyss in a crack of black smoke. But these ogres seem resistant to it."

"Thankfully, they're not resistant to a good bludgeoning,"

Levi added, cracking the hammer against the purple creature's hip. It howled and collapsed, only to begin dragging itself up again as the yellow creature covered it.

"Look out!" came Cuan's shout and we all hit the deck as the red ogre's fist, which it had again retracted, sailed over our heads and back into the churchyard wall. Quickly, it began rewinding again.

I looked around. There were seven of these ogres now, counting the hulking red one. There were four of us, and I wasn't even sure how much help I'd be. We needed a trump card.

Cuan seemed to be coming to the same conclusion. He swallowed hard. I knew immediately what he was thinking.

"You don't have to do it," I said to him. "Not if you don't want to."

"I don't think we'll make it through otherwise," Cuan said.

"What are you talking about?" Alexander asked. "What is he going to—"

As if in answer, Cuan titled his head back and howled. The howl echoed through the streets, carried on the wind, and all of the ogres stopped for a moment in surprise. It would have been a good opening for Levi and Alexander, except that they had stopped in surprise, too. I, however, took advantage of the opportunity to thwack the green ogre in the back of the head with the metal rod I had, and it fell forward.

Cuan, meanwhile, was pure white light. His silhouette stretched and changed, and when the light faded, there was Cuan in his werewolf shape, grey fur and long red mane, his vest and wushu pants stretched over his powerful muscles.

"You..." Levi gaped.

Cuan stretched tall, and then immediately whipped into a blur, striking out at the purple ogre before it could process what was going on. The purple ogre stumbled backward, clutching the shoulder that Cuan had slashed open, and immediately the gray ogre ran up to cover it.

"You... it's you..." Levi growled. "You're a monster, just like them!" He reared up with his hammer.

"Cuan!" I cried, and Cuan leapt sideways as Levi brought his hammer down where Cuan had been standing.

"Levi, what the fuck is wrong with you?" Alexander shouted.

"*Language*," Levi admonished, then rounded on Cuan. As he did so, the gray ogre rushed him from behind.

"Look out!" Alexander cried, but before any of us could act, the gray ogre roared with pain, reaching around to its back and scrabbling in vain to pull out the bright red crossbow bolt that was suddenly sticking out from between its shoulder blades.

"You need to pay attention to who your true enemies are," came a voice from the roof of the building across the street. I looked up to see Cedric standing tall, wide-brimmed hat shadowing his sunglasses-clad face, cloak billowing around him.

"Cedric!" I shouted, legitimately glad to see him.

Cedric nodded in my direction and then leapt from the roof, firing another shot at the gray ogre in the air before grabbing a lightpost with his free hand, bracing one foot against it, and spinning down it to the ground.

"You have a lot of nerve, showing yourself here," Levi glared.

"And yet, you would be grossly outnumbered without us," Cedric said.

"We're *more* outnumbered with you here," Levi retorted. "What, did you lead these creatures here to take our church?"

"What use would I have with your church?" Cedric replied cooly. He loaded another crossbow bolt and fired it at the orange ogre, which Alexander was currently working to fend off, but the creature dodged suddenly and the bolt missed its mark. The green ogre stirred, and I thwacked it on the back of the head again to keep it from rising. Cuan, meanwhile, had rushed back toward the red hulking ogre to keep it busy. The blue ogre seemed unsure of its next course of action, and waited warily.

"Hatred? Greed?" Levi postulated in response to Cedric. "Who knows what motivates someone like you?"

"I am here because the creatures seem intent on coming here," Cedric replied. "I cannot say I am sorry about it—not because they are targeting you, but because it does seem to have finally roused your Order to take some sort of action. But mark my words, I have no desire to set foot inside your wretched building."

"Of course not; you'd likely burst into flames."

I turned at the sound of this new voice and saw Father Jacob striding forth from the church building, carrying some sort of large glass sphere with a cross topper in his hand. The sphere had a long piece of cloth extending out from beneath the topper.

"Jacob..." Cedric muttered, hatred in his voice.

"Cedric," Jacob declared in a low voice. "Take your beasts and go."

"These ogres are not mine to command," Cedric replied.

"I am not talking about them," Jacob responded, nodding in the direction of Cuan. "You have a lot of nerve, bringing that monster here."

"He's not a monster," I replied angrily.

"You know *nothing*," Jacob replied. "No ungodly beast like that shall ever be permitted in the House of Christ."

"You are even more callous than I thought," Cedric growled.

"Such is the burden of the righteous," Jacob responded coolly. "Only the pure are deserving of mercy." He raised his hand, touching something to the end of the cloth, and suddenly it ignited. "The holy flames of purification consume the unworthy!" he shouted, and lobbed the sphere in the direction of the street. Levi, Alexander and I jumped back as the bottle landed and burst, scattering flames across the ground. One of these extended to a parked car, which exploded violently, and I recoiled as flames from the blast engulfed the orange and purple ogres.

"Holy, nothing," Cedric said. "That is a Molotov cocktail."

"They are the flames of heaven and the fires of judgement!" Jacob shouted wildly. "Levi," he commanded, "I must go visit these righteous flames on the others that are assailing us. Fall back and guard the entrance. Let *no one* through who is not of the Order." He paused briefly. "Except Cole. We of the Order protect our wards."

Then he was gone, and Levi followed him toward the door.

"You heard Father," he declared. "Alexander and Cole are welcome here. The rest of you, begone."

"It's not safe yet," Alexander protested. "If we retreat inside the church now, they'll just follow us."

"Then *do your job* and stop them," Levi ordered.

I looked around. Alexander had the yellow creature nearly at bay. Cedric was managing the gray. The only others still standing were the blue, and the red monstrous one. Just then, there was a blast from about a block away.

"That is where Bran and Bianca are," Cedric said. "Cuan, handle things here; I need to check on them."

Cuan nodded as Cedric dashed away. The gray ogre gave chase, leaving three.

"Cuan!" I shouted. "See if you can get that red one to fire both fists at once."

Cuan barked an acknowledgement and raced toward the red creature. I ran to the sidewalk as the ogre levelled a fist at the gray and red blur and fired. Cuan neatly dodged, and the fist blasted into the back of the yellow ogre that Alexander had been fighting, sending it and the fist into the wall. The yellow ogre's body absorbed most of the impact, but there was a nasty crack and the creature slumped to the ground and lay still. The red ogre roared and took aim at Cuan again, firing its other fist, but Cuan dodged again. This fist blasted into the churchyard wall, sending more stone flying.

Almost immediately, the creature began rapidly rewinding the chains. This was my chance. I ran toward the part of the chain lying in front of me before the slack had been pulled tight and thrust the metal pole I had picked up through one of the large links in the chain, then threaded the pole through a link in the other chain as well. I only just got out of the way before the rest of the chain tightened and the pole started to drag along the ground, fists not far behind it.

Cuan, meanwhile, was trying to get near the red ogre, but the blue creature suddenly seemed to focus on him, and began to pick up bricks and other debris and toss them at Cuan, who had to focus on dodging.

Finally the chain wound as far as it could, as the metal pole jammed up against the mechanisms on the creature's wrists. The chain had retracted so quickly, and the impact of the pole against the creature's wrists was so strong, that the metal bent, jamming the rod in place. The ogre roared, confused, whirling around madly, trying to free its arms. It yanked its body sideways and the metal pole punctured the side of a parked pickup truck. It must have hit the fuel tank because the truck exploded. The blast engulfed the red ogre and knocked the blue one toward me. The blue ogre tried to get its footing as it stumbled awkwardly along the sidewalk. I stepped out of the way as it lost its balance and fell face first, smacking its head on the pavement just behind where I had been standing.

I looked at the creature as it lay on the ground. Its sickly blue skin was blistered in places from the blast, and part of the ragged pants it wore had been torn asunder. Something caught my eye.

I heard Cuan running toward us, likely intent on finishing the creature off.

"Stop!" I shouted, bending down.

Cuan obeyed without question. I heard his footsteps slow and saw a shine of light out of the corner of my eye as I reached toward the creature's torn trousers and started lugging them downward.

"Alexander!" I shouted. "Come here!"

"Um, Cole?" I heard Cuan's voice next to me. "Why are you undressing this unconscious ogre? I mean, I'm generally not one to judge people's fetishes, but I have to draw the line at non-consensual—" he stopped once I got the rags past the blue ogre's ass, and stared.

I heard Alexander run up. "Cole, what's the matter? What— *holy fucking shit.*"

"Guys?" Cuan asked quietly. "Why does this blue thing have your names tattooed on its ass?"

There was no mistaking it. The writing was stretched and faded and the skin was distended, to say nothing of discolored, but the fancy script clearly read "Alexander" and "Cole", one name to a cheek.

"Because... we know him," Alexander said.

"That's Marcus." I blinked in disbelief. "This was the guy who found me when I was first unconscious. We'd apparently dated a few times."

"Wait," Cuan said. "This was a *human*?"

Alexander and I nodded.

Cuan whipped a case out of his pocket and opened it up to reveal his smartphone—the case, I figured, must have been quite something if it had kept the phone intact through all of that. Cuan punched the screen a few times and held the phone to his ear.

"Lester," he said. "Yes, I know you're busy. No, I don't care. I'm a block from the front of the church, on the street facing the entrance. Come here *now*." He tapped the face of his phone and returned it to his case, bending down in front of Marcus's big blue body as he did so. "He's alive," Cuan concluded, "Just unconscious."

"This... this is insane," I said.

"Marcus..." Alexander choked back a sob. He looked completely shattered. "What did they *do* to you?"

"You subdued them?" came a familiar voice. I turned to see Lester hurrying toward us, bag in hand. "Great, but that's what cleanup is for. Why the impatience with this blue one?"

"They know him," Cuan explained.

"What, as in he was in one of the other attacks?"

"No," I explained. "This is Marcus."

"It has a name?" Lester asked.

And so, I explained all I could, distraught Alexander filling in the details when he was able to manage. How Marcus was, as far as we knew, an ordinary human, how he'd been trying to date us, how he had a drug problem, how Alexander had sent him to a public clinic.

"I... I was just trying to help him," Alexander said, on the verge of a breakdown.

"Holy hell," Lester responded when we had finished. "Well, there's some good news. If this is human-based physiology, then..." He opened his bag and rummaged around, finally pulling out a giant syringe with a wicked needle and plunged it into Marcus's neck, forcing its contents into his blood.

"What the fuck are you doing!?" Alexander shouted.

"It's a formula I've developed. Tranquilizer plus anesthetic with a touch of adrenaline to keep the heart going. It took me a while to get the balance right, but it should keep your friend both sedated and alive." He sighed. "You realize, of course, that this probably means the other ogres were also inpatients in that clinic of yours."

I had realized that. From the way Alexander blanched, however, he must not have.

"Someone must be abducting people in the clinic, perhaps multiple clinics in the city. It'd be easy to inject the patients; they probably thought they were getting a fix, or perhaps a treatment like in a methadone clinic."

"That's sick," Cuan growled. "Those kinds of programs have enough trouble getting their legitimacy recognized without someone using them to fill their ranks."

"That's why these things seem to be coming out of nowhere," Alexander realized. "Whoever is doing this is preying on the weak and disenfranchised, the homeless and the outcasts.... The public were happy enough that they didn't see them on the streets anymore without wondering where they were ending up. And I... I sent Marcus..."

"You were doing what you thought was best," I said. "He needed the help. And this program *should have* provided that."

"And instead it did this," Cuan said. "Who... who would do such a thing?"

"Whoever it is," Alexander said, clenching his fists until his knuckles turned white, "I'm going to find them. And I'm going to stop them."

"I'll help," I said.

"And me," Cuan added.

"So will all the Hunters," Lester replied as he wrapped Marcus's disfigured blue body in what looked like glimmering gauze. He had seemed so callous when I'd first met him, but now he was careful, sympathetic, almost a different person. He *cared*. "Cedric won't stand for this," he continued. "This is a tragedy, but at least it gives us a lead as to where to start looking for answers." He returned to his bag, still businesslike. "I will transport your friend to the lab... or to The Hunters' Home, since the lab is farther away. We'll see that he's safe. In the meantime, maybe by examining him we can discern more about this transformation, and perhaps we can find a way to reverse some of the damage."

"I..." Alexander paused. He hesitated for several seconds, but at last he said, "Thank you."

"Hopefully we even can learn something to help the others at the lab," Lester added.

"Others?" I asked.

"Of course," Lester asked, almost affronted. "What do you think I do on cleanup? The ogres who are alive, like the ones Cuan's subdued in the last few days or greenie over there—looks to me like he was just knocked out—I keep under heavy sedation, basically in forced comas. Without more information, though, I haven't tinkered with any of them. But now that I at least know they have, or had, a human physiology, I can perhaps devise a treatment plan."

Alexander looked over his shoulder, back toward the church. "I need to get back." His voice was shaking. "Cole," he added, his voice a small plea, "I hope you'll come with me."

He turned and started to walk off. I turned to Cuan.

"Cuan, I—"

"It's OK," Cuan said. His sad smile was only a little forced. "Alexander needs you. You both knew this guy. Go comfort each other. Give him some pleasure to focus on instead of... this, and maybe he'll get some sleep tonight." He gave me a wink. "Knowing you, you'll tire him right out."

"Cuan..." I took his hand and squeezed it. Cuan stepped toward me and gave me a quick but enthusiastic kiss.

"Go on," he said, dimple forming in his cheek as he offered that half-smile. "Tomorrow, come to The Hunters' Home, and we'll get to the bottom of this."

I nodded and said a farewell, then turned and ran toward the church.

Levi, still standing at the doorway, let me pass.

I walked down the halls and to the rooms. I was tired, and

part of me just wanted to go into the guest bedroom and collapse, but I was worried about Alexander. I knocked on his door.

The door opened, and Alexander appeared. He had already taken off his hoodie, and was standing in a sweaty, royal blue T-shirt. He looked at me with a haunted expression.

"I came to check on you," I said.

Alexander stared at me in silence for a moment. Then he grabbed the front of my shirt and pulled me into his room, throwing the door shut behind him. He pulled me against him and kissed me deeply, my nostrils filling with the scent of chestnut as he did.

I pulled back, alarmed.

"Alexander, are you OK?" I asked.

"No," he said, brows knit. "I'm not OK. Here I thought I was helping Marcus, and look what happened. I have no fucking clue what's going on, but if someone in those clinics is taking advantage of one of this city's most vulnerable populations and giving those critical public service programs a bad name, then I'm going to fucking *crucify* them."

"Damn..." I said, both a little taken aback and a little turned on by this new edge to Alexander.

"But right now," Alexander said, "I don't want to think about all that. I just wanna get it all out of my head. And you're here. So let's do it."

"How romantic," I said dryly.

"Come on," Alexander said, frustrated. "I don't just mean that. I just saw someone I care about made into some sort of horrible monster, and I don't know if he's gonna be OK. I know you only remember knowing him for a few days, but I've known him a lot longer than that. And I *care* about him, even if he is a massive douche. But all this time I've just been sitting here afraid to even let him in the Church doors because of what he might say or do. And now I have you here, and I care about you, too. And all I can think about is how I don't wanna fuck up like I fucked up with Marcus, and miss all this stuff I could have had or done."

"Well... do you want to go somewhere?" I said. "I mean, no sex in church, right?"

"Fuck that," Alexander said. He yanked his shirt over his head and tossed it aside, where it knocked into the back of his desk chair and flopped to the floor. He stared at me, bare chest heaving with a mix of emotions, boring into me with his blue-green eyes. "So fucking what about what anyone says?" he continued. "Right now I don't give a shit about any of it." He pulled open his belt and let his trousers drop to the floor so that he was only in his briefs, the fine hairs on his legs glinting gold in the light. "I've had a fucking terrible day. I'm tired. I'm scared. I'm confused. Except about one thing: and that's what I want to do right now." He was so agitated that he was practically panting. "I want to *fuck*," he announced. "So fuck me, Cole. Pound me into the back of the bed. Fill me with cum until I can't see straight."

I stared at him for a moment. He was taking a risk, but I also knew that he needed to do exactly that. He needed this. So what if it wasn't about me? He cared about me; he was asking me. That was probably more than a lot of guys think about when they want sex. It was enough. Besides, this wasn't about me. It was about Alexander.

I nodded, reaching forward and pulling him toward me. I kissed his neck, his cheek, and then met his lips with mine. It was a deep kiss, and he returned it with the kind of passion that comes tinged with desperation. I placed a hand on each side of his chest and pushed him gently down onto the bed, following him with my body, keeping our lips locked as we moved. I gently brushed my thumbs over the hard pink nipples on his chest, and he moaned, loudly and deeply. I reached down with my right hand, tracing the muscles of his abs, feeling the softness of the golden down and the slickness of his sweaty skin, until I reached his briefs. I crept my fingers over the fabric, cupping his balls and the base of his fabric-trapped cock with my palm, teasing his scrotum with my fingers. He released the kiss and moaned his approval, then reached up and hastily unfastened the buttons on my shirt, almost pulling them open until the shirt hung loosely from my torso. He pulled it off, and I kicked off my shoes and socks before he reached down and got me out of my trousers and boxers. He slid his hand down my torso and, wrapping his fingers around my semihard length, began stroking it to attention, all the while taking in my bare body with his eyes.

It was very different from that other day on the estate grounds. Then, Alexander had been interested in exploring my body, discovering how I reacted, enjoying my pleasure. Now, his intention was expressly to get me hard. He needed me inside him in a deep, visceral way, and even though his demeanor was much more urgent than romantic, there was something about the intensity of it that turned me on. He didn't want something slow and sensual. He wanted me to pound him the way an evangelist pounded the Bible. I passed my eyes over his tan, glistening shoulders, over his chest, his abs, over his blue, piercing eyes, and finally looked down to where he was stroking me, drawing my foreskin up and over the tip of my cock and then pulling it down to expose my reddening head. Our chests heaved, my nostrils flooding with his chestnut scent. I was hardening quickly, and it wasn't long before my cock was standing firm and tall. Sensing that I was ready, Alexander released it and leaned back on the bed, and I reached down and pulled his blue briefs off. His cock, thick and gorgeous, was straining upward, dripping precum down onto his downy balls.

Alexander reached into his dresser and pulled out an open jar of what looked like Vaseline, slathering it on his fingers and then reaching down and, pulling his legs up, applied it liberally to his winking hole.

"Fuck me," he begged.

I positioned myself over him, feeling the tip of my cock slide between his ass cheeks, and then pushed into him, slowly but smoothly, his body making way for me while still holding my cock tightly in a hot, wet embrace. As I slid in, Alexander let out a low, loud, long cry of pleasure, his body tensing and releasing with each inch until I felt myself press against his prostate.

Somewhere far off in another room, an organ began to play. It was a loud, intense fugue, rolling through the walls with energy and vigor. Alexander paid it no mind, and so I didn't worry about it, instead letting the energy of the music drive me. I moved.

Alexander grunted, then moaned, then cried out unre-strainedly as I began to thrust against him, holding the backs of his knees for leverage as I pumped with my hips. Alexander made no attempt to hide his reactions, his voice straining against the torrential notes of the organ, the storm of sound drowning out any and all of my own vocalizations. It was a tempest of sex, and every thrust, every press of my body sent the storm crashing through us both.

Our intensity was increasing, our pace quickening, when suddenly he pulled back.

"Wait," he rasped, his voice ragged. He twisted his body, keeping me inside him as he did so. It was an odd sensation, feeling his ass rotating around me. He wound up on his knees, facing downward into his pillow, bracing his body with his right arm.

"More," he grunted, his voice muffled.

I complied, returning to thrusting, slowly at first, then harder. I wasn't sure I was still hitting his prostate at this angle, but Alexander cried out even more loudly than before, his head moving in and out of the pillow he was pressed against, as he began to masturbate frantically with his left hand.

"More," he demanded.

Alexander made no effort to squeeze against me, no effort to coax my cock with his sphincter as it moved inside him. He was totally focused on his own body, and I realized then that that was what he wanted of me, too. He didn't want me to worry about whether I was hitting his prostate or not. He didn't want me to think about maximizing his own sensations. He wanted me to worry about myself, to use his body and his ass for my own satisfaction. He wanted me to be selfish. *That* would maximize his pleasure. The roughness, the abandon, the intensity, that would clear the evening from his mind, would wash everything away, would make him see white.

That's right. That was my job: to pump him so full of cum that he couldn't see straight.

I obliged, grabbing him roughly by the hips, throwing my whole body against him, feeling my waist slapping loudly against the cheeks of his behind as I went balls deep in his ass again and again and again, showing only enough restraint to make sure I wouldn't tear anything.

Alexander came alive, body shuddering and heaving. I could see his left elbow working like a piston as he jacked himself off. We went louder and faster as the organ crescendoed, and I felt my balls tighten and Alexander's body tense.

Then, all at once, Alexander exploded.

"*OH GO~D,*" he screamed into the pillow as his body bucked and heaved, and I could hear the spray of his cum against his bedsheets. Now his body tensed against mine, the involuntary spasms of his orgasm gripping and squeezing my cock, and I fired as though he'd pulled a trigger, grunting and gasping as I blasted him.

The sensation of me cumming inside him sent Alexander to yet another peak, and he cried out again and again as I flooded him. My cum spilled out from inside him, running down his legs, dripping off of his balls, and still we continued, riding the orgasm long and hard.

Eventually Alexander released his own erection, planting his cum-soaked left hand against the bed to brace his body, and it was only a few pumps more before the convulsing subsided. Alexander collapsed onto the bed, rivulets of cum spilling out of his backside as he slid off of me, and he lay panting and gasping against the soaked sheets.

In another minute the organ subsided into a low, quiet drone, then went silent.

"Fuck-ing-hell," Alexander rasped as he lay on his stomach with his head turned to one side, still out of breath. The broad muscles of his back stretched and contracted as he breathed. "That was *exactly* what I needed. Thank you so much, Cole," he added with an exhausted smile. "You're the best."

"It was my pleasure," I said as I crawled on top of him, pressing my body against his, "and I mean that in every sense of the word."

He tilted his head slightly so that I could meet him with my lips, and we kissed, gently, sweetly, affectionately. When my lips left his, his smile was angelic.

"This is nice," he sighed, reaching to take my right hand in his and squeezing it. "But as much as I hate to say it... you should probably go back to your room. If Father finds you here... he'll probably kick you out. Or kill you."

"If he even notices me," I murmured.

"Good point," Alexander chuckled. "Well, then... stay here a few more minutes?"

I smiled, nuzzling against his back. He sighed contentedly.

And the next thing we knew, we were being gently awakened by the morning sun.

XVIII

PREPARATIONS

THE MORNING WAS A QUIET ONE. I assumed most everyone had slept in, considering the insanity of the previous night. Still, Alexander insisted that there would still be morning church, and so when the first beams of light awoke us, he instructed me to slip off to the showers while he stole away to the laundry with a bundle of cum-caked sheets.

And right he was. I toweled off, went back to my room and dressed, and Alexander had only just finished his shower when Levi appeared and announced service in ten minutes. His face looked haggard, as though he hadn't slept at all.

The sanctuary was oddly quiet, and suddenly I realized that it was because the only people present in it were me and the Order of Light: none of the usual locals were in attendance. Had they evacuated? Or were they just too scared?

When it was time for the service to begin, Levi appeared from the side door as usual, but Father Jacob appeared from elsewhere, somewhere behind the altar. The service was a short one, drawing heavily on Chapter 6 of Paul's letter to the Ephesians, which dictates not only that children should obey their parents but also that humanity must don the Armor of God to defend against the devil. The sermon was a two-pronged tirade on righteousness and self-control, with Father Jacob waxing on about how the only way the Order would be able to stand strong against the onslaught of Hell was if it banded together and redoubled its dedication to holiness.

After the service, I was preparing to depart when Father Jacob announced the resumption of communal brunch. Julia had a stony, tight-lipped expression, but she stood up and went toward the door to the hallway leading to the dining area. I exchanged a look with Alexander, and we followed.

I hadn't realized how hungry I was until brunch was mentioned. I hadn't had dinner the previous night, and considering how much exercise I'd had—both outside and inside the church—I definitely needed some sustenance.

As soon as we entered the dining room, Julia pulled Alexander and Paul aside to compare notes about what had happened at each of their posts the previous night. While they talked, I glanced toward the kitchen shutter, which was open, and noticed with interest that Thomas was inside, peeling vegetables. As I entered the kitchen area, Rebecca was leaving with a heaping tray of plated omelets. Thomas was busy over a pile of onions and potatoes.

"Well," I said, "You're not usually the one in the kitchen."

Thomas gave me a sidelong look. His eyes were watery and irritated, likely from the onions.

"It's my punishment for playing the organ at top volume in the middle of the night," Thomas explained. "Father was *not* happy."

"I heard," I said. "That was quite a performance,"

Thomas gave me a dry look. "I could say the same for you."

"Huh?" I asked.

"Well, I assume it was you, anyway. All I could hear was

Alexander. Our walls may be stone, but that doesn't mean they block sound."

I blanched. Then, suddenly, something occurred to me. "Wait a minute," I said. "Is that why you—"

Thomas nodded. "If this is my punishment for playing the organ, imagine what Alexander would have faced for what I can only assume was Olympic sex. To say nothing of you, who came in here as a guest and then I'm guessing came inside my brother. When the rest of the household showed up in the sanctuary and demanded to know what had gotten into me, I told them I had to blow off some steam after all the insanity of the night. But the primary reason was to cover the animal sounds coming from Alexander's room. I mean, seriously," he shook his head. "What I heard before I ran for the organ was loud enough, and I assume that was only foreplay. I can only imagine what it was like when things really got going."

"Wow," I said, genuinely moved that Thomas would cover for us like that. "Um... thank you."

"Eh, it wasn't entirely altruistic," Thomas shrugged. "I also wanted to get out of there. I mean, who wants to lie in bed hearing their own brother having sex?"

"Fair point," I said. "Um... sorry?"

"I'll bet you're not, though," Thomas said, the corner of his mouth curling up slightly. Again I felt a shot of familiarity. "Nor should you be," he continued. "But... really... having sex with abandon like that, right here in the Church of the Holy Guardian...?" He trailed off, but he sounded almost... envious?

At that moment, however, Rebecca returned from setting the table, and Thomas quickly turned his attention back to the vegetables.

"It's been quite a night," Rebecca said as she loaded up another plate. "Apparently Father Jacob and Levi didn't sleep a wink. They were up all night trying to formulate some sort of plan to keep this from happening again. It's clear our wards aren't keeping these things away." She picked up another tray and nearly walked into me.

"Look out!" I called and Rebecca stopped with a start.

"Cole!" She said. "I'm so sorry; I didn't see you."

"Can I help with anything?" I asked.

"Sure you can. Mind taking those two pitchers of juice over there?" She nodded in the direction of the counter. I walked over and picked up the containers. One was orange juice, and the other, I noticed with a wry smile, was pineapple.

Once the table was set and everyone sat down, Father Jacob said a quick prayer over the food, and then we began to eat. I was only two bites into what was a frankly delicious ham and cheese omelet when Levi looked across the table at Alexander.

"Alexander," he said, "Are you still set on doing what you said to me last night?"

"What's this?" Paul asked with interest.

"When Alexander was passing into the church last night, he announced to me that he was going to find the source of the ogres. Apparently, he... knew one of them?"

"Is this another Hunter thing?" Paul asked suspiciously.

"No," Alexander said emphatically. "Someone is taking people from those rehabilitation programs, and probably the homelessness programs too, and turning them into those... those monsters."

"Are you serious?" Julia gasped, aghast.

"I'm certain," Alexander said. "And we're sitting here with our heads in the sand while these people are being hurt."

"This is what they get for using public programs and eschewing the church's guidance," Jacob said gruffly.

"Now, that's just ignorant and callous," Julia declared. "These are *people*."

"People who, mind you, Father, are a threat to the church if we permit them to continue being transformed into these beasts," Alexander pointed out.

Jacob glowered, but said nothing. It seemed like something had hit home.

"I'm going," Alexander said. "Don't try to stop me."

"And," Jacob added, "I assume that THEY will be there?"

"It's possible," Alexander said. "They know that the ogres were humans once too, now. They'll want to get to the bottom of this. They're at least *doing* something."

"We are doing something, too," Jacob retorted. "We are protecting our home, the House of God."

"I'm going," Alexander repeated.

"And I'm going with him," I added.

"You are a guest here," Jacob said, his expression turning much more gentle as he addressed me, "and as such I will not presume to dictate what you can and cannot do outside of these walls. But you, Alexander," he said, his expression hardening as he faced him, "if you are set on doing this, very well, but you will not take Candela with you."

"What?" Now it was Levi who was aghast. "You'd deny your son his own defenses?"

"The equipment of the Order is for the purposes of the Order only," Jacob stated. "This vigilante excursion is not Order work. Besides, if he is truly faithful, the Armor of God will be all the protection he needs."

"This is too much," Levi protested. "Armor is armor, but armor is not complete without a weapon."

"My decision is final," Jacob said.

"Then I'll go, too," Thomas insisted.

"You will not," Jacob replied. "You will be here preparing dinner. Consider it part of your penance for your impromptu midnight recital. You and Rebecca will see to it that Cole and Alexander have a meal waiting when they return. Julia and Levi are to assess our equipment stores and make sure that both nothing is missing and that we have enough to weather another attack. If need be, you will bless more tools for the purpose.

Paul will assess the damages to the property and arrange repairs. Somewhere in this city there must be a God-fearing contractor or stonemason who sees opportunity where others are blinded by fear, and will be willing to perform repairs. And I will spend the day trying to reinforce our spiritual protections. We cannot afford to have these creatures attack again."

"Why were they so obsessed with the church, anyway?" Thomas wondered.

"Because we are holy, and they are not," Jacob said simply. "It is the natural desire of evil to try to destroy good."

"But if these were people…?" Rebecca started.

"Then they have fallen, tainted by the Beast. They are desperate to come here either because they hold the empty belief that stepping on this ground will grant them purification and entrance to the Kingdom of Heaven, or they seek to destroy us utterly. Both, of course, are fruitless wishes."

"But don't you believe in forgiveness and penitence?" I challenged.

"There are those who have made choices so egregious that they cannot be saved," Jacob replied.

"Choices?" Thomas asked. "If these people are being abducted from those programs, where is the choice *they* made?"

"They made those choices long before," Jacob said. "The choices they made that put them in the position of needing those programs in the first place."

"Don't go blaming the victim," Julia replied hotly.

"This is ridiculous," Alexander cried. "I *knew* Marcus. He made some mistakes, but he was a good guy. His heart was in the right place."

"Don't let your own personal failings cloud your judgement," Levi warned.

"That's right," Jacob said. "If you sympathize with sin, it is only because you have failed to reject the sin within you. Be careful on this crusade of yours, Alexander. You don't want to fall so far that you can never climb back up."

With that note of encouragement, we finished brunch, and I stood to clear the table.

"Be careful out there," Thomas said as I dropped off the last pile of dishes.

"Yes," Rebecca said, giving me a sad smile. "Do the Order proud, ok?"

I returned to the rooms, taking a moment to complete my morning routine in the bathroom and brush my teeth. When I left the bathroom, Alexander was leaving his bedroom with a familiar bundle in his hand. We hadn't taken three steps, however, before Jacob appeared in the hallway, holding out his hand.

"Give it here," he said.

You're *really* not letting me take Candela?" Alexander asked. "You would do that to your own son?"

"You know the rules," Jacob said firmly. "You are not above them."

Alexander begrudgingly handed over the bundle, and Jacob unwrapped it, inspecting Candela before wrapping the sword back up.

"You really would deprive your own son of protection?" I demanded in spite of Alexander's attempts to wave me down.

"You are not one of us," Jacob said simply, "so I do not expect you to understand this, but we of the Order realize that our decisions carry consequences."

"This isn't a consequence," I said; "it's a punishment, pure and simple."

Jacob ignored me, turning to Alexander. "I assume you are going to look where the creatures first appeared. Do you know where Cole first encountered them?"

"Um, I'm right here," I said.

"You said they were at the square, right?" Alexander asked me.

I nodded angrily.

"That's where we'll go," I said.

"And when the Midnight Hunters appear, which I am sure they will, be careful," Jacob said. "They may seem trustworthy, but Cedric will cut your throat if it suits his purposes."

Alexander nodded gravely.

"I do not condone this excursion," Jacob said, "but since you seem set on making it, let us know what you find. And be safe." He turned and walked out the open door to the rest of the church.

"He'd be a lot safer if you'd give him his *fucking sword!*" I shouted after him.

"Language!" came Jacob's voice.

I clenched my fists, but Alexander placed a hand on my shoulder. "It's fine," he said with a sigh. "Let's just go."

Once we walked out onto the street, I didn't head toward the square. Instead, I made a beeline for The Hunters' Home.

"Where are you going?" Alexander asked as I strode off. "Isn't the square in the other direction?"

When I explained where I was headed, he balked.

"We can't go there!" he shouted. "That's heading right into the belly of the beast!"

"The *square* is the belly of the beast," I said. "The Hunters' Home is reinforcements. I promised Cuan we would stop there. Besides, don't you want to check in on Marcus?"

That last question triggered an immediate shift in Alexander's demeanor. He turned and walked quickly alongside me.

"So..." he started. "What's so great about Cuan, anyway? I mean, he's a werewolf, isn't he?"

"So what if he is?" I asked.

"Well, I mean, yeah, his human form is stupid hot, but he's basically a monster, right?"

"He is *not* a monster," I said angrily.

"Ok, so not-a-monster-but-a-werewolf. And you like that? What, are you a furry?"

"It's not like that at all," I said. "Not that you or anyone would have any right to judge me if it were. But it's not. In fact, when he's in his wolf shape, that part of him kind of... turns off."

"And yet you know that tidbit," Alexander said, slightly gloomily. "Well, if you're not a furry, then why do you like him?"

"Because he's kind," I replied. "And why do you care?"

"Because he spends time in the company of those... people," he said, nearly spitting out the last word.

"Hey," I said, "at least 'those people' have a place for him. Or what, should he become a part of the Order of Light?"

"Oh, goodness no," Alexander said, shaking his head. "The Order would never accept someone like him."

"And there you go," I said. "So what makes your 'Order' any better, huh? It just seems judgmental and self-righteous to me."

"We are doing the work of God," Alexander said. "We don't need your approval. We have God's."

"And yet, I don't see any angels knocking on *your* door asking for help."

"And what's that supposed to mean?" Alexander demanded.

"Nothing," I muttered. Az had consented to reveal his identity to Cuan, but he clearly didn't wish it to become public knowledge. Plus, I didn't think it was my place to 'out' him without his consent. And anyway, with Alexander going on like this, I didn't really feel like clueing him in. "Besides," I added, changing the subject to something equally pointed, "The Midnight Hunters are the ones trying to save Marcus's life. What would your Order have done?"

Alexander sighed, suddenly deflated. "Nothing," he admitted. "Well, actually, not nothing. They would have slain him where he lay."

"And yet you're so quick to pass judgement on the Hunters," I said. "Why, because Daddy said so?"

"Not just because Father warned me about them, no," Alexander retorted. "I've also seen them continually put you in danger."

"Have you, though?" I challenged. "Or have they just been there for me when I was in danger?"

"Like shooting a crossbow at you in their basement?" Alexander asked.

Now it was my turn to sigh. "Ok, you got me there," I said. "But that wasn't Cuan."

"Cuan again. Seriously, is *one* person who seems decent really enough to make you overlook all the other totally sketchy people in the Midnight Hunters?"

"It is at the Order of Light," I responded, and he glared at me.

Just then, my phone dinged.

"It's Cuan," I said, looking at my phone.

"Well, speak of the devil and he appears," Alexander muttered.

The message read 'r u coming by today', and so rather than text back, I punched the call button.

"Hello?" Cuan asked.

"We're on our way now," I said.

"We?" Cuan asked. "Alexander's with you?"

"Yeah," I said.

"OK," Cuan said. "See you in a bit."

We said our goodbyes and I hung up. When we got to the street that The Hunters' Home was on, however, Lester was waiting in the middle of the sidewalk for us.

"Nope, nope nope," he said agitatedly, waving his hand at Alexander as he hurried toward us. "I didn't want a *phone* from you people in our house, and now Cole brings a *person*?"

"But Uncle Festeeeeeeer," I whined exaggeratedly, and Lester's eyes focused on my face as he glared at me.

"Is there a problem?" Alexander asked impatiently.

"Yes, there's a problem," Lester said emphatically. "The Order of Light denies that we even have a right to exist, and now Cole wants to lead you right to our doorstep. How do we know the Order isn't going to lead an assault on our home, huh?"

Alexander scoffed. "Like the Order would lead an assault on anything. When was the last time they've left the safety of those walls, huh?"

"Good point," Lester admitted. "And yet, you're here."

"Without their blessing," Alexander said. "I'm worried about Marcus. Is he with you? Is he OK?"

"Define 'OK'," Lester said.

"Um... is his condition stable?"

Lester paused. "He's unconscious; he's alive; but his blood is a mess. I won't be able to maintain him long without a transfusion."

"I can't help with that, unfortunately," I said.

"Ah, right," Lester said. "The STI test that needed experts to weigh in."

I glowered at him.

"And Cuan can't, either," Lester mused. "Or Bianca, or Cedric. Bran is Rh-Positive, so he's out..."

"What's Marcus's blood type?" Alexander asked.

"AB-negative," Lester said.

"I'm A-negative," Alexander responded.

Lester stared at Alexander for several seconds. His mind seemed to be making so many calculations that I could almost hear it whirring.

"Come with me," he said at last, walking down the sidewalk toward The Hunters' Home. I nodded at Alexander, and we followed.

We ascended the steps to the porch, where Cuan was anxiously waiting for us. At our approach, he looked visibly relieved.

"Oh thank God," he said as I gave him a hug. "I wasn't sure Lester was going to let you in."

"No time to talk," Lester said, grabbing Alexander by the arm and pushing past Cuan; "getting blood."

"You're drawing blood?" Cuan asked as he and I followed the pair up the stairs. "But... aren't we going to investigate the area under the Square later?"

"I'll be fine," Alexander said. We reached the top of the stairs and Alexander stopped dead, his arm slipping free of Lester's. Cuan and I came to a stop behind him.

There in the hallway was Bran, apparently fresh out of the shower, bare-ass naked. He had been walking away from us, toweling off his feathered hair. His dark skin glistened with water, his muscular back and his round, meaty ass on full display. Alexander gawked. I did, too.

"Get out of the way, Bran," Lester said impatiently, pushing past him.

"Oh, sorry, I didn't see you all there," Bran said, turning unashamedly toward us. Now suddenly he was all pecs and abs. And large, tight balls. And pendulous, uncut cock.

Holy shit, he was hot.

He just smiled.

"Uh, hi," Alexander squeaked.

"Sorry," Bran said, "I'll get outta your way." He ducked into a door on the left to what I assumed was his room, raising his hand and offering Cuan a "Hi, doggo," as he did so. Alexander continued to stare.

I turned to Cuan. "You used to hook up with him?" I whispered.

Cuan nodded.

"Lucky you," I said.

Cuan offered me his adorably dimpled half-smile and simply shrugged.

Suddenly, Lester popped his head out of a doorway further down the hall on the right. "What's taking you so long?" he demanded.

"Right, sorry," Alexander said, giving his head a hard shake. He tugged uncomfortably at the fabric at the front of his trousers, then hurried down the hall to the open doorway.

"Wait a minute," I said to Cuan as we followed him, "don't you all have ensuite bathrooms?"

Cuan shrugged again. "Bran says the shower across the hall has better water pressure. He likes to use that one."

"Well, I'm not complaining," I said, and Cuan gave a short laugh.

Inside the room, which looked like a makeshift lab, Lester was already preparing to put a line in Alexander's arm.

"Where's Marcus?" Alexander asked, looking around.

"He's in the next room over," Lester said.

"Why aren't you doing a direct transfusion?" Alexander asked.

"As I said, Marcus's blood is a mess. I'll have to run a test to make sure of compatibility."

"So... shouldn't you do that before you take a full pint of blood or whatever?" Alexander queried, his face skeptical.

"This is much more efficient," Lester replied, sliding the needle into Alexander's vein. The tubing immediately ran ruby red as it pulled Alexander's blood into a tidy little bag, onto which Lester scrawled "Alexander, A-" with a sharpie.

"So... what's the plan?" I asked as Alexander had his blood drawn. "I assume there's more involved than just wandering off in the direction of the square?"

"The square used to be the top of an old subway line," Cuan said. "It's been out of commission for a while now."

"I remember that line," Alexander said. "That shut down, what, seven or eight years ago?"

"And it's just sat abandoned ever since," Cuan said. "The city was really lazy about disconnecting it from the power grid, so parts of it even still had light, to say nothing of a dangerous electrified third rail situation. It became a kind of haven for the homeless, remember? They used to take shelter there against the cold and the weather. The previous mayor said that the 'infestation' of the subway tunnels was the one of the biggest health and safety problems the city faced."

"Oh, that's right!" Alexander said. "And his calling the homeless problem an 'infestation' was some kind of massive PR debacle."

"And let his opponent run effectively on a platform of providing shelter and rehabilitation," Cuan noted. "But now then, if someone were looking to exploit the homeless situation as bodies for... *that*," he gestured toward an adjoining door, "then the abandoned subway network would be a good place to start."

Alexander nodded. Then he looked toward the door as Lester removed the line from Alexander's arm and taped a cotton swab in place.

"Can... can I see him?" Alexander asked.

Lester walked to the door and quietly turned the handle. "It wouldn't be a good idea to go in there," he said. "But you can see him from here." He pushed the door open, and immediately we could see why Lester was insistent that we keep out. The room was a tangled maze of tubes and wires, monitors and machines. And in the middle of it all, on a big bed, was Marcus. He had been positioned on his stomach, and a tattoo was clearly visible on his meaty cheek. The room also *stank*.

"Why isn't he on his back?" Alexander asked.

"He was vomiting a bit," Lester explained. "Plus drool, bile, all that stuff. I made a makeshift donut pillow for him."

He gestured into the room and we could see Marcus's head face down on a pillow of some sort, beneath which was a long string of drool dripping into a big bucket.

"That's really gross," I said.

"Maybe," Lester said, "but it also keeps him from choking on it. I had to improvise a lot to keep him here. It might have been easier to keep him in the lab like the others, but then I wouldn't be able to monitor his condition as effectively. Perhaps it's unfair, but I'm giving him special treatment."

"Well, I appreciate that, I guess," Alexander said tentatively.

"Good," Lester nodded. "Now go down to the kitchen and get some food; you need to replenish your blood."

We made our way back downstairs, Alexander turning to look at Bran's closed bedroom door as we passed it.

The kitchen was as it had ever been. Cedric was in his usual place cooking by the stove, sunglasses on his face and hat on his head, while Bianca was lounging in her chair, this time wearing what I could only describe as black studded leather lace with a white frilly apron in front.

"Oh yay," she said dryly when we walked in. "Cuan's brought guests again."

"Hello, Bianca," I said.

Her eyes focused on me. "And Casper, too," she added. "Back to haunt us, are you? And you brought Church Boy!" She turned to Cuan with a look of mock sympathy. "Aw, poor doggie, did you get replaced? I guess man's best friend is an altar boy after all."

"What the fuck?" Alexander exclaimed. "What the hell's the matter with you?"

"Just ignore her," I said, waving dismissively. "She's crazy. I think it's the syphilis. I'm guessing she caught it while working at what is clearly an S&M housekeeping service."

"Fuck you," Bianca said.

"No, see, that's how it spreads," I said to her in my best

patronizing tone. "Remember, when you're doing sex cleaning, the rubber is for more than just the gloves."

Bianca crossed her arms and glared at me, but it was a look of begrudging respect and satisfaction.

"So... Alexander needs to eat something," Cuan said to Cedric. "He just gave blood for a transfusion for Marcus."

"OK," Cedric said, without missing a beat. "There are two unopened 32 oz. bottles of spring water next to the refrigerator, plus I am cooking up some pancakes. He needs iron, so get him some raisins from the pantry. Also, there is a little red crystal bottle with a red stopper in there; get that."

Cuan did as he was told and suddenly Alexander had two bottles of water and a pile of raisins in front of him. Cedric, meanwhile, plated a stack of pancakes each for Cuan, Alexander, and Bianca.

"You hungry, Cole?" he asked.

I was a little uncomfortable with his addressing me as though everything was back to being business as usual, but I decided not to deal with it just then.

"I had brunch a little while back," I said.

Well, one pancake, then," he said, plopping one on a plate. Then he turned to Cuan. "Open that vial and put three drops on Alexander's pancakes, will you?"

Cuan moved to pick up the vial, but Alexander waved his hands to stop him.

"Wait, wait," he said, "hold up. What's that?"

"It is a potion to replace lost human blood," Cedric explained. "Very useful."

"Nope," Alexander shook his head. "I'm not taking that. No offense, but I'm not drinking some pagan magic potion that's gonna restore my body but damn my soul."

"I take very much offense, thank you," Cedric retorted. "What are you going to do, then? Just go out toward the subway and faint away when things get exciting?"

"No," Alexander replied, slightly sanctimoniously, "I'm going to do this." He opened one of the bottles of spring water and placed his palm on the open bottleneck. Then he shut his eyes, and began intently whispering something in Latin.

I felt the effect before I saw it: a surge of energy seemed to well up around Alexander and then direct itself toward the bottle. A moment later the contents of the bottle glowed softly with a pinkish light, which faded into just the faintest hint of white.

"Well, well," Cedric said, legitimately impressed. "The Order taught you something useful after all."

"This'll take care of the blood loss," he said, gulping the drink down. Almost immediately his face looked a little less pale.

"Wait," I said. "You can do that, but you still needed to give your own blood for Marcus?"

"This only works on regular human blood," Alexander said. "Lester said Marcus's blood is kind of messed up. I don't know what it'd do to him. I'm guessing that's why you didn't use that sanguinary syrup you have over there?"

Bianca snorted. "That's actually a pretty decent name for the stuff," she said.

"But yes," Cedric replied. "That is exactly right."

"Ok, so now that that's sorted out," Cuan said, stuffing his mouth full of pancakes, "should we go over the plan?"

"There is not all that much to go over," Cedric said. "Just to the northeast of the square, there is an entrance to the abandoned subway. The city tried to seal it up, but we passed it yesterday and I noticed that the recent... activity in the area has caused it to reopen. That is your best point of entry. You three can enter from there; the rest of us will cover areas where ogres have appeared before in case we detect any new activity.

"Oh," Alexander said, looking back toward the stairs. "So... Bran's not coming with us?"

"No," Cedric said, raising an eyebrow. "He and Bianca will sweep the surrounding streets. I shall watch near where the massive collection of ogres appeared that headed toward the church. Az will keep a lookout near the square."

"What if ogres show up somewhere new?" I asked. "Haven't they appeared in different places most of the time?"

"Good strategic question," Cedric nodded. "Lester will be monitoring seismic activity in the area. Rumbles will likely mean that ogres are popping up."

"How is Lester monitoring seismic activity?" I asked, taking a bite of pancake.

"Hacking," Bianca said matter-of-factly.

"Huh?" Alexander asked.

"Lester has... access to the University's meteorology and geology department," Cedric explained. "It turns out the lab was keeping tabs on tectonic activity in the area. The computers are still running, and they have records of events that match each ogre sighting, so Lester has surmised that they will likely detect any future ones, too."

"And... nobody at the University has said anything?" I asked.

"They've evacuated, remember?" Cuan said.

"Right," Cedric added. "And if anyone is monitoring the system remotely, they have not posted anything anywhere that we have noticed. There is probably a graduate student in charge of the system who has been instructed to hold back data for a dissertation."

"Sounds about right," Cuan muttered.

"Anyway, we should move out," Cedric announced. "We do not know what we will find under the square, but if whoever is responsible for what is going on down there is keeping tabs on things, then we do not know how long we will have to wait for an opening to get down there. If you have anything else to take care of, do it now."

"Right," Bianca said, disappearing out the door to the front hall.

"Um," Alexander asked, "is there a bathroom?"

Cedric gave directions and off Alexander went.

"That's not a bad idea, actually, if we'll be waiting a while," I said, standing from my chair.

"Hold a moment, Cole," Cedric said. I turned and looked at him.

"What is it?"

Cuan watched us in tight-lipped silence.

"I hear from Cuan that you have been training to understand your powers under Az."

"What about it?" I responded coolly.

"Az has told me that you are progressing nicely."

"And?"

Cedric's brow darkened behind his sunglasses. "If you are looking for an apology, you will be disappointed," he said gruffly. "I think my decision was sound, and I do not believe I put you in legitimate danger."

"It sure felt dangerous to me," I said. "Are we done?"

Cedric visibly bristled, until Cuan cleared his throat loudly.

"*But,*" Cedric said, frowning. "I understand that my methods were—are—were... unacceptable to you. And it seems clear that it was not necessary to apply those methods for you to make progress, because you have found another means of training. Furthermore, I believe that you are both insightful and an asset to our ranks, and additionally we have yet to make good on our pledge to help you understand your past. So..."

"So...?" I asked.

"So if it came to be that you wished to stay here again, provided you understood and respected my role as leader of the Hunters, I would not see any reason why I would need to subject you to such training measures again."

I stared at him coldly for a moment. "That clearly wasn't easy to say," I said at last.

"It was not," Cedric admitted.

"But as an apology, it sucked."

"It was not an apology," Cedric stated.

"I am well aware," I said, turning to head to the bathroom. At the door to the hall, I looked over my shoulder. "I'll consider it," I said. "But this is the beginning of negotiations, not the end." And then I left.

XIX

WHAT LIES BENEATH

ONLY A SHORT TIME LATER, we headed out from The Hunters' Home toward the square. Bianca and Bran had apparently departed earlier, and Az was traveling to his post directly from the hotel. Cedric, Cuan, Alexander, and I walked together in tense silence, unsure of what the evening was going to bring.

After we walked two blocks, Cedric peeled off down another street, wishing us good luck as he did so. And then it was just the three of us.

"So... any idea what we're going to find?" Alexander swallowed as we walked.

"Nope," Cuan said. "But we'll know soon enough."

I nodded. We walked another block.

"So..." Cuan said, "you seemed rather taken with Bran."

"Um, w-what?" Alexander stammered, face going bright red. "What makes you say that?"

"Oh, please," I said. "'Where's Bran?' 'Will Bran be coming too?' You really couldn't be more obvious."

"So sue me for finding a guy attractive," Alexander said defensively. "I mean, we just came up the stairs, and he was just *there*, with that body and that ass and those pecs..."

"Yes indeed," I said, savoring the memory.

"Plus... did you see that cock? He had a *massive* cock."

"Knows how to use it, too," Cuan said with a smirk.

"Wait, what?" Alexander stammered, face turning even brighter red.

"I'll bet," I said appreciatively.

Alexander fidgeted uncomfortably.

"Still, you certainly seem to have changed your tune," I said to Alexander.

"What do you mean?" he asked.

"About the Midnight Hunters," I said.

"What, just because I think they have some hot guys?" Alexander asked.

"'Guys,' plural?" I asked pointedly, and Cuan's quiet smirk widened.

"Whatever, shut up," Alexander replied hotly. "And besides, just because I think that Bran guy is hot doesn't mean anything. I don't even know what he's like." He paused for a moment. "... What's he like?"

"He's... fine, I guess," Cuan said noncommittally. "He's friendly."

"Is he?" Alexander asked, looking at me.

"I couldn't really tell you," I admitted. "I've barely interacted with him."

"No, see, that's no good," Alexander said. "Personality is important. That's what makes Cole so great," he wrapped his arms around my left arm possessively. "Among other things," he added. "What do you think, Cole?"

"What is this, *The Dating Game*?" I asked. "What, do I need to list out my top ten traits I'm looking for or something?"

"Didn't you already do that in your online dating profile?" Alexander asked.

"Wait," Cuan interjected, suddenly deeply interested, "Cole has a *dating profile*? Why did I not know about this?"

"It's from before I lost my memories." I said.

"And where can I find this dating profile?" Cuan asked.

"Here," Alexander said, pulling out his phone and punching the screen. "I have it bookmarked."

"You have it *bookmarked*?" I asked as Alexander handed Cuan his phone. I couldn't decide if I was irritated at Alexander's suddenly putting me up on display or relieved that he was being something other than sulky and suspicious around Cuan.

"I may... um... enjoy looking at it when I can't sleep," Alexander admitted.

"Well, I can see why," Cuan said, a grin spreading across his face as he flipped through my pictures. "Storytime with Nerdy-Hunk21," he announced, holding out the photo of me equipped with nothing more than a book and a carefully placed sheet.

"Yes, yes, I get it, I'm hot," I said, rolling my eyes exaggeratedly. "Now can we focus, please? We're here."

Cuan and Alexander stopped walking and looked up, then ducked quickly against the wall of the building we had been rounding. About half a block in front of us was the entrance to the abandoned subway station. True to what Cedric had said, the big metal gate sealing off the entrance was hanging open from one hinge.

"Do you see anyone?" Alexander said quietly, clicking his phone off and putting it in his pocket.

"Not a soul," I said. Slowly we walked toward the station entrance, keeping an eye out for anyone nearby. As we approached, however, Cuan suddenly shot his hand out in front of us to stop us from moving.

"What?" I asked.

Cuan pointed. There, above the entrance to the subway, someone had hooked up a security camera. It clearly was newer than the rest of the entrance, as it was quite a bit shinier. Plus it was bolted up, and wires were clearly visible running down inside the subway, rather than concealed inside the walls as one would expect. The mount of the camera had been damaged in the recent chaos and it now hung straight down over the entrance instead of pointing slightly outward, but I could still make out a faint blinking red light that told us it was operational.

"Shit," I said.

Cuan nodded. "We can't risk being caught on camera by whoever that is. We have to find a way around it and then keep an eye out for more cameras inside."

"Well," I asked, "How are we supposed to get around that?"

"Leave it to me," Alexander said smugly. He raised his right hand, palm up, and slightly extended his thumb and first two fingers.

"*Lux,*" he declared, voice clear and resonant. Almost immediately, a little ball of light formed, balanced neatly between his fingers. Cuan and I stared as Alexander raised his hand higher and turned so it was pointed outward. "*Radius,*" he said firmly, and suddenly the ball of light burst forward as a beam, which sliced through the mount and the wires, sending the camera clattering to the ground.

"Holy shit," I managed.

Alexander grinned. "See? I'm not defenseless without Candela."

There were no other cameras as we crept down through the dark abandoned subway entrance. There were no lights, either, but thankfully(?) the square above had been damaged enough that some daylight filtered down into the sealed-off depths.

We descended a dark stairwell with a broken escalator, at the base of which was a landing with what seemed to be an abandoned ticket office and some shuttered stores. I could make out a donut place and a sub shop as we passed down. A sharp squeak made us all jump, and we turned to see the shadow of a massive rat scurrying away.

We climbed over the ticket gate and down a long hallway

leading to a subway platform. Here were the remains of what looked like a tent city, with rows of dilapidated tents and canvases along the back of the platform. The air was thick with the smell of garbage and body odor.

"This must have been where the homeless were," Alexander observed quietly. "I guess the city took them in to the shelters."

"Uh-uh." Cuan shook his head. "Something's not right. If the city were relocating homeless people to the shelters, the people would have taken their belongings, right?"

I looked again. There among the abandoned tents were sleeping bags, duffel bags, and trash bags packed with blankets, stuffed animals, and other worldly mementos. One stash of food had been ripped open and clearly devoured by rats. It was as Cuan said: something wasn't right.

We walked along the tent city and eventually found ourselves at what looked like a maintenance office. Here, however, Cuan stopped again. He pointed down.

"What?" I whispered.

"Look. The light under the door is different."

The light under the door was ever so dim, but visible.

"So what?" Alexander said quietly. "Perhaps there's another hole up above that light is filtering down."

"Nope," Cuan responded. "Outside light doesn't cycle every few seconds."

"Huh?" I said. I looked down again, more carefully this time. Cuan was right: the light under the door was dim, but the relative brightness of it changed very slightly every few seconds.

"Something's in there," Cuan said emphatically. We nodded. Slowly, he reached for the handle, and put his weight against it.

Nothing happened.

"Locked," Cuan said.

"Can we break it down?" Alexander asked.

"And make that much noise?" Cuan asked. "No way. If anyone else is down here, that would definitely draw their attention."

"Then what do you suggest?" Alexander challenged.

"I have an idea," I said. I turned and faced the door. Slowly, I breathed in, then breathed out.

"Cole, are you sure?" Cuan asked, guessing at what I had in mind. "What if you get sick? What if you get stuck in there?"

"I won't get stuck," I said. "But sick? Probably. Still, it's our best option."

I concentrated on my own body, on my clothes, on the bounds of my self-identity. Carefully, deliberately, I pictured myself, every detail I could think of. And then, just like I had with Az, I visualized the world around me melting away.

I felt the ground soften under my feet, and suddenly everything had a familiar afterimage.

"There," I breathed.

"You OK?" Cuan asked with concern.

I nodded. Then I slowly stepped toward the door. And through.

My eyes focused as best they could on the office beyond. Clearly, as Cuan had suggested, it was in use, though currently, mercifully, it was unoccupied. Two monitors danced with light at either end of a desk. It was hard to make out the images on the monitors with the afterimages they were leaving in my vision, but as far as I could tell, the monitor on the left, the brighter one, was cycling through security camera footage of each of the subway station entrances. One of these was a cloud of static, doubtless the one that Alexander had disabled. The second monitor, however, was both easier to read and more worrisome. On this monitor was a scrolling list of what seemed to be hexadecimal labels, and next to each of those, a status indicator. The scrolling was currently in the late 20s:

28> STABLE
29> EMPTY
2A> STABLE
2B> EMPTY
2C> EMPTY
2D> BREACH
2E> BREACH
2F> BREACH
30> BREACH
31> BREACH
32> BREACH

And on it went.

Between the monitors, on the desk, were some papers. There was just enough light from the monitors to make out a folder atop the rest of the messy pile. I struggled to read its cover, what with the dimness and the afterimages.

"What's in there?" Alexander asked through the door.

"All kinds of things," I said. "None of them good."

"Can you open the door?" Alexander asked.

"Maybe?" I said. "I just have to—"

"HALT! POLICE!" came a shout from somewhere outside the office.

"Shit," Cuan growled.

"PUT YOUR HANDS IN THE AIR!" Came a second voice.

"HANDS UP! HANDS UP!" Came the first voice. The shouting continued, getting louder.

"No, this is good," Alexander said. "We can show them what you found. We can expose this whole place."

Alarmed and doubtful, I looked rapidly around the office. My eyes fell on the folder on the desk again. This time, the left monitor was showing the bright white static snow from the broken camera, and the light was just enough for me to make out the cover of the folder, even with the afterimages.

"OPERATION CITYWIDE ENFORCEMENT", read the

title, and below that, "SOLDIER DEVELOPMENT DIVISION". Beneath that title were two images: the seal of the city, and the seal of the police department.

Holy fucking shit.

"Guys," I managed to rasp. "Get out of there."

"But they can help us," Alexander protested as the voices got louder.

"No they won't. They're not your friends."

"I won't leave you trapped in—" Cuan started.

"I can go anywhere," I said. "You need to get out of here. GO!"

The shouts were more frantic. Suddenly there was a gunshot. There was a clang as the bullet ricocheted off the door.

"*Scintillo!*" came Alexander's shout, and from behind the door frame I could see a bright flash. The shouts of "HANDS UP!" turned to intense cursing, and I heard Alexander shout "Split up!" as he and Cuan scattered, immediately followed by round after round after round of pistol fire.

Frantically, I turned my attention back to the office. I needed evidence. I reached for the folder, but my hand passed through it. Shit.

Then, suddenly, something occurred to me. When I had gone incorporeal, or 'faded', as I had been coming to think of it since Az's training session, my clothes had come with me. But that wasn't all.

I reached into my pocket and pulled out the smartphone. It had faded with me. As long as I continued to hold it, I reasoned, it would remain with me. And it was on.

The screen read "No Signal." No surprise there: I was underground in a subway, and even if I wasn't, an incorporeal phone probably wouldn't pick up cellular waves.

But perhaps it would pick up light. After all, when I faded, I didn't turn invisible. My body still blocked light—at least mostly.

I held my phone up and punched the camera button. On came the flashlight as well, which was extremely disorienting, but I managed to regain my focus. I pointed it at the monitor with the status report and hit the shutter button.

Satisfyingly, I heard a click, and an image of the monitor, albeit slightly obscured by the glare of the flashlight reflection, appeared on the screen.

Running footsteps stopped outside the door to the office.

"I think they split up," came one voice.

"Check the main entrance, where the camera was broken," came the other. "I'm gonna look in here. I thought I heard a third voice shouting from inside."

Immediately the handle jiggled, then there was the rattling of keys.

I wasn't sure if whoever was outside the door would notice me if they stormed in. But they had heard my voice, and they were therefore looking for me. Those seemed to be two possible prerequisites for being aware of my presence. I wasn't about to take any chances.

Holding the phone as steady as I could, I shined the flashlight on the folder on the desk and snapped a picture. Then I retreated through the rear wall of the office, my body sliding through a foot of thick concrete before reaching an open space.

I was in what looked like an abandoned subway line, except that it was lined with big, empty vats. Some of them were broken. There were no lights, but I could nonetheless see thanks to the slivers of evening light trickling down from a gaping hole in the ceiling far above. I tried to navigate through the space, but it was hard with all the debris and piping and tracks leaving afterimages before my eyes. However, suddenly, I spied something familiar: a huge chain with a giant ball attached to the end. The ball itself was on a pile of debris, but under that debris was a limp blue hand, and I realized that this was probably the blue ogre that had first surfaced after I had helped defeat the phantom. I felt a twinge of sadness at the realization that it, too, had likely been a person at one point.

Then I saw it, caught in a tight loop in the chain: a pair of khaki pants. I hurried over to it and plunged my hand into the pocket. When I reached, I felt my hand pass frustratingly through a set of keys, and then through a wad of cash. I groaned. I couldn't reclaim my keys—and, therefore, my apartment—while I was incorporeal, but if I regained my solidity, I'd be too disoriented to escape.

I groaned again. It occurred to me also that, perhaps now that I was better at shifting my phase, I could probably gain entry to my apartment, but I couldn't very well unlock it and leave it that way, and getting confused and nauseous every time I entered and exited did not sound appealing. No, the only long-term solution would be keys. I glared at the pair of pants, frustration welling up within me, trying to decide what to do.

Within seconds, however, the decision was made for me. I heard shouting from farther down the tunnel, then rapid footsteps, then lights flashed to life above me, some of them flickering rapidly. The sudden change in brightness made the afterimages all the more disorienting, and I threw myself toward the wall of the subway, becoming engulfed in the thick brick and solid ground.

It was dark. I felt the earth pressing into me. And only then did I realize that if I wanted to get out, I would need to go up.

I remembered the feeling of flying through the air after the ogre had thrown me during one of my previous experiences with incorporeality. The ground had stopped me then simply because I'd let it. It was a different viscosity, and I'd reached my hands into it to slow my travel. Perhaps the same concept would work here. I needed to grip the earth, to feel it instead of move through it.

I needed to swim.

So swim I did, awkwardly, upwardly, keeping the edge of the open subway tunnel to one side to keep my sense of direction. Eventually I lost the tunnel, and then I was just passing through dark earth.

I didn't dare breathe. I didn't dare think. I didn't dare imagine what it would be like to regain my solidity in such a space. I just concentrated on moving.

And, suddenly, I felt pipes. Then pavement. And, at last, air.

I was in an alley. I had no idea where I was beyond that, but there was no sign of a subway entrance, no sound of police.

I was probably safe. And, more importantly, I was exhausted. I was out of breath; I gasped for air, but my incorporeal lungs had trouble pulling it in. I had been holding my breath while trying to get to the surface. I needed air. I craved it. I needed to be able to breathe.

And suddenly, as if in response, the afterimages coalesced and overlapped, and the world was abruptly solid again.

My previous experiences with incorporeality had been brief. This time, however, I had faded for several minutes, and had engaged in much more activity than before. When the world became solid again, it hit me hard. The fog was thick. The air was cold. I could barely see. It reminded me of what it had been like to regain consciousness immediately after losing my memories, and that recollection scared me. Could that have been what happened? Had I pushed myself so hard that I had forgotten everything when the world snapped back into place? Was it going to happen again? I tried to concentrate. I didn't want to lose my memories again. I didn't want to forget the people I'd met. Alexander. Cuan. I tried to picture them, struggled to keep them in my mind as I stumbled down the street, gasping for breath. Vertigo hit and I dropped to my knees.

The images in my mind wavered. Was I forgetting them? Or I was I just losing consciousness?

Then, suddenly, I felt warmth. I heard a voice. A familiar voice.

".o..."

The blackness in my head stopped thickening. In my mind, I struggled toward the voice, strained toward it.

".o..."

That was my name. It was my name. I knew my name.

".ol.."

I hadn't realized that my body had been shaking until then, until it stopped.

".ole."

"Cole."

The world snapped back into place. The fog melted away. And there was Cuan, holding me as he always held me.

"Hi," I said weakly.

"Hi," he said back, golden eyes glinting in the lamplight. I realized suddenly that it was dark, but I didn't look around. I only had eyes for him.

"You found me," I said.

He tapped his nose, his half-smile widening into a grin. "I'll always find you," he said. "Can you stand?"

"I... think so," I responded, rising to my feet.

"Good," Cuan said. "We should find Alexander and get out of here."

"Yeah," I agreed. Cuan propped me up on his shoulder as we started to hurry down the street as quickly as I could manage. "We have to talk about what I found. You'll never believe it. I found papers. With the city's official seal and—"

Suddenly, there was a quick, dull noise, and Cuan's eyes widened as his body stiffened.

"Cuan?" I asked. Cuan coughed. He reached his arm toward his back and staggered. Now it was me holding him up.

"Cole..." he managed as he slumped to the ground.

"CUAN!" I screamed.

Footsteps approached. Quickly.

"Cole? Cuan?"

It was Alexander. Immediately he was at my side.

"I was coming around the corner when I heard you scream. What...?"

He stopped short, mouth agape. I looked at him, then followed his eyes. There was a dart sticking out of the back of Cuan's right shoulder. A dart with a cartridge of some sort in it.

"Cole..." Cuan gasped again, looking at me. His eyes unfocused as he started to shake. "What... what happened?"

"I... I don't know," I said, panic pushing at the edge of my senses. I fought to press it back. "You've been shot."

"Sho...t?"

"What happened?" came a voice as a woman rushed to our side.

Julia.

"What are you doing here?" Alexander asked.

"Levi and I were worried, so we followed you," she explained. "What is going on?"

"Cuan got hit by some kind of dart," I said frantically.

"Let me see," she demanded. Her movements were sharp and precise, like a field medic. She turned Cuan over, pulling the dart from his shoulder. His shuddering continued.

"Cuan!" I shouted.

"This is... aconitine," Julia said, looking at the dart in horror. "What in the hell?"

"Aconitine?" I asked.

"From monkshood. Wolf's-bane." She said.

Wolf's-bane. Poison.

"Cuan, can you hear me?" I asked, clutching him as he spasmed. "You have to shift. You have to purge your system."

"I... I'm try..ing." His voice was shuddering and shaky. "I... can..'t."

Panic took me. What the fuck what the fuck what the fuck.

"At this dosage he'll be dead within hours," Julia said frantically.

"I can..'t... feel my arms..." Cuan managed.

"What's going on?" came another voice. Az was at my side.

"It's Cuan," Alexander said immediately. "Wolf's-bane."

"The aconitine got directly into his bloodstream," Julia said. "You need to filter his blood."

"Cuan!" I shouted again. "Please shift!"

"I..." he managed. "Why...can't I..."

"What in the hell?" Julia said again, looking at the capsule more closely.

"Heal him!" I demanded of Az.

"Healing... isn't really my purview," Az explained, kneeling next to me. "I can delay his death, but it'll be agonizing."

Cuan nodded, eyes on mine but directing his assent to Az, then braced himself as Az placed his hands on him. His pain seemed to increase exponentially, but he focused against it.

My mind was unraveling. My body felt like it was about to overheat.

"There's something else in here," Julia said, still looking at the capsule. "A spiritual poison. Where the hell did they get this from?"

"What is it?" Alexander asked.

"It's a powerful binding ichor," Julia explained. "But it's curable. We need Seraphiel's tears."

"What?" Az and I asked in unison, looking at Julia.

"It can burn away the curse. It might even burn away the aconitine. We have a vial in the room behind the sanctuary. It's a green liquid in a bottle with a golden stopper, sitting on the altar."

"Behind the sanctuary... The Chamber of the Guardian?" Alexander asked, and Julia nodded.

"How did you obtain Seraphiel's tears?" Az demanded.

"One of the Order received them a century ago," Julia said. "They've been passed through the leaders to Jacob."

"Will they let us—" Alexander started.

"If there was ever a time to use them, it's this," Julia said. "We only need a drop."

"It's not safe here," Az said. "Lester has a machine for filtering blood that he uses for Bianca. I'll take Cuan back to The Hunters' Home and have Lester use it to start filtering out the wolf's-bane and keep him from death. You three find those tears and bring them to me."

"You two go," Julia said. "If there's someone around here with aconitine darts, then Levi is in danger. I need to find him."

"Good luck," Alexander said.

"You too," Julia replied, racing off.

Az stood, lifting Cuan from my arms as he did so. It was unbearable to let him go.

"Co.... le....." Cuan managed, looking over at me.

"I'll be right there," I said. My entire body felt as though it was about to ignite. "I promise."

And Azrael was gone. It felt like a part of me went with him.

I wanted to fall apart, but instead I turned to Alexander.

"Come on," he said. "There's a door in the back of the Sanctuary that leads to the Chamber of the Guardian."

I nodded and ran. And ran. My body burned as I sprinted through the streets, the world seeming to fall away around me, my feet seeming to barely touch the ground as my stride grew longer and wider. Alexander couldn't keep up, but that didn't matter. Nothing mattered but getting the cure for Cuan. Alexander would catch up once I got to the church anyway.

After minutes of running that seemed interminable, I arrived at the church, out of breath and panting. The stone building stretched imposingly before me, the structure somehow much less welcoming in the cloudless night. Light flickered dimly from the windows, so I knew someone had to be there. I made for the great front doors, prepared to pound on them, but to my surprise they were unlocked.

The sanctuary was empty, illuminated by candles on the torch of every pew, marking a silent passageway to the back of the altar. Something about the space seemed to prohibit running, but I strode to the back of the sanctuary as quickly as I could, stepping behind the altar, where I noticed that the stonework formed a single door.

I pushed it open, and inside was a dark room. I reached my arms to the sides inside, feeling along the walls for a lightswitch, knowing that I wouldn't find any—but nor did I need any.

I couldn't see much of the interior in the dark, but the dim stretch of candlelight from the sanctuary behind me illuminated the one thing I needed to see in the room: a simple altar, upon which sat a small golden box, and beside it a tall, ornate vial filled with green liquid that glittered in the flickering light.

Seraphiel's Tears.

There would be time for explanations and apologies later. I walked into the dark room, straight to the altar, reaching to take the liquid that would save Cuan's life in my hands.

Just before my fingers touched the vial, however, there was a loud rush of energy and a white flash, and found myself unable to move any further, as though I were running up against an invisible barrier.

Confused, I looked around as my eyes adjusted, and realized that I was standing in the center of what was now a glowing circle on the floor, etched and covered in symbols. Light flooded up from inside it, and suddenly I felt chains wrapping around my body, lifting me from the ground, spinning me around and suspending me in the air with my legs bound together and my arms outstretched, leaving me completely unable to move beyond turning my head. The chains glowed and hummed, freezing and burning at the same time, and I was unable to free myself from them.

I was now facing the door to the sanctuary, and in the light from the circle I could see that I was not alone in the room.

Jacob stood just inside the door, looking at me with a serenely menacing smile.

"Welcome, Cole," he said, voice smooth as ice. "Feeling larcenous today, are we?"

"Please," I said. "I need to use Seraphiel's Tears."

"Oh?" Jacob asked.

"I need them to save someone's life," I pleaded. "The Hunters were helping Alexander and me investigate the pit where the ogres came from. You won't believe what we found. But all that can wait for later—one of the Hunters was shot with wolf's-bane and some sort of other poison. We need the Tears to heal him."

"And so you came for them," Jacob said. "Good thinking. You did the right thing."

"So let me down so I can take them to him," I said.

"No, no, no," Jacob replied, shaking his head. "That wouldn't be right at all. Your place isn't with the Hunters. It is here with us. The Church of the Holy Guardian needs you."

"I need to save Cuan," I shouted. "What the fuck don't you understand?"

Jacob's face wrinkled in disapproval. "Language," he said.

Something stirred in the back of my head as I continued to struggle and fight against the chains. "Let me go!" I cried again.

"That would defeat the purpose of everything we did to get you here," Jacob explained. "It all worked so well."

"What worked?" I asked, confused and furious.

"After the attack the previous night, I knew we needed a stronger ward. A shroud. One only you could provide. When Levi told me last night that Alexander was planning to go search the square, I knew that you would go with him and that the Midnight Hunters would likely be there, and thus we had an opportunity. I didn't forbid Alexander from his little extracurricular excursion, but I forbade him to take Candela with him, allowing Levi to feign concern. That way, it would be easy for him to convince Julia that he was worried about you two and that they needed to provide support, knowing that after he slipped away and shot Cuan, she would immediately be able to identify the poison and send you here."

It was a trap. It was all a trap. The Order had set me up. And Cuan.

Cuan.

"You fucking second-rate Judas knock-off," I growled, ire boiling up within me. "I'm going to get out of here and save Cuan, and then I'm going to shove my foot so far up your ass that the two-foot pole you have up there is going to come flying out your nose."

I felt the now familiar shift of my body, the entire world melting to take on an afterimage. As before, my clothes came along with me, but unlike before, white flames licked up and down the chains and around the circle as my whole person faded into incorporeality.

But I still couldn't move.

Jacob's face had shifted into an expression of concern when the flames rose up, but now fixed back into his previous expression of sinister satisfaction.

"Spirit Chains," he said with satisfaction. "True to their name. That, plus the Key of Solomon, are enough to keep you right where we need you."

The Key of Solomon. Whatever had been growing in the back of my mind snapped forward. The circle. Being trapped. I had experienced all of this before.

My mind wracked with confusion as Jacob laughed quietly. The flames waned and flickered as I felt the chains finish adjusting to my incorporeal form and lock into place.

"You must be surprised," Jacob said. "But we need you. As we told you before, the forces that would destroy us are gaining in power, and our prayers and wards are losing their efficacy. The attack on our home should be evidence enough of that. But you... spirits and monsters seem to pass by without giving you a second glance. Not surprising, as you're clearly one of them."

He walked behind me and I craned my neck to keep him in view. "Which is why," he continued, caressing the lid of the ornate golden box on the altar with his fingers, "this vessel will be the perfect home for you."

I continued to struggle against the chains, to no avail.

"It's an age-old practice," Jacob crooned, "binding spirits and demons to physical objects. You will fulfil your true purpose here, putting your unnatural power to good use, hiding our entire church from the eyes of the Adversary and his thralls, so we can continue to pursue our good works in peace."

There was so much wrong with that sentence, I didn't know where to begin. Not like I could voice them anyway.

"Father?" came a voice from in front of me, and I snapped my head forward to see Alexander standing in the doorway, an ashen expression on his face. "What are you doing?"

"Saving all of us. Saving you," Jacob said.

"Leave Cole alone!" Alexander shouted, running forward.

"You will HALT!" his father roared.

And Alexander did, long-standing, automatic obedience winning out over everything else.

I tried to scream at him, to beg him to help, but no voice came. It was as though the Spirit Chains were choking the wind out of me. I succeeded only in agitating my bonds, sending flames of white whipping around the circle once more. I was becoming unhinged, losing all sense of myself—were the flames coming from the chains, the circle... or me?

"I am doing what needs to be done," Jacob continued. "You

will not question me. Surely you understand that the safety of the Order, of your own family, is paramount above all else."

Alexander walked toward the circle, fighting an internal struggle that only he really understood.

"Disturb this ritual and you relinquish your family and your place in the Order of Light," Jacob said. "You know nothing of the importance of what I am doing."

Alexander looked up at my face, despair writing across his features. It was then that I knew. In spite of everything, in spite of all his frustration and his growth and his desire for freedom, when faced with the choice of betraying me or betraying his Church, the weight of his past was too much to bear. Alexander had grown, yes, but not enough to throw off the shackles of his father and the fetters of this manipulative, all-consuming perversion of his Faith. The decision had been made.

But that wasn't what I cared about just then. That wasn't what I had come for. I craned my head, twisting back to the altar, casting my gaze at the gold-gilded vial of green liquid that glittered near the golden box.

I silently begged Alexander to understand. He walked slowly around the circle, his father watching him like a sheriff ready to mete out swift and violent judgement at the first sign of an infraction. He stopped in front of the green liquid, and lifted it in his hands.

"Seraphiel's Tears," Jacob said. "You can dispose of those; we have no need of them anymore."

Alexander took the vial in his palm and stepped backward, moving toward the door.

"If you're thinking of saving that wretched beast," Jacob said, "it would be less of a waste to dump them on the ground. Or would you prefer to defile your mother's memory," he added, a wicked edge coming into his voice, "by saving the monster that killed her?"

It was a fucking ridiculous accusation. Cuan and Alexander

were the same age; Cuan would have been a newborn when Alexander's mother died. It was a bald and transparent attempt at manipulation, but nevertheless Alexander's face blanched at the suggestion.

I struggled and tried to shout again, succeeding only in rattling my chains and sending more white flames spiraling through my magical cage.

"Now leave us!" Jacob demanded, and with one last look, Alexander was gone.

I craned my neck around again as Jacob smiled widely and creaked open the lid of the box. The space inside was like a vacuum, pulling me toward it, my body, my being folding in on itself as it slid toward the small vessel. I felt as though I were melting away, my spirit dissolving through the chains, slipping between the links, as I was sucked in toward the chamber.

"It's better this way," Jacob said smoothly. "It kills two birds with one stone. More, really, if we consider that we are getting rid of that wolf in human's clothing, too. You are clearly a terrible influence on Alexander, driving him to stoop to perversions, convincing him that there is more than one way to interpret scripture, and doing God only knows what else to him with your silver tongue. Your sacrifice here will protect this place for eternity."

My entire being was fully contained within the box now. Jacob peered in through the open lid, continuing to smile his snakelike smile.

"Don't think badly of me," he crooned. "A man must do what's best for his people. Think of my sons. After all, what would Jesus do?"

From somewhere deep inside me, my voice resonated, clear and defiant.

"Asks the man who's sticking me in a fucking tomb."

With a furious roar, Jacob slammed the lid shut, and then all was black.

XX

(RE)AWAKENING, AGAIN

THE WHOLE WORLD WAS DARK. Thick. Heavy. Closed.

Was I asleep?

Was I alive?

It felt familiar, and yet different. The blackness before had been when I was shut away inside of myself. But this... now I was *being* shut away, closed off from the world. How long it had been that way, I didn't know. At what point I became aware of the blackness rather than simply inhabiting it, I had no idea.

What had happened?

A sensation. A memory.

I'd been tired, exhausted. I'd been trapped. That much, I remembered.

Now I felt nothing.

But why was I suddenly aware of nothing?

Something had pushed against the corner of the blackness.

It pushed again. Was it a sound?

No. It wasn't a sound. It was... movement.

What was it? Where was it coming from?

Whatever it was, it was straining.

Something was out there.

I searched outward, toward the motion. I felt the darkness expand ever so slightly around me, then stop.

Something was in the way; something was separating me from the motion outside.

But it wasn't my body.

In fact, where was my body?

My body was gone. Or was it not gone, and just diffused?

I needed to open my eyes. But I had no eyes.

Open.

OPEN.

Nothing.

Had I been sleeping?

No. I hadn't been sleeping.

I had been trapped.

Trapped, and put to work.

I don't know how long it was before the motion came again. This time it was stronger, more intense. But it wasn't my own effort that caused it: this was coming from the outside. But it was enough for me to push back.

Push. Break. Break through.

Open.

The thin arc of light came back, and this time I caught my mind on it, willed it to stay.

More. Give me more.

And then, suddenly, the darkness gave way, and I spilled out into a field of light.

I gasped, coughed, sputtered.

If I was gasping, I was breathing.

If I was breathing, I had a body.

Right, I remembered: my body.

I pushed my awareness outward, felt it expand to fill my face, my limbs, my core. In some places, my body was cold. In others, it was warm. I searched my body and found my eyes. They were open, staring, but all they saw was gray.

And then I felt arms on me, something pulling me up, and I realized the gray I had been seeing was the floor. But the rest of the world seemed gray, too.

The arms around me were warm, reassuring. And then came the voice.

I couldn't understand it, but it kept saying a name.

A name. I knew that name.

".o..."

I focused. This was my name.

I just had to hear it.

".ol.."

".ole."

Almost there. Concentrate.

"Cole."

And the world came into focus.

"Uh..." I muttered.

"Oh my God, Cole, it's really you."

I knew that voice. But I felt disoriented. I couldn't place it.

Slowly, I turned my eyes up.

"Come on, honey," the voice urged. "Stay with me; we don't have a lot of time."

My eyes focused on the face above me, on the dark skin and intense, anxious brown eyes.

"Ju..lia?" I asked.

"Get up, baby," she said, pulling me to my feet. "Can you stand?"

I nodded, feeling the solidity of my legs under me.

"Wha... where am I?" I asked. And then, suddenly, I remembered. Everything snapped into place.

"Oh my God," I said; "how long was I in there?"

"Three days," Julia said. "Alexander told me what happened. He hasn't left his room in days, and when I went to check on him two days ago, he told me. I pieced the rest together. It must have been Levi who shot Cuan."

I blanched. "Cuan—"

"—received the tears," Julia said. "Alexander went straight there with them."

A deep, visceral part of me heaved with relief.

"He hasn't been permitted into the Sanctuary in days. Believe me, he's tried to get in. But Levi and Jacob are keeping a close eye on him. Alexander won't speak to them. His brothers don't know why. But," she added, "I do. I know. And they don't know I know. Even so, though, this was the first time I was able to get anywhere near here without anyone else around. So get out of here," she said. "Run."

"And what about you?" I asked. "What will they do when they discover I'm gone?"

Behind me, Julia slammed the lid of the hateful gilded box. "Maybe they'll never know," she said. "But fuck the lot of them. I'm OUT. I was already on the verge before, but this? Shackling you into a *box*? Nope. That's not Christianity. Fuck them all."

"Where will you go?" I asked.

"I have a place," she said. "But what is more important now is that *you* need to go. Right away."

I nodded. Then I hugged her, tightly. She was surprised, but after a second, she hugged me back. And then I ran, because I knew exactly where I needed to be.

I could feel it, a part of me that had been taken away, calling to me.

The world was still disorienting. I was dizzy, but I ran. I ran until a door barred my path. I didn't stop. I didn't knock. I just ran through it, the world solidifying after me.

The fog returned, but I didn't care. Perhaps it was my single-mindedness, perhaps it was adrenaline, but even the fog didn't stop me. My entire being was laser-focused on a single person, and as their image sharpened in my mind, the world sharpened around me.

I had reached a hallway. I knew this hallway. There was

another door. This door was shut, too, but this door, I knew, didn't have a lock. I reached for the knob and yanked.

I threw open the door and practically ran into the room, out of breath, heart pounding in my chest. All I wanted to see was him. He had been sitting on the edge of the bed, but as soon as I entered he stood, sharply, and stared at me. He held my gaze with those golden eyes as we looked at one another. That fiery red hair, that dark indigo sleeveless shirt that I knew hid a tightly muscled torso, the baggy pants that allowed him to move but were also adorable.

"Cuan..." I gasped.

I panted once, twice, before he crossed the space between us and pressed his mouth against mine, kissing me deeply, hungrily, like a starved animal.

I kissed him back desperately, tears almost coming to my eyes. I needed him. I needed him in a very real way, immediately, physically. I needed him as close to me as possible; so close that our bodies overlapped.

His lips left mine and went to my neck, teasing my nape. I gasped at the sensation, and Cuan pulled his face back slightly and glanced at my eyes, his breath hot and sweet on my face. I put a hand on his cheek, still convincing myself that I was really here, here with him. His gaze held a question, and I silently, ever so slightly, nodded an answer. It was all he needed to know how serious I was.

Wordlessly, he placed a hand on the front of my button-down shirt and, in a single, sharp motion, ripped it off me as he took a step back, sending buttons clattering across the floor.

I stood staring at him, my exposed chest heaving under the shreds of clothing as the back of the shirt fell away from my torso. I watched his eyes as he looked me up and down, taking in every curve of lean muscle. His gaze made my skin tingle as though a current was running through it.

He was drinking me in with his eyes, and I could tell that he was as desperate for the assurance of my body as I was for his. I stepped forward and pressed my chest against him, a silent indication that if he liked what he saw, he should take it.

His eyes met mine again, his gaze steely but deep, sharp and vulnerable and hungry at the same time. He thrust his hands out and grasped the sides of my chest, positioning them in such a way that his thumbs rested over my exposed nipples. I gasped at the sensation, feeling the blood flood into my groin as he pushed me backward, striding forward with me until my back was pressed into the wall. He teased my nipples as I twisted and moaned, grinding his pelvis into me as he kissed my face, neck, and shoulders.

I could feel him against me, hot and throbbing behind his baggy pants, even through my own trousers and underwear. I needed him inside me. I leaned forward and placed my hands on the sides of his shirt. As if on cue, he pulled his waist and torso back, and the shirt slid neatly over his head and arms, falling away on the floor. My hands immediately went to his firm, round buttocks, sliding inside the band of his pants and tugging them over his waist as I squeezed his ass. The pants slid down over his backside but caught in the front on his erection; he pulled them over the large red head of his cock, revealing the puff of soft fiery hair at the base of his pale, sculpted abdomen.

The pants fell immediately to the ground as he moved to the button of my trousers, yanking it open and then dragging them down to the floor. He reached up and grabbed at the waistband of my trunks and literally tore them from my body, the shreds fluttering around my ankles as we stood for a moment, completely naked, our hands running over one another's sides, looking into each other's eyes. And then we were kissing again, he pressing himself against me as though he wanted to push us both through the wall. Our slick, wet cocks slid against one another, and I heard Cuan let out a low groan as I placed a hand on his buttock and squeezed while the other grabbed his back. He frotted against me, both of us moaning into our kiss, until Cuan released my mouth and reached toward something on the dresser beside us, bringing his fist down on a tube and causing it to spatter onto the dresser surface, then slathering his hand in the mess. He brought his hand back, and I felt him smearing something slick and wet like coconut oil against the entrance of my ass. Then his hand went between us, his knuckles rubbing against my hardon as he applied the oil liberally to his own substantial length.

With one swift motion, he reached his arms under my legs and hoisted me up, hooking my knees over his elbows and grabbing the bottom of my ass, my back still plastered against the wall. He looked into my eyes, and I breathlessly nodded assent.

He slid into me in a single motion, not roughly, but not gently either. I let out a cry at the sensation, a mix of forceful tightness and sharp pleasure. The tight feeling died almost immediately; the pleasure did not—it only intensified as Cuan pulled partway out, then thrust back in, repeating the motion over and over with increasing force and intensity.

My head tilted back as wave after wave crashed through my body, letting out a small cry with each thrust, my vocalizations in sync with Cuan's own dark moans of pleasure and sex.

I was louder now, almost yelling in time with the rhythm as he slammed into me with even greater vigor, my own ramrod erection slapping against my torso over my tightening, darkening balls.

I felt the wave well up inside me, closer and closer as Cuan's speed and power increased, my feet haphazardly in the air on either side of us, toes curling until finally the wave was about to crest.

Our eyes met. That was all it took.

Cuan let out a half-growl, half shout as he exploded into

me, his hot cum flooding my insides like a tidal wave. I let out a loud, raspy cry of my own as I felt the orgasm burst forth, sending stream after stream of hot white semen firing out onto Cuan's torso, his face, myself, the wall, the light fixture.

Cuan kept pounding as we came, riding the spasms of intensity, shooting into me over and over until with each thrust I could feel the rich overflow splashing out around the edges of his cock to splatter against his balls and my legs, painting the wall and floor.

I cried out again and again, still cumming, perhaps cumming multiple times. We went on and on until exhaustion hit; Cuan's thrusts slowed, and my ass, now slick against the cum-splattered wall, slowed.

He leaned back, still holding me, still in me, lifting my back off the wall, pivoting, stepping, and then dumped me onto the bed. He slid out of me as I fell, and he fell on top of me, kissing me again as I wrapped my arms around him, feeling our slick, wet bodies hot against one another, feeling Cuan continuing to leak out of me onto the sheets.

Finally, eventually, he released my mouth, and pulled back to look at me with those golden eyes again.

I felt a grin spread across my face as I looked up at him. "Hi there," I said softly.

He smiled that lopsided smile of his, that charming dimple appearing in his cheek, his eyes glinting in the light of the cum-spattered lamp.

"Welcome home," he replied.

I held him. I just... held him, and he held me back, and we were together.

A short while later I awoke on his bare chest, dried semen gluing us together. Gently, I peeled my cheek from his skin and looked up at him. He stirred at the movement and tilted his face toward mine, grinning, the dimple in his cheek filled with my dried cum.

"Good morning," he said. "I'm glad you're here."

His face, his scent, his words… all of a sudden everything all hit me at once. Tears welled up in my eyes and I fell against his chest, heaving and bawling.

"I'm sorry," I said, the sobs wracking my body. "I'm so sorry I couldn't save you."

"Hey… hey now," Cuan said, his voice registering alarm but not surprise at my outpouring of tears. "You did save me. I've been bedridden for almost three days, but I'm OK. And you came back, just like you promised."

"But… But I wasn't there when you needed me. You were dying and I was trapped in some sort of Pandora's Box."

"Okay… we're going to need to talk about that box in a sec," Cuan said, "But you most certainly were here when I needed you."

"No… no…" I said, shaking my head as I sobbed into his chest, my tears melting the dried semen and causing it to run in a salty stream down his side onto the bed.

I felt his hand on my cheek, lifting my face up, fixing me with his intent, golden eyes.

"I could feel you," he said. "The whole time. I don't know how to explain it… it was like a white flame burning in my soul."

White flame. The words caught my immediate attention.

"I know it was you," Cuan said. "Your voice… you kept repeating my name, calling to me. I could feel you, sharing your strength with me, willing me on."

My sobs subsided, and I stared at him, the tears on my face dripping from my chin onto his skin.

"Alexander and Az and Lester and the others," Cuan continued, "they all did their part to keep me from dying. But you, Cole… You kept me alive."

The tears came again, but now for an entirely different reason.

The part of me that I'd felt go with Azrael when he had taken Cuan—it hadn't just been a sensation.

Cuan clutched me to his chest.

"Besides," he said, "I'm the one who should apologize. I wasn't there for you."

"That's ridiculous," I retorted. "You were fighting for your life while I was in that box."

"That's not what I was talking about," he said, "but again, we are going to need to discuss that. But I mean Cedric's training."

"You didn't know," I said. "And as soon as you did, you immediately understood why I needed to leave."

"I should have done more," he lamented. "I made excuses for him. His brutal training methods are all I've ever known. I didn't... I hadn't comprehended how awful they were. Cole, he *shot* at you." He shuddered. "If he'd killed you... hell, if he'd hurt you, I would have lost it. I'd have straight up attacked him, whether he raised me or not."

His grip on me tightened, and I leaned into him.

"It's OK," I said. "He won't do it again. He knows he doesn't need to."

"But he didn't apologize, either," Cuan said. "He doesn't think he did anything wrong. He's still him. I should have stood up for you more. Or I should have left with you. Instead I just let you go. I don't ever want to let you go again."

"So don't," I said, resting my head against his chest. "I want to be with you, Cuan. Tomorrow I'll talk to Cedric. I think we understand each other now, even if we aren't always in agreement. I'll lay out my very clear terms. None of his violent bullshit training, no treating you like a dog—no offense—and if he agrees, I'll respect him as leader, and I'll stay and become a Midnight Hunter."

"And if he disagrees, I'll leave with you," Cuan nodded. "I can live with him treating me like an animal—"

"You shouldn't," I said.

"But I can," he said. "But if he—if ANYONE—ever hurts you, I'll tear them apart."

"Well then... you're really going to have a bone to pick with the Order of Light," I said.

Cuan leaned up and looked at me, his face equal parts question and alarm.

And the story came out, everything that happened, in every bit of detail, from the moment he was hit with the dart until I burst into his room.

"That fucking sanctimonious, self-righteous, Bible-thumping sack of garbage," Cuan growled after I finished, flexing his hands in agitation. "I'm going to find him and see how he likes being stuffed into that golden box."

"It's a very tiny box," I said.

"I am aware," Cuan replied, eyes smoldering.

I placed a calming hand on his chest. "I appreciate the sentiment; believe me, I do," I said quietly. "But we can't just storm the Church of the Holy Guardian. The Order of Light is a big organization, and they will hunt you down, and me, and Bianca and Bran and everyone, if you attack one of their leaders. Right now, we might have an advantage: chances are they still think I'm trapped in that little box. Besides, beyond Jacob and Levi, we don't know who else, if anyone, was even aware of the plan to trap me."

"Alexander," Cuan said.

"He definitely didn't know," I responded.

"He didn't rescue you."

"He rescued *you*," I pointed out. "And that's more important to me. You know how hard it is for you to stand up to Cedric? Well, I imagine it's orders of magnitude harder for Alexander to defy his father. I'm not ready to write him off just yet."

"You just like his ass," Cuan muttered.

"I won't lie, it is pretty nice," I admitted. "Clearly you must have noticed that yourself."

Cuan scoffed, but I could tell he had.

"Being hot doesn't excuse his leaving you," he groused.

"No, it doesn't," I agreed, "but leaving me to deliver you Seraphiel's Tears does. If it comes to me or you, I would have preferred he saved you."

"He could just as easily have saved both of us," Cuan observed. "Why are you making excuses for him?"

I stopped. "I... I don't know, really," I admitted. "I mean, you're right. When it comes down to it, he betrayed me. But... not everyone can stand up to the person who raised them, the one they've been conditioned to depend on. I mean, I know that it's not at all the same as you and Cedric, but... maybe there's enough similarity that you can sympathize a bit?"

"I wouldn't have let Cedric keep you, or *anyone*, captive like that," Cuan growled.

"I know you wouldn't have. Because you're incredible. But Alexander is growing. I won't be able to forgive him, not right away. It'll take a lot of growth and a lot of work to regain my trust. But I'm not ruling him out. He's a good guy, Cuan. And it's because of him that you're here, and that counts for a lot. Especially because of what Jacob said to him... about how you killed Alexander's mother."

Cuan scoffed again, this time in earnest indignation. "How the hell could I have killed Alexander's mother?" He asked. "He's like the same age as me."

"That was exactly my reaction," I nodded.

"I mean, what does he think, that I was some kind of were-puppy on the warpath?"

The image of a ferocious tiny Cuan made me burst into a fit of childish giggles. "Scrappy-Cu," I cried gleefully.

"Shut up," Cuan said, but he burst into laughter alongside me. He reached under my arms to tickle me, and we rolled around mirthfully for a few minutes like a pair of schoolboys. Except of course that we were naked and had just had sex... so make that a pair of British boarding-school schoolboys.

Eventually we collapsed against each other, having tumbled from the bed onto the floor, most of the sheets having come with us. I looked into his golden eyes as he smiled back at me with his cockeyed smile, and I knew that there was nowhere else I wanted to be. Cuan was right: I was home.

"We still have a lot to figure out," Cuan said. "About your memories. About the Order of Light. About what's going on in the city and how it relates to everything else. But I want to help you figure out all those things. So let's do it. Together."

"Together," I agreed, leaning in and kissing him. "But tonight, let's sleep. Together."

I had known Cuan for about a week. A week. But that night, I already knew that I wanted him with me always.

The next morning, I became a member of the Midnight Hunters.

THE END

COLE'S STORY CONTINUES IN *LIGHT & MIDNIGHT BOOK II: THE WINGS OF DAWN*

ABOUT THE AUTHOR

Cort Channon loves stories: collecting them, creating them, and sharing them. He is a historian, theologian, and sociologist, but above all, a writer. A world traveler who hates the actual process of traveling, he has lived on three different continents and speaks multiple languages—some of them even well. He has worked as a game designer, researcher, illustrator, and author, but throughout it all, he strives to infuse his work with spiritual consciousness, social awareness, and sex-positivity. That, or he just really likes writing cute guys having lots of hot sex. Cort currently resides in the Pacific Northwest with his beloved spouse, Casey, and their two cats.

ALSO BY CORT CHANNON

Light and Midnight:

Book I: Midnight Hunters

Book II: Wings of Dawn